The Map *of* Bones

BOOK FOUR

of

The Joubert Family Chronicles

BY THE SAME AUTHOR

The Joubert Family Chronicles

The Burning Chambers

The City of Tears

The Ghost Ship

The Languedoc Trilogy

Labyrinth

Sepulchre

Citadel

Other Fiction & Short Stories

The Cave

The Winter Ghosts

The Mistletoe Bride & Other Haunting Tales

The Taxidermist's Daughter

The Black Mountain (Quick Reads)

Non-Fiction

Becoming a Mother

The House: Behind the Scenes at the Royal Opera House, Covent Garden

Chichester Festival Theatre at Fifty

An Extra Pair of Hands

Warrior Queens & Quiet Revolutionaries: How Women (Also) Built the World

Plays

Syrinx

Endpapers

Dodger

The Taxidermist's Daughter (adaptation)

The Queen of Jerusalem

KATE MOSSE

The Map of Bones

MANTLE

First published 2024 by Mantle
an imprint of Pan Macmillan
The Smithson, 6 Briset Street, London ECIM 5NR
EU representative: Macmillan Publishers Ireland Ltd, 1st Floor,
The Liffey Trust Centre, 117–126 Sheriff Street Upper,
Dublin 1, D01 YC43
Associated companies throughout the world
www.panmacmillan.com

ISBN 978-1-0350-4215-9 HB
ISBN 978-1-0350-4216-6 TPB

1 3 5 7 9 8 6 4 2

A CIP catalogue record for this book is available from the British Library.

Map by ML Design

Typeset in Stempel Garamond LT Std by
Palimpsest Book Production Ltd, Falkirk, Stirlingshire
Printed and bound by CPI Group (UK) Ltd, Croydon, CR0 4YY

MIX
Paper | Supporting responsible forestry
FSC® C116313
FSC www.fsc.org

As always, for my beloved

Greg, Felix, Martha, Ollie and Finn

For the first Huguenots in southern Africa

and every refugee, past and present, fleeing

persecution and war in the hope of a safer life

'Words strain,
Crack and sometimes break, under the burden,
Under the tension, slip, slide, perish,
Decay with imprecision, will not stay in place,
Will not stay still.'

'Burnt Norton'
Four Quartets, T. S. Eliot

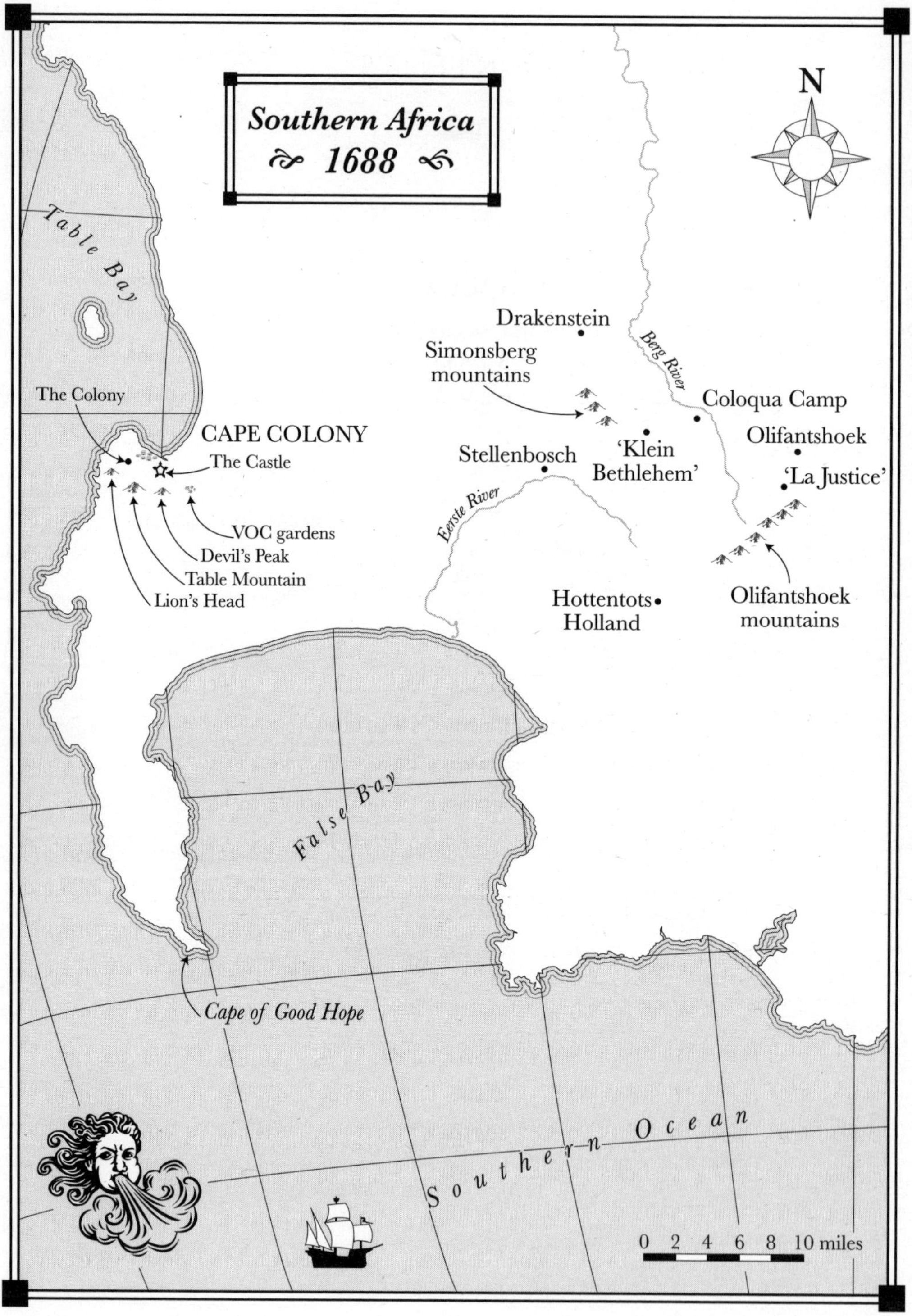

Southern Africa
1688
N
Table Bay
The Colony
CAPE COLONY
The Castle
VOC gardens
Devil's Peak
Table Mountain
Lion's Head
Drakenstein
Simonsberg
mountains
Berg River
Coloqua Camp
Olifantshoek
'Klein
Bethlehem'
Stellenbosch
'La Justice'
Eerste River
Hottentots
Holland
Olifantshoek
mountains
False Bay
Cape of Good Hope
Southern Ocean
0 2 4 6 8 10 miles

CONTENTS

Author's Note

The Map of Bones is the fourth and final book in a series of novels* about the Huguenot diaspora, a narrative of sixteenth-century France to the Cape of Good Hope in the nineteenth century by way of Amsterdam and the Canary Islands. Each novel is inspired by one of the four elements – fire, water, air and earth.

The sequence of religious civil wars between Catholics and Huguenots in France began on 1st March 1562 and ended – after several million had been persecuted, slaughtered or displaced – with the signing of the Edict of Nantes on 13th April 1598 by the previously Protestant King, Henri IV or Henri of Navarre. On 22nd October 1685, his grandson Louis XIV revoked the edict, precipitating the exodus of those few Huguenots still remaining on French soil. Though the first Huguenot refugees had begun to arrive in the Cape of Good Hope as early as 1671, the majority arrived in southern Africa on eighteen ships setting sail from the ports in the United Provinces between June 1687 and June 1688. The *spiegelretourschip* the *Berg China* – referred to in Dutch records simply as the *China* – arrived in Table Bay from Goeree, under the aegis of the Rotterdam Chamber, on 4th August 1688. The names of those first families – including Jourdan, de Villiers, Roux, Joubert, du Toit, Retief, Malherbe, Meinard, Jacob, Grange – are still present in South Africa today. My Joubert family is fictional and not related to the real Joubert

*The Joubert Family Chronicles: *The Burning Chambers*, *The City of Tears*, *The Ghost Ship*

family of South Africa (originally Jaubert) from Motte d'Aigues in Provence.

The Commander of the Colony, Simon van der Stel, initially set aside land for Huguenot settlement in the Drakenstein Valley. The land was poor and the refugees petitioned for farmland on the banks of the Berg River in Olifantshoek, the first being allotted to Heinrich Müller from Basel in 1692. He named it 'Keerweder', meaning 'turn back'. Many of the wine farms in today's Franschhoek still bear the names given to them by their original Huguenot owners, including 'La Motte', 'La Cotte', 'Cabrière', 'La Dauphiné', 'Bourgogne', 'La Terra de Luc', 'Champagne', 'La Bri' and 'La Provence'.

After years of conflict, the British finally wrested control of the Cape from the Dutch for good after the Battle of Blaauwberg in 1806 and, in the Anglo-Dutch Treaty of 1814, Cape Town was permanently ceded to the United Kingdom. In 1713, Olifantshoek was renamed *le coin Français*, the 'French corner', and was known as Franschen Hoek (and, briefly, as Roubaixdorp) before the Dutch version of its name, Franschhoek, was settled on. The name 'Cape Town' started to be used from 1733. For the sake of the narrative, I have taken certain liberties in my descriptions, topography and history of Cape Town, Stellenbosch, Drakenstein, Franschhoek and Joubertsgat Bridge.

On the question of language, to strike the balance between historical veracity and modern usage, I have used both 'enslaved' and 'slave' when unavoidable within the text. Hottentots Holland remains a place name in the Republic of South Africa. There were many different and shifting groupings within the indigenous peoples of the Cape during the seventeenth century and there is much debate among historians and scholars about nomenclature. I have focused on the Khoi, and used Khoi and San in the text rather than Khoikhoi or Bushmen. When referring to the language, I have also used Khoi rather than Khoe (or Nama). There is also discussion about the word 'leader' being preferable to 'chief' or 'headsman'. Because this is historical fiction, I have occasionally used 'headsman' as well as 'clan leader' as being more appropriate to the time in which this novel is set.

The influence of the Huguenots is extraordinary, a diaspora that took them as skilled immigrants all over the world – one branch of my family, also. Every country which accepted the refugees – including the Dutch Republic, England, Ireland and South Africa – was enriched by their presence despite their relatively small numbers. The word 'refugee' comes from *refugié*, a French word first used to describe the Huguenots. For those readers who would like a fuller history, I recommend Pieter Coertzen's *The Huguenots of South Africa 1688–1988* and *Huguenots at the Cape* by Philippa van Aardt and Elaine Ridge, both published by the Huguenot Society of South Africa.

Central to this novel are the operations of the United Dutch East India Company – the VOC (*Verenigde Oostindische Compagnie*) – which was established in March 1602, granting it a twenty-one-year monopoly to carry out trade activities in the Far East. Their modus operandi was not to establish colonies, but rather refreshment stations to provide the VOC ships with fresh food and water on their voyages to Batavia (Jakarta) and beyond to places such as China and Japan. The one exception to this was the Cape of Good Hope, which was a colony built on the labour of enslaved people brought from other parts of East and West Africa, as well as from Madagascar, India and Indonesia.

At the heart of *The Map of Bones* is a belief in the power of words, that unless women's stories and testimonies are included alongside those of men in the historical records, it cannot really be called history at all.

There is no Joubert Family Archive and Reading Room in London, nor was there a ship called the *Gouw*. The wine farm 'La Justice' in Olifantshoek, owned by the fictious Barenton family, does not – and never did – exist, nor does Klein Bethlehem. All the characters in *The Map of Bones*, unless otherwise specified, are imagined, though inspired by people who might have lived: ordinary women and men, struggling to survive and flourish against a backdrop of religious war and displacement.

Then, as now.

Kate Mosse
Chichester
April 2024

Principal Characters

In The Cape Colony (17th century)

Suzanne Joubert
Florence Amiel (*née* Reydon-Joubert), Suzanne's grandmother & Louise Reydon-Joubert's cousin
Driek Holsteen, sailor
Lars Eltorp, mercenary
Adriaan van Dijk, VOC official
Marie Lombard, refugee
Pieter Odendaal, *landdrost*
Anke Odendaal, his sister
Tia Nemen (Kroket), a Khoi servant
Harrie Nemen (Khemy), a Khoi interpreter
Kmame, the Cochoqua headman's son
Shansi, a female elder
Fala, a midwife
Khasso, a Khoi guide
Théodore Barenton, settler

In Stellenbosch & Franschhoek (19th century)

Isabelle Joubert Lepard, writer
Mrs Müller, landlady
John Turner, guide

Hans van Aarnhem, farmer
Griet van Aarnhem, his wife
Piet and Jan van Aarnhem, their sons
Andries Barenton, settler
Xavier Barenton, settler
Maya Barenton, Xavier's wife
Magdalena Barenton, his daughter

Historical Figures

Pierre Jaubert (recorded as Joubert in VOC records), refugee
Isabeau Jaubert, his wife
Pierre Grange, refugee
Jean and Louise Meinard, refugees
Jean Prieur du Plessis, barber-surgeon
Judith Verbeek, orphan (though her relationship with Adriaan van Dijk is imagined)
Catrina Janse van der Zee, orphan
Petronella van Capelle, orphan
Wilhelmina de Wit, orphan
Simon van der Stel, Commander/Governor of the Cape Colony (1679–1699)
Johannes van Andel, Dutch pastor of the Cape Colony (1688–1689)
Johannes Neethling, Dutch pastor in Stellenbosch (1858–1904)
Alexander Macmillan, Co-Founder of Macmillan & Company (1818–1896)
Lily Watson, novelist (1849–1932)
Samuel Watson, solicitor (1839–1921)

PROLOGUE

La Rochelle
May 1687

Rue des Gentilshommes
18th May 1687

Suzanne could hear them rampaging through the house. More like animals than men, except animals did not destroy wantonly. These men, *dragonnades*, were uncouth and violent bullies: Catholic soldiers billeted with Protestant households and given licence by the King to intimidate, humiliate, abuse, thieve. Huguenots were no longer citizens in their own country.

Kill or be killed.

She froze at another huge crash below. A splintering of wood, a cacophony of metal striking the tiled floor of the main hall, discordant chimes. She clenched her fists, suspecting the lawless soldiers had pulled down the lantern clock from the wall, simply because they could.

Suzanne had never before felt such rage, such fear, as over this past week. *Dragonnades* had been coming to the rue des Gentilshommes several times a day on the pretext of searching for Huguenot 'malefactors', as they called them. Then, five days ago, the soldiers had moved in and behaved as if the house was a muster camp on the battlefield: slashing portraits with their swords; shattering the Venetian wine glasses that had been in the Joubert family for generations; fouling the yard at the back of the house so the air stank. Drinking and drinking and drinking. Her grandmother, Florence, had sent their servants away, unwilling to put them at risk, so it was just the two of them left. Yesterday, as Florence was bringing food to the table, one of them had stuck out his foot and she had gone sprawling.

'What kind of man takes pleasure in humiliating an old woman?' Suzanne protested sharply. The soldier had laughed, then slapped her face for her insolence. Who was there to stop him?

Florence was not hurt, but she was badly shaken and had remained in her chamber for the rest of the day. Suzanne had thought herself civilised, but now she knew she would kill every one of them were it not for the fact that it would leave her grandmother unprotected.

She checked the door to her bedchamber was locked, having made sure Florence was secure in her room. The nights were the worst, listening to the rough voices getting louder and more strident, arguing and fighting, then an uneasy silence falling as the soldiers collapsed into an inebriated stupor. As a child, she had lain in this same chamber hearing the sounds of customers being ejected from the taverns at the port. Ugly sounds, aggressive voices, but she had felt safe.

Now, the threat was inside her own home.

From below, she heard a sudden bellow of triumph. 'Hey, will you look at this!'

Suzanne heard a new and unwelcome sound, the unmistakable scrape of the heavy walnut table in the hall being dragged away from the panelled wall. Her heart sank. She had moved it there after the first visit of the *dragonnades*, in the hope of concealing the small door down to the wine cellar. She had prayed that, once they had eaten and drunk the pantry dry, the *dragonnades* would move on to find another household to terrorise.

In despair, she knelt on her *prie-dieu* and muttered the same words over and again.

'*Post tenebras lux.*' After darkness, the light. Perhaps, tonight, God would be on their side?

After a while, she moved to sit on her bed. Below, the sounds of carousing grew louder. It went on so long that she eventually fell into a troubled half-sleep.

A little later, Suzanne awoke with a jolt to see that her candle had burnt right down. She heard the bells of the *grosse horloge* striking three o'clock, then realised the house was silent: no shouting, no singing. Instantly, Suzanne was on her feet. She tiptoed to the door, carefully turned the key in the lock, and opened it a crack.

Not a sound. Could it be that they would make it through another night? Then, across the landing, she saw the tray she had left outside her grandmother's door was still there. Unease trickled down her spine. She did not want to wake Florence if she was lost in the comforting arms of sleep, but what if she had been more hurt than either of them had realised? What if she was lying in her bed in need of help?

Suzanne hesitated, then stepped out onto the landing.

In her stockinged feet, she moved as quietly as she was able towards her grandmother's chamber. She could not stop herself glancing down, then wished she had not. The hall looked as if an army had marched through: glass everywhere, a flagon lying on its side with the last dregs of wine dripping red from the neck and pooling like blood on the tiled floor. One soldier was sprawled in the high-backed armchair, stains down his uniform jacket; another was slumped over the table with his head on his arms; a third was at the bottom of the stairs, his shirt patterned with vomit.

Revolted, Suzanne turned away and tapped on Florence's door.

'*Gran'mère?*' she whispered. '*Ça va?*'

There was no answer but, when she pressed her ear to the door, she could just hear gentle snoring. Relieved, she turned away. Then her breath caught in her throat. Standing at the top of the stairs, between Florence's chamber and her own, was the fourth soldier. She had foolishly assumed him to be in the yard.

Their eyes met: the hunter and his prey.

Suzanne leapt forward, but he was quicker. He encircled her waist with his arms, then pulled her towards him. She struck at him with her fists, beating against his chest, urgently trying to prise herself free.

'Come, come, I'm only after a kiss.'

Suzanne recoiled, striking out with her stockinged feet. Her assailant was briefly knocked off his stride. She took the chance to slip free, running across the landing towards her room.

He laughed, pawing at her skirts, dragging her back towards him.

'No harm in a kiss,' he wheezed, and she realised that her resistance was inflaming his blood.

'Let me go,' she murmured, scared to make a noise in case she woke her grandmother. Or, worse, his unconscious companions.

Suddenly, she remembered something she'd seen down in the port when she was a girl. One of the doxies who frequented the waterfront when the ships came home from the sea had been manhandled by a customer. The woman's face had been red and furious, Suzanne remembered, when she suddenly brought up her knee between the man's legs. He had fallen screaming and writhing to the floor. She hadn't understood at the time, only that the woman had bested him.

The soldier's lips were now on her neck, his hands groping at her bodice, fumbling with the hooks and eyes.

With all the strength she could muster, Suzanne lifted her leg and brought her heel back. Kicked. It wasn't enough. He gasped, but tightened his grip.

'Wild little cat, aren't you?' he hissed, with a cold edge to his voice.

In a last desperate attempt to free herself, Suzanne twisted and clawed at his face. She gouged his cheek, drawing blood. He froze, then his expression changed, transforming things from a rough game into something darker. Before she had the chance to duck, he pulled back his fist and punched her on the jaw.

The pain reverberated around her head, disbelief too, as she felt herself falling. Then another explosion of pain as her temple hit the newel post at the top of the stairs.

Suzanne could not have been unconscious for more than a few moments but, when she came to, the man was on top of her. Her chemise had been torn open – she could feel the night air cool on her bare skin – and her skirts were pushed up around her waist. Suzanne panicked. She couldn't breathe, she couldn't move. In vain she tried to push him off, but he barely seemed to realise she was there. His eyes were closed and he seemed in the grip of some violent turmoil.

Pinned, she stopped struggling, now wanting more than anything for it to be over. Praying that her grandmother would remain in her room and not have to witness what was happening. She felt a final, tearing pain between her legs, then the soldier collapsed on top of her. Suzanne felt her ribs were cracking, as if her whole body was being crushed. There was something wet on her cheeks. She stuck out her tongue, thinking it would be blood from the wound on her temple, but tasted salt.

Suddenly, the man rolled off her. Suzanne gulped at the air, rolling onto her side. Now he was tying his breeches and shrugging his arms back into his uniform jacket. She didn't move, not wanting to provoke him to some other assault.

Something cold struck her cheek. She turned her head and saw a silver coin lying bright on the floorboard beside her.

'For your trouble,' he said.

Was it her imagination, or was there shame in his voice? Then he turned and staggered down the stairs, leaving her lying on the floor.

Suzanne did not move. She was stunned. Numb, as if this horror had happened to someone else. Then, as always, thoughts of her grandmother took over. She couldn't risk Florence waking and finding her like this. She was an old woman and, though she had survived much in her long life, Suzanne would not inflict another ordeal on her.

She stood up, setting her head spinning. She steadied herself, then staggered to her bedchamber, pulled off the sullied clothes that had not protected her and rolled them into a bundle beneath her bed. Taking a plain garment from her chest, she dressed quickly and laced her boots. She cleaned herself, wiped the blood from her temple, washed her hands with water from the nightstand and tidied her hair so it hung in its usual curls on either side of her face.

She would not let this man take anything more from her. She would not let him win. But she knew that if such a thing could happen once, it could happen again.

The trauma of what had been done to her caught suddenly in her throat. She closed her eyes, willing herself to be strong. Suzanne took a few deep breaths to compose herself, then knocked on her grandmother's door. This time, she was more insistent.

'*Gran'mère*,' she whispered, as loudly as she dared, 'let me in. I must speak with you.'

Still bleary with sleep, Florence opened her door. 'What's happened?' she said, taking one look at Suzanne's face.

'One of . . .'

Instantly, from the unnaturally stiff way that her granddaughter was standing, from her pallor, from the effort she was taking to hold her emotions in check, she knew.

'Did he hurt you?'

'I tried to fight him off, but I . . . I should not have opened the door.'

Florence grabbed her granddaughter's arm. 'No! It is not your fault, don't ever think that. That is what wicked men say to make women responsible for *their* treacherous actions. It is not your fault, Suzanne, do you hear me?'

Looking dazed and distant, Suzanne nodded. Florence's heart twisted in her chest for the pity of it.

Thinking furiously, she issued instructions. 'Go to your room. Put on warm clothes, garments with pockets, and conceal anything of value that is small enough to carry beneath your cloak. Bring your wooden casket with your mother's jewels, but not too much.'

'Are we going to allow ourselves to be driven from our own home?'

Florence put her hand on Suzanne's shoulder. 'This is no longer our home. Only our lives matter. Quick, now.'

While Suzanne returned to her own chamber, Florence looked around the room that had been her refuge for nearly sixty years. She had come here with her own father many years ago – to her cousin Louise's house – and, for the most part, she had been happy in La Rochelle.

Florence gathered a few precious trinkets that she could not bear to leave, family heirlooms, then put on her plainest cloak and bonnet over the crumpled clothes she had slept in. Her old fingers fumbled over the laces of her boots but, at the same time, she felt a new lease of life. Being trapped here by the *dragonnades*, unable to move against them for fear of putting Suzanne in more danger, had been unbearable. She would rather die, than live like this any longer.

The two women, one not yet twenty and the other in the twilight of her life, moved silently down the back stairs and away from the magnificent turreted stone house overlooking the rue des Gentilshommes, then slipped into the side streets, leaving behind their lives, their memories. Florence held Suzanne's hand, drawing her back into the shadows at the sound of soldiers' boots on the cobblestones, then hurrying her forward when the coast was clear.

'What are we going to do?' Suzanne whispered. 'The gates will be bolted for the night and there are patrols everywhere.'

Florence put her finger to her lips.

La Rochelle was shrouded in a white mist come in from the sea, filling everything with a strange, other-worldly light. As they passed beneath the *grosse horloge*, the clock tower that divided the city from the port, the bell began chiming for four o'clock. Soon, the fishermen and the ostlers would be stirring.

'Where are we going?' Suzanne asked. 'We are not allowed to leave.'

This time, Florence was relieved to hear a little of her old spirit in her granddaughter's voice.

'Just follow me.'

She led them away from the two main towers that guarded the entrance into La Rochelle harbour towards the Lantern Tower where prisoners were held. It was said that many scratched their initials on the wall to leave a record of their incarceration.

Luck was with them. There were no candles burning in the

houses overlooking the sea wall and no one to notice them at the water's edge. She signalled for Suzanne to wait, then approached one of the painted fishing boats tethered in the water.

'Monsieur?' Florence hesitated, then spoke a little louder: 'Monsieur, *c'est moi.* Florence Amiel – *la fille de* Jean-Jacques Joubert.'

This time, there was a rustling beneath the nets and a man's head appeared from the depths of the rowing boat. A hushed conversation began, full of entreaty and gestures. Finally, a few coins changed hands.

'Come, *petite*,' she said gently, leading Suzanne to the little boat. 'We are going to hide here for now. It will be light soon. The captain will take us to the Île de Ré as soon as it is safe.'

Suzanne still looked dazed. 'But why would he help us?'

'Because my father, Jean-Jacques, once helped him,' Florence replied, keeping her voice as steady as she could. 'Lie down here. Try to rest. It is going to be all right.'

But as Florence joined Suzanne beneath the nets, with the smell of fish and the sea in her nose, she knew they were taking a very great risk. Any Huguenots caught trying to leave France would be executed, or the men condemned to the slave galleys and the women confined to a convent for the rest of their lives. And she was relying on the captain's debt from the past to not betray them.

All the same, in the black and early morning chill, she smiled. The women of the Joubert family were made of strong stuff. If they could make it to the Île de Ré without being caught, from there they could seek passage on a Dutch ship sailing north.

She felt Suzanne reach out and take her hand. '*Post tenebras lux*,' she whispered into the darkness. After darkness, the light.

PART ONE

Fifteen months later

THE CAPE COLONY

August 1688–March 1689

CHAPTER ONE

TABLE BAY
Wednesday, 4th August 1688

White sails against a grey sky. Salt air and wind, the slap of water against the hull of the ship. Singing in the rigging and the snap of the red, white and blue flag of the United Provinces atop the three masts and prow. Two o'clock in the afternoon on the fourth day of August in the year 1688. Winter in the south, a time of storms and rough seas. Gulls shrieking overhead to guide the *China* into Table Bay.

Suzanne Joubert stood with both hands on the taffrail, trying to imagine how it would be to feel the earth beneath her feet. No longer the sway of the ship, the ever-changing vastness of the ocean, but solid, unshifting ground. How it would feel to no longer be confined to a few hundred feet of deck or the squalid sleeping quarters down below. The seasoned mariners, who'd sailed this route before, warned her she would feel land-sick at first, as if it was the world that could not stay still. She hoped she would be all right, but she gripped the rail more tightly all the same.

After the excited chatter when the coast of Africa had first been sighted, the passengers were mostly silent now. In a ship of more than three hundred souls, seafarers and soldiers, there were twenty-eight passengers, including Suzanne and her grandmother. This was the place they were to learn to call home, as different from the villages of Provence or the canals of Amsterdam as could be. A 'wild and desolate land', Jan van Riebeeck, the first commander of the Cape, had called it in his writings.

Suzanne thought it majestic: the sheer scale and the size of the vista coming into view, the endless sky and the dwellings dotted on the plain as tiny as children's toys in the nursery. Rocks to one side, sandy beaches to the other. Most of all, the mountains. Though the ship's cook had described it, Suzanne had still gasped when Table Mountain came into view and she saw the famous floating white drape of cloud, crisp like a laundered linen tablecloth, lying across it. Beside it, she could make out the summit said to resemble a lion sleeping and the ragged outline of the formation known as Devil's Peak.

'*Laat het anker zakken.*' Drop anchor.

Suzanne registered the shudder as the chain rattled, then began to grind and stutter as it started to unwind. Slowly at first, then fast and faster as it gathered momentum under its own weight, until the huge metal hook found the sea bed. She felt a lurch, then a coming-to-rest as the anchor bumped along the bottom. Finally, a sharp jolt when it found purchase.

The *China* rocked on its chain. Suzanne heard the whistle confirming the ship was secure and the shouted orders and sounds of the crew clambering up the masts to furl the sails. Still, she did not turn round. She kept her gaze fixed upon the shore, as if it might disappear if she looked away.

The *China* gave a gun salute, covering the deck in a cloud of white smoke. Foreign ships were obliged to discharge all their weapons on entering harbour but, for a VOC ship coming into a VOC harbour, a single shot would suffice. An answering salute came from the shore, and the crew cheered. Even Captain van Groll was smiling.

At last Suzanne felt she could breathe more easily. The voyage was over and, with it, all the heartbreak and the wonder, the friendships and the moments of joy. The stories of exile and despair, of experience and hope. She'd seen a wedding on board and a birth, the black sky scattered silver with stars below the Equator. The solitude of the night watch.

She thought of the waves, white-crested like frosted hills in winter, the shifting colours of green and blue; leaping silver-flanked sword-fish and dolphins racing alongside; sea dogs, and translucent jellyfish hovering below the surface of the water; ugly creatures with gaping mouths. Suzanne had never before seen such sights outside the pages of a book or the painted surface of a seafarer's globe.

Perhaps here, in the Cape, she would learn to feel joy again?

Her feeling of relief faded as the darker events of the voyage came back to her. Suzanne blinked away the memory of the bodies wrapped in dirty shrouds – refugees, sailors and soldiers, children too – twenty dead in all, each thrown overboard in tarpaulins weighted with stones:

'*Een, twee, drie, in Godsnaam* . . .' One, two, three, in the name of God.

She remembered the stench below deck, the lack of fresh food and the crust of salt upon their skin. The storms, with the ship rearing and plunging through the rutted depths until it seemed as if the *China* would crack in two. Waves as high as a house. Later, the eerie times when they were becalmed or suffocated by burning red sands blown from the coast of West Africa. She could still hear the silent weeping of the Dutch orphan girls sent to be married to settlers they had never met and see the despair of the young Frenchmen when they remembered the villages they would never see again: La Motte d'Aigues; Saint-Martin-de-la-Brasque; Cabrières d'Aigues. Mothers, fathers, cousins, brothers, wives, sisters, all praying they would find kindness and tolerance in this distant Christian corner of the world. A place to lay their heads without fear of persecution.

Friends, now.

Suzanne was not like them, despite the empathy she felt for all they had lost. She felt exhilaration, not dread. Although she and her grandmother, Florence, had also been forced to flee their home in La Rochelle, they were the last remaining members of one of the great Huguenot families of France. They had bought passage on a ship sailing from the Île de Ré to Nantes, then travelled overland to Chartres, avoiding the King's soldiers hunting Huguenots for sport, making it to Reims and into the Spanish Netherlands, and on until they were safe.

Once in Amsterdam, the elegant van Raay house in Warmoesstraat had been waiting for them. They had shelter and they were safe. They might have stayed – perhaps they should have stayed – except Suzanne knew that she would never have been able to settle. She was a traveller, not a refugee. She had boarded the *China* with a heart full of anger, and a mission.

Besides, wasn't the sea in her blood?

Suzanne had grown up hearing stories about her cousin, Louise Reydon-Joubert, a woman who had lived and died many years before she was born. Louise had bequeathed her house in La Rochelle to her uncle – Florence's father – as well as a wine business in which she had an interest and Suzanne herself had been born in the elegant building in the rue des Gentils-hommes.

During the winter in Amsterdam, trying to bury the memories of what had happened in La Rochelle, Suzanne had found Louise's prison diary and read her account of being put on trial for murder. After that, thoughts of Louise had become Suzanne's constant companion in her fractured life. She had scoured the records from the old van Raay shipping offices now archived in the library in Warmoesstraat and found the evidence of Louise's ownership of a *fluyt*, a trading ship, called the *Old Moon*. Even now, such a thing would be extraordinary, but then? A woman who lived on her own terms in a man's world, a woman of courage and principle. A woman who had turned pirate, a she-captain, hunting down slaver ships on the high seas.

A history written in blood and betrayal.

The *Old Moon* had left Gran Canaria bound for the Cape of Good Hope in October 1621. Louise's friend, Gilles Barenton – rumoured to be her husband – was on board, as was Louise's half-brother, a man by the name of Phillipe Vidal. They had dropped anchor in Table Bay seven months later. That much was on record. But neither Louise herself – nor her two companions – had ever been heard of again.

No word, no story, no grave.

The *Old Moon* had been sailed back to Amsterdam by Louise's first lieutenant, on her instruction, but the Englishman maintained to his dying day that he had no idea where his lady-captain had been headed nor why she had forsaken the ship she loved. It was he who'd handed the prison diary into the keeping of Louise's elderly aunt, Alis, in Warmoesstraat sixty-five years ago. The diary Suzanne carried with her now.

Her hand slipped to her leather satchel containing not only the diary, but also a Tarot card, wrapped in a piece of threadbare white linen. It was a constant reminder of what she had come to do. She was on a quest, as much as Achilles or Hercules ever had been.

'Next!'

Suzanne jolted back to the present, as the ship's first officer called out the names of the passengers to be taken ashore in the rowing boats. She hoisted her satchel higher across her shoulder, then moved to stand beside her grandmother.

'Remember, *petite*,' Florence murmured, 'you must try to speak Dutch now.'

'I know.'

She stood patiently in line, waiting while her grandmother was helped down into the boat. Despite the dull day, Suzanne's copper hair shone bright. Broad and powerful in stature, her colouring linked her to the Dutch side of the family. Only her unusual eyes, one blue and one brown, spoke to generations of Joubert women whom she resembled in spirit – Minou, Marta, Louise, Florence – adventurers, all.

'Suzanne Joubert?'

'*Hier ben ik*,' she replied clearly. I'm here.

Holding her portmanteau tight, Suzanne climbed down into the boat and settled herself on the wooden bench beside her grandmother. She took a deep breath, feeling her nerves singing with excitement. Apprehension, too. The sea was choppy, but she was accustomed to the roll and swell of the waves.

As the oarsmen started to row, Suzanne smiled.

'*J'arrive*,' she muttered under her breath, as the gulls continued to screech above their heads. 'I'm coming. I'm coming to find you.'

CHAPTER TWO

The instant the rowing boat pulled away from the shelter of the ship, Suzanne realised the sea was far rougher than it had seemed from the deck. She squeezed her grandmother's arm and looked straight ahead. Florence, though in her ninth decade, showed no sign of fear.

'Should we not wait until the sea is calmer?' Suzanne shouted up to the helmsman.

He shook his head. 'There is a storm due. Conditions will worsen as the afternoon closes in. We need to disembark everyone now or wait until the weather has passed through.'

'But is it safe?'

'I've known worse. If you are sickened, fix your eyes on the shore.'

The tiny boat battled forward in the broiling sea, until a monstrous wave broke over the gunwales, almost capsizing them. The youngest of the Dutch orphans, Catrina, screamed. Though they came from a country built on waterways and dykes and rivers, few could swim, and none of them had ever set foot outside of Rotterdam before this pilgrimage to the ends of the earth. Another arc of seawater thundered over the boat, swamping the boards. The sailors began to bail water as some of the other girls, dressed alike in their grey orphanage pinafore dresses, began to weep.

The land seemed very far away.

'There's nothing to worry about, it's just the usual mischief of the sea in winter,' Suzanne shouted over the swell. 'The Cape of Good Hope, that's what they call this point of land – "good hope" – and that's what it will turn out to be. Mark my words.'

'*Beloof je?*' Catrina whispered. Do you promise?

'I am certain of it,' Suzanne replied firmly, as another wave crashed over the prow of the boat. Next to them, the oldest girl, Judith Verbeek, though green around the gills, mouthed her thanks.

As they heeled violently to port, Catrina screamed again. Suzanne and Judith pulled the girls away from the seats at the bow and pushed them down into the bottom of the boat, shouting at them to hold on tight.

'And pray for God to have mercy on us,' Judith murmured.

The oarsmen continued to struggle to make headway against the current, as the craft was tossed and shaken by the rolling waves, driven off course. But the helmsman, though drenched and blinded by the spray, held steady. Little by little, as the shoreline drew closer, the sea became less wild. Finally, protected by the curve of the bay, the pilot brought the rowing boat safely to the wooden pier, where hands immediately reached down to pull the bedraggled new arrivals up onto the jetty.

In a babble of Dutch and French – refugees who had travelled on the twelve VOC ships that had sailed the 'wagon trail' before them – were ready to welcome their brothers and sisters. But they stood back when they saw the Dutch orphans. These were not their kin. They folded their hands to wait for the next boat, bringing their co-religionists to shore.

'*Dank u*,' Suzanne said, as an official reached down to help her, remembering her grandmother's advice. He nodded, assisted with her portmanteau, but said nothing.

She felt a flutter of nerves in her stomach. Though they were Huguenots too, they had paid their own way as passengers. She was young and unmarried, and the Colony was known to be lacking in suitable wives for VOC men. It should mean she would be welcomed with open arms. But then, Suzanne had not come to the Cape to be a farmer's wife.

THE CAPE COLONY

They were instructed to walk to the end of the jetty and wait on the shore.

For a moment, Suzanne couldn't move. She stood, with her legs braced, as the jetty beneath her feet seemed to sway, praying the sickness would pass. She shivered, soaked through by the spray. Her skin felt tight with saltwater and her head was spinning.

Though the waterside was noisy, everything was muffled by the low-lying grey mist and a drizzle that reminded her of the squares and cobbled streets of Amsterdam. The air seemed to glister white, like the shimmering over the canals in autumn. For Suzanne, though, everything was vivid and bright. The smells, the sounds, were all tantalisingly familiar, yet all utterly strange: the rattle of barrels over the wooden boards of the jetty; men's voices raised in command or anger; gulls; sooty black wading birds with bright red legs and beaks, oyster catchers, she thought.

Suzanne was used to a stew of languages and mingling with travellers from all over the globe – she had always and only lived in harbour cities – but she was struck by the porters come to carry their luggage. Men with skin as black as ink, tall and majestic. Others were lighter skinned and dressed in working clothes, their features speaking of homes in Madagascar and Bengal and Sri Lanka.

The rumour was that the Commander of the Cape Colony

himself was the grandson of a freed slave, and yet the captain of the *China* had boasted of how the number of enslaved people here was already twice that of the VOC employees settled at the Cape. Suzanne had held her tongue and tried not to let her revulsion show. Slavery was illegal in the United Provinces, though not in its overseas territories, and she was sickened by the thought of humans being bought and sold like cattle.

From the Van Raay archives in Amsterdam, she'd learnt that Louise herself, Louise's great-aunt Alis and Alis's companion, Cornelia van Raay, had spoken out against enslavement. But a few lone women's voices had not been enough to sway the men who ruled Holland – the Lords XVII. They had adjudged that, with the trafficking of human beings, would come riches and influence. Time had proved them right. And Suzanne knew that the growing Cape Colony could not function without these stolen people.

Behind her she heard a smattering of applause. Suzanne turned to see the second of the rowing boats, carrying the first of the refugees, pulling up to the pier. The small crowd surged forward again, hoping to see the faces of long-lost family and neighbours. She saw their smiles of relief, hands reaching down, heard their prayers in French thanking God for their friends' and relatives' safe deliverance from the sea.

Once all twenty-eight passengers had disembarked, an official in the colours of the VOC stepped to the front of the crowd and clapped his hands.

'This way.'

Suzanne moved forward, beckoning for others to follow her towards a large cavernous shed. Before being allowed to sail to the Colony, each of them – even paying passengers like Suzanne and Florence – had had to swear an oath of allegiance to the

United Provinces, to obey Dutch laws, to be good and loyal subjects and to promise to remain at the Cape for a minimum of five years.

Having spent more than four months at sea with her co-religionists – and knowing their knowledge of Dutch customs was limited – Suzanne doubted if any of her fellow travellers had any idea of what they had committed to. They were masons and farmhands, weavers and coopers. They had grown up in the warmth and simplicity of Provence, among peach groves and vineyards and olive trees, where tiny interlinked hamlets nestled in gentle, green hills and river valleys, bound to one another by centuries of marriage and kin. Most of them had never even seen the sea before they boarded the *China* and few could sign their own names, let alone read the documents put in front of them.

'In here, if you will,' said the official.

Suzanne stepped through wide wooden-latched doors into a shed as large as anything at the shipbuilding yards of Amsterdam. A long and basic rectangular structure, fashioned from planks and sealed with tar, there were high open windows at the top for ventilation and long benches set down both sides. At the far end was a line of narrow trestle tables with oil lamps, resembling a court of justice where the officials, like a line of black crows upon a fence, sat ready to begin the process of registering the new arrivals. On the wall behind, the flag of the United Provinces hung between two larger pennants proclaiming the authority of the VOC. Suzanne gave a discreet smile. The size and positioning of the flags made it clear where the real power lay: with the merchants rather than the far-distant Lords XVII.

'Sit,' the official said, gesturing to benches on their left. 'Wait until your name is called. When it is, make your approach to the desk and answer the questions put to you.'

The eight orphans sat down in a shivering huddle of grey, then stood up again, fearful of doing the wrong thing. No one else had moved. The official had spoken clearly, but Suzanne knew that most of her fellow passengers would struggle to understand. They had picked up very little Dutch during their time at sea, tending to remain in their own quarters and communicating mostly between themselves, even when Suzanne had offered to teach them. Now, they were weary and they were scared. Their relief at having survived the voyage had already given way to fear of a greater kind: the fear of the unknown.

'Hurry,' the official called impatiently. 'You are all to sit.'

Suzanne stepped out of the line. '*Mijnheer*, perhaps I might help?'

He ran his eyes up and down her filthy, sodden clothes. 'You speak Dutch?'

'My great-grandfather's family was from Amsterdam.'

His eyes narrowed. 'Yet you are a refugee?'

A shake of her head. 'A traveller, *mijnheer*. We paid our own passage.'

'We? Where is your husband?'

'My grandmother and I,' she replied in a level voice. 'She is rich in years but yet, she too, wished to play her part in building this new corner of the Dutch Empire.'

She was aware of the picture she painted. A young woman in shabby travelling clothes, her bonnet stained and skirt sea-soaked. But the cloth was expensive, her cloak embroidered, her boots of soft Spanish leather, and she knew the man would recognise their worth. For all their formidable airs and graces, the VOC were traders above all else. They knew the market value of everything.

'What do you want?' he asked suspiciously.

'Merely to assist.'

Suzanne gestured to Judith and the other seven girls. 'They are from the orphanage in Rotterdam, but most of my co-religionists do not speak your language. I could translate for them.' She waited politely, hoping she had not been too forthright. Her time in Amsterdam had taught her that most of the minor officials within the VOC were easy to flatter. But perhaps the men of the Cape – pioneers, after all – were harder to please? 'I consider it my duty to be of service,' she added.

Duty. That he understood. He nodded. 'Come with me.'

CHAPTER THREE

'I have offered my services as interpreter,' Suzanne whispered to her grandmother.

'Do not be impertinent,' Florence cautioned. 'Men do not admire women with a sharp wit. They think it makes them look foolish.'

'Most do not need our aid in that!'

'Suzanne . . .'

She held up her hands. 'Don't worry, *Gran'mère*, I will guard my tongue.'

Suzanne kissed her grandmother, then hurried to follow the official. Her boots seemed over-loud in the echoing space despite the beaten-earth floor. The other clerks paid her no heed, but she was aware of the eyes of her fellow passengers tracking her with interest as she walked up the middle of the chamber. She smiled at Judith, standing with the other orphan brides like a mother hen, hoping to reassure her. An angular girl of nineteen years, her friend returned the smile.

The official came to a halt in front of the long trestle tables. Motioning to Suzanne to stay where she was, he stepped towards a man sitting in a high-backed chair. The *regisseur*, she supposed. His grave demeanour gave her an uneasy feeling of being judged, as if this was a tribunal rather than a welcoming committee. Which, in a way, Suzanne supposed it was. She and her companions were not individuals to this man and his officials, but numbers on a list to be processed and allocated to a parcel of land: labourers, farmers, vintners, breeders.

Suzanne did not imagine this was Simon van der Stel himself – the Commander would hardly concern himself with so mundane a task – but the *regisseur* bristled with importance all the same. A brass inkpot and quill in his hand, he was the twin for any of the VOC officials she had come across in Amsterdam. He wore a long black *justaucorps*, black breeches and stockings, a white flat falling collar, and his hair was combed back from his forehead. The only sign of flamboyance was a large, drooping moustache that framed his thin lips.

The official who'd brought her to the table was still whispering, and glancing back over his shoulder. The *regisseur* leant to one side, so they were both now staring at her. Suzanne did not smile, but remained standing with her hands folded in front of her, a picture of demure patience, until she was waved forward.

'You speak Dutch, *juffrouw* . . .?' the *regisseur* asked, leaving the question of her name hanging.

'Joubert,' she replied. 'Suzanne Joubert. I have travelled with my grandmother, Florence Reydon-Joubert.'

'But you are French?'

'My family is of French and Dutch heritage and settled in Amsterdam at the time of the Alteration.' She paused. 'Indeed, my great-grandfather played a part in the liberation of the city from Catholic oppression.'

The *regisseur* raised his eyebrows, but Suzanne knew the comment would find its mark. A significant wave of Huguenot refugees had fled to the Netherlands after the Paris massacre in 1572, bolstering the Protestant resistance in the Netherlands to Spanish rule. Six years later, the town hall had been stormed by Calvinists and Huguenots, who took control of the council – and hence Amsterdam – without a single death.

'Did he indeed? And why have you travelled here, *juffrouw* Joubert?'

'Most of our relatives have been killed by the Catholics in the latest persecutions in my homeland.' She gave the slightest of shrugs. 'There was nothing left for me in France, nor any family remaining in Amsterdam, so . . .'

The *regisseur* looked at her for a moment longer. Suzanne could read his narrow mind in his eyes. Why would a woman, allegedly from such a well-born family, make the perilous journey to the Cape and without a male escort? But pragmatism overcame his curiosity.

'Very well. You may assist.'

Suzanne smiled, understanding she was supposed to be grateful, despite the fact that he was getting the better of the bargain.

'*Dank u, regisseur.*'

She approached the first family waiting on the benches: Jean Meinard and his wife Louise, who had lost two of their children during the voyage. They came from one of the tiny villages in Provence, Saint-Martin-de-la-Brasque. She explained to Jean, a gentle man of six-and-twenty years, what was to happen, and offered her services as interlocutor. His wife accepted on their behalf, and gave him a loving nudge in the back to encourage him forward. Meinard straightened his stained jerkin, rubbed his boots on the backs of his stockings, and stepped up.

'Name?'

'*Ton nom de famille*,' Suzanne whispered.

The Frenchman nodded, and answered. Tall and bowed, he held his battered felt hat in his hand. His hair hung lank, framing a lean face. He showed no impatience. Suzanne knew this was what being a refugee meant, how a man's independence and individuality were stripped from him. Those who had been leaders in their home villages were now reduced to the status of supplicants; always having to be grateful, never making demands, being obliged to wait for whatever scraps might be given. Suzanne's heart broke for them, these men and women of Provence who found themselves in this alien country. It was a refuge, they were alive, but at what cost?

As the time passed, however, Suzanne had to admit that the process was thorough and, by its own lights, fair. Nothing was left to chance, there was nothing of favour or prejudice: each head of household was given a loan from monies raised by settlers, provided with tools and allocated a plot of land. The Colony needed people to grow fresh fruit and vegetables to supply passing VOC ships, men to establish wine farms and distil brandy and vinegar, and families to grow the population. The Company needed the refugees as much as the refugees needed a safe place to hang their hats.

After Jean Meinard, came the Jourdans and the Malans, the Courbons and the Goirands. The questions were the same each time, delivered in the same monotone by the official, who rarely lifted his eyes from the ledger.

Pierre Grange, a man of great dignity and gravitas, was one of the oldest of the refugees. The strain of the journey, and the insecurity of his position, showed in the deep lines on his face and the way in which his clouded eyes darted between Suzanne and the *regisseur* with every word spoken. Twice, she was obliged to ask him to raise his voice a little.

Suzanne requested that the girls from Rotterdam be called as a group, and that Judith Verbeek be allowed to speak for them all. Her petition was granted. To her great relief, for the first weeks at least, the eight girls were to be billeted together before being handed into the care of their new husbands.

'I will come and see you as soon as I can,' she muttered to her friend. 'To make sure you are settled in appropriate lodgings.'

'We will be all right for this first evening, I think,' Judith replied. 'It is what comes later, when we are separated. Catrina, Petronella, they are so young . . .'

'*Ik begrijp het*,' Suzanne said softly. I understand.

As the afternoon wore on, Suzanne's voice grew hoarse with talking. Her legs began to ache and her stomach still felt uneasy. She gazed enviously at the jugs of brandy and sweet biscuits on plates set at regular intervals along the officials' table, but no one thought to offer her any sustenance.

Finally, only one family was left to process. Pierre Jaubert came from the village of Motte d'Aigues. After a perilous journey over the mountains separating France from Germany, he had finally arrived in Rotterdam in the spring of 1688. He had joined the *China* with his new bride. Sweet and young, she had succumbed to a fever a mere week after boarding. With unseemly haste – or so it appeared to Suzanne – Jaubert had married another woman, who had also been widowed on board.

To begin with, Suzanne had avoided them. But as the weather changed, with the *China* leaving the Bay of Biscay and sailing down the Portuguese coast to the Islas Afortunadas, Suzanne found herself drawn to Jaubert's company. Though he could not read or write his own name, he was an amusing storyteller and his tales of his escape from his home to Geneva, his flight along the Rhine and the Maas rivers, kept everyone captivated on deck at night. The story always finished with a flourish as Jaubert produced his New Testament from his jerkin, a bible no larger than a man's hand, and brandished it above his head like a hell-fire preacher.

'This book,' he would say, 'this holy book, has travelled with me the length and breadth of France. It is this book –' at this point, Jaubert would press it to his chest – 'it is this holy book that has kept me safe, kept the soldiers' eyes averted.'

Though the details varied with each telling, the bare bones remained the same: unwilling to leave behind his sole family heirloom, but knowing that the possession of a French bible would mark him as a Huguenot and, so, hand him a death sentence, Jaubert had wrapped it in a waxed cloth and hidden it inside a *boule* of bread.

'And so here I stand, on this good ship *China*, knowing that God's light is still shining upon me. Amen.'

Suzanne had also come to admire his new wife, Isabeau. She was not given to words unless she had something of value to say, but she was steady and loyal. Suzanne thought she would be the perfect settler wife for the flamboyant and sociable Jaubert.

'*Juffrouw* Joubert, *alstublieft*. If you please.'

The *regisseur* was waving his hand impatiently. Suzanne realised she had allowed her concentration to lapse. She invited her friend to stand beside her.

'This is Pierre Jaubert. He is travelling with—'

'Never mind that,' the *regisseur* snapped, no doubt also thinking of his supper.

Jaubert, like most of the refugees, spoke Provençal rather than Parisian French, so Suzanne spoke slowly and carefully. 'Pierre, you will be given, as head of the household, two hundred and ten *eight-reales* and a plot of land in a place they call Drakenstein.'

'Where is that?' he asked, but was silenced by a fierce stare from the *regisseur*.

'I will tell you presently,' Suzanne replied. 'It is where most are being settled.'

'Is the land good?'

'I hope so.'

Jaubert nodded.

'They will also give you,' she said, as the *regisseur* read down his list, 'an axe, a sickle, seven bags of corn, a spade, a pound and a half of lead, a flintstone—'

'Good, good.'

'– as well as a half-share in a cooking pot, a half-share in a chisel, a boring tool and a brace-and-bit.'

'But what is my wife to do with only a half—'

'Pierre, please,' Suzanne murmured, then continued: 'Also, a half-share in a musket with a pound of gunpowder, a third-share in eight cattle—'

Jaubert snorted.

'– and a third share in a plough. It would be wise to thank him,' she finished sternly.

'*Dank u*,' Jaubert said loudly to the *regisseur*, as if talking to an idiot child. It was all Suzanne could do not to laugh.

'Sign here,' the *regisseur* instructed, pushing the document to the edge of the table.

It was only now that Suzanne saw that he had spelled Pierre's family name incorrectly, no doubt because he had been speaking her own name all afternoon.

'It is Jaubert,' she tried to say, 'with an "a", not Joubert with an "o".'

Her friend waved her concerns away and signed with a cross at the bottom of the page.

'It hardly matters, so long as I receive what they promise me.'

Despite her fatigue, and her parched throat, Suzanne smiled. She had no doubt that Pierre Jaubert – now Joubert – would thrive in this harsh land.

CHAPTER FOUR

Night had fallen over the Colony.

It had been a long afternoon but, finally, everyone was accounted for and assigned somewhere to stay for the first few weeks. As an unmarried woman Suzanne had been offered a small stipend. She'd refused it, knowing it would stand her in better stead with the authorities if she was not seen as a drain on their resources. She had given her valuables into VOC safe-keeping – her little jewellery casket, some gold and silver coins she had managed to smuggle out of France – to be deposited in a vault in the Castle of Good Hope. It was a service offered to all travellers to the Cape.

Most of the new arrivals were billeted in lodgings behind the Company buildings near the harbour, in huts made of clay and straw. The Provençal families were happy to be close together, even if their quarters were little better than the cramped conditions onboard ship. They were safe, they were on dry land. The Dutch girls were a few streets further back from the water's edge.

Suzanne and Florence had been allocated a single-storeyed house, sitting between the main square and the Company gardens. It was in a pleasant quarter of the town and close to the new hospital. The house itself belonged to a wealthy merchant who had sailed to Batavia with his wife last April and was not expected to return for twelve months. A verandah and a painted front door led into a small entrance hall with a wooden bench, an occasional table and rough whitewashed walls. There was a parlour with a shuttered window overlooking the street, two wooden upholstered armchairs and a square dining table with four woven-backed chairs, a chest of drawers and a settle with cushions. There was also a tiny kitchen with a hearth and a pail of water for washing, and beyond it, a bedchamber with a large rough-hewn bed with a straw mattress. The floors were tiled throughout, so it was clean and dry. Suzanne loved it on sight, though was disappointed to discover there were no books.

She had changed from her travelling clothes into her *robe de chambre* and she and Florence were sitting at the dining table, the remains of their meal between them – a loaf of bread and some cured meat, a dish of salted cabbage and watered-down brandy. A single candle in a brass holder sent shadows dancing across the polished wood.

'*Gran'mère*, tell me plainly, do you wish we had not come? That we had stayed in Amsterdam?'

Florence smiled. 'I do not.'

Suzanne traced the whorls of the woodgrain with her finger. 'I worry that I should not have accepted your offer to come with me. It was wrong of me to think only of myself.'

'I weighed the matter, and made my choice.'

'But the journey was so hard, especially for a woman of your years.'

'Nothing is right in these troubled days,' Florence replied, with a rare spurt of anger. 'We could not remain in La Rochelle after what –' She broke off. 'Besides, I never had any love for Amsterdam once my father and aunt were gone. It was more painful to be there without them than to be somewhere new, a place with no memories.'

Suzanne nodded. 'That I understand.'

'Besides, how could I sit alone in Warmoesstraat wondering

every hour of the day if your ship had gone down, wondering if you were even alive or dead? There is nothing worse than not knowing, my grandmother taught me that. So, I decided it would be better to make the journey with you, however hard, than spend the rest of the days God has allotted to me in ignorance of your fate. And, of course,' she added, her milky eyes twinkling, 'you persist in seeing this mission of yours as being something to do with you only.'

Suzanne found herself blushing. 'Mission?'

'Do you think I am ignorant of the true reason you are here?'

'Whatever can you mean?'

'Louise.'

The name fell like a stone into the silence, disrupting the air. Though Suzanne spent much of her time thinking about Louise, to hear her name spoken aloud was somehow shocking.

'But how—'

Florence laughed. 'Your face is an open book, *petite*. Didn't I bring you up from the cradle? When you are plotting something, you have the same expression you had as a child. The tip of your tongue sticks out, you frown, just as you used to do when plotting how to get away with not saying your prayers at night.' She smiled fondly. 'And all the time in Warmoesstraat this past winter, when you disappeared into the library for hour upon hour, did you believe I thought you had turned philosopher? You forget that I knew Louise. I was not often in her company, but I have vivid memories of her in Paris, and of us visiting her in Amsterdam.'

Suzanne was silent for a moment, realising she was eager to hear her grandmother's memories, recollections from someone who had loved her.

'Did you know Louise's mother, too?'

'Marta, no. Though my father was fond of his older sister,

he was wary. She was lost as a child in Paris, so they spent little time together.'

'What about his younger sister?'

Florence sighed. 'Bernarda was a difficult woman. My father was dutiful – they were only two years apart in age and grew up together in Amsterdam – but she never quite fitted within the family. Bernarda was uncompromising, one of those austere Calvinists. She disapproved of Marta and, later, disapproved of Louise, too, Marta's child born out of wedlock.'

'Jealous, perhaps?'

'Perhaps so. My father was always trying to be the go-between, but Bernarda did not want to be part of the Joubert family – the flighty, immoral, French side of the family.'

'She and her husband had no children?'

Florence shook her head. 'None, which is why the old Joubert home on Zeedijk passed out of the family. When Bernarda died, having outlived Frans by some years, she left the house to the Dutch Reformed Church.'

Suzanne felt she could almost see them, these family ghosts – Minou, Marta, Louise, Bernarda – some benign, others not.

'My own mother was a discontented woman, too,' Florence continued. 'Always finding fault and wishing for a different life. My baby brother died when he was barely a year old and my father was away so much – he was in the service of the great king, Henri IV – so she was much on her own. I regret to say she paled in comparison to Louise, who was determined and quick-witted. Louise was the mother I wished I'd had and I felt guilty for wanting that.' Florence gave a deep sigh. 'So, here we find ourselves on the other side of the world. Like you, *petite*, I have always wondered what happened to Louise. She would be more than one hundred years old now, you realise she cannot still be alive?'

'I know. I just need to discover where she lies. Make sure that she is remembered, I suppose.'

Florence took her hand. 'You see this as your mission to discover what befell Louise, but I would not go to my Maker ignorant of what happened to her either. For good, or for ill.'

Suzanne stood up and walked to the window that faced in the direction of the Castle of Good Hope. Through the slats of the shutters, she could see braziers on the five bastions flickering.

'Why did you not admit you knew what I intended?' she asked, aware she had underestimated her grandmother. 'Once we'd set sail at least. Why wait until now?'

Florence sat back in her chair. 'There is little privacy on a ship and I wanted you to confide in me when you were ready. But curiosity got the better of me. You are considerate and mindful of my years – too mindful, and that leads you to try to shelter me. There is no point in that. My hair might be grey, but my mind is as sharp as ever it was. I have seen much in my life, survived much. Will you not tell me what you intend?'

Suzanne felt something shift inside her. Her sense of purpose sharpened, as if some kind of bargain had been struck. She returned to the table, unhooked her leather bag from the back of the chair, pulled out Louise's diary and sat down. It was her bible, in a way, a talisman as much as Pierre Jaubert's Holy Book.

'I don't yet know. But this is where we start. With Louise's own words.'

CHAPTER FIVE

The sound of men's voices reverberated against the wooden walls of the tavern, the volume rising with every measure of brandy served. Driek Holsteen could barely hear himself think.

At the end of every voyage, he promised himself that he would not disembark and head straight for a hostelry. Driek had sailed the so-called 'wagon trail' before. After more than four months at sea, drinking bumboo and watery ale, he knew he didn't have a head for the rough Cape wine. Ease yourself back in, he told himself. King for a day or six, a week's onshore leave before the *China* sailed on to Batavia, her final destination. It was to be his last voyage. He had served ten years in the VOC fleet. He would get his lump sum, enough to settle down and find a wife.

'But where?' he slurred aloud, pointing at his own reflection in the mirror set above the door.

Batavia was too hot, too many flies. He wasn't cut out to be a farmer and the character of the officials in the Cape wasn't to his liking – too pious, too obsessed with rules and regulations – no good for a happy-go-lucky fellow like him.

'A good man, mind,' Driek told the mirror, tapping his finger to his chest. 'Not a saint, but . . .' He could hold his hands up to having made mistakes. 'But with a heart of a lion,' he murmured, remembering the words of a pretty doxy lying in his arms in a room in Rotterdam.

He might wed her, if she was still free. Could he remember

her name? Driek drained his tankard and tried to summon up her features.

'No need to rush,' he slurred, knowing the damage was already done. He was drunk.

The tavern grew ever noisier as more and more of his comrades from the ship – soldiers and sailors both – pushed their way into the confined space. Though little more than a shed, it was popular because it was the hostelry furthest from the Company buildings that lined much of the waterfront. A long and narrow room, with a counter at the end running the width of the building, there were no windows, though the wide double doors were pinned back to let in the cool night air. Driek laughed. After four months odd at sea, anything the land had to offer was sweet. Sailors brought their own tankards and, though there was nothing to eat, not even dry biscuits, the rough wine and brandy kept flowing so long as a man had *eight-reales*, pieces-of-eight, in his pocket.

Driek sighed. What he wouldn't give for an honest quart of Dutch ale, a comfortable stool and a full pipe. He was a man of simple needs. He looked down into his tankard and saw it was empty. He tipped it upside down, unwilling to believe the evidence of his own eyes, then scrambled in his pocket for a coin.

Nothing. He would have sworn on his mother's life he'd had another. Driek peered around, hoping to see a familiar face, yet somehow all the Rotterdam men had vanished. But it was too early to withdraw.

'The night is young,' he mumbled.

He stood up, a little unsteady on his feet. Perhaps he had spent all his coins already? Driek surveyed the clientele, all hard-working men like him looking for a little good cheer after the travails of the day. No officials here, not fancy enough, but solid labouring men who wanted nothing more than to whet their throats and perhaps, later, a little female company to help the night pass.

His eyes fixed on a table he hadn't previously noticed, away from the door, with four drinkers huddled around it. They looked like pioneers, not the sort of lily-livered excuses for men who passed their days with a quill and parchment.

Driek pulled himself up. They were short like him, with pale skin. He narrowed his eyes. Dutch, surely? He took all fellows at face value – he wasn't one of those who hated anyone who wasn't of his race – but he preferred his own kind. Wouldn't they help out a countryman in need? Lend him a little something to tide him over?

Taking it one careful step at a time, he made his way over to the table. Four sets of eyes stared up at him, not exactly friendly, but without open animosity.

'*Heren*,' he said, concentrating on enunciating each letter. 'Gentlemen, friends, I have information that might please you! If you stand me a drink.'

A man with a thick black beard looked up at him. 'Is that so?'

Driek put his hands on the table to steady himself. 'I came in on the *China* and sail on to Batavia in a few days.' He dropped his voice to a conspiratorial whisper. 'But do you know what we brought with us?'

'The pox?' the bearded man said, and his friends laughed.

'Another swarm of French rats,' a cadaverous man with red hair added. 'They can't even speak our language. This is our land, they turn up with their airs and graces, and they're not even grateful. Peasants, all of them.'

Driek tapped his nose. 'Girls,' he said. 'Young, unaccompanied, pure as the day they were born. Eight of them, ripe for the taking.' He licked his dry lips. 'And I know where they are billeted.'

There was a pause, then the ringleader held out his hand. 'Lars Eltorp.' He clicked his fingers, summoning a resigned-looking serving man. 'A quart of ale for our friend. Sit.'

Driek sank happily onto the stool. 'Don't mind if I do.'

CHAPTER SIX

Suzanne smoothed the first page of Louise's diary flat and read aloud, though she knew the words by heart.

'"*Today I am sentenced to swing. Before the sun rises, I will be taken from here to a place of execution and there, hanged by the neck until I am dead.*"'

She paused, allowing Louise's voice to echo through the chamber, then continued.

'She began writing this diary when she was imprisoned in Las Palmas de Gran Canaria, accused of a murder she claims she did not commit.'

Florence raised her eyebrows. 'She claims?'

'I am determined to keep an open mind, not take anything on trust. Having said that, I am inclined to believe her in that Louise does admit to other murders.' She pointed to the words lower down the page: '"*I confess I have killed, but only ever in self-defence or to protect those I love.*" Why would she lie? This is a private record of her hopes and fears.'

'Not intended for other eyes.'

Suzanne nodded. 'Exactly. And she writes of how it was her grandmother, Minou, who impressed upon her the importance of women speaking for themselves.'

Florence smiled warmly. 'Minou kept journals throughout her life. I never read them – they were lodged in Amsterdam in Alis's care and we were in Paris, then La Rochelle – but I know that Minou believed in bearing witness, in the power of the written word. She recorded not only her own story, but that of our whole family during the turbulent times through which they were living.' She waved her hand. 'Listen to me! You learnt all of this when we were staying in Warmoesstraat.'

'It is good to hear your thoughts, *Gran'mère*. But yes, I read everything I could find in the archives. It is fortunate that Alis kept everything.'

Florence nodded. 'Alis was the baby of the family – some twelve years younger than Minou – and outlived her older sister by some years. She saw herself as the keeper of the flame.'

'That was my impression, too.'

Suzanne closed her eyes and was instantly transported back to Amsterdam, picturing the five-storeyed red-bricked merchant's house on Warmoesstraat with its elegant neck gable and ornate pediments. A painted tile set between the stone-arched windows showed a richly dressed man, standing in front of a cargo ship bearing the van Raay family ensign, grain slipping through his fingers into a basket. Steps led up from street level to a narrow front door and into the entrance hall where stood a lacquered and ancient globe. To the left, was the library.

Suzanne inhaled, as if she might catch the smell of the wax as the candles burnt low and the scent of leather bindings. She remembered reading every page, every piece of correspondence, until the last vestiges of light had gone from the sky and her hands were stiff and blue with cold. Instinctively, she rubbed her fingers together. Then, she opened her eyes and was back in the Cape damp winter's night.

'Even in those of Minou's journals that have survived, there are gaps,' she continued. 'Times when she did not, or could not, write. But the story of how Louise came into her inheritance in Paris when she was twenty-five years of age, and Minou's fears for her granddaughter, she set down in detail.' Suzanne looked back to the diary on the table. 'Louise, on the other hand, was less disciplined, so all we have is this one diary. But it is a rich source of information. She writes of her eleventh-hour reprieve in Gran Canaria, of how the clerk to the court ran with the stay of execution in his hand when she was already standing at the gallows. She writes of her beloved Gilles and of her half-brother, Phillipe, who negotiated her release . . .' Suzanne glanced up. 'I had hoped to find an explanation of how Phillipe came to be on the Islas Afortunadas in the first instance, but Louise only begins at the moment they met –'

'Though we know some of that from Alis.'

'Yes. Alis recorded how Phillipe arrived in Amsterdam in search of Louise and of how she, and her companion, Cornelia, told him she had sailed to Gran Canaria on the *Old Moon*. Forgive me for repeating what you know, *gran'mère*, but it helps me to order my thoughts.' Suzanne took a sip of her brandy and grimaced. 'Lord, it is a good thing that Commander Van der Stel is encouraging our countrymen to the Cape to produce palatable wine! I cannot imagine a single Frenchman who would willingly fill his belly with this!'

Florence laughed. 'Though it is better than that foul bumboo on the ship.'

Suzanne shuddered at the memory of the sickly mixture of rum, sugar, water and nutmeg the crew drank from dusk until dawn.

'Alis and Cornelia only discovered that Louise was still alive when the *Old Moon* arrived back in Amsterdam two years later, bringing her diary with it.'

'But there is no explanation for why she stayed behind and sent her ship back to Amsterdam under the command of her lieutenant?'

'None, nor why Louise asked him to take her diary back with him.'

Florence frowned. 'I imagine Louise wanted to entrust it to Alis's safekeeping, and for her family to know what had happened to her. Though why she did not write a letter, I cannot say.'

'Nor I.'

'And what of the Tarot card?' Suzanne said, drawing the shabby square of white cloth from her satchel. 'It always seemed to me out of character for Louise to have such a thing.' She unfolded it. The Justice card, though worn from its travels, nonetheless lit the room with its bright colours: red, yellow, white and blue. 'Nothing I read suggested that Louise was a superstitious woman. It's possible that the card wasn't even hers. But it clearly meant something, otherwise she wouldn't have concealed it inside the diary and sent it back to Amsterdam, too.'

Florence carefully turned the card over in her hands. 'You have found no hidden message, no alterations?'

'I cannot discern that it has been tampered with in any way.'

They fell silent. Outside, Suzanne could hear the sounds of the Colony. Out at sea, a faint rumble of dry thunder could be heard. She supposed the storm had passed them by. She felt oddly at home, though she wondered if she would ever get used to the way the world was upside down here – that August was midwinter and December the height of summer. Or that the sun at midday was in the north.

Suzanne sat back in her chair. 'What I think is this: that Phillipe, by saving her from the gallows, considered he had some claims of ownership over her. Louise acknowledged that debt and would not have wanted to offend him. But, increasingly, she writes of how she and Gilles both resented Phillipe's demands. There was clearly bad blood between the two men.'

Florence considered. 'Would that not mean he would turn

his anger against Gilles, or vice versa, rather than against Louise herself?'

Suzanne's face darkened. 'There's many a man who destroys what he cannot have rather than let another enjoy what he might not. It is a matter of possession, not affection.' She paused, collecting herself. 'Louise also notes that, as a way of persuading her to permit him to sail with them, he claimed he had letters of interest to show her—'

'Between whom?'

'I surmise – though she never says so directly – between her mother, Marta, and their common father, Louis Vidal. The more I think about that, the more I wonder if that was a ruse. Certainly, Louise writes about how, whenever she asks to see the letters, Phillipe bids her to be patient.'

'You don't think they existed?'

Suzanne shrugged. 'I don't know, perhaps? Whatever the reason, Louise goes from wanting to attribute honourable motives to Phillipe's accompanying them to questioning his true purpose. The *Old Moon* had been a happy ship under her command. His presence appears to have set everyone at one another's throats.' She paused. 'But it is her final entry that preys on my mind. Once I had read it, I could not but re-interpret the entries that had gone before. I think Phillipe's presence became less of an inconvenience and more of a problem to be solved. A threat, even.'

She turned the diary around so Florence could read the entry for herself.

I think he means me harm.

CHAPTER SEVEN

Judith Verbeek checked the window and the door once again. She had done everything she could to secure their lodgings, but she still did not feel safe. It was a low-lying clay house with a straw roof, a single door without a lock or bolt, a narrow window with wooden shutters and no latch.

Once she was sure the other girls were sleeping, curled up together on the platform like kittens high above the gusty floor, she dragged the heavy wooden chest across the door to serve as a barricade, then sat to keep watch. Eight young women with no chaperone or protection – she knew word had spread like smoke through the Colony. The winks and leers of men in the street, as the VOC official had accompanied them to the lodgings, were evidence of that. Everyone knew they were here. She felt like a woodcock in a trap, waiting for the fox to come.

Judith hoped she was wrong. Perhaps things were different here in the Colony? Still, her experiences in the orphanage had led her never to let down her guard.

On board the *China*, despite the sickness and the stench below deck, she had felt secure. She had slept, confident that there was always a pair of eyes upon them. The sailors and soldiers, though foul-mouthed and vulgar when the officers were not in earshot, did not bother them. And she had been in the company of other women, many of them mothers, whose quiet but watchful attention made her feel safe. Now she was on her own and it was many hours until daybreak.

Judith pulled the candle closer, and prayed for the light to come.

Driek Holsteen stumbled along in the wake of his new drinking companions. The slight feeling of uneasiness he pushed to one side. He had promised to show them where the Dutch girls were staying – just to have a look, just to liven up the evening – but he was no longer sure where he was. It was four years since he had last come on shore in the Colony and everything had changed. A white moon, the same red earth, but so many more buildings, paths leading this way and that.

He blinked and tried to reorientate himself. They were still somewhere in the narrow alleyways between the harbour and the town, heading towards the main square but, in the dark, every street looked the same. It was oddly reminiscent of the streets around the Oude Kerk in Amsterdam and the canal-side dwellings low in the water. Here, in the Colony, the mood was the same: desperation, inebriation, loneliness, menace. He wished he was in his bed.

Then he realised that they were near the Slave Lodge, a windowless brick structure. A little further ahead, a door opened and a rectangle of light painted the ground. A woman came out, glanced over to them, pulled her headscarf over her face then started to walk quickly away in the direction of the water.

'*Hoi!*'

One of his companions, sallow of complexion and with a weeping eye, stopped dead in front of him, causing Driek to barrel into him. 'Hey you,' the man yelled again. 'Lady.' There was a guffaw of laughter from another, quickly silenced by a jab to the ribs. 'Am I not addressing you?'

The woman had reached the junction ahead of them. Even

in his ale-soaked state, Driek could see she was respectable. Not a woman to be bought. She pretended not to hear.

'Why do you pay me no heed, lady? My money not good enough?'

'It's not your money that's the problem,' one of the other men jeered.

Driek wheezed with laugher. 'That's good,' he slurred, 'very good.'

The first man lurched forward. 'I have *reales* enough. Look.' He thrust out his hand, sending the silver coins scattering on the earth. Falling to his knees, he began to scrabble in the dirt.

'Get up,' Eltorp hissed.

Instantly, the mood in the group changed. Driek had been in their company for long enough to know that whatever Eltorp said was law. If he laughed, they laughed. If he raised his fist, they cowered.

'*Hoer!*' Eltorp shouted, clicking his fingers. Whore.

The woman turned, enough for Driek to see a spark of terror in her eyes, then she started to run.

Eltorp picked up his pace. 'You should be grateful you have caught my friend's attention. Or is a white man not good enough for you?'

Driek found himself looking at his feet. He didn't want any trouble. It was only high spirits, letting off steam after four months at sea. He knew nothing about the standing of his drinking companions in the Colony, only that he couldn't afford to be arrested and thrown in the brig.

'Do not turn your back on me,' Eltorp shouted again, picking up one of the spilt coins and throwing it at her back.

'My friend, I don't think the lady is for—' Driek began, but events overtook him.

Eltorp grabbed at the woman's arm. She gave a sharp cry,

and tried to shake herself free. His three other companions lumbered behind him, nervous and uncertain. Lars spun the woman round and grabbed her chin between pinched fingers.

'My friend only wanted to talk to you, but you have offended him.' His grip tightened. 'Do whores have no manners in the Colony?'

Driek heard the sound of Eltorp's belt buckle loosen and he felt a stab of alarm. Shame, too. Surely he wouldn't make an attempt upon the woman here? He was suddenly aware of the stink of stale wine on his own breath, and was repulsed. Without meaning to, he heard himself speak.

'There are others more willing,' he stammered, pointing ineffectually towards the harbour. 'This way. I'll show you.'

Eltorp's arm moved so fast, Driek did not see it coming. The blow of knuckle on bone, the explosion of blood in his mouth.

'Stay out of this, Dutchie.'

Someone gave a nervous laugh as Eltorp took a fistful of the woman's hair and pushed her back against the wall.

'Someone needs to teach you a lesson.'

Driek's ears were ringing. He didn't know what to do. A good man would not walk away. But then, he wasn't a good man. He turned and hurried away in the direction they had come. He hammered on the door of the house the woman had come out of, hoping to alert someone to the mischief, then slunk away into the shadows.

Once he was out of sight, he rested his hand against the wall to catch his breath. Then, he heard the woman scream – a single, desperate sound that pierced the night, followed by the sound of shutters snapping open, like the retort of a gun, then other voices shouting. Men's voices, yelling in the language of the spice island they called Madagasikara, a pirate stronghold now. At least, he thought that was right. Not Dutch, certainly.

The street behind him suddenly filled. He heard the rasp of a blade being drawn and all Driek wanted was to be as far away from the fracas as possible. He stumbled forward, unaware of the thud of running feet at his back, until he felt his arm grasped.

'Show me where they are?' Eltorp demanded. 'I will not have this entire evening wasted.'

Driek tried to pretend he didn't know what he meant, but now there was the tip of a knife at his neck. 'I can't remember—'

'You lie,' Eltorp sneered. 'Besides, white meat is more palatable.'

The point of the blade jabbed harder. Driek felt a drop of blood trickle down his neck to the collar of his jerkin.

'This way,' he mumbled, staggering forward and wondering how he could lead Eltorp away from the orphan girls and yet still save his own skin.

Judith heard the shouting from the Malagasy quarter, only a few streets away.

Quickly, she pulled the candle close and blew, extinguishing the flame, then sat in the darkness with her heart thudding. She prayed that none of the girls would wake up, or cry out. That this trouble would pass them by.

She started to pray, though, in all her nineteen years on this earth, God had never listened to her nor shown her any kindness. Her life had been hard, and full of sorrow. But she kept reciting the words, praying desperately that this time He was watching over her.

CHAPTER EIGHT

'Did you hear something?' Suzanne said, bolting upright in the bed, her heart thudding. For an instant, she forgot where she was. Then she turned to her grandmother lying beside her, and remembered: they were in the merchant's house on the main square in the Colony at the Cape of Good Hope.

She was safe.

Florence was sleeping. She looked so defenceless in repose, so small and vulnerable. Their evening's conversation had been stimulating, but Suzanne's sense of guilt at having dragged her grandmother halfway across the known world was no less sharp.

Then she heard another sound outside and her chest tightened: men's voices, near at hand. Lying in her bedchamber in La Rochelle, listening to the taverns empty around the port, it had often been hard to tell the difference between good companionship and something uglier. In the end, it turned out that the greatest threat could come from inside one's own home. As always, she pushed the memory to the back of her mind. She could not survive otherwise.

Now wide awake, Suzanne swung her feet down to the ground, threw a shawl around her shoulders and tiptoed from the bedchamber into the parlour. She checked the bolt to the front door was shot, then crept back to the window and carefully pushed the shutter open a little until she could see out. Horizontal shafts of moonlight flooded the room.

She could see nothing amiss. Then, from a little further along the street, she heard footsteps hurrying in their direction.

Quickly, Suzanne pulled the shutter back into place to leave no more than a crack, then pressed her eye to the gap.

There were two men, walking close together: one with an untamed black beard, a rough-looking fellow, she did not recognise; the other was a sailor she remembered from the ship, seeming the worse for wear. What was his name? As they drew level, she saw the bigger man had pinned the sailor's arm up behind his back. Suzanne gasped. With his other hand, he was pressing a knife to Driek's neck. Yes, Driek, that was his name.

'How much further?' the man hissed.

'In truth, I kn-know not,' Driek stammered. 'It was tittle-tattle, I mi-might have misheard, I might have—'

'You were the one who traded information about the girls for the price of a jug of brandy. You will deliver on our bargain or . . . Do I make myself clear, Dutchie?'

The answering whimper from Driek suggested the knife was earning its keep.

Suzanne shrank further back into the shadows, waiting until their steps echoed into silence. Then the night was once again quiet. Relieved, she turned to go back to bed, then stopped.

'The girls . . .'

Cold fear trickled down her spine – the man couldn't have meant Judith and the Rotterdam orphans, could he? Suzanne shook her head, as if to dislodge the thought. She was making something of nothing. But then she remembered how the sailors and soldiers had whispered about where the girls would be lodging, and how long it would be before each was allocated to a husband. Nudges and winks, crude gestures.

Suzanne poured herself a half-measure of the rough Cape brandy, swallowing it down in one gulp. No reason for 'the girls' to be 'her' girls. Like any harbour city, there would be flophouses and doxies. Wasn't it more likely that Driek's companion meant that? Except Driek had only just come ashore. Even if he was a seasoned traveller to the Colony, what information would he possess that a local man wouldn't have already? Whereas new arrivals . . .

The longer she paced, the more her thoughts spiralled. And if her fears were justified, Judith would be no match for a drunken and violent man – the knife against Driek's neck spoke to that.

She looked through into the bedchamber. Gentle snores spoke to the fact that her grandmother was still sleeping soundly. Suzanne took quill and ink from her travelling chest, penned a brief note and propped it against the jug on the table where Florence could not fail to see it should she awaken. Then, quickly dressing and tightening her stays, she put on her cloak and boots, and slipped out into the hallway. She knew what she was doing was unwise, but she saw no alternative. She stepped out into the street, locked the door and posted the key back under the gap.

'*C'est dans le besoin qu'on reconnaît ses vrais amis*,' a phrase her grandmother often used. It is when in need that one recognises one's true friends.

She would be that friend to Judith, for better or worse.

'*Onze Vader die in de hemelen zijt*,' Judith murmured, saying the words of the Lord's Prayer over and again. 'Hallowèd be Thy name . . .'

Someone was hammering at the door. Heavy, single blows like the tolling of a funeral bell. Petronella, a pretty girl with yellow ringlets, lifted her sleepy head from her mat on the platform and looked down.

'What's happening? Is the ship sinking?'

Judith leant up and patted her shoulder. 'It's just a bad dream, we're not at sea any more. Go back to sleep.'

The hammering was getting louder. Catrina also woke and began to cry. Now, the latch was being rattled. Wilhelmina put her arms around the younger girl and tried to soothe her.

'They must have mistaken the house,' Judith said, struggling to steady her voice. 'The noise will stop in a moment when they realise their error.'

But she watched in horror as the bar began to lift. The chest would not hold whoever it was at bay for long. All seven girls were sitting up now, staring wide-eyed at the door. Steeling herself with a courage she did not feel, Judith spoke calmly: 'Move to the very back of the platform, put your blankets over your heads and don't say a word. Whatever happens, don't come down until I say. None of you, do you understand? Quickly, now. Not a sound.'

She put her finger to her lips and tried to smile, hoping to reassure them. Used to obeying the orders of the matron of the orphanage, and then the officers of the ship, the girls did as they were told without question.

Judith smoothed down her skirts, made sure her cap was covering her hair, then stepped to the barricaded door. '*Wie is daar?*' Who is it?

The only answer was a guffaw of laughter then, to her horror, the door opened a crack as the chest began to move inexorably into the room.

'It is late,' she cried. 'You cannot come in.'

At this, she heard a savage kick, and the chest slid further into the chamber. One of the girls screamed, quickly hushed by another.

'You cannot come in!'

A figure was standing in the open doorway. Judith could see little in the darkness, but she could hear his ragged breathing and make out that he was tall and broad, and holding a knife.

He dragged another man into the room beside him, smaller and rocking slightly on his feet. A sailor she recognised from the ship.

'Sirs, please leave.'

Judith took a step back, but the bearded man came further into the room. She could smell his ale-soaked breath.

'Look at you, your colour is high. Under your drab exterior, you're all the same.'

To Judith's horror, he reached out and fumbled at the buttons on her bodice.

'We all know what you Dutch bitches get up to behind closed doors.'

Judith pushed him away, but far from quelling his attack, her sudden resistance heated his blood.

'You may be plain, and still as ripe with the stink of the ship as Driek here, but your skin is unpocked,' he muttered, his dark eyes lit with the thrill of the chase. 'And he says you're clean.'

Without warning, he thrust his hand between her legs. Judith was torn between fighting back and not wanting to terrify the girls by screaming. She tried to push him off.

'Please, no,' she whispered. 'There are children sleeping.'

Inflamed by lust, he let the knife drop from Driek's neck. The sailor saw a chance to escape and tried to slip past, but tripped over the corner of the chest and, instead, stumbled into his companion.

The big man roared and spun round, snatching up the knife again. Judith saw the blade flash in the gloom.

Driek threw up his hands. 'Lars, no! It was a mistake. I slipped.'

But the man was in no mood to listen. He struck. The blade missed. Judith smothered a cry, praying the girls would have the sense to stay hidden. Driek was backing away, holding up his hands in apology. Lars lashed out again. This time he hit his mark. For a moment, the seafarer stood with a look of bewilderment on his face. Then his hands went to a jagged wound at his throat. He seemed to register the burgeoning splash of blood on his stained shirt and then, as if in slow motion, fell forward over the chest.

Lars stood stock still, as if surprised by what he had done, suddenly sober. He stared at Judith, then spat in her face, shoved past the chest and disappeared out into the night.

Shaking, Judith slammed the door shut behind him and dropped the latch. Then she forced herself to look at Driek. What was she going to do? He was not a kind man, but he had left them alone on the ship and occasionally stepped in when other sailors were bawdy. Even though he had brought Lars to their door, she couldn't bring herself to bear him ill will. Nor could she let him die without prayer.

'For Thine is the kingdom, the power and the glory, for ever and ever. Amen.'

Her hands trembling, Judith put a cloth over his face, then wrapped her arms around herself to try to stop the shaking. She heard a creak on the ladder, then felt birdlike arms go round her waist and looked down. Petronella's sweet face was looking up at her.

'Never mind,' the young girl said, with a wisdom belying her years. 'He can't hurt anyone now.'

Judith gave a wild laugh, then clamped her hand over her mouth. If she gave way to hysteria now, she would never stop.

CHAPTER NINE

Determination had driven Suzanne from their lodgings. But now she was walking across the main square, barely lit by a thin moon and with the cool night air on her face, her courage was seeping away. She had not even thought to bring a lamp.

Stupid, stupid, stupid.

The word marked time with the pace of her feet. A solitary woman, walking alone in an unfamiliar town at night. She tried to summon the spirit of Louise to give her courage, but Louise did not answer. And still the mocking voice in her head would not let her be.

Stupid.

Suzanne knew nothing of the customs of the Colony. She wasn't even entirely sure of where she was going, though the official's description of the house where Judith and the girls were billeted had been clear enough: a small dead-end street, the shutters unpainted, in one of three roads behind the main VOC administration buildings at the harbour.

She tried to calm herself. Unlike the medieval cities of La Rochelle and Amsterdam, with their chaotic narrow streets and canals that wound back upon themselves, the Colony was laid out like a grid in the distant shadow of Table Mountain – efficient and logical: the Castle by the water's edge, the main streets and buildings to the north; the Company gardens to the south. Further away, a separate development where Khoi and San, who worked for the VOC, lived. It ought to be simple to find the street she wanted. But her nerves would not be calmed and her heart continue to hammer as if it might burst through her ribs.

Suzanne pressed on all the same, letting the half-moon light her way. Hadn't she faced the worst, and survived? Hadn't she learnt to evade the soldiers hunting Huguenots for sport? Hadn't she travelled halfway across the known world? Surely she was capable of navigating the streets of the Colony at night, provided she kept her wits about her?

Besides, if not her, then who?

It was that thought that kept her going, past darkened wooden shutters in the white mist, until she found the right place. She would reassure herself Judith was fine and that the girls were in no danger, then she would return home to her bed.

Suzanne raised her hand and knocked gently on the door.

'He's come back!' Catrina wailed, looking down from the platform.

Judith twisted round, trying to screen Driek's body so Catrina wouldn't see the blood pooled on the beaten-earth floor. Then, from the other side of the door, came a welcome and familiar voice.

'Judith? It's Suzanne, are you there?'

Almost weeping with relief, Judith opened the door and dragged her friend inside.

'This will sound absurd,' Suzanne began to say, then blanched when she saw the body doubled over the chest. She swallowed hard. 'Who is it?'

'Driek Holsteen. From the *China*.'

'Did you . . .?'

Judith waved her hands. 'No, no. He came here with a man – Lars, I think he called him. They were both in their cups. Driek could barely stand. There was an altercation and

Lars . . . well, he . . .' Tears finally started to roll down her cheeks. 'All I was thinking was how to keep him away from the girls . . .' Her words trailed away.

Suzanne closed her eyes, trying to banish the memory of La Rochelle: the fear of it, the shame. The pain. She counted to ten until she was sure her voice would hold, then opened her eyes again.

'You must have been terrified,' she said steadily. 'Did he . . . did he hurt you?'

'No. He touched me where he should not have, but . . . no.'

Suzanne sighed with relief. 'Where is Lars now? Where did he go?'

Her friend was folded in on herself, arms twisted in a knot around her narrow frame.

'He left. I don't know where. When you knocked, I thought it was him returned.'

Suzanne looked down at the dead man. 'We have to tell somebody.'

Judith shook her head. 'I don't want the girls upset further.'

'Someone has to remove Driek's body and you will have to tell the authorities what happened. You can see that, Judith. We need help.'

The Dutch girl was still in shock, but finally she nodded. 'What do you want me to do?'

'Pass me a blanket.'

Petronella responded quickly, scampering up the ladder and pulling down the one nearest to hand. Suzanne laid the rough brown cloth across the body and the chest, so only the soles of Driek's boots were visible. 'There. Now, do you have something for the girls to drink, or eat?'

'Yes.'

'Good. It will keep them distracted.' Suzanne dropped her voice. 'Did they witness the murder?'

'I cannot say.' Judith hesitated. 'I told them to hide at the back of the platform and cover their eyes. Certainly, they will have heard everything.'

'It is important you explain things to them before the authorities come. Tell them that the men mistook their way, they did not intend to be here. That they were lost. A fight broke out between them and one was killed. It's close enough to the truth.'

Judith understood. 'It will quash the idea that Driek and Lars were looking for this house in particular.'

'Yes. It won't take away the distress of what they might or might not have seen and heard, but it should make them less fearful.'

As Suzanne turned to leave, Judith tugged at her arm. 'But what can you do at this time of night? Can't you stay with us until it's light?'

Suzanne could hear the panic in her friend's voice.

'I'm sorry. I'll be as quick as I can.' She put her hand to Judith's cheek. 'You will be all right,' she said. 'You are strong, Judith. You need to stay strong. The worst is over.'

The Malagasy quarter was silent again. There were bloodstains on the ground after the fight, though the neighbours would claim to have heard nothing. Nothing at all.

Two men were dead – one of Eltorp's erstwhile drinking companions and a Malagasy man who had attempted to protect his sister from the white aggressors. Two others were injured. The local man had been spirited away into the house where his wounds were being treated by the woman Eltorp had attacked. Her murdered brother, too. They would look after their own. The dead sailor and his injured friend with red hair had been dragged to the alleyway behind the small United Reform Church and abandoned.

The third sailor had fled back to the anonymity of the harbour tavern, praying that Lars Eltorp would not get to hear how his drinking companions had been set upon by a gang of Malagasy men and come off the worst.

No one wanted the authorities involved.

CHAPTER TEN

Standing alone in the street, Suzanne let her own tears fall. She was weeping with relief for Judith, with impotent rage at a world where the worst of men brutalised women. She was weeping for herself and all that had been lost.

She allowed herself a few moments of weakness, then she wiped her eyes. Enough. She was not some green girl, afraid of her own shadow, she had a task to accomplish. Judith was relying upon her.

But what if they didn't believe Judith? A young woman with no money and no influence, brought here to be married to a man she had never met? What if they thought Judith had wielded the knife having invited Driek to her lodgings?

No matter. She had to try.

Suzanne took a breath of cool night air, pulled back her shoulders and set out, her racing thoughts keeping pace with her steps. She doubted there would be anyone in the VOC administration buildings at the harbour at this time of night. Wiser to head to the Castle – not that any of this was wise. She would speak to the night watch and make her report. Then, the matter would be out of her hands. She had no choice but to report Driek's death, just as she had to believe that, in this frontier land, there would be justice.

The bell began to toll the mournful hour. Four o'clock and nothing's right with the world, Suzanne thought, but she didn't turn back.

*

Adriaan Van Dijk listened to the hour fading into silence.

He was cold, his feet damp from tramping up and down outside the walls. Though a high-ranking and valued member of the administration, he took it upon himself to do this guard duty once a month, so as not to drift too far from the experience of the common soldier. Tonight, he was regretting his decision. He looked up in the direction of the bell tower, willing time to pass more quickly. Only two hours more and his watch would be over.

Adriaan shifted the musket in his hand, adjusted its position on his shoulder, then turned and retraced his steps along his section of the walls between the Leerdam and the Oranje bastions. At least by this time in the morning, when the taverns and flophouses were quiet and all decent citizens were in their beds, Adriaan could hear the sound of the waves lapping on the shore and against the jetty, and that reminded him of home.

Like so many men, far from their native lands, his sentimental thoughts took him back to his mother and his childhood in Rotterdam in a narrow townhouse close to the dam. His father had worked for the VOC in the Rotterdam Chamber, an administrator not a fighting man, and expected his four sons to follow the same path: Adriaan's eldest brother had been a soldier, killed during the *Rampjaar*, the disaster year of 1672 when Britain and France had nearly overrun the Netherlands; his second brother had been lost at sea when his ship went down just a year later; the third, no more than a few months old, had been taken in the plague that swept through Rotterdam in the cold early months twenty years prior to that. Though he had loved his mother dearly, Adriaan knew she had quickened him into life to replace the child she had lost. Sometimes, at night, when she was tired or had soothed her nerves with laudanum, she had murmured the name of his dead brother rather than his own as she rocked his cradle.

Adriaan turned back towards Leerdam. He was alone now, the last remaining member of the Van Dijk family, and he supposed he might as well be here as in Rotterdam with his ghosts. But he missed the old country and was resolved, when his service came to an end, to go home and build a different life for himself.

A less lonely life.

Suzanne peered through the mist at the Castle, shimmering in the drizzle.

'Choose wisely,' she muttered.

Whomever she approached might make a difference to the outcome: a dismissive, impatient man would react differently to someone more prepared to listen to a foreigner – and a woman, at that. For all that her Dutch was fluent, they would hear her French accent and mistrust it. Although the first Huguenot refugees had been welcomed, in recent years France had been making attempts on the United Provinces and the Netherlands was becoming increasingly protective of its borders and resentful of those seeking sanctuary: a drain on resources, too many mixed allegiances, too many spies in the pay of the French king. A shared religion did not make them Dutch.

Suzanne stared at the Castle walls. There were two sentries at the main gate. She rejected approaching them, thinking she would have a better chance explaining herself to one person alone. She headed instead for the section of the walls closest to her where a solitary guard was on patrol, his weary steps suggesting that he might be slower to put his finger on the trigger.

Suzanne stepped out to where she might be seen.

'*Mijnheer*, if you please,' she called. 'Could I speak with you?' She saw him stop and turn, as though expecting a trick. His fingers tightened on his musket, though the gun remained on his shoulder. 'I have come to report a crime.'

He pointed his musket in her direction. 'Show yourself.'

She took a careful step further into the light.

'Who else is with you?'

'No one,' she whispered, and heard him catch his breath.

'You walked across open land alone without a lamp, are you deranged?' He kept the gun trained on her. 'Who are you?'

'My name is Suzanne Joubert, I arrived on the *China* last afternoon with my grandmother.'

'A refugee?'

'No, we paid our own way.' She held up her hands. 'I am not armed.'

The soldier hesitated, then let his musket down. 'What is it you want, *juffrouw* Joubert?'

'I have come to report a murder.'

'What! Do you take me for a fool?'

'Not at all. Some two hours ago, two men – one a sailor from the *China* by the name of Driek Holsteen, the other unknown to me – forced their way into the lodgings where eight orphans from the same ship are billeted. Both men were inebriated. When the stranger tried to take advantage of one of the girls, Judith Verbeek, Holsteen intervened. In that struggle, he was mortally stabbed.'

'This is a very grave allegation.'

Suzanne met the sentry's gaze. He had a pale but determined face, with kind eyes. Startlingly blue, the colour of cornflowers. Wearing the distinctive long blue jacket with red lapels and lining of the VOC regiments, with white breeches and stockings, he was a man of perhaps thirty years, though with the air of one who spent his life behind a desk rather than on the battlefield.

'It is, nonetheless, true,' she said. 'We need help.'

'What is your part in this?'

Suzanne had been wondering how to account for her presence. If she admitted that a few overheard words and female intuition had led her there, he would not take her seriously.

'I heard men talking outside my window. Their words concerned me. Judith and I became friends during the crossing. I wanted to be certain she – and the other girls – were safe. None of them has ever left Rotterdam before. It is hard for them.'

The soldier's eyes widened. 'Rotterdam, did you say?'

'Yes. They come from the orphanage there and have been brought here to become part of the Colony as wives. Judith, as the oldest, acts as a guardian to them.'

'Grey dresses,' he said softly, with a new tone in his voice, almost wistful. 'I remember . . .'

He turned to look up to the bell tower as if assessing the hour. Then, to Suzanne's astonishment, he took her by the elbow and steered her back towards the town.

'Show me.'

CHAPTER ELEVEN

At a loss to account for the soldier's sudden urgency, Suzanne struggled to keep up with his long stride.

'How many people know where the girls are lodging?' he asked.

'Certainly everyone on the ship – crew and passengers alike – knew they were to be billeted together until the time came for them to be separated and taken to their permanent homes.'

'Which are to be?'

'They have not yet been told,' Suzanne replied, a little out of breath. 'They are to be married to settlers, but know nothing more than that. In terms of where they are staying, anyone present when we were being processed might have heard the address. That's to say, anyone who understands Dutch would have heard. Most of my co-religionists do not.'

'Ah,' he said. 'You are she.'

Suzanne stopped. 'I beg your pardon?'

'There was talk that a Frenchwoman from the *China* stepped in to act as interpreter. That was you, was it not?'

'It was,' she said, unable to tell if he disapproved.

'Surely a guard was set? Eight young ladies with no chaperone?'

'They were given no protection.'

'Ridiculous . . .'

'I agree.' Suzanne paused. 'I gave you my name, *mijnheer*. I am originally from La Rochelle, though more recently a citizen of Amsterdam. Might you do me the courtesy of telling me yours?'

He turned to look at her. 'Forgive me. I am Adriaan van Dijk, originally from Rotterdam.'

'Ah.' Suzanne smiled, now understanding his interest. For a moment, the two new allies looked at one another. Then they continued the rest of their way in silence until they reached the rough, dead-end street.

Judith was waiting immediately inside the door. Suzanne could see that, in the past hour, the shock of what had happened – and what might have happened – had hit home. She remembered having that same delayed reaction. Her friend's eyes were glassy from shock, there was a sheen of sweat on her skin and she kept picking at a loose thread on her grey sleeve. The other girls were sitting on their mats on the platform, as far away from Driek's body as it was possible to be in such confined quarters.

'Judith,' Suzanne said gently, 'this is Adriaan van Dijk from the garrison. He, too, comes originally from Rotterdam. He has offered to help us. *Mijnheer*, may I present Judith Verbeek.'

At first, it seemed as if she had not heard. Then Judith remembered her manners and gave a slight curtsey. 'That is very kind.'

Van Dijk bowed, then gestured to the trunk. 'May I?'

Judith stepped back as he lifted the blanket. Suzanne saw Driek's skin was now the colour of wax and the wound on his neck was gaping.

'Will you tell me what happened, *juffrouw* Verbeek?'

Judith blushed at the courtesy of his address, then began to recount the events of the night. Her voice was clear and without an excess of emotion, Suzanne admired her self-possession.

When she had finished, Van Dijk asked: 'You recognised Holsteen from the ship, that is correct?'

'I did.'

'But the other man was unknown to you.'

'I did not know him. He was tall, much bigger than Driek, with a full black beard and blue cape. He was called Lars – at least, I think that's the name Driek used. There was so much shouting and—'

'Ah! Lars Eltorp, I'd wager. I know of him.' Van Dijk turned to Suzanne. 'Does this sound like the man you saw previously?'

'It was dark, but I think so.'

'Eltorp is a blow-in from one of the pirate ships, a Zeelander. He has been a guest at the Castle on more than one occasion.'

Judith turned to Van Dijk. 'You do believe me, *mijnheer*?' she said. 'That I did nothing to occasion this, that I didn't invite them here or—'

Suzanne touched her friend's arm to calm her. 'Hush.'

'I am confident you are innocent of any wrong-doing,' Van Dijk replied. 'I am only sorry that your first impression of the Colony has been so unfavourable. I would that you had seen us in a better light.'

'Sinner that he was, I prayed for him,' Judith said softly, glancing down at Driek's body.

Van Dijk nodded. 'He is in God's hands now.' As he spoke, Suzanne noticed, with gentle amusement, that the tips of the soldier's ears had turned pink.

He quickly recovered himself. 'I will fetch some of my colleagues to remove the body,' Van Dijk said briskly. 'Then, we must find you better lodgings. This is not a suitable quarter of town for young ladies. There is a chance that Eltorp might return.'

Judith became even paler. 'Do you think so?'

Van Dijk held up his hands. 'It is a precaution only, *juffrouw* Verbeek. The miscreant will be lying low in one of the boarding houses at the port, no doubt, but we'll find him. Have no fear.'

He turned to Suzanne. 'Can you remain here until I return?' He gestured towards the corpse. 'I wish it were not so, but . . .'

'Of course, we will manage.'

He gave a slight bow. 'Very well. Ladies, I will take my leave.'

For a moment after he had gone, they stood in silence. Then Suzanne exhaled.

'He is taken with you,' Judith said quietly.

Suzanne smiled and took her friend's hand. 'It is not me who has caught his eye, my innocent Judith.'

CHAPTER TWELVE

Thursday, 5th August

Adriaan van Dijk was as good as his word.

By the time the bell was ringing for six o'clock and the changing of the watch, he had returned with two soldiers to remove the body and to take Judith and the girls to their new lodgings.

Suzanne was intrigued. Van Dijk appeared to have more influence than any regular soldier might be expected to have: in a matter of hours, he had not only arranged alternative accommodation for the girls but had also settled it so that Judith would not have to appear before a magistrate.

'Everything has been taken care of,' was all he said.

A pale winter sun rising behind grey clouds was giving shape back to the streets as they made their way through the waking Colony.

'The new house is closer to where you are living,' he said, turning to Suzanne. 'Perhaps your grandmother might help *juffrouw* Verbeek with the girls?'

'She would consider it a pleasure. Is there any news of the assailant?'

Van Dijk lowered his voice. 'It seems – though no one in the Malagasy quarter is talking – that there was some kind of fracas there last evening involving three of Eltorp's known associates. The bodies of two – one dead, one close to death – were found together with a Malagasy man, also deceased, behind the Slave Lodge. All had been stabbed.'

'By Eltorp?'

'More likely in a general affray between the two groups. There is an order of arrest out for Eltorp and a fourth man who was seen drinking with him at a tavern earlier in the evening. Though no one is talking, we will find them.'

'Why will no one talk?'

'They are mostly freed slaves in that quarter, men and women brought from Madagascar or Bengal. They do not trust us.'

'Are they right not to?'

Van Dijk thought for a moment, then nodded. 'Regrettably, it is the case that some of my compatriots believe that a white skin indicates a truthful, an honourable, nature, whereas a brown or Black skin the opposite.' He cleared his throat. 'My experience has been there is good and bad everywhere, as the loathsome behaviour of Eltorp and Holsteen attested last night.'

Though it was in her nature to be cautious, Suzanne was growing to like this man from Rotterdam who had gone out of his way to help them. Van Dijk clearly had the ear of someone higher up within the VOC, so would surely be able to find out what was intended for the eight brides-to-be. 'Do you know where the orphans will eventually be sent?'

'Not the specifics of each case, no. It will not happen immediately. These things take time.'

'That will be a great comfort to Judith. It is said that the Colony has a surfeit of men and fewer women. Is that true?'

'It is.'

'You, yourself, are not married?' Suzanne asked eventually.

It was Van Dijk's turn to hesitate. 'I was. It was a marriage of convenience between our two families. We were young, sixteen apiece, but we suited one another well enough. When my wife died in childbirth, the infant too, I left Rotterdam and came here.'

'I am sorry.'

Van Dijk shrugged. 'It was more than ten years ago. I have grown used to being alone.' He picked up the pace, then turned to look back over his shoulder at Judith and her flock. 'Grey dresses,' he murmured, and Suzanne wasn't sure if he was still thinking of Rotterdam, or about the real flesh-and-blood young woman walking behind them.

The comfortable new lodgings were only a few minutes' walk on the far side of the square from Suzanne and Florence's house.

'This is far better,' Suzanne said with approval.

Judith smiled shyly. 'You have been more than charitable, *mijnheer*. There is nothing I can say that would adequately express my gratitude, but you have my thanks. If there is anything I might do to repay the debt, please do not hesitate to ask.'

Van Dijk met her smile with his own. 'If I might be permitted to call upon you from time to time – to see that you are passing well – that would be repayment enough.'

Suzanne took great pleasure in seeing they were both now blushing, and marvelled at the way of things. She hoped it would not lead to sadness, for either of them.

Back outside in the street, Suzanne suddenly shuddered as the horrors of the night caught up with her. She wanted nothing more, now, than to sleep.

'I must add my thanks to Judith's, *mijnheer* Van Dijk, not least for believing me.'

'You were very persuasive, *juffrouw* Joubert. And brave.'

'Foolhardy, my grandmother would say.' She shivered again. 'I must go home. Home! That seems so presumptuous a word to use after a mere eighteen hours in the Cape.'

Van Dijk looked uncomfortable. 'I'm afraid I have been asked to bring you to Commander Van der Stel.'

Suzanne's stomach lurched. 'Because of the murder?'

'I presume to thank you for your service yesterday. You should not worry.' He began to walk. 'Shall we?'

'With respect, *mijnheer*,' she protested, looking down at her clothes, 'I cannot appear before the Commander like this. And I would not have my grandmother wake and find me still not home.'

Van Dijk considered her words, then nodded.

'Very well. I will meet you at the main gate of the Castle at ten o'clock. Do not be late.'

CHAPTER THIRTEEN

By half past nine, the clouds had cleared and the sky was blue over Table Mountain.

Suzanne had endured a scolding from Florence – who had woken before dawn and been beside herself with worry – but the glory of the winter's morning made her spirits sing. She had dressed her hair, curling strands around damp pieces of cotton so it now hung in auburn ringlets beneath her best narrow-brimmed hat. She was wearing her finest cloak, bodice and skirt, and her boots were clean. If she was to meet Commander Van der Stel, she wanted to look her best.

Suzanne walked through streets now thronging with people of all colours and ages. She came to the site where a new church was being built on the foundations of the original wooden chapel. A white overseer was shouting at a line of Black slaves, who were transporting stones on their bare shoulders, and yelling abuse at free labourers who were carrying granite, slate and sandstone. The resigned expressions on the faces of the workers, and the whip in the overseer's hand, angered her, and she hurried past.

Van Dijk was waiting at the gated entrance to the Castle.

'See there,' he said, pointing up towards Table Mountain. 'The scrub that covers the lower slopes is known as fynbos. Beyond the limits of the town, you would see protea bushes with spiky flowers as big as my hand – red, pink, cream, yellow.' He turned his gaze to Devil's Peak. 'And in the valleys between the mountains there are leopards – huge cat-like creatures with dark markings – and lions, caracals, grysbok and duiker, all part of God's magnificent creation.'

'You like it here?' she asked, moved by the enthusiasm in his voice.

'There is much to admire and marvel at in nature, but—'

'But?'

'There is good, and bad, in any situation. Come.' He turned abruptly and walked into the compound. 'It does not do to keep Commander Van der Stel waiting.'

'How long have you been stationed here?' Suzanne asked, as they hurried through the gate beneath the bell tower.

'Nigh on ten years,' he answered. 'I had been intended for Batavia. My father was an administrator in the VOC and I was following in his footsteps. But I sailed with Commander Van der Stel, and he requested me to remain here.'

'And became a soldier instead.'

He grinned. 'No, that was never my calling. I am assigned to the administration offices.'

Suzanne frowned. 'Then why are you in uniform?'

'Once in every month, I take a watch with the guard.'

'To stay in touch with the common soldier?'

'Something like that, yes,' he replied a little awkwardly. 'Every man here should be ready to defend the Colony should the need arise, as able to use a musket as a pen.'

'Is there an imminent danger of tribal wars?'

'That, yes, but also against a possible attack by the British, or the French. Even the Portuguese are a potential threat, though their influence in the area is vastly diminished now.'

Suzanne had lived her entire life under the shadow of violence and death. She had been born in the plague years, when the French king was accelerating his persecution of Huguenots, and had grown up knowing that, at any moment, they might have to pack their belongings and flee for their lives. A trauma handed down from generation to generation, the fear was carried in their very bones.

When she and Florence had reached Amsterdam last autumn – finally safe from the *dragonnades* and king's men – she had slept deeply for the first time in many months. Suzanne had hoped that there might be some greater measure of security in the Colony. That she might escape from the memory of what had been done to her. But listening to Adriaan van Dijk, hearing as much in what he did not say as in the words spoken, she realised she had been naive.

There and then she resolved that she would learn to handle a gun, that she would never again be caught without the means to defend herself.

As they walked through the central courtyard, Van Dijk explained how the Castle of Good Hope had been built on the foundations of a much older fort. Expanded, fortified and modernised in recent years, its stone façade was the shape of a pentagon. The buildings were painted yellow on the interior to minimise the fierce rays of the sun. Within the compound there was a bakery, workshops, living quarters for the garrisons, and holding cells for prisoners. The Castle was a town within a town.

'There is also a chapel,' he added, 'which is currently serving as the main place of worship for the Colony while the new church is being built.'

As they walked past the colonnades and shaded walkways, Suzanne felt she could have been back in the Netherlands. It was a wholly Dutch development set incongruously in the vast African landscape. Only the birds gave the lie. All around them, rotund speckled creatures were pecking at the ground: white spots on black, blue helmets and a red crest. She found them oddly appealing.

'Guinea fowl,' Van Dijk said. 'Pretty markings, but very stupid birds.'

They walked up stone stairs and into a panelled chamber with polished floorboards and a longcase clock. Woven tapestries of sea battles lost and won hung on the walls. Carved wainscot armchairs were set at intervals below them.

'Stinkwood,' Van Dijk muttered in her ear, 'a highly prized timber from the high forests. There is never enough wood in the Cape.'

At the far end of the room, on a raised dais, a fleshy man in a black robe and white jabot sat writing at a long oak refectory table. His hair was so long and curled, so thick, that she wondered if it was a wig.

'Just answer his questions truthfully,' Van Dijk whispered as they came to a halt. 'He is not a man who suffers fools.' Then he raised his voice: 'Commander, may I present Suzanne Joubert.'

For several minutes, or so it seemed, there was silence. Suzanne forced herself not to fidget. Finally, Simon van der Stel laid down his quill.

'Are you interested in the natural world, *juffrouw* Joubert? This country is extraordinary – the colours, the flora and fauna, it is like nowhere else on earth. A botanist's dream.'

Whatever she had expected, it wasn't this.

'From the little I have seen, it is glorious,' she replied cautiously. 'I very much hope to travel into the interior and see for myself.'

'You are French.'

'I am of Dutch and French parentage.'

'Your colouring favours the Dutch side. Do you know anything of wine?'

Suzanne blinked at the abrupt change of subject. 'My family had an interest in a wine business in our home town of La Rochelle. Lost, now.'

'No brothers?'

She held steady. 'No brothers, nor family surviving beyond my grandmother and I.'

'I have planted vines at my estate at Constantia. Europe is a dying continent. War after war after war. Here, in the southern hemisphere, this is where the future lies.' The Commander tapped the table with his forefinger and Suzanne saw the tips of his fingers were stained black with ink. 'They have named a town after me – Stellenbosch. Yet I would rather be remembered as the man who cultivated the highest quality wine in the Cape. My farm is barely established, but it is already yielding grapes the quality of which your French vintners would envy. I wish I could do more, but this –' he waved his hand to take in the chamber – 'occupies too much of my time.'

Not knowing how best to respond, Suzanne held her tongue.

'Your co-religionists, do they have the skill to tend vines?' he went on. 'Our local wine is undrinkable, the brandy only just passable, our vinegar close to poison.'

Suzanne nodded. This she could answer. 'The families who sailed on the *China* are all from a small region within Provence. It is a place of valleys, orchards, vines as far as the eye can see. If they have the tools, and the fertile land – and water, of course – they will succeed.'

'Good. That is good.'

Seemingly satisfied by her answer, the Commander leant back in his chair and closed his eyes. Suzanne became aware of the ticking of the clock as the pendulum swung to and fro in its case.

Suddenly, Van der Stel's eyes fully opened, his gaze direct

and clear. For the first time she saw signs of the man who was admired, but also feared. He jabbed a finger at her across the table.

'Tell me, Suzanne Joubert, what has really brought you here?'

CHAPTER FOURTEEN

For an instant, under Van der Stel's piercing glare, Suzanne was almost tempted to tell the truth. To admit that she had come in search of her ancestor, Louise Reydon-Joubert, and to honour – or avenge – her death.

Caution prevailed.

'As you say, Commander, Europe is dying,' she replied steadily. 'The Catholics slaughtered every last member of my family, save my grandmother and I. France is lost to us and Amsterdam, though it was the birthplace of my great-great-grandfather, Piet Reydon – and the city that gave refuge to earlier generations of my family – that city is not my home. Huguenots are less welcome there than once we were. I want to live for the future, not mourn the past.'

Van der Stel continued to fix her with his stare, as if looking for evidence of deceit. 'I do not approve of women taking on the habits and responsibilities of men,' he said, jabbing his inky finger in the air. 'And I do not approve of you travelling unaccompanied. A woman's role is to marry and bear children, that is her highest calling. However, I believe we owe you a debt, *juffrouw* Joubert, for your assistance yesterday.'

'It was my honour to help,' Suzanne replied in a tight voice. 'During the course of our voyage, I became fond of my fellow travellers. I would they should thrive here.'

He scowled. 'Yet they have made no attempt to learn our language.'

'They will in time.'

'Are they good men? Are they sober and law-abiding and hard-working? Men who will be a credit to our Colony?'

'They are honest and hard-working *women* as well as men,' she said with spirit. 'If treated justly, they will serve the Colony faithfully. They are grateful to have this chance to build a new life – as am I.'

'Do you have any reason to believe they will *not* be treated justly?'

Suzanne flinched at his belligerence, but answered truthfully. 'Far from it, Commander. Everything upon our arrival has been measured and fair.'

Van der Stel grunted and started to tidy his papers. 'Until there is a man who might do this work, I would like you to do the same service for the other arrivals, if there are more refugees who do not trouble to speak Dutch. As I regret there will be. The *Zuid-Beveland*, which sailed from Middleburg in April, is due to dock in a fortnight. Two further ships are expected in October.'

Suzanne was elated at Van der Stel's request, though did not let her satisfaction show. 'It would be an honour.'

'I shall see you are recompensed for your time. A fair price for a fair day's work. My thanks, *juffrouw* Joubert, and for bringing the unfortunate matter last evening to our attention. When the miscreant is found, he will be punished, along with any who shield him.' He looked down at his papers and made a shooing motion with his hand. 'If there is nothing more, Van Dijk will see you out.'

Suzanne took her chance: 'If you please, there is something.'

'Indeed?'

'In the case of the Rotterdam girls, I know they are to be married.'

'What of it?'

His tone was not encouraging, but she persisted. 'The youngest is only fifteen.'

'They are all of age.'

Suzanne held her ground. 'They are, but they are innocent for their years and far from home. It would be a great solace to Judith Verbeek – she acts as their chaperone and is a very measured person – to have some involvement in where they are to be sent. So that she can continue to keep a watching brief over them.'

Van der Stel scowled. 'They will become the responsibility of their husbands.'

'But until such time as they are wed, might Judith be consulted? It will help her to make sure the girls settle here. It can only serve the best interests of the Colony in the longer run.'

At her side, she felt Van Dijk stiffen. Had she overstepped the mark? Suzanne held her breath, and waited.

'I perceive no objection to your request,' Van der Stel finally pronounced. 'Van Dijk, see to it that *juffrouw* Verbeek is kept appropriately informed.' He pointed at Suzanne. 'Contented wives make steady husbands. Think on that, young lady.'

As Suzanne and van Dijk retraced their steps across the courtyard, she saw her companion smiling broadly. It had the effect of making him look younger, less severe. She, however, was furious.

'May I congratulate you, *juffrouw* Joubert. You impressed the Commander. He can be a hard man to please.'

'Especially where women are concerned,' she replied irritably. 'But, I admit, he seemed fair.'

Van Dijk laughed. 'He is, and he is not. He is irascible, prone to bouts of ill temper – men from Amsterdam to Batavia have been at the sharp end of it. He left his wife in Amsterdam when he was posted here – there were rumours of ill-use – and instead brought his wife's sister to care for his six children. His elder sons are expected to take over the running of the Colony, in time. And when he considered progress on the *drostdij*, the courthouse, in Stellenbosch was moving too slowly, he had the master carpenter put under house arrest and the brick-makers shackled in irons.'

Appalled, Suzanne shook her head and sighed. 'Is it true the town is named for him?'

'Quite true, though the Commander actually named it himself. When he took up his post nine years ago, he took it upon himself to visit all the free burgher farms and the furthest extremes of the Colony's outposts. On a subsequent expedition, he came upon an untouched and fertile valley, with plentiful woods. He set up camp on a tiny island in the middle of the Eerste River, and called it Stellenbosch. It became a town three years ago, when a *landdrost*, Pieter Odendaal, was appointed to take control of the rapidly growing community.'

'But what of those people who lived there before?'

Van Dijk's expression hardened. Straight away, Suzanne knew she had asked the wrong question.

'There are two local peoples – the Khoi and the San, with many groupings within each community. The Khoi are herders, moving their cattle from place to place. The San, the oldest inhabitants of the region, are what you might call hunter-gatherers. Neither build fixed settlements, so—' He paused. 'I can assure you, negotiations with their leaders were fair. Many of the Khoi now work for us.'

Suzanne wondered about what the original stewards of the land really felt at seeing their patrimony stolen by the white settlers, but knew it was not her place to say so. Mindful of her grandmother's advice to listen rather than talk, she knew she was still ignorant about the customs and traditions of the Colony. She would learn, all in good time.

But it made her think. Each Huguenot family was to be given land to farm in Groot Drakenstein, the valley named, or so she had been told, for another Dutch Cape Commissioner who had visited three years previously. How simple it was. By the mere act of renaming a place, the Dutch took possession of the land just as surely as if they had used guns and force.

They walked out through the gate, following the route, she realised, their steps had taken them last night. The open plain, Suzanne now saw, was a parade ground, where a battalion of soldiers was being drilled.

'Was the Commander in earnest about wanting my help when the next ship arrives? That is, until a *man* can be found . . .'

Van Dijk laughed again, his good humour seemingly restored. 'You should not take offence. His views are traditional. We are not all so backward-looking.'

Suzanne refused to be diverted. 'But did he mean it?'

'Certainly. I will let you know when the *Zuid-Beveland* is due to make shore. A French pastor is on board. God willing, he will have survived the voyage – his arrival is very much anticipated by the refugees.'

'That will be a great comfort to them.'

'Yes, although the expectation is that they learn Dutch and so will be able to participate in our services instead.'

'And will the Commander keep his word about the Rotterdam girls?'

'He does not make promises lightly. If he says it will be so, then his word is law. Also, although it is true people marry earlier here than back home, these are not dynastic marriages, but practical. A child-bride will be no use to a farmer. They need helpmeets, women capable of working the land. If *juffrouw* Verbeek can help prepare her charges, then that will be to the benefit of us all. It is unlikely anything will happen until the new year.'

Suzanne smiled. 'That is reassuring. I will tell Judith.'

'No need,' Van Dijk replied. 'I am happy to inform her of the Commander's ruling. I need to visit the hospital. It is not out of my way.'

'But—' Suzanne began, then stopped herself. Who was she to sabotage his excuse to visit? 'I am sure Judith will be very grateful.'

He looked pleased. 'What will you do this morning?'

Suzanne looked ahead at the streets glittering and inviting in the milky winter sun, and grinned. 'Explore.'

'You will find the town pleasing, but do not venture further than the city limits. Things are different here. There are areas not suitable for a gentlewoman – for any of us, in point of fact.'

'I'll be careful,' she said lightly, and smiled.

He raised his eyebrows. 'I mean it. And there are snakes.' Suzanne's eyes widened. 'Oh yes. One must take care. There are many breeds of venomous snakes who find their way into town: cobras, boomslangs – they can be longer than I am tall – and a bite from a puff adder can be fatal.'

'I will be careful,' she said again, this time meaning it.

He held her gaze. 'As I said, things are different here.'

CHAPTER FIFTEEN

Several hours later, Suzanne stepped out of their house, leaving her grandmother to rest. The promise of the morning had faded and the sun was now covered by dark clouds. A persistent drizzle cloaked everything in a grey mist. Suzanne felt bilious. If anything, her land-sickness was worse now than the previous day. But she was determined to orientate herself and get the measure of the town in daylight.

She tried – and failed – to imagine how it might have looked when Louise first had set foot upon these shores sixty-six years before. In truth, she was finding it impossible to imagine Louise here at all. Almost every image she had, saw Louise standing proud on the bridge of the *Old Moon*, looking out to sea. Or, sometimes, in the prison in Las Palmas, her description of her trencher and night pot, a blanket lousy with fleas and her initials – LRJ – scratched upon the bricks. Not here, in this frontier land.

As she explored, Suzanne noticed one or two finer homes built alongside the more basic clay and straw buildings. White houses with the occasional gable and wooden windows, reminding her of Amsterdam and the grand canals of Herengracht, Keizersgracht and Prinsengacht.

Minou had written in her journals of her excursions into Amsterdam after the Joubert family had fled to the city after the St Bartholomew's Day massacre. She had found the adjustment to Dutch society difficult. Her pleasure in their narrow four-storeyed house on Zeedijk was tempered by her grief at having lost her eldest daughter, Marta, in the chaos of Paris.

She wrote of how she missed the mountains and had to become accustomed instead to a world defined by water, a city contained by broad canals and the floating palisade of the tall ships in the harbour. The difference was that Minou was regretting the loss of her previous life – in Puivert, in Paris – and wishing she was home. Suzanne had no home. What happened in La Rochelle that night had stolen that from her.

Her wanderings led her back into the main square. Here, in the Colony, everything was new. Was it discomfiting to be in a place so unrooted, or a liberation? Had Louise felt free here to be somebody different, no longer shackled to her past? Is that why she had come to the Cape rather than return home? More to the point, Suzanne thought as she turned back towards the main square, why she had stayed?

Then came another thought, cold and unforgiving. What if Louise had not stayed? What if she had sailed on to Batavia where a Dutch colony had already been established and made a home there, among the palm trees and merchants of the east? What if Suzanne was searching for Louise in the wrong place altogether?

She returned to their lodgings feeling out of sorts. It was Louise who had brought her here, but what if she never found her? Never found any trace of her? It was early days, but the thought filled her with despair.

Lars Eltorp was skulking around the waterfront, keeping to the shadows behind the VOC buildings.

He had no doubt that there would be a warrant out for his arrest. Commander Van der Stel was known for administering swift and brutal justice for any who broke the rules of the Colony. He considered pleading self-defence – the victim was a sailor, inebriated, straight off the ship, looking for trouble

– but knew that his own record would stand against him. The last time he was charged with a breach of the peace, he had received ten lashes and a week in gaol.

Eltorp ran a calloused hand over his matted beard. All the same, a plea of self-defence might still work, painting Driek as the aggressor. The only witness was the girl. The whole mess was her fault. If she had not been coy, pretended to virtue, then no one need have been hurt. His eyes narrowed. He should have killed her, too, not left her wagging tongue free to condemn him.

It was unfinished business.

Eltorp shifted position. There were men enough in the Colony who either owed him allegiance, or were too afraid to turn him away. There was a farm where a settler he knew would turn a blind eye to comings and goings if appropriate remuneration changed hands. If he could reach the countryside, then the VOC soldiers would not find him. But to make it across the sand dunes, he would need a gun. Three men he knew of had been killed by lions in the past month. His knife would be no good there.

Eltorp continued to weigh up his options, but found his bitter mind returning again to the girl. He knew it would be lunacy to go back, but the idea took hold.

Her fault. She need not have made such a fuss.

Women caused trouble, plain and simple. His anger started to rise and, with it, a desire for revenge that overwhelmed self-preservation. It would be wiser to leave town, but he had to secure her silence one way or another first. Then, he'd acquire a musket and leave. He'd head for Gallows Hill. No one went there at night. An ancient site, it was said to be haunted by all the unshriven souls of the slaves buried under the sand and by the miscreants cut down from the gibbet. He would surely be safe there . . .

CHAPTER SIXTEEN

At six o'clock by the Castle bell, Suzanne and Florence left their house and walked arm-in-arm to the meeting house. There was to be a gathering to welcome the new arrivals, organised by the more established French refugees. The women gathered most days in a small wooden building once attached to the old church, where they could speak in their own language without fear of reproach. The men, so Suzanne had been told, tended to congregate in the tavern close to the VOC stores frequented by farmers and settlers come into town for provisions.

Suzanne was looking forward to it. Her melancholy had lifted and she was excited to start asking about Louise. Although none of the ladies had been in the Colony that long, they would have heard gossip. She would put her faith in any group of old women knitting by the fire to know more than half a dozen government spies. They listened, they observed, they saw everything.

'*Bienvenue, entrez.*'

A small, birdlike woman with black smiling eyes and fluttering hands, came forward to welcome them.

Suzanne let Florence take the lead. The older Frenchwomen exchanged family names, identified their home towns – their host, Madame Niel, was originally from Dauphiné – and the ships which had brought them to the Cape. Suzanne and Florence were encouraged to fill their plates with cured meats, cheeses and chopped apples, then steered to a table.

'You must meet Madame Lombard. She is one of the oldest,

and longest-serving, residents of our community, the fount of all knowledge.' Madame Neil held her hands respectfully together. 'Madame, here are two more arrivals from the *China*.'

There were three women already seated at the table: a mother and her daughter also from Dauphiné – the woman's husband was in Groot Drakenstein – and Madame Lombard, a woman of sixty. Clearly the matriarch, she was stocky, with leathered skin and heavy-lidded eyes. She patted the empty chair beside her. Suzanne settled Florence, then asked Madame Lombard for her story. To her surprise – most refugees liked nothing more than to talk about their experiences – she waved the enquiry away.

'I am better off here,' she said brusquely. 'My husband was a thief and a brute, only a Huguenot for the advantage he thought it would bring – the local Seigneur was a God-botherer of the Protestant persuasion, do you see? Morals of an alley cat.' She paused, then to Suzanne's delight, winked. 'My husband, that is to say, not the Seigneur. He was a rogue of a different order, but that's another story.'

Suzanne laughed, delighting in the old woman's bluntness.

'My so-called dearest was always tugging his forelock, wheedling to ingratiate himself.' She snorted. 'When, all the while, the Seigneur had no more blue blood in him than do I. He won the living of Puivert in a game of cards, would you credit it? I'm better off without all that. At least, here, you know where you stand. An honest day's work for a fair wage, none of that bowing and scraping.'

Suzanne sat up straighter. 'Did you say Puivert?'

'I did.' Madame Lombard peered at her. 'Why, do you know it? I was told you were from La Rochelle.'

'I am,' she replied, 'we are. It's just—'

'Talk sense, child.'

Suzanne took a breath. 'My family originates in Languedoc and lived in Puivert some generations back. I have never visited, but my great-great-grandmother is buried there.'

'Is that so? What was the family name?'

'Joubert,' Suzanne replied. 'My great-great-grandmother was Minou Reydon-Joubert. She inherited the Château de Puivert from her birth mother, though the estate was lost in the religious wars after the massacre in Paris in 1572.'

Madame Lombard sat back in her chair with her hands folded across her ample belly.

'Well, well, well! I never thought to see the day.'

'Madame?'

The older woman slapped her hand on the table. 'My maiden name was Noubel. My grandmother and grandfather served the Joubert family. They talked often of the *châtelaine* of Puivert, how the family left for Paris to attend the royal wedding with their little ones, and never returned.'

Suzanne had read about this in Minou's journals. She leant forward, her eyes bright with excitement. 'That's right. Only her sister, Alis, remained in Puivert. She was one of the few to survive the sack of the castle.'

Madame Lombard's face darkened. 'Almost everyone was murdered by the Catholics, many of the old village families. Cut down where they stood by their neighbours, men they had grown up with, boys they had dandled on their knees.'

Suzanne shook her head. 'My great-great-grandmother wrote of it. The only thing we still have from those days is a family tapestry of my great-great-grandparents and their two older children, Marta and my great-grandfather, Jean-Jacques. Alis smuggled it out when she finally escaped. We have it still. It hangs in the house in Amsterdam where she lived for the remainder of her life.'

'Who would have thought such a thing,' the old woman said, shaking her head at the ways of Fate. 'Minou Joubert was a great lady. No one had a bad word to say against her. She treated everyone the same, pauper or prince. And here we are together on the other side of the world.' She pointed up towards heaven. 'Perhaps there is someone up there after all.'

Suzanne decided to seize the moment before anyone interrupted their conversation. 'In point of fact, I am not the first of our family to make the journey here,' she said, watching Madame Lombard's face carefully.

'You have relatives here who sailed before you? On which ship?'

'Not that. At least, not quite. Minou's granddaughter was called Louise Reydon-Joubert. She arrived at the Cape in May of 1622.'

Madame Lombard scoffed. 'How can that be? That was thirty years before the Colony was founded.'

'Well, VOC ships – and others – had been stopping here to replenish their stores before,' Suzanne began to say.

'I know that,' the old woman snapped. 'I have lived here for some twenty-five years, young woman. There's little I do not know. I know more than all these milksop VOC officials who can't see further than the tips of their noses.'

Suzanne held up her hand in apology as Madame Lombard continued with her history lesson.

'The Portuguese were first, then the British, French, Dutch and even Danish ships came and went, but no one stayed. Then, in 1647, the *Nieuwe Haerlem* ran aground at the Cape of Good Hope. The seafarers were stranded here for a year and it was that incident which encouraged the VOC to set their grubby sights on a more permanent settlement. Five years later, Jan van Riebeeck was dispatched to establish a refreshment station here.' She waved her arms to take in the room. 'So, here we sit.'

'You must have seen many changes, madame,' Suzanne said, hoping to soothe the Frenchwoman's ruffled feathers.

'Some for better, some for worse,' Madame Lombard grumbled. 'Well, come on, then. Tell me about this ancestor of yours. How did she get here, you tell me that?'

'Louise sailed her own ship, the *Old Moon*.'

'Nonsense! No self-respecting seafarer would sail under a woman. Whoever heard of such a thing.'

'Yet, they did,' Suzanne replied. 'Louise's own diary attests to it, and the recorded testimony of her lieutenant. He sailed the ship back to Amsterdam on her instruction.'

'If that is so, what happened to her?'

Suzanne dropped her voice in a conspiratorial whisper, hoping to draw the irascible old woman in. 'That is what I have come to find out.'

For a moment, Madame Lombard was silent. Then, to Suzanne's joy, she whistled like a fishwife.

'Well, well, another adventurer. Like me, like your Louise. They told me I could not travel alone, that these wild lands were not suitable for a woman.' She slapped her hands on her lap. 'Yet here I am, having buried two husbands in this red earth, and I'm still here. I own my own house, I sleep when I like, eat when I like, and will never again answer to any man.'

Suzanne laughed. 'Louise felt the same. She did not want to be beholden to a husband either. She was courageous and loyal to her crew, running down slaver ships. But after she disembarked in Table Bay, she vanished. No one ever heard of her, or from her, again.'

'Why do you care so much? You never even knew her.'

The old woman's bluntness pulled Suzanne up short. She had

asked herself that question many times since reading Louise's diary.

'It gives my life purpose,' she heard herself saying, and was surprised by the words. 'After everything that has happened to my family – to me – finding out what happened to Louise gives me a reason to keep going.'

For an instant, the two women held one another's gaze, bound by their mutual suffering, by the horrors they each had witnessed, by their determination.

'You are honest, at least,' Madame Lombard said.

She fell silent again, but this time Suzanne realised she was searching through her fading memories, trying to recollect half-overheard stories. 'Well,' the old woman said eventually, 'in those first months, when the Colony was little more than a few tents around Table Bay, I believe I did hear rumours about a white woman, with a red scarf and a dagger at her waist. Might that have been your Louise?'

'Yes, indeed! Many descriptions talk of her red scarf and how she carried a silver blade with a single green emerald. My great-grandfather gave it to her on the occasion of her twenty-fifth birthday.' Suzanne hesitated. 'Though it cannot have been the same weapon. That was confiscated by the court in Las Palmas when she was put on trial for murder.'

Madame Lombard's bushy eyebrows shot up. 'Murder, eh! Well, the Khoi called her a she-devil, other times the she-captain or the pirate-commander. Braver than any warrior. Yes, it is coming back to me. A white woman who lived in a valley near Olifantshoek, some said.' She shook her head. 'At least, I think that's right, it was a long time ago.'

Suzanne leant forward again. 'How long ago was it that you heard these rumours?'

'Oh, five-and-twenty years, or more.'

'Was she said to live alone? Or were there others with her?'

Madame Lombard frowned. 'There was talk of a white man, a husband or a son, perhaps?'

'Just one companion?' Suzanne asked, realising it could be Gilles Barenton or Phillipe Vidal.

'From what I can remember. But I tell you this. If it was your Louise, she must have been under the protection of the Khoi to have survived alone in the interior, even though relations between white and Black were more cordial at the beginning. Before they realised what the VOC were up to.' Her hooded eyes blinked. 'Truth be told, I paid the stories little heed. I thought they were tales made up to keep errant children in their beds and the hunters from the valley.'

'But if there—'

Madame Lombard held up her hand. 'All this remembering has worn me out. I will think on it and, should I remember anything more, will send for you.'

Suzanne sighed. 'Thank you, madame. We are lodging—'

The old woman waved a stubby finger. 'I know where you are. Have patience, child. We adventurers must stick together,' she said with a twinkle. 'Now, I would make the acquaintance of your grandmother. Florence, did you say?'

'Yes, she was named for Minou's adoptive mother.' She got up and went around to join her grandmother at the other end of the table. '*Gran'mère*, there is someone who remembers our family from Puivert. Might I introduce you to her?'

CHAPTER SEVENTEEN

Thursday, 19th August

Suzanne quickly became accustomed to the pattern of life in the Colony.

Damp days and moonlit nights passed quickly as she visited the VOC stores to acquire provisions, took short walks around the streets with Florence on her arm, and solitary longer walks to the sand dunes and back, and down to the water. She regretted the lack of books, but she called upon other families from the *China* and visited Judith and the girls. Suzanne was pleased to hear how Adriaan van Dijk had paid several visits and that he had even offered to accompany Judith to the United Reform service in the Castle chapel on the coming Sabbath.

For her part, Florence had become a regular at the ladies' *rendez-vous* in the afternoons, and this new-found companionship helped ease Suzanne's guilt. Florence seemed to be thriving, the burdens of their recent life in La Rochelle finally lifting from her shoulders. The refugees gossiped about how very hard life was for the settlers, how the land in Groot Drakenstein was not suitable for planting vines and how the resources put aside for the refugees were inadequate. It seemed they were as poor here as they had been in France, and as little regarded. Commander Van der Stel had been petitioned to apply to the Batavia Fund for more funds to distribute, but the ladies held out little hope. And more ships were expected, bringing destitute Frenchwomen and men to the Cape. Who was going to pay?

Suzanne used these visits to pursue her researches. But no one other than Madame Lombard had ever heard of the she-captain with a red scarf. She came to the conclusion that she might have better luck in the taverns. If it was true that Louise had settled near Olifantshoek, the men who travelled the grassy veldt and on through the mountain passes, the settlers and the farmers, were more likely to have heard rumours. But such a thing was impossible. As a respectable woman, she could not visit a tavern and Commander Van der Stel's edicts did not permit free conversation with the Black or Malagasy residents of the town.

'It is early days,' she told herself, but she felt her mission had stalled before it had ever got going.

Early on the morning of Thursday, the nineteenth of August, fifteen days after the *China* had dropped anchor in Table Bay, there was a knock at the door.

They had no servant, so Suzanne was cleaning the house herself. Besides, her conscience baulked at the thought of an enslaved person working for them.

'Are you expecting a visitor, *Gran'mère*?'

Florence looked up from her sewing. '*Pas si tôt.*' Not this early.

Suzanne removed her apron and straightened her cap, put the cleaning cloths in a pail and pushed it under the table, then went out into the hallway. She opened the door to find Adriaan van Dijk standing there, no longer in the uniform of a soldier, but rather in the black *justaucorps*, narrow breeches with white stockings and black polished shoes of the senior VOC officials. The attire suited him better and Suzanne could understand why Judith admired him.

'*Dag, mijnheer.*' Good morning.

He tipped his hat. 'Forgive me for calling on you unannounced, and at such an hour. Might I come in?'

'Of course.' She ushered him into the parlour. 'May I offer you something to drink?'

He held up his hand. 'Nothing, thank you. I am here on official business.'

Suzanne's heart skipped a beat. Their papers were in order, but the legacy of many early-hours calls to their house in La Rochelle by the *dragonnades* had left a scar.

'This is not then,' she muttered.

'Are you unwell, *juffrouw* Joubert? You are turned quite pale.'

'It's nothing,' she said, vexed to have given herself away.

Van Dijk raised his hat to Florence in her armchair, then gestured to a chair at the table. 'May I?'

'Please.'

He waited until Suzanne had sat down, then did the same.

'In point of fact, I have two pieces of business. One official, one less so. This afternoon, all being well, the *Zuid-Beveland* should drop anchor in Table Bay. We have been tracking its progress from the shore these past two days. I am here on behalf of Commander Van der Stel to request your assistance in interpreting for those refugees who cannot speak our language—' He stopped. 'That is to say, Dutch.'

Suzanne smiled. 'I am not offended, *mijnheer*. And, of course. I gave my word.'

'We would be in your debt, not least because Pierre Simond, the Huguenot pastor the refugees have been waiting for, is on the ship. I will send someone to accompany you to the harbour.'

'There is no need. I have the measure of the town now. I can find my own way to the jetty.'

'The harbour is not a suitable environment for a lady. I would prefer to know you were safe.'

Suzanne raised her hand in submission. 'Very well.'

'Second, there is also a piece of intelligence I would share with you.' He dropped his voice. 'Several nights ago, the lodgings where *juffrouw* Verbeek was previously staying with her charges was broken into. Some degree of damage was done. We have reason to believe that it was the work of Lars Eltorp. He has been sighted at several locations within the town, but I regret to say remains at large.'

Suzanne turned cold. 'Was he looking for Judith, do you think?'

'We have pieced together the events of the night of the murder. Eltorp was seen drinking with three companions in a tavern by the water. The tapster identified him and confirmed that Driek Holsteen joined them.'

'In other words, you have proved Driek and Lars Eltorp were together.'

'Precisely. But *juffrouw* Verbeek is the only witness to the murder – he does not know that you also saw him. I fear he went looking for her.'

'Have you told her this?'

Van Dijk met her eye. 'I saw no reason to worry her until we knew for sure.'

Suzanne nodded. 'What would you have me do?'

'Keep close to her,' he said. 'It will not take Eltorp long to find out where the new lodgings are if he sets his mind to it.' His brows furrowed. 'She is a young woman of a sweet and gentle nature. I would not wish any harm to befall her.'

Lars Eltorp watched the VOC man leave the merchant's house on the square.

Over the past fifteen days, fellow blackguards and shifters within the town had been persuaded, at the tip of his knife, to give him shelter and assistance. In this way, he had acquired a musket, paid a boy to retrieve his belongings from the boarding house at the harbour, and kept his belly full.

The longer he evaded capture, the more Eltorp's confidence had grown. During the day, a cooler head prevailed – no sense drawing attention to himself. But by nightfall, once his throat had been whetted by a quart or two, his burning head returned to thoughts of revenge, to silencing the one witness who could finger him for the sailor's murder.

Eltorp had gone back to the girls' lodgings, but had discovered the nest empty. In his temper, he had rendered it uninhabitable and then kept watch in case they returned.

Then, he'd had a moment of good fortune. He had previously observed this VOC cur hanging around and realised he might lead him to the girl. This morning, Eltorp had tracked him to this more salubrious part of town. Although the merchant's house looked too fine to be housing a brood of orphan-brides, he was prepared to wait. The girls might be here. For all his fiery temper and his lack of restraint when he was in his cups, Eltorp could be patient.

CHAPTER EIGHTEEN

After Van Dijk had taken his leave, Suzanne left Florence with some warm milk and brandy and went to visit Judith.

She discovered her friend exhausted, though uncomplaining as ever: Catrina was running a fever and Petronella was waking several times a night, but mostly the girls were exhibiting no ill-effects from what they had witnessed a fortnight ago. At least, none that could be easily seen.

'In truth, they are more concerned about what is to come, although *mijnheer* Van Dijk says I should not worry.' Judith bit her lip. 'Now we are in this house, I am growing to like the town. It is not Rotterdam, but there is a pattern to life that suits me. I don't want to leave. I have never lived in the country and, well . . . I am used to company.' She tailed off, then stared out of the window. 'The weather, of course, helps. This rain and drizzle are familiar friends. I had expected the heat of the tropics, sun that burns your skin and renders any activity a trial.'

'That will come. It is winter now.' Suzanne laughed. 'So has *mijnheer* Van Dijk visited often?'

Judith's eyes lit up, transforming her aquiline face. 'Once or twice. But there is nothing improper in it, I give you my word.'

'I am not suggesting for a moment there is. I am merely glad you have a friend and that his attentions are welcome.' She paused. 'Are they?'

'There is nothing that gives me more pleasure.'

'Then I am glad,' she said, putting her hand on her friend's arm. 'Now, I came to ask if you would accompany me to the harbour this afternoon. Another ship is due to dock and the Commander wants me to assist again with the refugees who do not speak Dutch. I wondered if you might like to come too. Be relieved of your nursemaid duties for a while.'

Judith's eyes brightened, then clouded again. 'I would like nothing more than to go further than these few streets, but I can't leave the girls alone.'

'My grandmother would be delighted to have their company for the afternoon. If it pleases you, we could take them there now.'

Judith clapped her hands in a rare moment of girlish delight, then hurried to the back of the chamber where her charges were sitting at a table sewing clothes more suitable for the southern climate. It appeared Adriaan van Dijk had suggested that they should forsake their grey pinafores and had even provided the cloth for new dresses.

'Ladies,' Judith was saying, 'we are going on an adventure. Brush your hair, gather your shawls and caps. Make yourselves presentable. You are to spend the afternoon with Suzanne's grandmother. Quickly, now. Before the heavens open.'

By the time two soldiers arrived to escort Suzanne to the harbour to greet the *Zuid-Beveland*, Florence had the seven girls sitting on chairs in a circle sewing and playing a counting game. It was too childish a pastime for the older ones, but it worked as a way of occupying their minds as well as their hands. Suzanne and Judith left to the sound of laughter.

'It is good to hear them happy,' Judith said, as she stepped out into the stormy air behind Suzanne. The wind had picked up and she had to raise her voice to be heard. 'They ask questions of me all the time – where they are to live, when they will meet their husbands – and it grieves me not to be able to answer.'

'Whatever the plans are, I am sure they will have been thought through thoroughly,' she replied, hoping her confidence was justified. 'Commander Van der Stel seems an honourable and upright man. And *mijnheer* Van Dijk, I am sure, will tell you anything he knows, if he can.'

'He is a good Christian,' Judith replied, then added: 'He has said he will accompany us to chapel this coming Sunday. I am most grateful to him for I had not felt able to attend before.'

Suzanne nodded as a plan took hold. Increasingly she had realised the VOC man might help her uncover intelligence about Louise. It could do no harm to ask.

Despite the rough weather and the north-westerly wind howling over the bay, there was a lively atmosphere at the port. There was a bustle of commerce and trade: stalls selling cooked meat, bread and brandy, hawkers with tawdry peacock feathers and strings of wooden beads. The disembarking refugees might be poor, but the officers and sailors were not. Black stevedores, the blue, white and red of VOC soldiers, Malagasy porters and dark-eyed women with vivid cloth headscarves with baskets of fruit and bread. A chorus of languages, the clicking and whistling and yelling of men who had found a way to communicate in order to barter and trade. Despite the dismal weather, there was so much life, so much colour. Even among the Huguenots, there was almost a carnival atmosphere. Suzanne put it down to the fact that the French pastor was on board.

Pierre Simond was from Dauphiné, like so many of the refugees including Madame Niel, who had welcomed them to the meeting rooms on their first evening. The exiles had been deprived of regular worship and spiritual leadership, despite having sacrificed much for their faith, so his arrival was keenly awaited. A man of God, one of their own, bringing solace and hope to his flock in this strange land.

As she and Judith slipped through the crowds towards the VOC registration building, Suzanne marvelled at how familiar it already seemed and how quickly she had become acclimatised to life in the Colony. Only two weeks ago, she had been the person standing at the taffrail, seeing Table Mountain and the Castle of Good Hope for the first time. Now, here she was, greeting her new friends, reacquainting herself with her fellow travellers: she waved to Pierre Jaubert and Pierre Grange, passed the time of day with the Malan family. She felt as if she had been a resident of the Cape for months, not just a handful of days.

Suzanne made herself known inside the registration building and was relieved to find she was expected. This time she was greeted with courtesy by the *regisseur* who had previously looked down his nose at her. She felt a moment of pride and belonging. Here, at least for the next few hours, she had a purpose and a value. And remembering the abruptness of their welcome a fortnight ago, the coldness in the eyes and voices of the official who had taken them to be registered, she determined to do better for those about to set foot on African soil for the first time.

CHAPTER NINETEEN

Lars Eltorp could not believe his luck. Invisible in the crowd, while all VOC eyes were on the ship as it dropped anchor, he had spied the girl. She was in the company of another young woman with red hair and a green cloak, more prosperous in her attire. He had watched the pair enter the registration building then, some quarter of an hour later, come out and make their way towards the pier itself.

Eltorp followed. He had cut off his black beard and was wearing a chandler's cap pulled low over his brow. He had stolen a pair of tan breeches from a washing line and exchanged his jacket for one of a different cut. His knife was concealed on his belt and ready to use. Anyone who knew his features would recognise him, but he thought he had done enough to disguise himself from the VOC soldiers.

Keeping the taller girl with red hair in his sights, he pushed roughly through the mass of people. Then his quarry turned, and he smiled. Though he had only seen the orphanage girl at night, her profile was unmistakable.

Out at sea, the *Zuid-Beveland* gave a single-gun salute and the ship was enveloped in white smoke. Eltorp drew close enough to touch his quarry's shawl. As the answering salute sounded from the Castle, and everyone cheered, he drew his blade from its sheath. At the last moment, the girl turned to speak to her companion, twisting away from him. But the knife was in and out before the cloud of smoke had dispersed.

He turned, and was swallowed up by the crowd. All eyes

were fixed on the ship in Table Bay, not on a lone working man trudging along the pier. His aim had been less than true, but he was sure he had done enough. He would collect his belongings and musket, and be halfway to Gallow's Hill before the girl even knew she was hit.

Without warning, Judith stumbled. Suzanne grabbed her arm to stop her from falling.

'What is it? Are you faint?'

Judith tried to straighten up. 'Someone pushed against me, that is all. An elbow, or the edge of a basket.' She pointed out to sea. 'Look, the first of the rowing boats is being lowered into the water.'

A gust of wind threatened to tear Suzanne's bonnet from her head and she had to shout to make herself heard. 'I hope they have an easier crossing of it than we did.'

If anything, she thought the swell looked even worse than it had been two weeks previously. The little boat was some way from shore but, once it had pulled away from the lea of the ship, Suzanne could see it was bobbing wildly, being tossed from side to side. Banks of waves whipped up by the gale seemed to be building higher and higher. The tiny craft battled bravely forward, heeling from side to side, until a black-green wave seemed to swallow it whole. A cry went up from the crowd, as the boat disappeared from sight, only to bob back into view a few moments later.

But the wind was relentless. A massive surge of water hammered over the gunwales and the boat finally capsized.

'They will drown,' a woman cried. 'They will all drown.'

'Someone must do something! We cannot leave them!'

Other voices joined in the call for a boat to be launched from the shore though, in truth, the sea was too wild and they were too far away. Everyone knew it. They could only watch helplessly as the hull of the upturned boat sprang back to the surface; only watch in hope as the *Zuid-Beveland* attempted to launch a rescue vessel only to pull back; only watch in despair as drowning men waved desperately in the water until, one by one, they sank beneath the surface. A moment of silence fell, then the sound of women's voices wailing and praying lifted on the wind.

Suzanne felt Judith's hand heavy upon her arm.

'There, there,' she said, putting her arms around her friend's shoulder.

Judith murmured. 'Those poor men. Those poor, poor men. May God have mercy on their souls.'

'Come, you need to sit down.'

Suzanne turned around and steered her friend back through the stunned crowd, knowing the images of the drowning men would be imprinted on their minds forever.

'Don't concern yourself with me,' Judith said, though Suzanne could hear she was struggling to catch her breath. 'You cannot leave. You have a task to do.'

She shook her head. 'They will not launch a second boat now. They will wait until the wind has dropped and the swell has calmed. I will take you back to our lodgings, then return here. There is time. You have had a shock. You need to rest.'

'I own I do feel faint,' she wheezed. 'I am sorry to be such a trouble.'

'Nonsense. It is no trouble. You will be as right as rain with a little food and a sup of brandy. Anyone would be affected to see such sights.'

But as they made their way along the pier and back into the town, Suzanne's concern for her friend grew. Judith was becoming paler with every step. Her pulse was racing and she seemed to be gasping for air. The further they went, the heavier she felt in Suzanne's arms.

Petronella opened the door. 'What has happened?' she asked in her sing-song voice. 'Is Judith unwell?'

'She has had a shock, that is all,' Suzanne answered, stepping into the hallway. Then she dropped her arm to Judith's waist to better support her, and felt something sticky. She glanced down at her hand, then turned cold. Blood. It hadn't been a sharp elbow at all.

'Petronella,' she said calmly, 'where is my grandmother?'

'Madame Joubert is in the parlour, but she has a visitor.'

'Fetch her please. Quickly, now.'

The moment she was gone, Suzanne carefully lowered Judith onto the bench and felt a fresh gush of warm blood on her fingers.

Florence appeared in the doorway with Madame Lombard beside her.

'Petronella said—' she began.

'*Gran'mère*,' Suzanne interrupted, 'we need to take Judith to the bedchamber. Keep the younger girls in the parlour, and send one of the older ones to fetch a physician . . . The first of the boats from the *Zuid-Beveland* capsized, losing all on board. We saw them drown. I thought that was why she was faint, but then—' Suzanne stopped, aware she was gabbling. 'Is there a . . . someone in the Colony, a physician? We need—'

'Suzanne, you are making no sense at all,' Florence said. 'Calm yourself and start from the beginning.'

But Madame Lombard pushed past and put her hand on Judith's neck, her lined face creased in concern.

'What happened, child?'

Suzanne swallowed hard. 'I – I think she has been stabbed. I didn't realise.'

Florence's hand flew to her mouth. 'Whatever can you mean?'

Madame Lombard took charge. 'My father, his father and his father before him were apothecaries in Puivert. I can help.' She bent down, took Suzanne's hand and pressed it against Judith's side. 'Keep the pressure here. We need to prevent the girl losing any more blood.'

She turned to her friend. 'Florence, if one of the older girls can be trusted to keep her tongue in her mouth, get her to fetch some hot water, a pail and strips of cloth. We need to clean and bind the wound.'

'But she was talking to me,' Suzanne said, dazed, unable to believe what was happening. 'She was walking. How can that be?'

Madame Lombard paid no heed as another pulse of blood gushed from the wound. 'Press harder, her life may depend on it. Do you have any valerian or brandy?'

Florence nodded. 'Brandy, yes.'

'Should we not take her to the bed?' Suzanne asked, struggling to keep her voice steady.

'Moving her could cause the wound to open wider. Put your cloak beneath her head to make her more comfortable.'

'She cannot die, she cannot.'

Madame Lombard pursed her lips. 'She will not if I have anything to do with it. Is there anyone we should inform?'

'There is one person,' Suzanne heard herself saying. 'A VOC official who has been particularly kind.'

'Send one of the girls to get him,' came the brusque reply. 'There's enough of them sitting here twiddling their thumbs. Now, we need to remove her dress. Gently does it.'

Once Florence had returned with cloths, water and brandy,

and one of the older girls, Wilhelmina, had been dispatched in search of Adriaan van Dijk, Suzanne knelt down beside her friend.

'How goes it with you, Judith?' she asked, and nearly cried with relief when her eyes flickered open at the sound of her voice.

'Forgive me for being a nuisance. It is just the thought of those poor men.'

'Your charity does you credit,' Suzanne said, glancing at Madame Lombard, who nodded her permission. 'But you did not faint. You have been injured. A knife, we think.'

'Oh.'

'We are going to remove your outer garments and chemise so I can treat the wound,' said Madame Lombard. 'It may hurt.'

Judith closed her eyes once more. 'So sorry for the trouble.'

Suzanne felt hysteria building in her throat at the girl's humility. 'Don't speak any more. You will feel better soon.'

'What's this?' Madame Lombard gently peeled back the blood-sodden clothing and pulled out a slim volume, which she handed to Suzanne.

'A collection of psalms,' Suzanne said, wiping the smears of blood from the cover with her sleeve.

Judith struggled to sit up. 'When I heard *mijnheer* Jaubert on the ship talking of concealing his bible, I thought I would do the same. It is the only thing I possess that belonged to my mother. She left it with me at the orphanage gates. I did not want to lose it.'

Madame Lombard gave a hollow laugh. 'Many a life has been lost to faith. Too many. In this instance, it is more than likely that your piety has saved you.'

CHAPTER TWENTY

'Where is she?' Adriaan van Dijk cried, rushing into the house, Wilhelmina trailing in his wake. 'Where is Judith?'

'*Mijnheer*, lower your voice,' Suzanne said. 'The girls are in the parlour. We are trying not to alarm them. Wilhelmina, will you join them please. Say nothing of what has happened.'

'I will kill him. I will hunt him down and—'

'Adriaan!' she said sharply, using his Christian name to focus his attention. 'This will not help. Judith is resting in bed. She is comfortable. Madame Lombard has dressed her wound and sees signs of hope.'

'Who is Madame Lombard? Why did you not send for a physician?'

'I would have—'

Having heard the commotion, Madame Lombard had come out into the hallway. 'I am she and there was no time to waste, young man,' she said, surprising Suzanne by speaking Dutch. 'And such ungoverned behaviour does not reflect well upon you.'

He exhaled. 'Forgive me, madame. It is merely that the girl did not say how serious the situation was and, well, I feared the worst.'

'It is serious enough, but then I have skill enough. I do not know what *juffrouw* Verbeek is to you but, provided there is no infection, there is no reason she should not make a full recovery.'

Van Dijk put his hand to his chest. 'I am in your debt.'

Madame Lombard held his gaze, then nodded. 'You have extraordinarily blue eyes, young man,' she said, then jabbed a finger towards Suzanne. 'In point of fact, that was why I called today. I remembered something else said about your Louise. It was said she had mismatched eyes, one brown and one blue. Like your own. You should ask if anyone remembers that.' Then before Suzanne could react, she swept back into the parlour without another word, closing the door behind her with a firm click.

'Is Judith really going to be all right?' Van Dijk asked, forsaking the proprieties.

Suzanne sank exhausted to the bench as the events of the afternoon finally caught up with her. 'Madame Lombard says so. She comes from a long line of physicians.' She gave a sigh. 'When you said you would kill him, you are assuming her attacker was Lars Eltorp?'

'Who else?' Then his expression softened. 'Can I see her?'

Suzanne looked up at him. 'Better not. People might talk. Besides, she is sleeping.' Seeing the disappointment on his face, she took pity. 'As soon as she wakes, I will tell her that you came. I know that will please her.'

'Will it?'

Suzanne smiled: '*C'est dans le besoin qu'on reconnaît ses vrais amis.*'

Van Dijk pulled a face. 'Forgive me, my French is rather rudimentary. I can negotiate the price of cattle, little more.'

'"It is when in need that one recognises one's true friends",' she translated. 'It is a phrase beloved of my grandmother. You have been that friend to Judith, *mijnheer*. She will be grateful for your kindness.'

His blue eyes glittered with hope. 'Grateful? Nothing more?'

Suzanne hesitated, then asked the question that had been on

her mind ever since the young man had first set eyes on Judith. 'Why do you care so deeply?'

Van Dijk flushed. 'Have you not read the works of your countryman? Five hundred years ago, Chrétien de Troyes wrote of love, of how it might immediately pierce the heart.'

Suzanne stared at him. 'You are saying that Judith is your Guinevere? Come now, *mijnheer*, the torments of love as writ in pen and ink are very far from the realities of it in our harsh world.'

'It is true, though. At least, in part.' To her surprise – he was usually so formal – he sat down on the bench beside her. 'When I was a boy in Rotterdam, my route used to take me past the gates of the orphanage – the "gates of charity", as they were known. I would sometimes stop and watch the children playing inside. The boys in breeches and caps, the girls in their plain grey pinafore dresses and bonnets. Although I knew they were to be pitied, in truth I was jealous. I was lonely, a solitary boy, whereas they at least had companionship.' He sighed. 'There was one particular girl who would always smile when she saw me.'

'What was her name?'

'I never knew. Then, one day, she wasn't there any more. I was just a child, there was no one I could ask – I had no *right* to ask – but I felt my world had ended.' He gave a light laugh. 'Twenty years ago, but it could be yesterday. How odd that I remember it now.'

'Not at all. The memories of childhood burn brightest, for they are the purest and least contaminated by time and experience.'

He nodded. 'It is not that Judith – if you will forgive my presumption in referring to her with such familiarity – puts me in mind of my first love. She was blonde, whereas Judith has hair the colour of –' he thought for a moment –'the colour of autumn leaves. And Judith has a profile and bearing of some nobility, do you not think, while the girl in Rotterdam had cheeks as pink as any milkmaid and a face as round. But when I first saw her, something moved me. I am no poet, I have no skill with words, I cannot explain it better.' He put his hands on his knees. 'I hardly expect you to understand. I can't even account for it myself.'

'But she is promised to someone else,' Suzanne said quietly. 'That was the condition of her passage, you know that.'

Van Dijk turned to face her. 'It is not so clear cut,' he replied quickly. 'I have been thinking on it. If you agree that Judith might come to care for me, as I care for her – not as a brother or a friend in times of need, but as a husband – it could be arranged.' He took a deep breath. 'If you were to tell me there was even the slightest chance, then I would speak to Commander Van der Stel and ask for his blessing. None of the marriage licences for any of the girls from Rotterdam have yet been issued.'

Suzanne considered what he'd said. 'Would the Commander agree to such a thing? He did not strike me as a man who would put sentiment ahead of practical considerations.'

Van Dijk leant back against the wall. 'I cannot see he would refuse it. My term here is fifteen years. I have served ten of those years and had indicated my intention to return to Rotterdam at the end of my service. If Judith would do me the honour of becoming my wife, I would withdraw my resignation. And stay.'

'And you would do this for her?'

'If it meant that we could be together, I would walk to the ends of the earth and back.'

Suzanne closed her eyes. She was exhausted by the calamities of the afternoon, from her emotions – fear, despair, relief. She did not want to say the wrong thing and there was a delicacy to such nascent emotions that could so easily be crushed. She did not believe in love at first sight, how could she after what had happened to her? But then she thought of how Judith's cheeks flushed when she talked of the Dutchman's cornflower-blue eyes, remembered her shy pleasure when she confided that he was to call for her on Sunday to take her to church. And from what she knew of Adriaan van Dijk, his sobriety and his steadfast faith, she knew he and Judith were two of a kind. He would be a good match for her friend.

'I cannot speak for Judith, you understand—' she began.

'Yes?' he said, failing to keep the hope from his voice.

'All the same, I would not be misleading you to say that Judith enjoys your company. Very much so. I do not know if it is love, but there is a growing affection, certainly.' She held his gaze. 'I believe she would welcome your suit, provided she knew there was nothing improper in it. And that it had a purpose.'

'You have made me happier than I could imagine.' He leapt to his feet, grinning. His joy made him look younger. 'I must make an appointment to see the Commander. He, too, will be pleased – for I know he did not want to lose me back to the Fatherland.' He opened the door, then smacked his forehead with the palm of his hand. 'I cannot believe this all but slipped my mind! I am bid to ask you to return to the harbour at four o'clock this afternoon. They are going to disembark the *Zuid-Beveland* then, when the wind has dropped and the sea is calmer.'

'How many were drowned?' Suzanne asked quietly.

'Eight in all, three officers and five sailors.'

Suzanne shook her head. 'But not pastor Simond?'

'No. He remains safely on board, so far as we know.'

'That is, at least, good news.' Suzanne made to stand. 'I will be there at four. I will leave Judith in the care of Madame Lombard and my grandmother. I will be fine on my own,' she added quickly before he offered her another escort.

Van Dijk opened the door and was about to step out into the street when Suzanne called him back. 'There is something you might do for me.'

He turned, still clutching his hat. 'Anything.'

'There is someone who came to the Cape some years ago, a relative of mine, whom I am eager to trace.'

Van Dijk waved his hand, as if it would be the easiest thing in the world. 'Give me his name and I will do what I can. There will be records.'

Suzanne smiled. '*Her* name,' she said. 'Louise Reydon-Joubert, Captain and Commander of the *Old Moon*.'

And by saying her name, Suzanne felt the air shimmer.

CHAPTER TWENTY-ONE

Wednesday, 15th September

The rains of August gave way to a mellow September, bringing with it the promise of spring: soft morning air, a warming sun, apricot skies at dusk. The Colony was coming back to life after the long cold and wet winter.

The passengers and crew of the *Zuid-Beveland* were also quickly absorbed into the day-to-day life of the expanding refugee community. Pierre Simond held an outdoor service of thanksgiving for their deliverance from the sea, and for the country they were all to learn to call home. Sanctuary, faith, hard work, gratitude; these were the pillars on which the Huguenot community in the Cape would be built. Since no further ships were expected until October, there was a sense of stability in the town: a breathing out, a moment of settling. Of peace.

Cared for by Madame Lombard and Florence, Judith gradually recovered. Adriaan van Dijk was now a regular visitor to the Joubert household. Having secured Commander Van der Stel's blessing for his marriage, he had offered his hand and been accepted without hesitation. The marriage banns had been published and the wedding set for a date three weeks hence.

Judith had nothing to bring to the marriage, and Suzanne knew this worried her. But several of the women from the meeting rooms presented her with a square of unbleached linen and coloured cotton thread, and so Judith was working in secret to embroider a sampler to present to her betrothed on their wedding day. The border was patterned with ivy to symbolise steadfast love, faithfulness and fertility; a sparkling vine clinging to a tree a symbol of marital love and dependence – and a reference to the country in which they would build their family. She stitched two peacocks, top and bottom, as an allusion to future prosperity. In the centre, exquisitely worked, was an inscription of Judith's own composition:

FAITH, UNWAVERING AND STEADFAST,
WILL STRENGTHEN BODY AND SOUL

For his part, Van Dijk presented Judith with a pair of gloves to seal their engagement – a Dutch tradition – to be worn on their wedding day. Fashioned from the softest kid, the cuffs were embellished with sea pearls and embroidered violets. A central motif of entwined hands and a basket of fruit spoke to their union and the hope of children to come. They were quite the finest gloves Suzanne had seen and she was astonished that Van Dijk might have acquired such a pair. To her knowledge, there were no glove makers resident in the Colony and few embroiderers capable of producing such delicate work. When she asked, he admitted he had bought the gloves from a merchant returning from the East and paid handsomely to secure them.

Madame Lombard surprised everyone by taking charge of the orphanage girls, moving into their lodgings while Judith was convalescing with Florence and Suzanne. She was brusque, sharp-tongued, wry, and the girls flourished under her firm – sometimes irreverent – guidance. Commander Van der Stel had been as good as his word. The girls now knew that none would be married until the new year at the earliest, so they were free to enjoy their days.

In this frontier colony, Suzanne realised she, too, was healing. The question Madame Lombard had asked her on the occasion of their first meeting – why Louise mattered so much to her – she was now not afraid to answer. She could not rewrite her own traumatic history, but she could do everything to bring Louise's story into the light and that gave her purpose.

Yet Suzanne could do nothing but wait for Adriaan van Dijk to give her any morsel of information – and he was bound up with preparations for his wedding – and that was a drain on her spirits. She persuaded him to bring her books from the Castle library, though they were mostly dull treatises about trade or moralising volumes to improve the Christian mind. All the while, she held firm to her conviction that Louise had come to the Cape and settled. Her determination to find her remained steady.

Venturing out whenever she could, Suzanne found something different to marvel at on each occasion and wondered if Louise had been moved by the same sense of awe. The fynbos had exploded into life and the ground was carpeted with flowers: red, white, yellow, purple, pink and blue. The world was alive with the chirping of grasshoppers and rock kestrels and black-shouldered kites twisted and turned in the warming air. She was careful never to stray too far from the accepted paths, and never to places where lions or baboons had been sighted. But she took her notebook and she recorded what she saw. Like generations of Joubert women before her, she increasingly found solace and purpose in putting her words down on the page.

Testimony of a new world.

Six weeks to the day since the *China* had sailed into Table Bay, a small congregation of celebrants gathered at the chapel in the Castle of Good Hope for the wedding of Judith Verbeek, spinster and orphan, to Adriaan van Dijk, son of Johanna Evets and Jakob van Dijk of Rotterdam.

The Dutch pastor of the Colony, Johannes van Andel, conducted the service in the presence of Commander Van der Stel, the groom's VOC colleagues and the bride's travelling companions from Rotterdam. Wilhelmina, Petronella and Catrina were flower girls. Suzanne, Florence and Madame Lombard were the only French guests.

In front of their witnesses, Adriaan and Judith exchanged their vows, swearing their troth on the volume of psalms that had saved Judith's life. Suzanne thought Adriaan had never looked finer, with his brown hair gleaming and his blacks laundered, his cuffs and collar bleached white. The bride wore a pale green dress, with open sleeves and a bodice exquisite with passementerie. She looked radiant in the chapel with her crown of flowers. Suzanne smiled, recollecting Adriaan's description of Judith's hair – the colour of autumn leaves – and wished she had the skill to capture it with paint and brush.

A simple wedding feast followed. The spiced wine known as 'bridal tears' was served in pewter cups and Adriaan had found someone within the Castle kitchens to bake bridal sugar, the sweetmeats that blessed every wedding table in Holland. It had been, Suzanne thought as she crept to bed some hours later, the most perfect day.

CHAPTER TWENTY-TWO

Monday, 18th October

Adriaan and Judith van Dijk settled into married life in his small, but comfortable, quarters in the Castle. Although the eldest of Van der Stel's four sons was expected to succeed him, the Commander increasingly relied upon Van Dijk's steady advice and proficiency.

For her part, the role of wife seemed to suit Judith. She continued to watch over the Rotterdam orphans as if they were her own children – though Madame Lombard now had sole charge of them. Her face grew plumper and her skin less sallow and, although her quiet and sweet nature was unchanged, she seemed to grow in stature. Judith had found her place in the world.

Suzanne had not.

The temperate climate of spring was giving way to a fierce summer. The sun blazed bright in the sky for twelve hours and more a day, forcing everyone inside. The town was attacked by flies hovering like black clouds over the earthen streets and, at night, the remorseless whine of mosquitos had every woman, man and child sleeping with a woven fan to swat them away. Suzanne was restless and, missing her previous intimacy with Judith, was suffocated by ennui. The heat and her own inaction made her ill-tempered and whatever her grandmother suggested to help pass the time did not help. What purpose was there to being here at all if she was just going to sit at home scribbling away in a notebook? She wanted to do something, *achieve* something.

The opportunity came a month after the Van Dijks' wedding, when Adriaan unexpectedly presented himself at her door.

'Good day to my favourite sister,' he said, raising his hat. 'The last two ships of the season are due to arrive soon: the *Prinseland* in a matter of days and the *Castricum* before October is out. Will you again help with the refugees? The request comes from the Commander himself.'

'You need hardly ask,' she replied, 'I am going out of my head with boredom. Will you come in for a while? I have seen so little of you these past weeks.'

Inside, Adriaan removed his hat and loosened his stock and the buttons on his jacket, accepted a measure of wine, and answered her tumbling questions about Judith, her health, their day-to-day lives, with good humour. Once the pleasantries had been dispensed with, and arrangements made for the arrival of the final refugees, Suzanne took her chance.

'I know you have had much to occupy you, brother, so I have not pressed you. But I wonder if you have had any success in looking into the case of my relative?'

He held his hand to his head. 'Forgive me, I have been remiss. I have been meaning to find the time to talk to you, but—'

'You have found something?'

Adriaan pulled a notebook from his pocket. 'I did look into our earliest records – some, as you may imagine, pre-date the establishing of the Colony and go back to the days when our ships simply anchored for a week or two to replenish their stocks, before sailing on. Those records are not extensive and many of the files dating from before the Castle was built, when there was no more than a wooden fort on the site, have been lost.'

'But there are some records?'

'There are. While I could find no mention of Louise's name, I did find three references to a person who fitted her description.'

Suzanne sat forward, elbows on the table like any trencherman waiting for his supper. 'Tell me.'

'The first was in a letter from a VOC captain to the governor general of Batavia dated the sixteenth of June 1622.'

'That is five weeks or so after Louise dropped anchor.'

'And some three years after we had repelled the English attack and were starting to build a city on the ruins of Jayakarta. As a consequence, many more VOC ships were sailing east and stopping to replenish at the Cape. The captain in question had put in at Table Bay for provisions and to negotiate with the Khoi, who were ready to barter cattle in exchange for iron, copper, beads, brandy. His onward departure was delayed because of a series of storms that were battering the Cape. He was obliged to take lodging in the Fort until such time as it was safe to continue. I assume the letter was to explain the hiatus, though why it was never sent, I know not. The point is that, in making his report of his trading with the Khoi, he learnt they were not the only Dutch ship to have arrived in the Cape that autumn.'

Suzanne realised she was holding her breath. 'Go on.'

'That earlier ship had drawn everyone's attention for several reasons: first, they had nothing to trade or barter. They simply replenished their supplies, then set off again almost immediately on the following tide to return to Europe. That was unusual.'

'Louise's lieutenant said she gave him orders to sail her ship back to Amsterdam without her,' Suzanne put in.

Adriaan nodded. 'Second, the captain appeared to be a woman.'

'*Appeared* to be?'

'The descriptions were vague. She was tall and broad, always with a red scarf around her head.'

'Louise often wore such a scarf.'

'And there was also much talk among the Khoi of a dagger with an evil eye. That could mean anything.'

Suzanne's eyes were now shining with excitement. Finally, she was getting somewhere. 'Louise had a dagger with a single emerald on the hilt. At least, she'd had it in her possession in Gran Canaria.'

Adriaan paused dramatically. 'Third, it is told that she had two male companions. One of the men is said to have had a devil's mark, that's to say – so far as I can tell – a strip of pure white in his hair.'

Suzanne took a deep breath. For the first time, this was independent confirmation that all three had survived the voyage and come on shore. 'Phillipe Vidal. He was her half-brother. Where did they go?' she asked keenly. 'Did the captain write of that? Did they stay in Table Bay?'

Adriaan held up his hand. 'Slow down. The Khoi claimed that they went into the interior. Towards the elephant's valley.'

'Where is that?'

'We call it Olifantshoek, where the elephants go to calf. It is beyond Stellenbosch, a distance of some fifteen leagues from here as the crow flies. That's to say, the distance to Stellenbosch and as far again. But the formidable mountain passes are dangerous, the valleys wreathed in shadow and every manner of wild animal can be found there. Few white settlers have ventured that far.'

Suzanne thought for a moment. Olifantshoek. This married with what Madame Lombard had told her. 'Did they travel together, did the captain write of that?'

'He says that reports varied. Sometimes it was two men, sometimes it was a woman and a man, sometimes three men. That is where the letter ended. The storms cleared and, I presume, the good captain sailed on to Batavia.'

She refilled his cup and, this time, poured herself a measure too.

'You said there were two other references.'

'Yes. It is fortunate that, even then, we were keeping meticulous records of our trade with local people. It is so important to—'

'Adriaan, please,' she interrupted, seeing the zeal in his eyes. 'I do not care about the VOC arrangements with the Khoi.' Suzanne checked herself. 'Forgive me, of course I do. But not at this moment.'

He took the rebuke in good spirit. 'The second reference is more fleeting. In the quartermaster's stores, there was a ledger from the November three years later, 1625. In it, a white man – name unrecorded – is described as coming to the harbour to trade peacock feathers for paper and ink. It is noted because he had travelled from the interior. In other words, not a sailor or a merchant, but resident up-country.'

'Is there any record of where, precisely?'

'No.'

Suzanne frowned. Could it have been Phillipe? Gilles? Or even Louise herself? From her diary, she knew Louise sometimes wore breeches.

Adriaan continued. 'But it is the last reference that is the most intriguing. It took some finding, I can tell you.'

Suzanne grinned. 'You know that I am grateful, brother.'

'I do.' His blue eyes glinted. 'And it makes my wife happy that I should help you, so . . .' He smoothed the pages of his notebook flat. 'In the autumn of 1630, the Khoi chief Autshumao, who also appears in VOC records as Harry the Strandloper, was taken to Batavia. There, he learnt English and Dutch, in order to work as an interpreter between the settlers and his people. He was, by all accounts, wealthy and influential. His niece, Krotoa, was also an interpreter, an extraordinary and gifted woman. As a matter of fact, she was a ward of the first commander of the Cape, Jan van Riebeeck.'

'Adriaan . . .' Suzanne chided.

He hushed her. 'This is relevant, sister. Autshumao returned two years later, first based on Robben Island working as a liaison and post officer for European ships, before coming back to the mainland. He might have been a prisoner on the island, it's not clear. We have no records in his own hand – it is not certain if he could read or write – but his achievements are well-documented.' He tapped his notebook. 'So here we come to it. In May of the year 1644, Autshumao talked about meeting two white men near Olifantshoek. One is described as in middle years, the other a young man with a streak of white in his hair.'

'Gilles would have been in his middle years,' Suzanne calculated. 'But Phillipe would have been fifty years of age by that time, so hardly young.'

Adriaan shrugged. 'I am only telling you what was written down.'

She drained her cup and sat back in her chair. What *did* it mean? That Louise had died by then, or that she simply was not with them that day? That Gilles and Phillipe were in one another's company, allies presumably? Was it possible she had read something into Louise's diary that was not, in fact, there? Misled by the final entry: *I think he means me harm.* She had always assumed that 'he' to be Phillipe, but perhaps she was mistaken?

'Both men were white,' she clarified. 'Not *mestiço*?' It was the Portuguese term still used in the Colony to describe someone of mixed heritage.

'According to Autshumao's testimony, yes.'

Suzanne fell back into contemplation. In the somnolent atmosphere, she became aware that Adriaan was becoming restless. Still, she didn't speak, not wanting to break her train of thought. Running out of patience, he closed his notebook, slipped it back into his pocket, and stood up.

'Forgive me, Adriaan, there is so much to think on,' she said, 'I hardly know where to start. But, thank you for all of this. It must have taken time and effort.'

He pushed his chair back under the table. 'It was my pleasure. Now, if there is nothing else, I will let you know when the *Prinseland* is due to drop anchor.'

Suzanne also stood. 'There is one more thing.'

'No, no.' He held up his hands in surrender. 'I cannot face another afternoon in the archives, not in this heat.'

She laughed. 'No, not that. This is something else entirely. I need to know how to handle a gun. Will you teach me?'

CHAPTER TWENTY-THREE

Hottentots Holland

The light was fading over the plain.

Lars Eltorp raised the musket to his shoulder. It was an old weapon, traded with an acquaintance, and the weighting made long-distance shots inaccurate. But it was adequate for his purposes.

For two weeks, he had been living in the area a half-day's ride south-east of Stellenbosch on a settler farmstead. The farmer's wife gave him a wide berth, and kept her daughters away, but he had sailed with her husband some years ago on a Barbary corsair ship and those bonds were hard to break. For now, Eltorp was comfortable enough, he had plenty of brandy and, if he landed his shot, there would be fresh meat tonight.

In the dusk, some eighty yards ahead on the low-lying plain, was a herd of grysbok, the smallest of the antelopes that inhabited the region. The red fur of the male seemed to catch the last rays of the sun and set its thin antlers gleaming. They were shy creatures, only coming out at the end of the day to graze. But the meat would be welcome and an unbutchered carcass could be carried by one man over his shoulders.

Eltorp took aim, and fired.

The herd scattered, fleeing back to the thicket and dense shrub. He cursed loudly, fumbling to prepare his next shot, but the clearing where the grysbok had been stood empty. He kicked the ground and cursed the rogue who had sold him a gun not fit for purpose. His hand went to the knife at his belt. He preferred to cut. He liked to see the whites of his victim's eyes, man or beast.

He had laid low for the past weeks, keeping his ear to the ground, but had heard nothing. No VOC lackeys had been sighted in the vicinity, no one asking questions up-country. He was not surprised. Though both his victims had been white – Driek was just another sailor who couldn't hold his drink, and the girl? A nobody shipped halfway across the world? She mattered little more than the Black devils under the overseer's whip or incarcerated in the Slave House each night.

He laughed, a raw and ugly sound in the quiet of the plain. He'd outwitted them all. For all their airs and graces, they weren't real men, these merchants and secretaries. They didn't know how to fight, or hunt, or use a knife. He skimmed his finger along the blade, then slipped the weapon back into his belt.

Eltorp waited a while longer before accepting the grysbok would not return. No matter, he had bagged a brace of hyrax on his trek out here. They were small grubbing animals, and full of bones, but some meat was better than none. At his feet, the blood of his catch was seeping through the hessian of the sack, staining the green grasses red.

CHAPTER TWENTY-FOUR

Gallow's Hill
Wednesday, 20th October

Two days later, Adriaan van Dijk presented himself at the Joubert household wearing an unseasonably heavy black cloak.

'If the Commander hears so much of a whisper of this,' he said, 'he will have my head.'

Suzanne ushered him into the hallway, which was barely cooler than the street outside. A dense column of flies was spiralling in the still air, twisting and turning on itself. She had given up trying to get rid of them. It was easier to pretend she could not hear their incessant buzzing.

'Officially, I am here to tell you that the *Prinseland* is expected to drop anchor tomorrow. In this calm weather, it should be an easy matter to disembark the passengers.'

'And unofficially?'

He opened his cloak to reveal a musket and a bag of ammunition.

'To teach you to handle a gun. I have grave misgivings, but my wife says you would not have asked if there were not a very good reason for it.' He paused. 'Is there a good reason?'

She met his gaze boldly. 'It can only be wise for a woman alone to be able to defend herself. Common sense, in fact.'

Adriaan looked unconvinced. 'There is nothing more to it than that?'

'What could there be?' Aware that she had not allayed his

suspicions, she gave him her most innocent smile and opened the door. Louise would be proud of her. 'Lead on.'

Some half an hour later, they were at the north-eastern boundary of the town in the area known as Gallow's Hill.

Adriaan told her that the sandy wilderness of dunes and grasses was known to be an ancient burial ground, throwing up the bones of women and men who had long lain in the ground. Khoi once used the coastal plains for grazing which, in turn, brought lions down to the sand. It was intended in the future to build graveyards for the city – for freemen and enslaved alike.

'It is said that the spirits of the evil dead haunt the plains, which means most people, Khoi and settlers alike, avoid coming here.'

'Perfect for our purposes.'

'Quite.'

He led her to a series of sand dunes where they were shielded from the eyes of the town. From his sack, he produced several cracked earthenware pots. 'For target practice,' he explained. He set them in the sand, then came back to where Suzanne was waiting. 'Have you ever fired a gun before? A pistol, a musket, anything?'

She shook her head.

'Very well.' He unpacked the sack and laid the contents on the sand for her to see. 'This,' he said, holding up a leather sash-cum-belt, 'is a bandolier. It holds your ammunition, the firing balls.' He picked up a long, thin piece of wood. 'This is what we call a scouring stick, used for packing the black powder – that's to say, the gunpowder – into the muzzle.' He pointed to some small twists of paper. 'The gunpowder is carried in individual cartridges—'

'So one knows how much to put in?'

Adriaan nodded. 'Exactly so.'

Suzanne was concentrating so hard that it was a while before she realised that her face was burning. It was early, yet, but the sun was already fierce in the sky and she did not want to have to lie to her grandmother when she asked why her cheeks were so red. She dragged her bonnet lower on her forehead.

'Now I'm going to take you through each section of the musket itself. It's a flintlock mechanism – most pistols and muskets have them. Watch carefully, then I'll show you how to load it.'

'And then to fire it?'

He smiled wryly. 'All in good time, my impatient sister. You cannot fire a weapon unless you have properly prepared it. Most muskets, or any flintlock firearms, are generally loaded via the muzzle like a cannon. You push the gunpowder into the muzzle, using the scouring stick, right down to the bore where it settles at the breech, above the trigger and below the pan. An experienced soldier will be able to tell by eye how much is needed for a successful fire but, when you have a cartridge like weapons such as this, then the measure is already set.'

'I understand.'

'Then a cloth wad is placed over the muzzle and the lead ball is pushed in on top. The wad helps to ensure the ball is airtight within the barrel so it will not roll back out. An airtight chamber is much more effective.'

Suzanne nodded.

'You will then need to prime the gun before you can fire it. You do this by lifting up the frizzen. Here.' He tapped the top of the weapon. 'You will put the priming powder into the pan. It creates less smoke than gunpowder, so there is less danger of your view being impeded. Once this is done, you lock down the frizzen like so, to protect the primer from the elements – essential when it is raining – then the next step is to pull back the cock. Can you see?' He pointed to the hammer-like mechanism attached to the trigger that held the flint.

'I see it.'

'Once the gun is fully cocked, you are ready to fire. You just aim and pull the trigger. Easy.' He turned and handed the musket to her. 'Now, would you like to try?'

Suzanne felt a flutter of nerves in the pit of her stomach, exhilaration too, as she took the gun. It was heavier than she had expected, its length causing the muzzle to dip.

'You need to raise it just so,' Adriaan said, helping her to manoeuvre the weapon into position. 'The force will drive the musket back into your shoulder, so it is important to set it right otherwise you could end up with a broken bone.'

Suzanne did as he instructed.

'Now, bend your knees and set your feet further apart,' he continued. 'No wider than your shoulders. The first rule of marksmanship is that the position and hold must be firm enough to support the weapon.' He paused. 'Are you comfortable?'

'I suppose so.'

'Then raise your right arm, straight in front of you. The gun's got to point naturally at the target. Otherwise the recoil will knock you off balance.'

'It feels all right.'

'Good. Now, close your left eye, focus with your right. Look down the barrel. Make yourself breathe, slowly, in and out, get used to the position.'

'Can I fire?'

Adriaan laughed. 'Never rush your shot, unless there is no choice. A musket is accurate for some fifty yards or so, after that it is about putting the ball where you want it to go and praying. Now, slowly, very slowly, squeeze your finger towards you; you're gently pulling the trigger, not jerking at it. Squeeze it. Keep your eye on the target all of the time, don't look at anything else. Then, and only then, when you're ready, shoot.'

Suzanne felt a strange calm suffuse her. She exhaled, then slowly squeezed. But at the last moment, the muzzle jumped and the shot went high.

'Ow!' she cried, feeling the punch against her shoulder. 'What did I do wrong?'

'It's what always happens to start with. The ball must be released and followed through without any change to your firing position. You anticipated the shot, so at the very last second you lost your aim.'

'I did not,' she protested.

'It's a common mistake. You blink, your arm moves a fraction, the muzzle slips to one side, and you'll miss the target.' He held out a second paper cartridge and the scouring rod. 'You load this time.'

Suzanne went through the steps, Adriaan encouraging her, until the weapon was again ready to fire.

'Now, try again. Attempt the middle of the target, any one will do.'

Suzanne took aim. Determined to do it right, she counted down in her head, slow and steady, breathing in, breathing out. This time, she squeezed the trigger and imagined the ball shooting down the muzzle and out. An earthenware pot in the middle of the line shattered.

'There!' she said with triumph, turning round to face him.

'Though I still do not consider this a suitable pastime for a lady, that was not bad.' Adriaan grinned. 'Not bad at all.'

Suzanne tried again, and again, until all but one of the earthenware pots were lying shattered on the sand.

'One last time?'

Adriaan looked around. The sound of the Castle bell could just be heard in the distance. 'Better not.'

'But there's no one about.'

He shook his head. 'There is always someone watching in the Colony, looking for gossip to trade. My absence will be noted if I am away too long.'

Suzanne let the muzzle drop, but she knew she would dream of firing it in her sleep. Her shoulder was already sore, and she had no doubt she would feel the strain in her muscles tomorrow. But, while she was holding the weapon, she had felt invincible.

CHAPTER TWENTY-FIVE

CAPE COLONY
Saturday, 6th November

In the event, Suzanne was not to have a gun in her hand again for more than a fortnight. In the meantime, she read the books Adriaan brought for her and managed to secure a map of the region. It was roughly drawn, and not to scale, but it at least gave the relative positions of the Colony to the mountains, the mountains to Stellenbosch and Drakenstein, then the passes beyond that led east to Olifantshoek. She pored over the map at night when Florence was asleep, imprinting the lie of the land on her mind.

Adriaan managed to smuggle Suzanne into the Colony Registry to study the VOC records of births, marriages and deaths, having secured permission for her to visit her strongbox held in the Castle vaults. For form's sake, she confirmed that the gold, silver and jewellery she had deposited was all there and accounted for. But she learnt little in the registry, save for the fact that there were no records at all of Louise Joubert, Gilles Barenton or Phillipe Vidal. She asked if she might visit the archives, so she could see for herself the documents Adriaan had found.

That request was denied.

The arrival of the latest refugees on the *Prinseland* and the *Castricum*, the last two ships of the season, had swelled the population of the Colony by another four hundred people odd.

The disembarkations had been straightforward, though time consuming, as had finding lodgings for all who needed them in the town. In the flattening heat, tempers were short and the limited resources much under pressure.

When time allowed, Suzanne was coaching Adriaan with his French. He had finally accepted how useful it would be to be able to converse more freely with the growing numbers of refugees. He was an eager student and Suzanne enjoyed visiting their apartment armed with paper and pen.

Florence continued to thrive. It was now she who, with Madame Neil and Madame Lombard, hosted the regular evening event to welcome the new Huguenot arrivals. It pleased Suzanne that her grandmother had, in the autumn of her life, found a new role. In France, the women would not have been friends. They would have had nothing in common. Their lives would not have crossed. But here, refugees all, different alliances were being created. Only they knew what it was like never to feel safe, to understand that one's home was not always a sanctuary. Suzanne was happy for Florence – and it eased her guilt at having brought her to the Cape in the first place – but she was also a little wistful. She had found no such community. And, since that first evening when they had talked of her mission to find Louise, the subject had not been mentioned between them. Florence was filling her days with the present, not thinking about the past.

The fact was that Suzanne was lonely. Her one friend, Judith, as the wife of a senior VOC official, found her time occupied in hosting dinners for the captain and his officers, doing good works for the church whilst trying to make favourable matches for her Rotterdam girls. And, although Suzanne enjoyed Judith and Adriaan's company when they dined informally at their lodgings, there was little left of the intimacy between the two young women that had characterised their long sea voyage and their first month at the Cape.

On the evening of Saturday the sixth of November, Suzanne was pleased to find herself invited to the Castle to attend a dinner in honour of the captains of the *Prinseland* and the *Castricum*. She had no doubt that Judith had lined up yet another VOC officer she wanted her to meet. Suzanne had never shared the reason for her violent antipathy to the idea of wedlock, but however many times she said that she was not looking for a suitor, her friend refused to accept it.

'There are other paths to contentment,' Suzanne protested, but Judith just smiled and told her to 'wait and see'.

Shortly before eight o'clock, Suzanne left her lodgings and walked through the familiar streets, across the parade ground and bridge, to the Castle. Her hair was dressed in long ringlets which framed her face. She was wearing her favourite gown, a pale blue with a jewelled bodice, wide sleeves and lace trim at the neck, with her finest embroidered shoes. She feared they would be stained by the dust – it had not rained for weeks – but the occasion required it. Though not interested in any man Judith might put before her, she still wanted to be admired.

Having given her name to the guards at the gate, Suzanne was ushered under the bell tower and into the main courtyard. Lanterns had been set along the path towards the hall chamber, the flames fluttering in the gentle evening breeze sending shadows dancing along the yellow walls of the buildings. Everything seemed soft and enchanted in the apricot dusk. The guinea fowl were gone, replaced by four magnificent peacocks, their beautiful tails trailing across the cobbled surface.

Inside the building, she could hear the strains of courtly music slipping down the staircase. Viol and lute, the percussive plucking of the strings of a virginal. For an instant, she was back in La Rochelle in the days before the *dragonnades*, when chamber musicians would travel between the big houses filling the town with harmony.

Having paid her respects to the Commander and his sister-in-law, Suzanne was pleased to feel Judith's hand upon her elbow.

'You are placed beside Jean Prieur du Plessis,' Judith whispered. 'His wife is at home nursing their son. He was barber-surgeon on the *Oosterland*, which arrived last April. Thanks to him, there was not a single death on board. I think you will enjoy his company.'

The name triggered a memory, but Suzanne couldn't place it. Du Plessis wasn't mentioned in Louise's prison diary, yet she was sure she had seen it written somewhere.

'Thank you. Who else is here?'

'That's the captain of the *Prinseland*,' Judith said, inclining her head towards a tall man standing by one of the open windows. 'And that man with the whiskers, he is the captain of the *Castricum*. They lost a fair few souls during the course of the voyage, a source of bitter regret for him.'

Suzanne looked around the chamber, recognising a few faces. She was surprised to see Wilhelmina, one of the Rotterdam girls. In a plain red gown, and with her hair styled, she appeared older and more assured.

'Wilhelmina?'

Judith's gentle face grew sombre. 'She met Corporal Biebouw at our wedding and he requested she should be invited tonight. My husband says he means to ask Commander Van der Stel for permission to marry.'

'You are not in favour of his suit?'

Judith's composure faltered. 'It seems that he has, for some time, had a relationship with an enslaved Malagasy woman he owned. Some say he married her – which made her a freewoman – but even so. There is a child, a girl, whom he had baptised and he himself is named as the father.'

Suzanne frowned. 'But if that is the case, how can he marry again?'

Judith lowered her voice. 'Many of the first enslaved women married Dutch settlers – though Corporal Biebouw is, in point of fact, German – but it is now prohibited.'

'So the marriage is not seen as legitimate.'

'Exactly so. I cannot see such a man will be a good husband for Wilhelmina, but her heart is set upon him and Adriaan says the Commander will give his blessing. Maybe she will reform him.'

'Only God can reform man's baser nature,' Suzanne said wryly.

Judith nodded. 'It is true that I have yet to see Corporal Biebouw in chapel of a Sunday.'

Suzanne was about to ask more, but now Adriaan was standing in front of them. He smiled lovingly at his wife. 'My dear, I would introduce you to the captain of the *Prinseland*.' Then he turned to Suzanne and dropped his voice. 'Meet me at the main gate at ten o'clock tomorrow morning, sister. Wear travelling clothes.'

'Are we going back to Gallow's Hill?'

He looked around, as if fearing to be overheard. 'No, we ride for Stellenbosch. I will explain tomorrow.' Then he raised his voice for the benefit of any eavesdroppers. 'Might you be good enough to excuse us, *juffrouw* Joubert?'

Suzanne stared as Judith was swept away, brimming over with curiosity and excitement. At last, she was to travel into the interior. She had no idea why or how Adriaan had arranged she should accompany him – nor what the purpose of his visit might be – but it didn't matter. At last, she would see something of life beyond the Colony, riding the 'wagon trail' to Stellenbosch.

And beyond that, Olifantshoek.

Unable to stop herself from smiling, Suzanne waved her fan, stirring the warm air, then mingled with her fellow guests. She picked up murmured snatches of news from the Fatherland: that William of Orange was leader of a Grand Alliance of Protestant countries alarmed at the expansionist ambitions of the king of France; that there were rumours William might even take the throne of England to save the Protestant nation from the rule of the convert Catholic king James II; that an English composer by the name of Henry Purcell was taking London by storm.

Suzanne let the chatter float by, stories from another world. Her eye alighted on Wilhelmina, listening with pretty animation to one of the VOC officer's wives whilst constantly looking to see if Corporal Biebouw's eyes were upon her.

She liked Wilhelmina, and wished her well, but wondered if anyone had considered the feelings of Biebouw's common-law wife in the matter. She thought of the Black and Malagasy women she saw in the town, with lighter-skinned children playing at their sides, and realised how many such liaisons there must be. Based on mutual affection, or something darker? That was the question, for what power could those women, enslaved or free, possibly have to turn down such advances?

Her ruminations were brought to an end by the banging of a huge brass gong. A Black servant dressed in VOC livery then clapped his hands and invited guests to take their seats at the table for dinner. Suzanne nodded a greeting to the gentleman on her left, an officer from the *Castricum*, and spoke a few words in French to Monsieur du Plessis. A man of some fifty years, he had a crumpled face, but his eyes shone with determination and resilience. She still could not remember why the name was familiar.

Then the pastor enjoined the assembled company to say the Grace. Suzanne bowed her head and tried to still her excitement.

'Tomorrow,' she murmured to herself, as she put a morsel of bread in her mouth.

CHAPTER TWENTY-SIX

THE CAPE FLATS
Sunday, 7th November

The bay mare crested the brow of the low hill. Mane and tail flying, the thunder of its hooves reverberated on the sun-baked sands.

Suzanne felt free, exhilarated, just as she had when standing on the deck of the *China* looking at the vast ocean. The limitless space, the glorious joining of land and sky, sailing to the ends of the earth. Out here, on the Cape flats, she felt something of the same. At her back, she heard Adriaan shouting at her to pull up and knew she should obey. Instead, she dug in her heels harder, wanting to hold this sense of liberty for a while longer.

When Suzanne had arrived at the Castle at the appointed hour, wearing her knee-height leather boots and riding gloves, Van Dijk had been waiting with two soldiers and four horses, one fitted with a lady's saddle. He had summoned a groom to bring steps so she could mount. 'I thought you might prefer this to a cart. We will ride due east, across the Cape flats, and should arrive in Stellenbosch by nightfall, all being well.'

'And you gained permission to take me with you. I cannot begin to thank you, brother.' She looked quizzically at him. 'How did you? Indeed, *why* did you?'

Adriaan raised his eyebrows. 'My dear wife says that you are finding time hanging heavy on your hands.'

'That's true, but even so.'

He swung his leg into the saddle. 'I have need of your assistance.'

'Does it concern Louise? You have discovered something more?'

'Possibly,' he replied. 'I will explain as we ride.'

At first, they had held a steady pace, heading past the Castle and following the valley of the Salt River that ran east across the plains. Then, Suzanne had not been able to resist giving her horse its head. The sun was high in the sky and the grasslands were alive with colour. It was magnificent to see the fynbos at closer quarters: yellow and white flowers, purple pelargonium with soft, heart-shaped petals, and bold-pink protea with sugarbirds perched on top, their long tail feathers hanging down to the green stalks of the flower.

Adriaan finally caught up with her. He pulled up his grey stallion beside her horse and grabbed the reins.

'Have your wits gone? How could you put yourself, put us all at risk, by galloping ahead?'

Immediately chastened, Suzanne bowed her head. 'Forgive me. I have been confined for so long.'

His expression softened. 'No harm done. But this is not France, riding out for sport or pleasure in gentle woodland. Here there are dangers everywhere.'

Suzanne saw nothing save a heard of antelope in the far distance.

'There are lions and jackals here,' he said, 'and although they cannot outrun a horse, those animals are killers. And though elephants live in the valleys, and are mostly indifferent to us unless we encroach on their territory, they are treacherous if roused.'

'Is that likely here?'

'Well, no,' he admitted. 'But as we establish settlements further up country, the animals move further inland and the more likely we are to provoke them. We also need to take heed of the settlers. There are increasing numbers of farms, in Drakenstein and the Liesbeeck Valley and along the Eerste River, which runs through Stellenbosch, managed by former VOC employees or settlers, so some of the animals are becoming more used to human presence. These free burghers are able to cultivate a piece of land, on which they must grow crops to be sold back to us. But only the VOC is permitted to barter directly with the Khoi for cattle and sheep and this is a source of tension. We have to be careful.' He paused to drink from his flagon, then offered it to Suzanne. 'The Khoi, as you know, are a nomadic people, moving their herds around between Table Bay, Swartland and Saldanha Bay. There are agreements in place about limiting hunting to protect their livestock.'

Suzanne heard the pride in his voice, though that did not stop her asking a question she knew would vex him. 'Are these trading agreements with the Khoi observed?'

'For the most part,' Adriaan replied curtly. 'You must understand that many of the local chiefs choose to barter with us and work with us, as interpreters and traders.'

'But what choice do they ha—' she began to say, then, seeing their escort had nearly caught them up, Suzanne dropped her voice: 'Why are we going to Stellenbosch? You promised you would tell me.'

Adriaan fixed her with a severe look. 'Only if you promise to pull no more tricks like that.'

'I give you my word.'

'Some two weeks ago, we received word that a white man answering to the description of Lars Eltorp was apprehended in Stellenbosch. It appears he, and a farmer living to the east of the town, became inebriated in a makeshift tavern near the river. A fight broke out between them and local workers. A great deal of damage was done, knives were drawn. It is only thanks to the swift reactions of the tapster and a couple of off-duty soldiers, that no one was killed.'

Suzanne looked at him with surprise. 'I did not realise you were still looking for him?'

'Eltorp attempted to ruin my wife, and then to kill her,' he said. 'Why would I ever stop trying to hunt him down?'

'If it is the same man,' Suzanne felt obliged to point out. 'He cannot be the only man called Lars in the Colony.'

'And that is why you are here. You can identify him.'

Suzanne's stomach lurched. 'And if it is?'

'Then I intend to see him hang.'

Despite the heat of the day, Suzanne shivered. 'You suggested that there was something more? Something to do with Louise?'

'In an attempt to escape the noose, Eltorp has been spinning tales.'

'He mentioned Louise?'

Finally, his expression relaxed. 'As ever, dear sister, you will have to be patient. I do not want to prejudice you. We will hear what the villain has to say for ourselves.'

CHAPTER TWENTY-SEVEN

STELLENBOSCH

They arrived in Stellenbosch at dusk. The air was still warm and, save for the constant whine of mosquitos, it was quiet.

Nestled in a fertile valley below the Stellenbosch mountains on the banks of the Eerste River, the temperate climate and the resources allocated to build a settlement here, meant that the Cape's second town was thriving. It was already functioning independently of the Colony. Adriaan had told her it had its own magistrate, as well as a church, a school and a newly established theological seminary. The main street boasted a few fine houses with verandah-trailing bougainvillea and lines of oak trees planted on Van der Stel's orders to provide shade.

'We will go straight to the *drostdij*,' Adriaan said. 'The holding cells are there and the *landdrost* is expecting us. Once our investigations are over, we will stay overnight, and return to the Colony in the morning.'

Suzanne felt a flutter of nerves.

They dismounted and led their horses across the narrow footbridge connecting the street to the little island in the river where Van der Stel had first set up camp, and their soldier escorts handed them into the care of a groom. Adriaan and Suzanne brushed the dust and sand from their clothes before going inside the impressive building to present themselves to the magistrate, Pieter Odendaal. A florid fellow of some five-and-thirty years with whom Adriaan was acquainted, he appeared puffed up with the importance of his own position.

Within a quarter-hour of their arrival, Adriaan and Suzanne were walking through the courthouse to the holding cells. She felt saddle sore and dirty from the journey.

'In truth, we have little need of cells,' Odendaal said with a measure of self-satisfaction. 'We have no trouble here. A stable community of hard-working Dutchmen, no sailors to disturb the peace, few conflicts with the tribesmen.'

'A model town,' Suzanne observed, wondering at the absence of women in his description.

Odendaal looked sharply at her, as if suspecting a criticism.

'If it pleases you,' she continued, as meekly as she could stomach, 'on what charge is the man being held?'

'Affray, in the first instance. Brawling in a tavern, damage to property and persons. When we brought him in, we discovered several items that could only have been acquired in trading with Khoi.'

Remembering how Adriaan had explained that only the VOC itself was permitted to trade directly with the local people, Suzanne nodded.

'I think perhaps . . .' Odendaal said to Adriaan, 'the young lady should return to the house. The gaol is hardly a suitable place for female sensitivities.'

'I am quite—'

Adriaan interrupted her. '*Juffrouw* Joubert is the only one who can identify the villain. We need to be certain if justice is to be done.'

Odendaal looked unconvinced, but he raised his hand. 'As you wish.'

He led them down three steps into a small internal courtyard, contained on all sides by a high brick wall with shards of pottery set along the top. On the far side, there was a squat straw-and-brick building with no windows. Two torches flamed beside the door, sending distorted shadows up and along the walls.

Taking one of the torches, Odendaal shot the bolt and led them inside.

Suzanne instantly put her kerchief over her mouth and nose. The air was foetid and hot. Ahead of them was a large iron grille, fixed floor to ceiling, leading to the area where prisoners were kept. She saw metal cages either side of a corridor and chains affixed to the walls, shackles for wrists and for ankles.

Odendaal took a large ring of keys from his belt, unlocked the grille, ushered them through, then secured it behind him. He held the torch up to reveal a huddled heap of filthy clothing in the corner of a cell. Suzanne peered into the flickering gloom. Was this the man who had menaced Judith, who had put a knife into her side? He looked no threat at all.

Odendaal banged on the iron bars. 'Get up, Eltorp. You have visitors.'

The man did not stir. Then, with a lazy insolence, he raised himself on an elbow and glared towards them. Instinctively, Suzanne shrank back. His face was bruised and one of his eyes was swollen shut, a mane of black hair hung down either side of his bearded face. A villain, no doubt, but could she be certain he was the man who had walked past her window that first night holding a knife to Driek's neck?

Adriaan looked at her, the question in his eyes.

Suzanne shook her head. 'I cannot see clearly enough.'

'Get up, man!' Odendaal shouted.

This time, the prisoner complied. Though his clothes hung like rags, stained and stinking of the cell, there was something threatening in the way he moved. Waves of hatred, of violence, seemed to emanate from him.

He gave a mock bow. 'To what do I owe the pleasure?'

Suzanne jolted. It was the same voice, overheard in the darkness, she would swear to that.

'Enough of your impertinence,' the *landdrost* said. 'Speak when you are spoken to, otherwise hold your tongue.'

'No, let him speak,' she said.

Eltorp sneered. 'My, my, you've brought me a lady to sweeten my days.'

'Enough!'

Odendaal banged on the bars again, but Suzanne had heard enough. 'It is him,' she whispered to Adriaan.

'Certain?'

Suzanne nodded. 'I am.'

Eltorp pointed at the *landdrost*. 'You have no right to hold me all this time. No right at all.'

Odendaal laughed. 'I have every right. You've been bartering illegally, no point denying it.'

'No worse than any half a dozen other men around here. Why not give me a flogging, and be done with it? Waste of VOC hospitality keeping me in victuals these past days.'

'It will go better for you if you cooperate, Eltorp,' Odendaal warned, his colour rising.

Eltorp came closer. Instinctively, Suzanne took another step back. She knew the bars were secure, but she did not want to be within spitting distance.

The prisoner looked at the magistrate, leered at Suzanne – sizing her up as if she was a doxy for sale – then addressed himself to Van Dijk.

'I cannot see why my paltry dealings would be of interest to such a fine gentleman like yourself, but to please my dear friend . . .'

'Get on with it!'

Adriaan put his hand on Odendaal's arm. 'I'm listening, Eltorp.'

Eltorp cleared his throat. 'The *landdrost* here, has persuaded himself that I have been a naughty boy. That is to say, that I have been bartering pelts directly from the Khoi in return for . . . well, he hasn't seen fit to furnish me with that information.'

'Four quagga pelts, Eltorp. You had them on you when you were arrested.'

Suzanne saw Eltorp's eyes flicker between the two men, assessing how his performance was going down.

'I am a plain man,' he wheedled. 'I may not have all the book learning you gentlemen do, but I know my rights as a free citizen of the Colony.' He jerked his head towards Odendaal. 'I've told him until I'm blue in the face that all my transactions, shall we call them, were with a white man, not a heathen. He came from further up-country, from Olifantshoek, he said.' He fixed the magistrate with an insolent look and tapped the side of his head. 'Sawdust between the ears.'

'I am warning you . . .' Odendaal snapped. 'I will come in there and flog you myself.'

Eltorp crossed his heart. 'It's God's own truth.'

Adriaan cut in. 'There are no farms that far east.'

'I do not know if the trader was speaking the truth,' Eltorp retorted, 'but that's what he told me. And he was here in Stellenbosch, as certain as I stand before you now. I happened to have a pistol I no longer had the need of – I have a perfectly good musket, bought fair and square, before you ask – and he had four fine quagga skins that I thought would suit me just fine. So, we came to terms. A perfectly honest trade between two white gentlemen, nothing prohibited by the venerable VOC.'

'What was his name?' Odendaal asked, 'this illusory trader who appeared from nowhere?'

'In matters of business, a man's word is his bond.' Eltorp laughed, a cruel bark that sent a shiver down Suzanne's spine. 'A handshake was all I needed, not a name. I'm not going to be paying house calls.'

'I don't believe he ever existed,' Odendaal said, turning to Adriaan. But Suzanne could see he was taking the story seriously.

'Describe the man,' Adriaan said.

'Well, he was about your height, *mijnheer*, and about your girth. Twice the age of my friend the magistrate here. Sixty years or so.'

'Are you sure?' Suzanne asked, unable to help herself.

For the first time, Eltorp appeared to stop and think. 'Yes, though he did not carry himself like a man in his autumn years. It was only the lines on his face that spoke to his age.'

Odendaal threw up his hands in frustration. 'You could be describing anyone. Half the men in the Colony.'

A sly look came over Eltorp's face. 'Ah, but there was something special. Something worth a sip of clean water, perhaps?'

Adriaan looked around and saw a barrel on the wall with a wooden cup beside it. He half filled it and passed it through the bars to Eltorp, who savoured it as if it was vintage wine.

'Get on with it, Eltorp,' Odendaal growled.

Eltorp wiped his lips on the back of his filthy sleeve. 'His hair was grey, but with a white stripe down the middle.' He folded his arms in triumph. 'Never seen such a thing before and I wager neither have you.'

'Phillipe Vidal,' Suzanne murmured under her breath, suddenly understanding the other reason Adriaan had brought her here. Except how could it be? Phillipe would be much older.

'Is there anything else you can tell us?' Adriaan asked calmly. 'More precisely where this man had come from? The tenor of his voice?'

'He spoke Dutch, but perhaps there was an accent?'

'What else?'

'Isn't that enough?' Eltorp snapped, then his face darkened. 'Time to end this pantomime. You have nothing against me.'

For a moment, no one spoke. Then Adriaan stepped forward.

'Lars Eltorp, you are accused of the murder of Driek Holsteen on the night of the fourth of August in the year of our Lord 1688.'

Now Suzanne saw fear ignite Eltorp's eyes. 'You can't pin that on me.'

'Furthermore,' Adriaan continued in the same steadfast voice, 'you are accused of the attempted violation of a young lady that same night, and an assault upon that same innocent person on the dockside on the afternoon of the nineteenth day of August.'

Eltorp's temper erupted. He kicked the bars, cursing and ranting. 'There are no witnesses,' he ranted. 'How could the girl speak when I—'

Van Dijk pointed at him. 'You condemn yourself from your own mouth, Eltorp. Know this. Your knife did not take her life.'

Now Eltorp started to bluster. It was pitiful. Pleading, cajoling, betraying himself by talking about the crush at the harbour, about how he had not been there, how he had never been near the girl in the grey dress.

'I do not recall mentioning how she was attired,' Adriaan said, with devastating calm.

'She was nobody!' Eltorp screamed.

Suzanne saw a look of contempt cross Adriaan's face. 'All of God's children matter, especially in this instance. The woman you attempted to rape, then murder, is my wife.'

Suzanne flinched at the word as if she had been struck. Rape.

For a moment, she saw another man's cruel face looking down at her.

Eltorp laughed in disbelief, until he saw the steel in Adriaan's eyes. Then he staggered back, his hands out in supplication. '*Mijnheer*, I had no—'

Adriaan cut him off. 'Therefore, with the authority vested in me by Commander Van der Stel, I sentence you to be hanged by the neck until you are dead. Your carcass will be left upon the gibbet as a warning for any who would violate the rules of the Colony, to be picked bare by the crows and the vultures.'

'No!' Eltorp howled and started to hammer on the bars of his cell. 'No, no, no.'

Suzanne was frozen to the spot, sickened both by the terror in Eltorp's voice, and Adriaan's cold determination.

'I will stay to see the sentence carried out tomorrow, then leave the matter in your hands, *landdrost*.'

Suzanne felt Adriaan's hand on her arm. For comfort, or for support, she did not know. Her legs felt hollow and her nerves wrung out. She closed her eyes to try to blot out her revulsion at the stinking cell, the horror of it all.

Without another word, Adriaan turned and steered her away, with Odendaal following in their wake. Suzanne threw a last glance at the condemned man, then left with Eltorp's desperate shrieks of rage and terror ringing in her ears.

CHAPTER TWENTY-EIGHT

When they returned to the *drostdij*, it appeared they were to dine with four valued members of the community who, with Odendaal, comprised the *Heemrade*, the town's council.

'I am sorry I had to subject you to that,' Adriaan said, 'but we had to be sure. I hope you understand.'

Suzanne felt sick to her stomach. She had no appetite, how could she? She wanted nothing more than to be alone with her thoughts.

'Shall we go in?'

'Adriaan, I cannot,' she protested.

'Odendaal's sister will be there. I would not have brought you to a house with no female chaperone. I would not sully your reputation.'

'It is not that. I have nothing to wear, my head is aching and that . . .' She gestured in the direction of the cells.

'You do not believe the sentence is just?'

'No, I do. But I would be poor company, Adriaan. Eltorp was so pitiful. It was like watching an animal caught in a trap. The terrible sound . . .' Her words tailed away. 'The man he described sounds like the person you found referenced in the archives twenty years ago. Liar though Eltorp might be, villain he undoubtedly is, but I cannot think he could have fabricated the description of his hair.'

Adriaan nodded. 'I agree. That's why I wanted you to hear it for yourself.'

She paused, then took a deep breath. 'Must Eltorp hang?'

Adriaan fixed her with a look. 'That is the penalty for murder.'

'But what if he knows more?'

'He would have told us everything. He was bargaining for his life.' Adriaan glanced towards the door where the sound of voices suggested the dinner had already started. 'I must join the others. I will give your apologies and ask if a tray might be sent up.'

Suzanne nodded her thanks. 'The last thing I would want would be to compromise you in any way, Adriaan, but when we return to the Colony, could you please, please find a way for me to visit the archives for myself? Now we have this additional piece of information, perhaps it will unlock something you missed. I know I presume a great deal of our friendship—'

He looked at her, then smiled. 'Given it was your courage and love for your friend that brought my dear Judith into my life, I will do my best.'

'Thank you. And after that—'

He put up his hands. 'I know, "one last thing"! It always is.'

'Am I so predictable?'

Adriaan laughed. 'That I cannot answer for fear of causing offence.'

Finally, Suzanne smiled too. 'Given what Eltorp said about this man having come from Olifantshoek, and given we know from what you found in the archives – that Louise and her companions had gone into the interior soon after they arrived – might it be possible to talk to the local people?'

'Khoi, do you mean?'

'Well, yes. You tell me that many speak Dutch – and I dare say some of your men speak their language. It stands to reason that if there is a lone white settler living in the valleys beyond Stellenbosch, the Khoi would know. And,' she added, remembering her first conversation with Madame Lombard, 'if Louise did settle in the interior in 1622, she must have done so with their blessing. Otherwise, how could she – how could they – have survived?'

He thought for a moment. 'The challenge will be to find someone prepared to talk to us.'

'But will you try?' she pressed. 'Perhaps even find someone prepared to take me there? Several times, Olifantshoek has been mentioned. If I could only see for myself—'

At that moment, a maid appeared in the hallway, bringing the conversation to a close. She was wearing a blue dress with a bib apron and cap, dazzling white against her Black skin.

'The master has bid me tell you dinner is served,' she said in perfectly executed, though strongly accented, Dutch.

'*Juffrouw* Joubert will not be joining us. Please show her to her chamber and take her some light supper.'

'Very good, *mijnheer*.' The maid bobbed a curtsey. 'Will you come with me, miss?'

Suzanne turned to Adriaan. 'Will you?'

'I will think on it. Good night, sister. Sleep well.'

In her chamber, Suzanne took a sip of wine and felt her sore arms and shoulders relax a little more. A new plan started to take shape. Perhaps she should base herself in Stellenbosch for a while? It would make sense for her investigations and make it all the easier to make an expedition to Olifantshoek. Although she doubted if her grandmother would want to come with her, she had no concerns about leaving her in the Colony for a week or two. Florence's friendship with Madame Lombard sustained her, and gave her a social anchor among the growing Huguenot community.

Perhaps Adriaan could arrange for her to stay in the *drostdij* for a week or two? Odendaal's sister was here, so she could serve as chaperone if she would be amenable. One thing was for sure, Suzanne couldn't let this lead go cold.

Louise was suddenly within her reach. She could almost see her, feel her presence at her side. Guiding her on.

Suzanne exhaled, taking pleasure from the stars in the upside-down sky and the gentle cries of night-time birds. A nightjar, she thought, and an owl calling to her mate. Today, she had learnt something that pertained to the present not to the half-distant past. It was only two weeks ago that Eltorp claimed to have seen the man with a white stripe in his hair.

The more her thoughts danced in her mind, the more the identity of this man troubled her. Louise, Gilles, Phillipe – one woman and two men had disembarked the *Old Moon*. But Phillipe Vidal would be more than fourscore years and ten, an exceptional age. Surely even Eltorp would not mistake a man of such advanced years for one thirty years younger?

There was another explanation – that Phillipe had fathered a child and the man Eltorp had traded with was Vidal's son. But if that was the case, then who was the mother? He was a white man, Eltorp had been certain about that. She pushed the idea away. But somewhere deep inside, the thought took hold, like a splinter, under her skin.

CHAPTER TWENTY-NINE

Suzanne woke refreshed. Outside, she could hear singing in the fields. Enslaved people, she knew, but somehow the melodies sounded sweeter here than in the crowded streets of the Colony.

Then, with a clenching feeling in her stomach, she remembered the reason they were in Stellenbosch. This morning, Lars Eltorp was to hang. Overnight she had made peace with the idea that he had nothing more to tell. She had no pity for him, he was a violent and treacherous man, but she would that it were over and done with.

There was a knock at the door.

Suzanne sat up and straightened her bedcap. 'Come in.'

The maid from last night stood in the doorway. 'The master and other gentleman would like to know if you will be accompanying them to the hanging.'

Having no stomach to witness Eltorp's reckoning, Suzanne shook her head. 'No, I will remain here.'

The girl was looking at her with steady brown eyes that gave nothing away.

Suzanne smiled. 'What is your name?'

'Tia, miss.'

'Is that your given name?'

She thought she saw a spark of interest in the maid's eyes, but it was quickly extinguished. 'Yes.'

Suzanne was reluctant to let her go. At home in La Rochelle, they'd had a small but loyal household staff. In Amsterdam, the same. Here, she disliked not understanding how things worked. And surely Tia could not be her birth name? She had learnt that Khoi women and men who worked for the VOC were given Dutch names.

Was she a slave or a servant? Then, she remembered that Khoi were not allowed to be enslaved. The women and men with Black skin she saw in the Colony had been seized from other countries in Africa and brought to the Cape in ships. With the men on the building sites, in the fields, the distinction was clear: from their clothing, from their demeanour. Suzanne hated to see the lines of enslaved workers, bare to the waist, toiling in the vicious heat of the day. Inside a prosperous house, it was harder to discern the difference.

'Will you be wanting breakfast, miss?'

'That would be nice.'

She watched as the girl took her night pot from under her bed, covered it with a cloth, took the jug to refill with water, then withdrew without speaking another word. She pondered how old Tia might be – perhaps eighteen or nineteen – and how long she had worked for the *landdrost*.

Suzanne had dressed and was sitting at the occasional table by the time the girl returned with a tray of pancakes and a pot of tea with milk. A very Dutch meal. She wanted to ask more questions, to try to establish some kind of friendship as she would have done with servants back home, but there was something in the girl's bearing that did not encourage confidences.

'Will there be anything else, miss?'

'No, thank you,' she said, then repeated it in Khoi. It was a word she had heard Adriaan use. '*Gangans.*'

Again, she saw a reaction in Tia's eyes, but she said nothing. She simply bowed her head and left the room, quietly closing the door behind her.

Despite everything, Suzanne found she had an appetite.

Having eaten everything on her plate, she walked to the long window facing east. Only then did she realise that it overlooked the courtyard between the *drostdij* and the cells.

Pieter Odendaal and Adriaan were standing in silence in a slant of sunlight, only about thirty paces away. Beside them was a man in the black clothes and white stock of a pastor. The door to the gaol opened and two soldiers came out, pulling Eltorp between them. Now Suzanne saw that a heavy rope was hanging over the highest branch of a tree in the corner of the courtyard. The noose swayed slightly in the hot morning air on its twist of rope, sending an elongated shadow against the whitewashed walls.

She opened the window a crack and heard Adriaan's voice repeating the charge laid against Eltorp. It was already hot and the air seemed to hang heavy, even this early in the morning. It suddenly crossed her mind how it was odd that Eltorp was being executed here. Adriaan's judgement yesterday had made it clear that the culprit's body was to be left on the gibbet as a lesson to others. That being so, why was the execution not taking place somewhere more public where there were people to see it?

Suzanne put her hand on the window sill, unable to turn away, as Eltorp was dragged forward and thrown onto a cart. As the hangman stepped forward with the hood, the prisoner suddenly began cursing, damning their souls, struggling wildly. But the soldiers held him fast and, with his hands tied behind his back, Eltorp could not prevent the hood being pulled over his face, and the noose set and tightened around his neck.

Odendaal nodded and the soldiers dragged the cart away. Eltorp screamed as he fell, but only for a heartbeat until the rope choked his voice from him. Suzanne watched with horror as his legs thrashed, trying to find purchase, as the weight of his own body pulled the noose tighter. The pastor raised his voice in prayer, not for the soul of the hanged man but for the officers of the VOC who had condemned him. After what seemed like an age, though was no more than minutes, Eltorp stopped struggling. The rope creaked on the gibbet as his body swung, finally coming to rest. She saw Adriaan cross himself and heard his murmured words.

'May God have mercy on his soul.'

He turned away from the scene and Suzanne saw his blue eyes dulled by the savagery of the moment. But she knew Adriaan had no doubts that he had exacted just punishment for the violence done to his beloved wife. She understood: 'Life shall go for life, eye for eye.'

Wasn't that what the Bible preached?

CHAPTER THIRTY

CAPE COLONY
Monday, 22nd November

The two weeks after returning from Stellenbosch passed quickly as Suzanne put her plan into action to make an expedition to Olifantshoek. The first step was to persuade Adriaan to speak to Pieter Odendaal.

Adriaan was reluctant. She was aware she had made a poor impression on the *landdrost*. In consequence, the magistrate was disinclined to invite her to stay as a guest. Like the Commander, he did not approve of women with opinions of their own.

Suzanne decided to enlist Judith's help.

Her friend was suffering with a malaise, brought on by the oppressive heat, so did not venture out from their quarters within the Castle. Suzanne wondered if she was lonely. Judith had lived her whole life in the orphanage surrounded by people. Here she was alone for much of the day. But on this particular Monday, Suzanne and Florence had been invited for tea, so she hoped there might be an opportunity to lay out her plan before her friend.

'You will forgive me if I do not get up,' Judith said, as they were shown into a pleasant room on the first floor of the Castle. 'I find I am quite giddy much of the time and as nauseated as if we were back at sea.' She smiled weakly. 'But it is a pleasure to see you both. Thank you for taking the trouble to come to me.'

'It is kind of you to invite us, my dear,' Florence replied, settling herself into an armchair. 'I am sure you have many demands on your time.'

Suzanne bent down and kissed Judith on the cheek. 'You look well,' she said, less than truthfully. 'The married state suits you.'

'I am well, except for this sickness, and this terrible fatigue. This heat. And because Adriaan is much valued by the Commander, so often called upon, he is not always at home . . . But there is much to occupy my time: I am helping to design a school's programme for the children of VOC officials: the new hospital requires funds; and the building of our new church is not progressing as quickly as the Commander would like. Of course, the older ladies are experienced and instruct me, but I like to think that I am making some small difference.'

Judith rang the bell and a Black maid soon appeared with a tray of tea and sweet biscuits. 'You will find it has a very delicate aroma,' she said. 'It is a Chinese blend.'

Suzanne marvelled at how this shy, humble orphanage girl had become a purposeful young woman. But the dark rings beneath Judith's eyes worried her and she hoped her friend was happy. It couldn't be easy to be surrounded by other VOC wives determined to remind her of her humble origins.

'How do you fare, Madame Joubert?' Judith asked.

'Florence, please. We are married women both, though I have been a widow for longer than a wife.'

Judith smiled. 'I have barely seen you these past weeks, confined as I am to these chambers.'

Suzanne laughed. 'I barely see *Gran'mère* either! Like you, she finds much to fill her days.'

'How do things fare with our friends from the *China*?'

Florence put her tea cup down on the table. 'To speak plainly, my dear, many of them are struggling. They came with nothing, and the resources here to support them are stretched to breaking point. I do what I can and Madame Lombard is a great help. She works tirelessly to make sure that no child goes hungry and cares for your girls like a mother. But many of the refugees do not even own a pair of shoes. It doesn't matter so much now, but come the winter . . .' Florence stopped, not wishing to bring a note of disquiet into the convivial gathering. 'The refugee council has made petition to the Commander and he, I am told, has applied again to the Batavia fund for more money, but things are difficult.'

'I am sure he will do his best,' Judith replied carefully.

'The other issue is making sure each family has what they need in preparation for their journey to Groot Drakenstein. The Malans, the Jourdans, Pierre Grange and Pierre Jaubert – forgive me, Joubert – and his family have already left. The others are to follow in the New Year. But there is concern that the tools they were promised are of inferior workmanship, and a greater concern about the quality of the land. They are saying it is not suitable for planting vines or wheat.' A mosquito landed on Florence's hand, which she slapped away.

'It must be hard,' Judith said, still refusing to be drawn.

Suzanne was not surprised. Judith would not say anything that could be construed as a criticism against the VOC and, by extension, a criticism of her husband, but she was certain that Florence had made her point.

'Tell me about my girls?' Judith said, her face brightening. 'How are Petronella and dear Catrina? You will have heard that Corporal Biebouw's suit for Wilhelmina's hand has been accepted?'

'Yes, indeed,' said Florence, raising her eyebrows. 'Madame Lombard keeps me apprised of everything.'

Suzanne sat back and let the conversation drift. Outside, she could hear the sounds of the Castle going about its business: the never-ending cry of the starlings lined along the roof; shouted orders from the guards; servants running up and down the stairs. The afternoon sailed softly on.

'But what of you?' Judith asked, suddenly turning her attention to Suzanne. 'It was kind of you to go to Stellenbosch with Adriaan. He says he wouldn't have been able to conclude the matter without your assistance.'

Suzanne hesitated. There was no point trying to explain to Judith the horror she had felt when she had come face to face with Lars Eltorp, nor the emotions she experienced when she had watched him hang. Adriaan protected his wife from any unpleasantness. Who was she to do otherwise?

'If I was able to help see justice done, then I am glad.'

'I sleep more soundly because of it,' Judith said. 'It was silly of me, I dare say. Adriaan would not let any harm befall me. But knowing that villain is no longer able to inflict suffering on anyone else has given me peace of mind.'

For an instant, Suzanne felt a flash of anger, unfair as it was. She had rarely known a time in her adult life where she had slept deeply without fear of what the night might bring. Judith, for all her deprivations in the orphanage, had not grown up dreading that every night might be her last.

'Adriaan says you wish to return to Stellenbosch,' Judith continued.

Suzanne pushed her unkind thoughts aside, grateful her friend had raised the subject of her own accord. 'You remember I have talked of my ancestor, Louise, before?'

'Of course.'

'She came here thirty years before the Colony was established. But, with your husband's help, we managed to piece together a few fragments of information. Madame Lombard who, as you know, is the longest-serving resident of the community, contributed a few recollections, too. Then, in Stellenbosch, Lars Eltorp gave us a fresh lead.'

Judith was nodding. 'Adriaan told me all about it. But you surely cannot intend to go into the interior yourself? A woman alone.'

Suzanne felt a glimmer of hope. If he was talking to Judith about her request, then maybe he was considering it?

'I cannot let this chance go, Judith. It was only two weeks ago, this encounter. The only possible way for me to discover anything more is to travel to Olifantshoek and try to find this man Eltorp claims to have met.'

'But it is such a large area to search.'

'It is, and I could not go without a guide.' She looked her friend in the eye. 'But if Adriaan gives me permission and assistance, it could be done.'

'What could be done?' Adriaan said, striding into the room, his polished boots loud on the wooden boards. He dropped a kiss on the top of his wife's head, gave a half-bow to Florence, kissed Suzanne on the cheek, and then stood directly below the fan and loosened his collar. 'If you will excuse me, it is as hot as a furnace in the council chamber. I have fled here for a little civilising company.'

'Suzanne is hoping to travel to Olifantshoek,' Judith said, answering his question. 'She will need a guide and horses, and papers giving her permission to travel.' She gave a delicate shrug. 'I don't know what is required, husband, but I am certain you do.' She smiled up at him. 'Can you help? I would not lose my only friend in the wilds of Olifantshoek.'

Adriaan sighed. 'Not this again.'

'I give you my word, brother,' Suzanne said quickly, 'that if you help me with this one last thing, then I will never ask anything more of you. Upon my word.'

He laughed. 'Even if I believed that – which I do not, for you are the most tenacious person I have ever met – it is too dangerous.' His expression grew serious. 'There have been deaths in the valley – men brought down by lions, jackals, by elephants protecting their calves, baboons. And you would be trespassing into Khoi lands.'

Suzanne met his gaze. 'That is why I would need a local guide and the authority of your office. If you could persuade *landdrost* Odendaal to allow me to stay in the *drostdij* for a day or two initially, and perhaps again at the end of my expedition, and facilitate the hiring of a guide, a horse and provisions, that would be enough. I have money, you know that. And I would be doing no harm.'

'Except possibly to yourself, and those who love you.'

Judith reached her hand out to her husband. 'You know that she will never let this rest, Adriaan. It might be better for your peace of mind to concede.'

Suzanne saw the look of love passing between them and, for the first time, felt something like envy.

'And you give me your word that, whatever you find, this will be the end of the matter?' Adriaan sighed.

'In so far as I can make such a promise, I do.' Suzanne turned to her grandmother. 'It is not only for me. *Gran'mère* knew Louise. She, too, would have some measure of peace knowing what had happened to her older cousin.'

Florence gave a wistful smile. 'The end of the story is to make sense of its beginning.'

'And you would give Suzanne your blessing to undertake such an expedition?'

Florence gave a shrug of her thin shoulders. 'I am old,

mijnheer. What I have learnt in my long life is that we each must follow the path laid out before us. Calamity is as likely to befall us in our own home, as traversing the plains of Africa. All of our brief lives are full of risk. It is up to us to decide how we face those challenges. We are in God's hands.' She smiled at her granddaughter. 'I trust Suzanne to know her own mind. She believes she has an obligation to Louise and she is determined to fulfil it. She has come halfway across the world to do so. So, yes, I give her my blessing, even though I will not rest from the moment she rides away until the moment I see her beloved face once more.'

It was quite the longest speech any of them had heard Florence make. Suzanne felt her eyes brim and, when she looked at Judith, she could see her friend similarly moved.

'Forgive me,' Judith said, waving her hand. 'Everything provokes me to tears at the moment.'

'Thank you, *Gran'mère*,' Suzanne said. 'But, rest assured. I have every intention of coming back.'

Judith looked to Adriaan, who was now pacing the room. 'Well, husband?'

Suzanne watched him look around at each of them in turn. Finally, he sighed. 'Very well. I will see what I can do.'

Suzanne ran to embrace him.

'That's enough, that's enough,' he said, disentangling himself. 'If only every problem was so easy to solve as this. Alas, my labours await me. If you ladies will forgive me, I will leave you to finish your tea party.'

'When—' Suzanne began.

He put up his hand to stop her. 'I will set things in motion. As soon as the arrangements are made, I will let you know.'

She pressed her hands together. 'Thank you.'

Adriaan kissed his wife and bowed to Florence. 'Good day,

Madame Joubert. I hope you will not think it forward of me to say that you are a most remarkable woman.'

As soon as he had gone, the three women sat back in silence. Then, Florence leant forward in her chair and took Judith's hand.

'To take Suzanne's words for my own, there is "one last thing". I think you will find that a little ginger taken in brandy at the start of the day will help your sickness. It will pass.'

Judith's face flooded with colour. 'How did you know?'

Florence smiled. 'My dear, it is as clear as day you are with child.'

Judith smiled. 'I did not want to say anything to Adriaan until I was sure. I prayed to God for it to happen, and He listened.'

Suzanne surprised everyone, not least of all herself, by bursting into tears.

CHAPTER THIRTY-ONE

Monday, 29th November

A week after the tea party, Suzanne met Adriaan by appointment at the Castle to raid her strongbox. Not only did she have to withdraw funds enough to pay for the expedition, but she needed to arrange for Florence to have access to the vault in her absence. Suzanne was hoping not to be away for more than a month, but wanted to ensure her grandmother would have sufficient funds in the interim.

It was ten o'clock in the morning, yet already the heat was punishing. Even the birds were silent and the workers kept to the shade around the corners of the building. The stench of rotting seaweed on the shore permeated every nook and cranny, and clouds of mosquitoes hovered in the sluiced-down alleyways behind the VOC buildings at the harbour. Day or night, it was impossible to escape the stink. Suzanne would be glad to be up-country where the air was sweeter.

Adriaan was in good humour. 'Madame Joubert's remedy is working,' he said as they walked across the sun-flattened courtyard. 'I am most grateful to her. My wife is no longer prone to sickness in the mornings and the feelings of fatigue are passing. Every day, she returns to full health.'

'I am glad of it,' Suzanne said. 'And when might the baby come?'

Adriaan smiled awkwardly. 'Judith thinks it will be mid-June. Jean du Prieur du Plessis will deliver her.'

'There are several *sage-femmes* among the refugees,' Suzanne said delicately, 'not least of all Madame Lombard, if Judith might prefer a woman attend her. A familiar face.'

He thought for a moment. 'I will suggest it. Whatever Judith wants, she shall have.'

They walked past the slave quarters into the inner courtyard, then to the administration building where the vaults were situated. Every free citizen of the Cape had the right to take advantage of the secure storage offered by the VOC. It discouraged house-breaking in the town, since burghers could store their valuables and gold in the vaults rather than in their homes. Suzanne suspected it worked to the VOC's benefit too, allowing them to keep a watchful eye on the growing wealth of the inhabitants.

They walked down a long and dark corridor, lit only by high fanlights, and arrived at a heavy wooden door guarded by two soldiers. They stood to attention when they recognised Adriaan, but Suzanne showed her papers all the same.

'No need to wait for me,' she said. 'I will be quite all right on my own.'

Adriaan nodded. 'Come and visit Judith tomorrow. I will be occupied most of the day and she would be glad to see you.' He touched his hat, then walked back the way they had come.

Suzanne was shown through into a small counting house with a cadaverous clerk sitting behind a high secretary's desk.

'Box seven hundred and two,' she said. 'Suzanne Joubert.'

The clerk stamped her papers, then handed her a heavy silver key and gestured to a table at the side of the chamber. 'Take a seat, *juffrouw* Joubert, I will bring the box to you presently.'

Suzanne had barely settled herself on the bench when a boy appeared carrying a rectangular iron box. Bound in riveted strapwork, with wrythen bale handles to make it easy to transport, the front and back were smooth so the box could be stacked. On the underlip of the lid, there was an elaborate steel lock shooting four bolts. It would not prevent someone from stealing the box itself, of course – should they manage to infiltrate the building in the first place – but it made it impossible to open without the key.

Suzanne turned her key and heard the mechanism shift, then a pop as the lid unfastened. She had come for a bag of guilders, intending to exchange it for *eight-reales*, the most widely used currency in the Colony. She had worked out what she required: the cost of a horse; funds to pay a guide; money to buy a gift for *landdrost* Odendaal, and something for his sister, to express her gratitude for their hospitality. She would also need enough to purchase provisions for her expedition. She had pleaded with Adriaan and, finally, he had agreed to purchase a musket for her and a bandolier to hold ammunition and powder, and these were expensive.

It was dark in the room, so Suzanne paddled her fingers in the box until she felt the black felt purse. As she lifted it out, she saw two other precious items at the bottom of the strongbox.

The first was an eyeglass. She had found it in Alis and Cornelia's house in Warmoesstraat, lying dusty on a shelf in the library. She did not know to whom it had belonged – it could not be Louise's, since surely she would have taken hers when she sailed – but Suzanne realised it would be useful. The second was her small casket, the only thing of value she had brought with her from La Rochelle. A carved wooden box, lined with silk, it held the jewellery she had inherited from the mother she had never known. Mathilde had died bringing her into the world, but they shared a birth month – her mother had been born on the last day of January and Suzanne on the very first.

Gently, she gently lifted out the tiny casket and opened the lid, releasing a scent of sandalwood. The pale silk looked faded, as if it had lost its lustre in the blindness of the vault, but the gems within shone as bright. A silver necklace with a garnet, her birthstone, as red as a prick of fresh blood on a finger, and matching ring. Knowing that they had belonged to Matilde made them precious, but Suzanne had never yet found the courage to wear them. They spoke to her of loss, of her mother's silence.

She slipped the ring onto her finger and held it up. Then a new idea came to her. Suzanne's great-grandfather had presented Louise with a dagger, her birthstone set in the hilt – an emerald – for her birth month of May. How much more practical, more useful, than something of purely decorative value. Suzanne tilted her hand, watching how the stone glistered even in the dull light of the vault, then slipped it off and into her palm. If she could find a silversmith in the Colony, she could ask him to remove the garnet from the head of the ring and reset it in the handle of a knife. Just like Louise's.

Pleased with her idea, Suzanne added the cost of a dagger to her list of purchases to be made, then locked the box and left it on the table.

'I am travelling upcountry,' she said to the clerk, as she handed back the key. 'In my absence, my grandmother – *mevrouw* Florence Joubert – is to have access to the box. Here is the authorisation.'

The clerk read the letter Adriaan had provided, then stamped it without comment, and passed it back.

'Thank you for your assistance,' she said.

Then, unable to keep the smile from her face, she ran back down the corridor and into the blazing sunlight, with her purse, the eyeglass and Matilde's ring in her bag.

Finally, the expedition could begin.

CHAPTER THIRTY-TWO

Thursday, 16th December

Three weeks later, on the third Thursday of December, Suzanne Joubert was ready to leave for Stellenbosch. It was a month since she had last left the Colony, and so much had changed. This time, she was in charge of her own destiny.

Wearing her lightest travelling clothes and a broad-brimmed hat, she had a leather sheath attached to her belt with a short-bladed knife, the garnet now set in its hilt by a Huguenot *couteleur* in the Colony. She hoped she would not have cause to use it for anything other than hunting. In her satchel, the eyeglass, an old map of the interior and provisions for the day's journey jostled for space with Louise's diary and the Tarot card in its white linen wrapper. Suzanne had intended to leave them with her grandmother for safe-keeping but, at the last moment, changed her mind. She wanted something tangible belonging to Louise to carry with her and, though she did not yet know what she might discover, the Justice card felt like a powerful talisman.

Florence, Judith and Madame Lombard had come to see her on her way, with the two youngest of the Rotterdam orphans. Now dressed in Cape summer attire, and their complexions touched by the sun, they looked as if they had been born and bred in the Colony.

As before, she was waiting at the gate for Adriaan to bring the horses round. He had decided to ride with her to Stellenbosch, with two soldiers, on the pretext of a tour of inspection. He would stay overnight to see Suzanne settled at the *drostdij*, and to help secure the services of a local Khoi guide, then return to the Colony the following day. After that Suzanne would be on her own.

'I shall lack your company,' she said to Judith, holding out her hands.

She was delighted to see the bloom had come back to her friend's cheeks and, though there were not yet any outward signs of her pregnant state, she seemed softer.

'And I yours,' Judith answered. 'These weeks seeing one another so regularly have been quite like our first weeks here. Do you remember? Everything seemed so strange. Impossible.'

Suzanne grinned. 'And now look at us. You, a married lady, and me a pioneer. I hope you will forgive me for taking your husband from you again.'

'I would not have it any other way. God speed, dear Suzanne.'

They embraced, then Suzanne turned to Madame Lombard. 'You will take good care of *Gran'mère*,' she said. 'Catrina is going to lodge in our house so my grandmother will have an extra pair of hands while I am away.'

Madame Lombard prodded a finger at her. 'You take care to come back to us, do you hear me?'

'I will.'

The old woman harrumphed. 'Mind you do, girl, mind you do.' She leant forward and whispered in her ear. 'You have a gun, don't be afraid to use it. Man or beast, shoot first, ask questions after.'

Suzanne laughed. 'Good counsel indeed. For this, and many other kindnesses, my thanks.'

Finally, Suzanne turned to her grandmother. 'I don't know how to take my leave of you. No words seem enough, yet there seems nothing I can say.'

Florence smiled. 'You are the greatest gift of my life, Suzanne. I am proud of you, proud of what you are doing. But remember this. Louise's story is not your story. You suffered a great injustice, something no woman should have to endure, and yet have kept your character. Do not sacrifice yourself for the idea of a dream.'

Suzanne frowned. 'Do you think it is wrong of me to go?'

Florence put her veined hand against Suzanne's cheek. 'Not in the slightest. But whatever you find out, if you discover anything at all, it only matters for what it means to you now. The past is gone. Revenge, loss and grief for a person you never even knew, these are things that can make us forget that we are here today. You are not Louise, *ma petite*. Find out her story, bring her back to life in order to lay her to rest, by all means. But then come back here and let yourself live again.'

Not knowing how to reply, Suzanne kissed her grandmother's cheek. 'I love you, *Gran'mère*. For everything you have given me, for your faith in me. For showing me the meaning of courage.'

CHAPTER THIRTY-THREE

Stellenbosch
Friday, 17th December

Although Pieter Odendaal was courteous, the coolness of his welcome left Suzanne in no doubt that it was only Adriaan's patronage that had secured her lodgings at the *drostdij* for a second time. His sister Anke, a nervous and worn-out woman, was unable to look Suzanne in the eye, said a few ineffectual words of greeting, then scuttled immediately into her sewing room. It was left to the same maid, Tia, to show her to the chamber she had occupied previously.

Later, the four of them ate a stilted meal, with Adriaan valiantly attempting to keep the conversation flowing. Beyond his obvious antipathy, Odendaal seemed preoccupied. His sister kept darting anxious glances at him, then dropped her soup spoon when he shouted that her fidgeting was getting on his nerves. He all but ignored Suzanne and gave the most perfunctory of answers to any direct questions Adriaan put to him. He ate little and drank a great deal of wine.

'Thank you, Odendaal, *mevrouw* Odendaal,' Adriaan said, as their host rose from the table when the meal was over. 'It was kind of you to lay on such a feast.'

'So long as she does not expect it every night,' the *landdrost* replied ungraciously, flapping a drunken hand in Suzanne's direction.

'I would not presume further on your hospitality, *landdrost*,' she said.

Adriaan dropped his napkin onto the table. 'Shall we take the air before we retire, sister? There are one or two matters about your expedition to discuss before I return to the Colony.'

Grateful for the chance to be out of the poisonous atmosphere, Suzanne politely excused herself to Anke Odendaal, then fetched her bonnet and cape.

Once they were beyond the bridge, and out of sight, she took his arm.

'Well! He could not have made his displeasure any more obvious.'

'I am sorry about that. I regret to say he is one of those men who becomes morose when he is in his cups.'

'More than morose. His poor sister. To be dependent on such a man – she could barely hold her napkin without trembling.'

'Are you having second thoughts?'

'Not a bit. But it makes me all the keener to be away from Stellenbosch as quickly as possible.'

The evening air, after the heat of the day, was soft. The wind had dropped to a gentle breeze and there was no one about as they strolled down the main street. Beside them, the Eerste River sang its song, racing over the rocks and stones, and around the island on which the *drostdij* was situated.

'I did wonder if the *landdrost* had something on his mind that caused him to be so . . . distracted,' she said.

'I gather that two slaves have gone missing.'

'They have run away, do you mean?'

'It appears so.' He exhaled. 'It is rare, in truth, for where would they go? And the penalties are harsh. Odendaal appears to see it as a slur on his character, a personal affront. And he has decided—'

'– that someone within his own household must have helped them.'

'That is observant of you.'

Suzanne glanced at her friend. 'Is it possible he is right?'

Adriaan kept his eyes straight ahead. He knew that she abhorred the practice of slavery and, though his Christian heart rebelled against it, his practical head spoke otherwise.

'Without knowing the particulars, I cannot say. It is possible, I suppose, but it seems unlikely. All enslaved men working in the town are housed in the *slavenhuis*. They have no freedom of movement, rather they are released each morning to their tasks and taken back in the evening when the day's work is done. It is hard to see how two men would abscond without being seen.'

'Or someone is turning a blind eye.'

'That's the rub.'

They reached the outer limits of the town, then turned to retrace their steps.

'But who would help them?' Suzanne asked. 'They would be putting themselves at risk.'

'Not to mention putting their standing with the VOC at risk. That is why it seems less than likely to me.'

'And you have told the *landdrost* this?'

'I have tried to impress upon him that his best course of action is to wait. More likely than not, the runaways will be found by a settler. Or returned by Khoi hunters.'

'Why would they do that?'

'There is a reward.'

'Ah.'

Suzanne was silent, hating a world where a human being could be considered another man's property, his life measured in those terms and those alone.

'What will Odendaal do?'

An expression of distaste crossed Adriaan's face. 'He has already sent soldiers out to search. He will not let it rest. His sister knows it, the household knows it. Everyone is walking on eggshells. Well, as you saw.' She heard him draw in his breath. 'I confess, sister, I am not altogether happy leaving you here while things are so unsettled.'

'I will be here only for as long as I have to. I will stay out of his way. I have no desire for his company, nor that of his poor sister. Do not worry. He can hardly bear even to look at me.'

'Even so—'

Suzanne interrupted his protestations, not wanting him to change his mind and withdraw support for her expedition.

'Before we left the Colony, you said you would secure the services of a guide. Have you been able to do so?'

Though clearly still anxious, Adriaan nodded. 'Yes. A decent fellow, a Khoi interpreter who knows the land well. He will report to you the day after tomorrow.'

'Thank you. I assume he can speak Dutch?'

Finally, Adriaan laughed. 'Dutch, French, English, a little German and Portuguese as well as Khoi, and no doubt other local languages. He is one of the most gifted linguists I have come across.'

'What is his name?'

'He goes by the name of Harrie Neman.'

'And his Khoi name?'

Adriaan gave a wry smile. 'Khemy, I believe.'

They had arrived back at the *drostdij*. Suzanne hesitated a moment, reluctant to go back into the unhappy house. 'And Harrie – Khemy – will be here on Sunday?'

'That is right. So, if you can keep out of trouble for another day and a night, all will be well.'

Not for the two poor souls who chose to flee into the interior rather than face another day in the slave house, Suzanne thought, but did not say so. Whether the men were caught by Odendaal's men, attacked by wild animals, or brought back by those who would see a little extra money in their pockets, she feared their future was bleak.

CHAPTER THIRTY-FOUR

Sunday, 19th December

Adriaan left Stellenbosch at dawn.

Although Suzanne had made light of the situation, she felt uncomfortable in the *drostdij* without him and was sorry to see him go. She intended to stay out of Odendaal's way so far as that was possible. His dislike of her seemed to spread through the house like a bad smell. She could not imagine what she had done to warrant such loathing, but she had no interest in finding out. In a spirit of building bridges, she did, however, offer her company to his sister, but was turned down flat.

'Oh no,' Anke said hastily, 'my brother would not like it. Not at all.' She darted a browbeaten look at Suzanne. 'I do not mean to offend.'

'No offence taken,' Suzanne lied. 'May I ask, though, if there is something I have done to upset your brother? I would make amends, if I can.'

Anke Odendaal looked, if anything, more terrified than before. 'I cannot say, I dare not,' she stammered. Then, to Suzanne's astonishment, she rushed from the room leaving her sewing on her chair.

Suzanne spent the remainder of the long hot afternoon in her chamber, laying out her equipment for the expedition, even though she had checked it a hundred times already. From time to time, shouted instructions filtered up to her room, and the sound of slamming doors. Twice, she heard the grille to the gaol being unlocked but, when she looked, there was no one in the courtyard.

At dusk, when the mosquitoes were at their worst, Tia came in to bring her a tray of supper. If she had not been so hot and frustrated at being cooped up inside all day, Suzanne might have laughed when she saw how meagre a repast was provided now Adriaan was not here: a little bread and salted meat, a handful of walnuts and a small glass of brandy.

The sooner she was away from Stellenbosch, the better.

Suzanne could hear the sounds of shouting in the fields and the barking of dogs. 'Have the men been found?' she asked, as Tia turned down the bed and closed the shutters.

Tia lowered her eyes. 'No, miss,' she said, then left before Suzanne could ask her anything more.

Suzanne settled herself at the table with her frugal supper before her. She thought of their rations on the ship, and Louise arriving in the Cape and having to barter for food, then ate every last scrap as if it was a banquet fit for a queen. Tomorrow, the guide would come and she would be rid of Odendaal – or, rather, he would be rid of her.

Suzanne was woken by the sound of hammering competing with the toll of the bell for the Sunday service. Slipping out of bed, she went to the window and looked down at the courtyard where, two weeks earlier, Lar Eltorp had been put to death. Two Malagasy men were securing a wooden post in the middle of the courtyard, one holding it straight while the other pounded it into the scorched earth with a mallet. When Tia came in with her breakfast tray, she asked what they were doing.

'The master says someone must know.'

'Someone?'

'The servants here, the slaves.'

Suzanne waited. 'And?' she prompted, when Tia did not elaborate.

'He means to beat it out of us,' she said, for the first time meeting Suzanne's eye.

'But that's appalling. And why would anyone know?'

'It is what he believes,' Tia repeated tightly, making it clear what little she thought of her master. 'Will there be anything else, miss?'

Distracted, Suzanne shook her head. 'No. No, thank you, Tia.'

In the distance, she heard the church bell slow to a single note to summon the last of the faithful to prayer. Looking out of the other window overlooking the street, she saw Odendaal rush down the front steps, with Anke scuttling behind him, and stride across the bridge towards the chapel. She was relieved they had not pressed her to join them. Suzanne turned away with distaste, wishing Madame Lombard was here. She would have sharp words for a man who so abused his household whilst pretending to piety.

Then, Suzanne realised she could venture from her chamber while Odendaal and his sister were on their knees before the pastor.

She dressed quickly and went downstairs. Straight away she could feel it. The atmosphere in the house was different. Like a sigh or a letting out of air, the air was no longer sharp with tension. She walked through the house, nodding to the maid dusting in the parlour and to the cook in the kitchen, then went outside. She found Tia at the pump.

'Is there something you need, miss?'

Suzanne shook her head. 'Just taking the air while I can,' she said, and was gratified to see a faint smile light Tia's lips.

'The air is fresher this morning, miss,' she said, then returned to her task.

Next, Suzanne went to the stable to talk to the groom, Jan, who was caring for her bay mare. Horses were valuable and still relatively rare in the Colony, so Adriaan had explained how Harrie – Khemy, as Suzanne was determined to think of him – would walk beside her rather than ride. He had also added that, although some Khoi had firearms, most still preferred to use a spear with a reinforced tip.

'With iron we obligingly provided,' he'd added wryly. 'Lethal.'

The sun was already too hot for her to remain outside for long. So having extracted a promise from Jan that someone would inform her as soon as her guide arrived, the sound of the church bell signalling the end of the service sent Suzanne hurrying back to her chamber. She had no desire to see either Odendaal or his sister. However, she found she could not avoid hearing him.

Within a half-hour of their returning to the *drostdij*, Odendaal was in the courtyard below her window shouting and issuing orders. Suzanne watched aghast as Black servants and Malagasy men were paraded in and forced to stand in the direct sun. Two soldiers stood with weapons in hand, ready to shoot at anyone who dared to move. Odendaal's face was puce and Suzanne could see rings of sweat on his white shirt.

'Are you all blind?' he shouted as he walked up and down in front of the line of men. 'Are you deaf? Are you dumb?'

Without warning, he struck one of the men in the face with his cane. The man cried out, but held his position. Suzanne saw how they all looked down at the ground, unwilling to catch the *landdrost*'s eye. All save one man, at the end of the row, who looked straight ahead.

'Until my property is returned to me, everyone will suffer,' Odendaal screamed, spitting out the words as if they were nails.

'Every one of you. There will be no food, no water, until you tell me where they have gone and who assisted them.'

He ran his stick along the bare upper bodies of the men, as if defying them to flinch, until he arrived at the proud man at the end. He was tall, broader than most of the Khoi men Suzanne had seen, and wearing Dutch clothes.

'Well?' Odendaal demanded, shouting in the man's face. 'Cat got your tongue?'

'There is no one who knows anything,' the man replied in clear Dutch. 'I have asked widely, and I give you my word.'

Odendaal threw back his head and laughed. 'Your word? How could the word of a savage possibly be worth anything?'

The *landdrost* raised his arm. 'I will teach you a lesson you will not forget.' He clicked his fingers. 'You, and you. Strip him.'

Two Malagasy men shuffled forward at his summons, not wanting to obey, but having no choice. Odendaal's victim gave a slight nod of the head, as if absolving them, then removed his own shirt rather than have it torn from his back.

'And the rest,' Odendaal shouted.

Calmly, and with grace, the man removed his breeches and stockings, until he was standing only in his undergarments. Suzanne feared his self-possession would inflame Odendaal further. The *landdrost* was attempting to exert his authority, but the other man's quiet dignity diminished him, and he knew it.

He walked calmly to the wooden stake and allowed his hands to be tied around it. Suzanne realised he was permitting the beating to happen. He wanted to spare the Malagasy men from having to drag him kicking and screaming as, Suzanne guessed, Odendaal would have preferred.

She averted her eyes as the *landdrost* delivered ten blows

across the man's naked back, each delivered with more ferocity than the last. But she could hear the whip of the cane through the air, the connection as the rod found its mark, and Odendaal's laboured breathing. His victim flinched with every blow, but he did not shout out.

At last, there was silence: that of the dispossessed when they have no power to prevent the injustice happening before their eyes; that of shame at having been forced to witness an act of undeserved punishment; the silence of self-preservation at not wanting to draw attention to themselves; and finally, gratitude that it was not their skin raw and bleeding.

Sick to her stomach, Suzanne turned back to the window. When the man's hands were untied, he staggered as if he might fall, but managed to hold himself.

'Now what do you say?' Odendaal was panting from his sadistic exertion.

In a clear voice, that carried as clearly into Suzanne's chamber as if the man had been standing directly before her, he raised his head and looked Odendaal directly in the eye: 'My answer remains the same, master. No one knows anything.'

The *landdrost* roared and struck him across the cheek.

'Leave him here,' he bellowed to the soldiers. 'Let's see if a little African sun will teach him to respect his betters.' Then he turned and stormed into the *drostdij*.

Straight away, the other men began to disperse, some pausing to speak to their injured comrade, others hurrying away as if terrified to be seen talking to him. The soldiers, too, moved away. One ignored him, the other spat in his face before following Odendaal into the house.

When the courtyard was empty, Suzanne saw the Khoi man allow himself to slump against the wooden post for support. Then, she saw Tia run out from the kitchen with a cup. She held it to the man's lips, put her hand on his cheek, then rushed back into the *drostdij*.

Suzanne closed her eyes. She had witnessed much cruelty, and knew what it felt like to be on the receiving end of a fist. She had seen men hunted down for sport in the streets of La Rochelle and the woods of northern France. But the cold deliberation of Odendaal's actions made it all the more brutal. She drew a deep breath, raging against the unfairness of the world that gave a bully such as him power over so many.

Yet what could she do? She had no authority, no influence to prevent Odendaal doing exactly what he wanted in his own house. Without Adriaan, her position was precarious. More to the point, if she tried to intervene, would it make the situation better or worse?

Then something occurred to her. Tia had been prepared to risk Odendaal's wrath by giving the man water. Might it be that she knew him? Suzanne had never seen him before, so did not think he was a servant in the *landdrost*'s employ. Perhaps if she could find out who he did work for, then she could seek his employer out and have him released? She knew in her heart it was a rusty plan – Odendaal was the most powerful man in Stellenbosch, so who would stand firm against him? But she could think of nothing better.

Suzanne hurried from her room and down the stairs. She found Tia in the kitchen, bent over a black cooking pot hanging over the open fire. It was like a furnace in the small chamber, the chicken boiling in the water, the flames spitting. The smell made Suzanne gag.

'Tia?'

The girl jolted, then composed herself before turning round. Straight away, Suzanne could see she had been crying.

'I saw what happened,' she said, making no move to comfort

her. She suspected the girl would resent her sympathy. 'I wondered if—'

'It's your fault!' Tia suddenly shouted, then clamped her hand over her mouth as if to prevent herself from saying more.

Suzanne flushed. 'Whatever do you mean?'

Now Tia was wringing her apron between her hands. 'Nothing, miss. I'm sorry, miss.'

Shaken by the girl's outburst, Suzanne took a step towards her.

'Please, Tia. I'm not angry. Tell me what you meant. I want to help, but I need to know more.'

The girl raised her eyes defiantly. 'He was only here because of you.'

Suzanne suddenly understood. 'That man is my guide? Is that what you are saying?'

Tia nodded. 'The master saw him come into the kitchen and accused him of passing a message about the missing men. Since he did not want to get me into trouble by naming me, he said nothing. And now look . . .'

'Who is this man to you?' Suzanne asked gently.

'Harrie is my brother,' Tia replied, then burst into tears.

CHAPTER THIRTY-FIVE

Suzanne had never known a time when it was not dangerous to be a Huguenot. She had grown to understand how everything about their lives was fragile, how at any moment a new law might be enacted to limit their freedom of worship, of movement, of existence. And how important it was to keep her emotions hidden.

Now, this ability to mask her true feelings stood her in good stead. She would have liked to feel the cold hilt of her newly jewelled knife in her hand. But she knew that any attempt to shame or call Odendaal to account would fail. He was a bully and, like all bullies, it meant he was a weak man, and a coward. Suzanne would have to use his own vices against him if she was to have a hope of having Tia's brother released.

She strode into the hall, heading for Odendaal's study. She knew he tended to spend the hour before lunch in there with his papers, though Suzanne suspected he did little. Laziness, too, she added to her tally of his failings.

Anke Odendaal was dithering in the hall, blocking her path.

'Oh, you should not disturb him,' she said, her thin voice quavering when she realised where Suzanne was heading. 'He is much disturbed. There has been an incident this morning. An act of disloyalty which has much upset him. Even I am not permitted to disturb him until the gong is sounded for—'

'An incident?' Suzanne said, trying to keep her temper in check. 'Is that what he told you?'

Anke's nervous eyes flashed. 'Don't go in. It will only make it worse.'

Suzanne felt a fleeting rush of pity for the woman, who so clearly lived in fear of her brother. 'I am afraid I have no choice,' she said, gently moving her aside from the door.

'What the Devil?' Odendaal stammered as she walked in, swinging his feet from his desk and sending a pile of papers scattering onto the wooden floor. As Suzanne had expected, there was a glass at his elbow and little evidence that he had been working.

'If I might beg a moment of your time, *landdrost*,' she said, taking care to keep her voice civil.

'No. You may not. I am occupied.'

Suzanne let her eyes slide to his glass, then back again and had the pleasure of seeing Odendaal's blotchy face turn a deeper red.

'It is a matter of a few moments.' She smiled.

Odendaal still did not do her the courtesy of standing up. 'I do not have time for women's frivolities. Whatever you want, speak to my sister. It is always possible she will be able to do something, fool that she is.' He jabbed a finger across the empty space between them. 'Get out.'

His words were sliding into one another. He was more inebriated than she had thought, and Suzanne knew this would make him less predictable.

'I wish for nothing more than to leave,' she said, holding her ground. 'It is you who is preventing me, *landdrost*.' Though it pained her to give him the respect due to his office, she adjudged it wiser to match his boorishness with courtesy. 'Adriaan van Dijk, to whom I believe you answer, engaged a guide to accompany me. That individual, I now discover, is at this present moment in your courtyard. At your bidding.'

'I have no idea what you're talking about. If you do not leave now, I will be obliged to call for assistance.'

Suzanne nearly laughed at the idea he would need someone to escort her from the chamber, but curbed her tongue. Her aim was to have Harrie released, not to beat Odendaal in a battle of wits.

'The man whom you punished this morning – I know not for what infraction – is, I regret to say, the very guide *mijnheer* Van Dijk hired to accompany me. I am therefore asking you, *landdrost*, to put aside whatever felony this individual has committed and release him, so that I might be on my way.' She paused. 'I cannot imagine that you would have allowed him to be chastised in such a manner had you known he was in Van Dijk's employ.'

Moving with a speed that caught Suzanne by surprise, Odendaal suddenly stumbled out from behind his desk.

'But your protector is not here,' he hissed nastily, twisting a strand of her red hair around his finger. He ran his hand down her cheek, then pinched her chin between his forefinger and thumb. 'I do not know who you think you are, *Mademoiselle* Joubert,' he said, using the French honorific as an insult, 'but here you count for nothing. You are a refugee. Your own king didn't want you or your kind, so we have to put up with you here, forcing us to take in the dregs France no longer wants.'

He squeezed harder. Thinking of Harrie in the courtyard, Suzanne forced herself not to make a sound.

'Or perhaps you are a spy, mademoiselle. They say your king is using French harlots to do his dirty work for him. What say you to that?'

'I am not a spy, *landdrost*, and I do not think it behoves your office to insult me in such a manner. However, I give you my word that, if you release my guide and let me leave, *mijnheer*

Van Dijk will hear nothing of this from me. Indeed, if it pleases you, I will travel directly from Olifantshoek to the Colony after my business is concluded, and will not trouble you again.'

Perhaps a sliver of common sense pierced his drunken mind for, without warning, he pushed her away and staggered back to his chair behind the desk. 'Then why was he seen coming into the house, you tell me that?'

'He was coming to see his sister,' Suzanne said, realising before the words were out of her mouth that she had made a mistake.

He leant forward, his eyes glinting with malice. 'Who?'

Desperate not to compound her error, Suzanne shook her head. 'I do not know. It is only what the servants are saying.'

'His sister!' He gave a bark of laughter. 'They are like bitches in heat, all of them. They'd open their legs to any man.'

Suzanne felt her hands bunch into fists. 'So, will you have the man released?' She swallowed her pride. 'Please.'

'Please,' he mocked. He peered into his empty glass, then seemed to lose interest. 'Fetch the maid to bring me more brandy. The pretty one, what's her name? Eva or Tia? That one.'

'She was sent to fetch water,' Suzanne lied, wanting to protect her from his drunken paddlings. She had no doubt that was his intention.

'Bah!' Odendaal slumped back in his chair. 'Send Hendrik to me.'

Suzanne hesitated. She knew one of the two soldiers was called Hendrik. Did this mean he was going to accede to her request?

'Thank you, *landdrost*,' she forced herself to say, 'and for your hospitality. I will not disturb you further.'

Her heart thudding, she left the room. Suzanne stood for

a moment in the hall to compose herself, then went to find Hendrik and delivered the message. She concealed herself in the corner of the hall, waiting until she heard Odendaal give the instruction to release the guide, then returned to the kitchen.

'Tia, he is going to release your brother—'

The young woman's eyes lit up. 'How?'

Suzanne put her finger to her lips. 'There is no time to explain. The *landdrost* asked for you. I told him you had gone to fetch water, but it would be wise to make yourself scarce. He is in an ugly mood.'

The expression on Tia's face – part revulsion, part resignation – confirmed Suzanne's suspicion that Odendaal did not keep his hands to himself.

'See to it that Khemy—'

Tia interrupted again. 'He prefers to be called Harrie, miss.'

Suzanne didn't understand why he would prefer the name the Dutch had foisted upon him, but knew this was not the time to ask. 'Very well. Bind his wounds and make sure Harrie is able to travel, then ask him to meet me in the stables. The groom has my mare ready. When the household is sleeping after lunch, we will leave.' She hesitated: 'You should come with us, Tia.'

The maid stepped back in surprise. 'I cannot, miss. This is a good job. If I leave, I would never find employment with anyone else, he would see to that.'

'It will not take the *landdrost* long to discover you are Harrie's sister. He will want someone to blame and he will pick on you, can't you see? Besides, I would be grateful for female company.'

'How will I live?'

'My grandmother and I have need of a maid in the Colony. You can work for us.'

'But you are French?' Tia said in disbelief.

Suzanne laughed. If nothing else, the experiences of this long, dreadful morning had taught her once and for all that the French were seen as of no account in the Colony. In everyone's eyes – Dutch, Khoi, even Malagasy – they were poor and disenfranchised, nothing but a drain upon this frontier nation.

'I am not a refugee, we paid our—' she started, then stopped. None of this mattered. What mattered was getting away from the *drostdij* before Odendaal changed his mind. 'I will look after you, Tia, as your brother will look after me on this journey.'

Suzanne held her breath, not wanting to rush the girl to a decision, whilst knowing that every second counted.

'I cannot be seen leaving with you,' Tia said, decisive now. 'And I will need some clothes.' The girl looked down at her blue dress, white pinafore apron, cap and shoes. 'These belong to *him*,' she said, infusing the word with contempt. 'I would not be branded a thief.'

Suzanne nodded. 'Come with me.' Upstairs, she found a shirt and chemise, clean undergarments. 'But I have no shoes that will fit you.'

'No matter, miss.' Tia took the clothes in her arms. 'I will meet you by the camphor tree on the far side of the river.'

'Where is that exactly?'

Finally, Tia smiled. 'My brother knows.'

CHAPTER THIRTY-SIX

For Suzanne, the waiting was interminable. At every moment, she expected to hear Odendaal's heavy tread upon the stair.

Having packed her belongings, she kept to her room, watching the shadows lengthening. Some while after Tia had left her chamber, Harrie was released. Another maid, whose name she did not know, came with a pail and strips of cloth to clean his wounds. She couldn't hear what they were saying in the courtyard below, but the girl was smiling shyly and Suzanne realised Harrie was trying to put her at her ease.

Suzanne approached the window and put her hand to the frame, keeping out of sight. She saw him brush the dirt from his clothes, stiffly pull on his breeches and lace his arms into his sleeves. Pinpricks of blood immediately started to spot the white fabric of his shirt. He grimaced as he put on his boots, his movements slow and precise, then he pressed his hands together as if to thank the maid for her assistance. Suzanne watched them go into the house and, shortly afterwards, heard the squeak of the kitchen door which she knew led out to the stables.

That was her signal to move.

Quickly, Suzanne gathered her things, pulled on her leather riding boots, tied the cord of her leather hat around her neck, then went onto the landing and looked down over the wooden bannisters to the hall below.

On her tiptoes, taking each step carefully, she came down the stairs, into the hall, and through the pass door into the servants' domain. The old cook was sitting in a high-backed wooden armchair, her hands folded across her bony ribs, gently snoring. Apart from her, the room was empty.

Her heart in her mouth, Suzanne crept towards the back door, almost feeling the pinch of Odendaal's hand upon her shoulder. Only when she was outside in the yard, did she allow herself a moment of respite. Then she saw, beneath the bench, a pile of neatly folded clothes – Tia's maid's uniform, her white cap perched neatly on the top – and she sighed with relief. Surely that meant Tia had managed to get away from the house unseen?

Apprehensive, still half expecting Odendaal to be lying in wait, Suzanne walked into the stable.

'Hello?' she called. '*Is hier iemand?*' Is anybody here?

To her intense relief, Jan appeared from behind the straw bales. 'Your mare is ready for you, miss.'

'Thank you. I am waiting for someone to join me.'

'I am here,' Harrie said, following Jan into the light.

Her first impression of the man who was to take her into the interior was that he was even bigger than she had thought, having only seen him from above and at a distance. He was tall and broad, his voice low and unhurried.

'I am sorry for what happened,' Suzanne said in a rush.

'It was not your fault.'

'Your sister believes that it was.'

Harrie slowly shook his head. 'Tia worries too much.'

'Are you fit for the journey? Have your wounds been properly bound?'

'I am able to travel,' he said, then cupped his hand to help Suzanne up into the saddle. 'Shall we?'

Suzanne mounted, passed her musket and saddlebag to Harrie, then picked up the reins. She fished in her pocket, found a coin, leant down and pressed it into the groom's hands.

'For your service, my thanks.'

'God speed, miss,' Jan said.

She and Harrie walked quietly out from the shade of the stable, over the bridge onto the main street heading east. Though she was anxious, she was calmed by the familiar rattle of clinker and bridle, the swishing of the horse's tail in the afternoon air. Neither of them spoke: Suzanne felt oddly self-conscious in Harrie's company; for his part, he seemed to have no need to disrupt the silence.

It was still very hot, so they kept to the shade beneath the trees when they could, walking in and out of the dappled sunlight to the sound of the heavy tread of her mare dropping her feet on the dry ground. Harrie moved with loose and long strides, seemingly in no hurry, and that was making her anxious. Suzanne felt this was the most perilous moment, when Odendaal might look out of his window and catch sight of them. However much she told herself that he had no power to stop Harrie leaving Stellenbosch, her nerves were still tight. Odendaal had malice enough to make it difficult.

It was not until they had reached the boundary of the town that Suzanne finally allowed herself to feel a burst of anticipation for what lay ahead.

'Tia is to join us,' she said in a low voice.

At her side, Harrie smiled. 'At the camphor tree, I know this.' He walked a few paces more. 'Thank you for that kindness. He is not a good man.'

'No, he is not. But we are free of him now.'

As they travelled away from Stellenbosch, the markers began to fade. Few carriages, few horses, came this far. A long dusty track lay straight before them leading towards rolling green hills and wooded valleys as far as the eye could see. Banks of white clouds were moving low and fast across the sky, blown by a wind from the north, and the buzzards circled in the hot air above their heads. They walked parallel to the Eerste River and Suzanne noticed, for the first time, how the stones beneath the racing river made the water appear red.

'Fire, water, air and earth,' she murmured. Having been liberated from the suffocating prison of the *drostdij*, she now felt equal to any challenge the journey might bring.

With their shadows striding before them, Harrie led them over the brow of the first hill. Suzanne turned in the saddle and could no longer see Stellenbosch, no sign of any human habitation.

'There she is,' he said.

Suzanne could see the outline of a person standing beneath a canopy of dark green leaves. Having never seen Tia without her maid's cap, she was surprised to see that the girl's hair was short, black twists cut close to her head. Looking self-conscious in her borrowed clothes, with a knife at her belt, she bobbed a curtsey to Suzanne, then ran towards her brother and threw her arms around him. He winced.

'Sorry, sorry,' Tia said, then began chattering in their mother tongue.

Only now did Suzanne realise that Harrie had been nervous, too. She saw his shoulders relax and heard the tone of his voice lighten as he talked with his sister. Suzanne thought Tia might have been scolding him, for he reached out, stroked her head, then placed a kiss on her cheek.

'We will ride on until the sun sets, miss,' Harrie said. 'This is almost the longest day of the year, so we have many hours of light ahead of us.'

'It is a day's ride to Olifantshoek?'

'Perhaps more, perhaps less. We will make our own tracks through the pass. When we set camp tonight, you will tell me what you know of the man you seek.' He looked at her with his deep and dark eyes. 'And I will tell you what I know.'

CHAPTER THIRTY-SEVEN

Harrie led them in a gentle curve through the fertile valley, lush even in the height of summer. The Hottentot Holland mountains were to one side and the Simonsberg mountains to the other.

'In our language, this is the *gantouw*, which means the antelopes' path.'

Suzanne was content to listen and to look, drinking it all in. The blue sky, the racing clouds above the hilltops, the sun turning from gold to white as the afternoon drew on. Here, rather than the rainbow colours of the fynbos on the plains, everything was a different shade of green. Suzanne had travelled through the forests of France, but here in Africa there was a scale that took her breath away. She felt as if she was riding through a virgin landscape, untouched by human hand and beneath the widest heaven. She tried to imagine Louise in this same green world, with her beloved Gilles at her side. With Phillipe, too?

'Do you see?'

Harrie's voice jolted Suzanne from her reverie. She stared in the direction of his pointing finger and, to start with, saw nothing. She twisted round to take her eyeglass from her satchel, then raised it to her eye. This time, her gaze found it – a pride of lions, lying languidly in the sun some distance away.

'They are creatures of company,' Harrie explained in his measured way. 'Several females and a male, protecting their territory. At this time of year, when food is plentiful, they mostly hunt at night and avoid the heat of the day. If we keep our distance, they will not harm us.'

Suzanne adjusted the sight for a clearer view of the pride. From skins she had seen in the Castle, she knew that the females resembled large cats, but the males had a mane of fur around their faces. Their roar was said to make the world shake.

'Lions are clever,' he continued. 'They will watch the vultures and go to where a kill has been made. They let other hunters do their work for them, then swoop in and claim the prey for their own.'

'There are leopards here, too,' Tia added. 'We are entering their territory now, where the Dutch and Portuguese were scared to come.'

'Some came,' Harrie corrected her. 'There are a handful of farmsteads, including the one where the dead man was said to be hiding.'

'Lars Eltorp, do you mean? You know which one it might be?'

'It can be one of only three.'

'Should we go there? To ask the owner what he knows? I assume you know the settlers who have farms this far out?'

'Some I do, some not.' He gave a wry smile. 'Many of these men will not wish to speak to me, and some will not wish to speak with you. They know that they are on Khoi land, and they hate us for that. I see their guilt in their faces. And they will hate you because you are French. They believe your nation wishes to take their land from them, as they took it from us.'

The idea that a few hundred French refugees constituted a threat seemed ridiculous, but Suzanne suspected Harrie's analysis was right. The good faith the Huguenots had been offered by the Lords XVII, the rulers of the Dutch Republic, was not shared by the Dutch settlers many thousands of miles from Amsterdam.

*

The hours passed. The land rose and rose as they travelled up into the hills. The track grew narrower, until finally it petered out.

Ahead of them was a canyon. Suzanne welcomed the coolness as they passed from sunlight into shadow, and shelter from the scouring wind. After the open green expanses, it was strange to be suddenly confined. Her horses' hooves echoed between the walls of rock as they walked in single file, Harrie leading the way and Tia bringing up the rear. They were both alert: Suzanne saw Harrie's hand was now on the shaft of his spear and Tia had drawn her knife from its sheath.

Their increased vigilance made Suzanne alert. On the plains, any animal could be seen from some distance away. But here, in the narrow canyon, they would not see a predator until it was nearly upon them. For the first time, she felt scared. She had seen men trampled by horses and, once, a child mauled by a bear that had escaped from a travelling circus. She dreaded to think what damage the claws of a lion or a leopard might inflict.

Then, out of the corner of her eye, she saw movement: above them to the right, a glimpse of something flashing between the gaps in the rock. A flash of tawny-brown and dusted yellow. Something was tracking them.

Her hand went to the musket she wore slung across her shoulder.

'Should I load it?' she said in a low voice.

'Your gun will be no use here, miss. There is no room for a shot. We must keep moving.'

Suzanne took a deep breath, winding her fingers around the hilt of her jewelled dagger instead. The red garnet stone was bright in the gloom. Then, she saw another flash of speckled colour above them.

'Harrie—'

'He has been with us for some time,' he whispered. 'Make no sudden movements, keep your eyes straight ahead.'

'But if it attacks?'

He did not answer. Her heart thudding, Suzanne did as she was told, forcing herself not to look up or to attract the animal's attention in any way. She thought she could hear it breathing, could discern the pad of its feet on the smooth grey surface, could sense a rasping sound in its throat like a saw cutting through wood.

'Is it a leopard?'

Tia answered. 'Yes. That is better. Leopards mostly hunt alone. Jackals hunt in packs.'

Suzanne wasn't reassured by the idea that there was only one dangerous predator tracking them. Then, the instant before the attack, she sensed the air shift. A tension, like a wire being drawn taut. Harrie felt it too. She saw the muscles in his shoulders tighten just before the leopard sprang, using the height of the rock to launch itself down into the canyon.

Without even seeming to turn, Harrie suddenly swung his arm back and threw his weapon. Suzanne heard the spear vibrate through the air, then the thud as the iron tip pierced the predator's chest.

The animal was still falling towards them, so close that Suzanne could see the speckled rosettes on its coat, its teeth wide in its mouth, the blacks of its eyes. She stifled a cry. But Harrie's aim had been true, striking the leopard through the heart. It dropped like a dead weight onto the path in front of them, causing her horse to rear up. Suzanne grabbed at the pommel, fighting to keep her seat. Tia sprang round behind her, pulled the leopard's ears back and sliced its throat to make certain of the kill.

For a moment, everything was still. Then Tia wiped her knife on the corner of her skirt and there was a sucking noise, like the tide on a pebbled shore, as Harrie pulled his spear from the leopard's chest. Suzanne could see spots of blood pricking on the back of his shirt where the exertion had ripped open the wounds from his beating.

'Hey, hey,' Suzanne cooed to her mare, calming her down. She dismounted to inspect the damage. The dead leopard's claw had torn the skin on the horse's left foreleg, but it didn't look too deep. Shaking, she pulled a cloth from her satchel and dabbed at the wound.

'I will lead her from here,' she said to Harrie, struggling to keep her voice steady, then added: 'Thank you.'

He had saved her life. Had saved them all.

'Will we take the carcass?' Tia asked her brother.

Harrie looked at the beautiful animal, then shook his head. 'It will weigh us down.' He crouched and, with his knife, cut away three large chunks of flesh. It was hard work, and Suzanne looked away. She understood that they needed to eat, but she couldn't imagine the taste of the meat in her mouth.

They walked on in silence, heading for the patch of daylight ahead at the end of the canyon. As they came out onto the plateau, Suzanne exhaled, relieved to be back in the open air again. To the west, the sun was now white in the sky and sinking fast, sending long shadows into the red twilight. A cloud of black flies hovered in the air, darting and irritating her mare, who kept shaking her head to keep them away from her eyes. Suzanne removed her hat and used it as a fan.

Then, a little way in the distance, she saw a small configuration of round huts. Low and conical, they were set in a circle, the openings facing inwards. Coming closer, it seemed to Suzanne as if the dwellings had been constructed from branches bent over and tied together, then covered with reed mats. Behind the huts, she saw a wooden pen. Around the perimeter was a deep trench, half covered in brush and scrub.

'To keep predators at bay,' Tia explained.

Suzanne nodded and carefully led her horse across the narrow band of earth into the centre of the abandoned encampment.

'Our brothers and sisters have moved on,' Harrie said, 'but, as I had hoped, they have left the *matjieshuis* standing for their return journey. Tia, fetch wood for a fire.'

'Is there water?' Suzanne asked.

'There will be a source nearby, otherwise they would not have set camp here.'

As Tia disappeared towards the scrub in search of firewood and water, Suzanne tethered her horse, removed the saddle and then let her out on a long rein to graze. She cleaned away a little of the sweat and dust of the ride with her kerchief, and allowed her muscles to relax. She looked at Harrie, worried at how his wounds would be after the long trek.

'Are you all right?' she asked, gesturing to his back.

He nodded, though he clearly did not want her pity or fuss. 'Soon we will eat,' he said.

Suzanne nodded. 'I will be glad of it. Food first, then we must talk.'

CHAPTER THIRTY-EIGHT

THE CAPE COLONY

'Come quickly,' Catrina cried, the instant Madame Lombard opened the door. Inside, Petronella and two of the other girls stopped what they were doing, and listened. 'Please, come.'

Frowning, Madame Lombard wiped her hands free of flour. 'What are you saying, child?'

'Madame Joubert has a cruel fever. She is shaking, first hot and then cold, and her skin is burning. All last night and the night before.'

The old woman threw down her cloth. 'Why didn't you come to me before?' she snapped.

'She said it was nothing,' Catrina wailed. 'She did not want to make a fuss. She was bad the night before, then it seemed to pass yesterday, but then . . . I think the Devil is in her.'

'Don't be ridiculous. The air is full of pestilence, the seaweed rotting on the shore is enough to turn the strongest of stomachs. It's no more than a reaction to that.'

'No.' Catrina was shaking her head. 'Her arm is badly swollen.'

'Her arm, you say?'

'It is so tormented that there is almost no unmarked skin left to see. Oh, please come. I think she is dying.'

Not even pausing to remove her apron, Madame Lombard turned to issue instructions to the girls.

'Keep kneading the dough, then prepare yourselves supper

and clear everything away. I will not be long. Petronella, you come with me.'

The small party rushed from the lodgings, heading out in the dusk towards the Joubert house. The hot wind of the day had dropped, but the air was thick with the stench from the harbour. Swatting away swarms of flies, Madame Lombard fired breathless questions at Catrina as they hurried across the main square: when had the fever come on? Had she bathed Madame Joubert's forehead? What ointments had she applied to her arm?

Question after question until Catrina burst into tears. Every answer the girl gave increased Madame Lombard's alarm: headaches, stiff limbs, plummeting temperature alternating with burning fever. It sounded as if she had ague, the debilitating sickness that seemed to afflict only the settlers. Some survived, most did not. No one knew how the malaise spread, only that this summer there had been many deaths.

'Madame Joubert,' she called out as she stepped into the house. Straight away, she smelt it: an odour of decay and sweetness, like lilies fading from bloom. And it was so hot in the house, barely cooler than the street outside. 'Florence?' she called, forgoing their usual formality.

'She is in the bed chamber,' Catrina sobbed.

Madame Lombard nodded. 'Stay here.'

Leaving Petronella and Catrina on the threshold, she went inside. The shutters were closed and the light was the soft grey of evening. Moving slowly, so as not to alarm the patient, she opened the window a little, then turned to the bed.

'Florence, *comment ça va*?'

Even from this distance, she could feel the heat emanating from her friend. Suzanne's grandmother had thrown off her bedclothes and her nightwear was rumpled. Worse was the sight of her right arm lying on top of the sheet, swollen beyond recognition. As Catrina had said, there was not a patch left unaffected. A mass of fierce, pustulating marks, scoured with scratches where Florence had tried to quieten her burning skin. There was another smell too, of nausea and bloody flux. Madame Lombard remembered it from her own journey through France to safety: too many people in one space, the foul stench from latrines dug too close to the refugee camps where people were sleeping. The despair that comes before the end, when a person no longer has the strength to fight.

She was not a praying woman, but she found the Christian words of her childhood coming into her head. Prayers of supplication and deliverance. Then, steeling herself, she approached the bed and put her hand to her friend's cheek. It was so hot that she all but snatched her fingers away.

'Florence?' she repeated. '*C'est moi.*'

Florence moaned, but did not open her eyes. 'Suzanne?'

'It is me, Marie.'

'Where is Suzanne? Where is my beautiful girl?'

Madame Lombard swallowed hard. 'She has ridden to Stellenbosch, you remember? She will be back presently.'

'Ah . . . Yes. I remember.' Her voice was faint, as if it cost her too much to speak. Her lips were chapped, the skin cracked and bleeding.

Needing to do something, Madame Lombard summoned the girls from the doorway. 'Petronella, fetch a pail with water and cloth. Then, find the French pastor. He should be at the chapel. Ask him to come urgently.'

'What should I tell him?'

'That Madame Joubert is very unwell.'

Petronella looked up at her. 'Is she going to die?'

'Water, then deliver the message,' she said firmly. She took another deep breath to steady her nerves, then turned to Catrina. 'What is there to drink in the house?'

'The milk has curdled, madame.'

'Then fetch brandy and a sponge.'

'We don't have a—'

'Then a cloth,' she snapped, fear making her sharp. 'Use your common sense, child.'

Catrina bowed her head and scuttled from the room. Madame Lombard did not have time to feel guilty. She was determined to do what she could to reverse the hold the ague had taken, but she feared it was too late.

'Is your head troubling you, Florence?' she asked quietly, and was rewarded with the slightest of nods.

'That was how it began,' the old woman replied, her eyes creased shut. 'As if I had a thousand flies buzzing inside my head, and the pain . . . I have known nothing like it.'

Madame Lombard took her left hand. 'And now?'

'Like the pounding of a drum,' she whispered, 'over and over.' She struggled to catch her breath. 'I thought I saw her, standing in the corner of the room? She looked so alive, so real.'

'Who, Suzanne?'

The faintest of smiles flickered across Florence's face. 'Louise. I have lost many people in my long life – my own daughter on the day my beloved Suzanne came into the world – but it is Louise who comes most often to me now. She is waiting for me, I think.'

Suddenly, she opened her eyes. Marie Lombard wanted to avert hers, seeing the mark of death in Florence's unfocused gaze, but sat down close to her on the bed. Her only hope was for the fever to break, but she knew it was too late. Once the fever reached the brain, there would be no way back. She had even seen it in the good air of the Pyrenees when she helped her father in Puivert. She had seen it on the road to Rotterdam, and here in the Colony. But she would do her best.

Petronella put the pail down beside her.

'Now be quick, child. Fetch Pierre Simond. Run.'

She dampened the cloth and held it to Florence's forehead, hoping it would provide a little respite. Catrina tiptoed back in with a cup of brandy and a square of fabric. Madame Lombard dipped the cloth in the amber liquid, then dabbed a little to the dying woman's lips. Florence cried out as the brandy stung her cracked lips, but Marie persevered until she had persuaded her to drink a little. The fever would take the moisture from her body, and the brandy might help numb the pain in her head. It might help her to sleep.

'Suzanne has gone to find Louise,' Florence said, suddenly fixing her gaze on her.

'I know.'

Florence gave a long sigh. 'In La Rochelle, I could not protect her.'

Madame Lombard squeezed her bony hand tighter, fearing what Florence needed to say, a story too commonplace to be shocking in these days of persecution. Knowing this might be Florence's last confession, so she could depart this life without it weighing on her conscience.

'Tell me, my friend,' she said gently.

'We were lucky for so long,' Florence murmured slowly, as if each word cost her a little bit of life to say. 'But, in the end, they came. *Dragonnades*, given licence by the King, to establish themselves in Christian households.'

'I know,' was all Marie said. What more could she say? The stories were legion. Every Huguenot family had suffered.

'Their behaviour, Marie, uncouth and vulgar. We sent our

servants away so that they should not be bullied or . . .' She stopped and Marie saw a precious tear run down her cheek. 'But I never thought . . . Not in France.'

'You do not have to tell me,' Madame Lombard replied, wanting to spare her friend.

'I have to tell someone. We never talked about it, you see, Suzanne and I. First, because our thoughts were only of getting away before we were discovered. Later, I was silenced by my guilt in not having protected her. And my beloved girl, for her part, did not want to distress me. All this time, it has lain there unspoken between us.'

Marie wetted the cloth again, squeezed it and placed it across her friend's forehead, felt the heat steam through the damp fabric.

'We tried to stay out of their way and we locked our doors at night, but one night, a *dragonnade* surprised Suzanne as she was returning to her chamber.'

Marie did not want to hear more, but knew she had to listen.

Florence closed her eyes. 'I didn't even know it was happening, not until it was over. She didn't want to cry out for fear of waking his comrades down below. She didn't want to scare me, scared that they might come and . . . When it was over, he tried to give her a coin. A coin, Marie.'

Madame Lombard felt sick to her stomach. 'And then?'

'She came to my chamber. I saw the blood, her face, and knew we had to leave. If it had happened once, it would happen again.'

'You slipped away?'

'Yes. We headed to the port. A fisherman, to whom the name Joubert still meant something, hid us beneath the creels and netting. He took us as far as the Île de Ré. We waited there, keeping out of sight of the Catholic patrols, until we could get passage on a Dutch ship.'

'Listen to me, Florence,' Marie said. 'There was nothing you could have done. Nothing. If anything, you might have made it worse. In too many of these cases, *dragonnades* kill the girl they violate rather than have them stand witness to the crime.' She hesitated. 'There was no child as a result of it?'

'No. No child.'

'That is good. I am sure Suzanne does not blame you for what they did, she is devoted to you. You know that. You should not blame yourself.'

'But it was my role to keep her safe,' Florence cried.

'And you have. Didn't you get her to Amsterdam? Didn't you come across the known world with her to build a new life here? She is strong and sure of herself. Suzanne will come back full of the stories of the interior and what she has discovered, just wait and see. Finding Louise is what gives her life purpose, she told me that. And she will revel in her adventures a second time by sharing them with you.'

Florence sighed. 'She thinks that by finding Louise she will find herself. Heal the darkness in her own heart.'

'And who is to say it will not. Sometimes, by saving others, we can save ourselves. Suzanne has much to give in her life. She is a survivor – no, a victor.'

Florence gave another long sigh. 'Ah, Marie. You are a good friend. Take care of my girl, do you promise me that? She does not belong here. Encourage her to go back home. To Amsterdam, if not La Rochelle. She must not stay here to keep watch over my bones.'

Marie blinked away the tears. 'I promise.'

They heard the Castle bell toll the hour. Then, moments later, Florence started to shake, and Madame Lombard knew the end was coming. Her thin old body wracked with spasms. Then, just as quickly as it had come, the fit passed.

Now Florence lay still, her breath coming in shorter and shorter gasps. Finally, it stopped altogether.

Madame Lombard bowed her head. Then she released her friend's hand, pulled the sheet up over her body and face, and let her own shoulders slump in sadness. She didn't know how long she sat there before Petronella's voice cut into the silence.

'The pastor is here.'

Madame Lombard wiped her eyes, straightened her shoulders, then turned to see Pierre Simond in his black robes, clutching his prayer book, standing in the doorway.

'You are too late,' she said brusquely. 'She's gone.'

CHAPTER THIRTY-NINE

The Khoi Encampment

Three people sitting around a fire, their faces lit by the flames: Suzanne, Harrie and Tia, each enjoying the crack of the wood, the lingering scent of roasted meat, the companionable silence that comes with a full belly and a slaked thirst.

Suzanne felt a sudden surge of emotion. How glad she was to be sitting beneath the upside-down stars, scattered silver against the black velvet sky. Harrie and Tia were not yet her friends. More separated them than united them – their position in the world, the colour of their skin, their experiences, the land of their birth. All the same, Suzanne felt more content than she could remember. She knew that they would protect her. Her experiences fleeing across France, and before, had made her a good judge of a person's character. Learning who to trust in the blink of an eye could mean the difference between survival and death.

In the air above her, she heard a sudden beating of wings. She turned to see a flash of white against the dark sky, lit by the fire, as a solitary bird flew out of the coppice and wheeled away towards the mountains.

'A white owl,' Harrie said. 'Very rare indeed. I have never before seen one.'

Suzanne watched the speckled wings wheel higher and higher, then swoop away into the cover of the woods. 'What does it mean to see one?'

Harrie looked up at the now empty sky. 'Some say it is a

good portent. Others, an omen of death. I would say that the natural world exists beyond the wills and desires of men. The bird cares nothing for us.'

Suzanne nodded, then sighed. She did not want to break the spell, but the time had come.

'We should talk about our plans.'

Harrie leant forward and took another handful of fragrant kindling to feed the fire.

'We are waiting for someone to join us.'

Suzanne felt a spark of unease. She was comfortable in the company of Tia and her brother.

'Who?'

'A member of my clan, the Goringhaiqua, as the Dutch call us. He has information that will be of interest to you.'

Suzanne looked at him in the firelight. 'What has *mijnheer* Van Dijk told you?'

'That you seek a white man who lives in the valley of the elephants.'

'That's right. He was seen near Stellenbosch some two weeks ago.' She hesitated. 'Though he is not the primary person I am seeking. I had a relative, a woman, who came to the Cape many years ago. She and her companions – one man, possibly two – travelled into the interior, but were never heard of again.'

'And you think this man might be either of those original travellers?'

Suzanne traced a pattern in the dirt. 'Possibly. Or perhaps a son . . . The man had a distinct marking, a stripe of white in his hair.'

'What of your ancestor?'

'She was called Louise. She captained her own vessel and ran down corsairs, disrupting the slaver ships on the Atlantic Ocean.' Suzanne paused, again marvelling at Louise's courage.

'She cannot still be alive, but to find out what happened to her is the purpose of my expedition.' She turned to Harrie. 'Has there been talk of such a woman among the Goringhaiqua?'

She saw brother and sister exchange a glance.

'When *mijnheer* Van Dijk engaged me, I spoke to other clans – not just our own – who travel between those lands and the coast. There are some I can trust.'

'And?'

'There were some who remembered such a woman, though perhaps their tales were magnified in the telling. A she-devil, they called her, a warrior. They remembered she learnt some of our ways and came to pay homage and to ask for permission to settle on our land.'

'When was this?'

'Twice the life-span of a man.'

Suzanne worked it out in her head. 'Sixty years ago?'

Harrie shrugged. 'Before the Dutch came.'

'The elders met her? Talked to her?'

He nodded. 'The leader of the clan that roamed the lands around the elephant's valley said she asked for his protection. She was travelling with one other, a man.'

'Just one?'

'That is what he said.'

'Did he describe him?'

'He was one of your people,' said Harrie, with the ghost of a smile. 'According to the elders, the headsman believed they were in flight. Certainly, they asked for sanctuary and negotiated his silence in exchange for copper and iron.'

'Did the old chief grant her shelter on his lands?'

Harrie nodded. 'He ordered his warriors to take them into the deepest valley, and that no one was to speak of its location on pain of banishment. He passed down this command to his eldest son, so that the oath would be binding. He was a man of honour.' He paused. 'Unlike his younger son. You understand that none of the elders are still alive, so I am recounting this story second- and third-hand.'

Suzanne smiled. 'But every word is precious.'

'It seems that the chief had only two sons. One, his favoured child, wished to keep separate from the white men from the sea. He did not trust them, did not believe their word to be binding. He wanted only for their ships to pass by. The second son wished for riches. Unknown to his father and older brother, he began to trade privately with the vessels that sailed from Holland to Batavia. He became greedy, always wanting more, selling information as well as cattle and ivory.'

'What sort of information?'

'The location of springs that never dry up, even in the heat of summer. Where the elephants go to calf, and where to go to plunder their ivory. Which plants are wholesome and which will kill.'

Suzanne began to understand. 'And he told someone where Louise and her companion were living. He broke his father's oath of secrecy?'

Harrie nodded. 'It seems that a third member of your ancestor's party was at the camp at the waterfront. Left behind, or had chosen to stay behind. The elders talk of him as being very rich and having a Devil's mark. That is to say, a white stripe in his hair. They remember him because he did not speak Dutch.'

A shiver went down her spine. 'Louise's half-brother. He was French.'

'All the same, he managed to communicate well enough to buy information, to secure a guide to take him and—'

'– went in search of them.' Suzanne stopped, trying to make sense of the sequence of events. 'And then what? Did he find them?'

'When my kinsman arrives, you will hear it from him. It is better.'

Feeling she could not bear another delay, Suzanne stood up and started to pace. 'When will he be here?'

'Soon.'

Suzanne knew that could mean anything from an hour to a day. She peered out into the inky darkness and saw nothing, hearing just the same night sounds, the same high howling of a jackal. More than one. The atmosphere now seemed menacing, the pack closer at hand. Despite the warmth of the evening, she wrapped her arms around herself, and kept walking to and fro beside the fire.

Back and forth, back and forth.

Suzanne didn't know how long they waited, but Harrie and Tia's kinsman arrived in silence and, it seemed, without movement. One moment they three were alone, the next he was standing before them. In his right hand, he carried a spear.

'*//Khore//hare*',' Harrie said, embracing the man, then added in Dutch for Suzanne's benefit: 'Welcome.'

The newcomer was dressed in the clothes of his clan: a sheepskin cloak around his shoulders that Suzanne knew was called a *kaross*, a smaller apron *kaross* around his waist and leggings of dried raw-hide. She had seen men and women dressed in this way in the markets in the Colony.

She listened as he and Harrie spoke in their mother tongue, an extraordinary music of sounds punctuated with clicks. Their visitor tilted his head to Tia, who pressed her hands together in greeting, then he turned to Suzanne and bowed.

'Welcome,' she said.

'This is Tshu,' Harrie said. 'He has a few words in Dutch, but not sufficient for conversation. He is the one who heard the stories from his father who – himself – was a boy when the white woman came to the valley. Tshu witnessed none of this himself, you understand?'

Suzanne nodded. 'I do.'

Tia added more scrub to the fire. They all sat down, then the conversation began, Suzanne asking a question, Harrie translating it, listening to Tshu's answer, then explaining the gist of his reply.

'So,' Harrie said, 'Tshu says that when the old chief heard his younger son had betrayed the white woman, and revealed her whereabouts to the man with the Devil mark, straight away, he sent men to the valley. But he was too late.'

'Why? What had happened?'

'The camp was destroyed, evidence of conflict, blood.'

The words sent a shiver down her spine. 'And nobody there?'

'Nobody, alive or dead.'

Suzanne picked up her cup. 'Will you ask him to tell you the whole story, then repeat it to me?'

'Years pass,' Harrie said after an interval, picking up the narrative. 'The old chief dies and his eldest son – the one closest to his heart – succeeds him. More and more ships are sailing to Batavia and stopping in Table Bay to take on fresh food and water. The new headsman of the clan holds to the old ways, travelling across the land, building and striking settlements as they move their herds of cattle. The younger son, in the meantime, has established a permanent base closer to where the Colony now stands, so as to be first at hand when a new ship docks. He builds up his personal wealth, not in honour nor cattle, but in the white man's goods: iron, copper, silver, china. His followers benefit, too. He learns to speak Dutch, all the better to drive a good bargain, and is one of the first to build relationships with the Colony when the Dutch establish a refreshment station.'

Suzanne interrupted. 'But what of Louise?'

'This is where the story is harder to follow. But it seems as if, at about this time, new accounts begin to surface about two white men living near to where the original settlement had been.'

Suzanne frowned. 'Two men, not a man and a woman?'

'Two men.' Harrie shrugged. 'Whether it is true or not, I cannot say. One of these men was said to have the Devil's mark. I am sorry. This is not what you want to hear.'

Suzanne could not allow herself to feel disappointed, not until she knew everything Tshu had to share.

'Which means either Louise died,' she said, talking as much to herself as to the others, 'or that one of them killed her.'

She sat and looked into the flames. Had Gilles and Phillipe formed an alliance and turned against Louise? But then she thought again of the way in which Louise wrote about Gilles in her diary, her love for him, and could not believe it.

'And Tshu knows nothing more?' she asked, when he had fallen silent.

'He has told me everything he heard from his father and grandfather. I have repeated it faithfully.'

'And I am grateful,' Suzanne said. 'Please tell him so.'

She waited while Harrie relayed her thanks.

'Can we go to the site of their original camp?' she asked Harrie. It seemed as good a place to start as any. 'Do you know where it is?'

'We can, but this all happened many years ago, before the Dutch wars. There will most likely be nothing there now.'

'All the same . . .'

Harrie nodded. He understood how the land held the echo of the past, the spirit of a person, how it preserved the truth of what had happened.

'And after that?' Tia asked, her eyes bright with interest.

'I will know when I get there,' Suzanne answered, hoping that it would turn out to be true.

CHAPTER FORTY

Monday, 20th December

When Suzanne woke the following morning, Tshu had gone. Tia was her usual bright self, but Harrie seemed to be struggling. The mark on his face where Odendaal's cane had struck seemed more pronounced. She wanted to ask how he was feeling, but suspected he would not welcome the question. He was a private man, and a proud one.

Suzanne stretched and looked out from the encampment to the vista laid out before them. It was going to be another beautiful day. An apricot dawn sky silhouetted the trees on the ridge to their left, the sun beginning to rise in the sky sending slants of light across the green land. She drank a little water, ate a sweet biscuit, banged her boots together to check no insect had taken refuge there in the night, and put her knife back on her belt.

Harrie saddled her horse, refusing all help though Suzanne noticed he was moving more stiffly than before. Then they doused the fire, stamping the last embers into the dirt until the red turned to grey. Wildfires on the plains and in the forests were a constant threat during the hot, dry summer months.

They set out as the sun was rising, walking east: Harrie led the way with his spear in his right hand, Tia brought up the rear, her knife at her belt, and Suzanne rode between them.

'Are we now going to where the old chief allotted Louise a parcel of land?' she asked.

'We are, but not directly,' Harrie replied. 'When you were sleeping, Tshu and I talked further. Although he knows nothing more from his own experience, he remembered something else.'

'Yes?'

'There is a clan who tend their animals to the north of here, towards the Simonsberg mountains. He remembered that there was a very old woman who claimed to have delivered a child to one of your kind.'

Suzanne felt a jolt in her stomach.

'Women hear different stories to men,' Tia said. Suzanne knew this to be true. She thought of Florence sitting with her friends in the meeting room, sharing every piece of gossip between them, and smiled, feeling a sudden longing to be in her grandmother's company. What stories she would have to share with her when she returned to the Colony. Perhaps she would even be back in time to mark her own birthday on the first day of the New Year?

'Where will we find this clan?' she asked.

'Tshu last had sight of them near the Groot Berg River.' He looked up at her. 'It will be the same, you understand. We will only learn something if the midwife passed on her story to her daughter and her daughter's daughter.'

'I do, but someone must have said something, for even a whisper to have reached Tshu's ears.'

'I agree.' Harrie nodded. 'We should be there by the time the sun is at its highest.'

Suzanne looked at the sky. By her reckoning, if they kept a steady pace, that should be in six hours' time.

They rode through the emerald landscape. Softly undulating hills, the land less dry as they made their way. Mile after mile, hearing the jackals that seemed ever present, but never visible.

Tia pointed out a herd of bontebok. Suzanne was pleased at how much she could identify for herself, knowledge amassed like treasure in the four months she had been in Africa. Then an embarrassed smile lit her face. The truth of the land lay far beneath the surface and would take a lifetime to understand.

Suddenly, Harrie stopped. Suzanne pulled up her horse, too, her heart speeding up. Tia came from behind to stand beside her brother, her hands pressed together almost as if she was praying.

'Look, miss,' she said in a voice full of awe. 'They have come to welcome us. The forceful ones.'

Suzanne followed the line of Tia's finger, allowing her gaze to narrow down, seeing the grey against the green, and caught her breath. She reached into her satchel, withdrew her eyeglass and adjusted the sight. Elephants. No description had done justice to these magnificent beasts. Even at a distance, she could appreciate their majesty.

'Can we go closer?' she asked in awe.

'A little, but we do not want to disturb them,' Harrie said. 'Can you see, many of the females have little ones? Your people, as well as ours, hunt elephants for their tusks – ivory is very precious – but not in calving season.'

'Do both male and female elephants have tusks?'

'They do,' replied Tia. 'The herd are ruled by the females, the males come and go.'

Suzanne could see the smaller animals beside the adult elephants, half hidden by their trunks and their vast grey ears, triangular like a lateen sail.

Silently, they moved forward until, even without her eyeglass, Suzanne could see there were six adults and four calves. They came as close as Harrie would allow and stood in silence. Then in a low voice, almost as if he thought the elephants might hear them, he whispered: 'We must go around them to go on.'

As they set a line to the left, then back through the valley, Suzanne thought about how hard it would be to give birth to a child in these surroundings, aided only by a woman who did not speak your language. Wondering how Louise would have felt, the fear of it and the pain. Assuming that Louise was the mother. For if not her, then who?

CHAPTER FORTY-ONE

The sun burnt bright in a cloudless sky as they headed north towards the Simonsberg mountains. The heat was almost more than Suzanne could bear. She could see Harrie was suffering too.

'We will stop when we reach water,' he said.

Finally, they came to the beginnings of a tributary of the Dwars River. Suzanne dismounted, then cupped the clear water in her hands and cooled her face. Harrie and Tia did the same.

'Where now?' she asked, standing in the shade of the trees.

'Tshu saw the clan camped close to the mountains,' Harrie replied. 'We will follow the path of the river upstream. That should lead us there.'

Walking single file beneath the green canopy at the water's edge, the song of the current was restful in the heaviness of the afternoon.

Finally, Harrie led them up onto open land. Here, the trees on the ridge were buffeted by the wind: yellow-wood with its long hanging leaves, wild peach trees and wild olives.

'That is where Tshu said they were,' Tia explained, pointing to a patch of higher ground.

Suzanne's heart sank. 'But there is no one here,' she said, seeing nothing in any direction. 'We have wasted time with this diversion.'

'Wait and see,' Harrie said, breaking into a long, looping run towards the abandoned encampment ahead. Suzanne watched him, as he neared the perimeter of where the huts had been constructed, then beckoned for them to join him by the burnt-out fire.

He rubbed the ash between his fingers. 'Still warm. They have not been long gone.'

'But how can we know where they are going? East, west, is there any way of telling?'

'At this time of year, they will be heading north,' he said. 'And their cattle will leave a trail.'

'But north takes us further away from Olifantshoek,' Suzanne protested.

'It is up to you, miss,' Harrie said. 'They cannot have gone far and they will be moving more slowly than us with the herd.' He met her gaze with his dark, steady eyes. 'If you want to hear directly the story Tshu heard rumour of, then this is what I advise. If, however, you wish only to stand where your ancestor once lived, then there is no need. The choice is yours.'

Suzanne looked out over the empty green horizon. The truth was it was no longer enough just to see where Louise had lived. If there was a child, then she wanted to know.

She nodded. 'We will continue north.'

Harrie's instinct was right. As the sun was beginning its downward path, they heard distant noises, carried on the wind over the rise and fall of the land. Harrie stopped and held up his hand, then cocked his head to the sound. Now Suzanne heard it too. Voices and the distinctive lowing of cattle somewhere up ahead.

'This way,' he said, adjusting their course to the right.

It was not much longer before they saw a knot of people in the distance. Suzanne lifted her eyeglass, then handed it to Harrie.

'Perhaps ten or twelve women and men,' she said.

'Yes, and some dozen cattle. I will go ahead. Pay my respects and see if they are, indeed, those we seek.'

Once he had gone, Suzanne slipped down from the saddle and stretched her shoulders. Then she patted the mare's neck and loosened the reins so she could graze.

'Are you tired, Tia? Walking so far in this heat?'

The girl laughed. 'This is nothing, miss.'

Suzanne tried to picture this landscape in the winter. She could not ever imagine being cold again.

'How did you come to be working for *mijnheer* Odendaal?' she asked.

Tia gave a shrug of her slight shoulders, but Suzanne did not think she resented the question for she replied quickly enough. 'There are only the two of us, my brother and I. Our parents, our kith, are dead or gone.'

'And Harrie is often away . . .'

'It is good that he works so hard, and he is so admired by the VOC for his skill with languages, but—'

'– it leaves you alone.'

'Yes. I want to marry, miss, but the right man. One who will treat me well. So, I decided to work in a big house until that time came. I thought – we thought – it might be safe there. But *mijnheer* Odendaal . . .'

'He is not a good man.'

'No, miss.' Tia flushed. 'And when the master of a house is –' she mimed wandering hands – 'then the other servants follow his lead.' She tossed her head back. 'But I can take care of myself, I know the tricks.'

Suzanne pulled a face. 'Me too.'

Tia looked surprised. 'You know such trouble, miss?'

'There are villains everywhere, Tia, where I come from as well as here. It is a man's heart that makes the difference, good or bad.' She grinned. 'Perhaps we should learn to live like elephants, then we would have no trouble.'

Tia burst out laughing. 'That's right. No men, no trouble!'

When Harrie came back, he found them sitting on the ground chattering away like birds in a tree. He looked from his sister to Suzanne, but wisely decided not to enquire.

'We are fortunate. The daughter of the old woman who claimed to have delivered a baby to a white mother so many years ago, is one of the elders of this clan.' He turned to his sister. 'They are not our people, but I think there is fellowship here.' Then he turned back to Suzanne. 'The mother's name was Fala; the daughter's name is Shansi. She is prepared to tell you what she knows.'

Something in the tone of his voice gave Suzanne pause. 'Do you not trust them, Harrie?'

He took a moment to answer. 'I think it would be wise to be on our guard,' he replied carefully. 'This clan is an off-shoot of the Cochoqua, one of the largest groups. They played a leading role in the second war with the Dutch and hate the VOC with a vengeance. It would be wise to leave anything we carry of value here. Your horse, certainly. The musket too, perhaps. You can stay here on guard, Tia. I will walk *juffrouw* Joubert to the encampment, then bring her back as soon as the talking is done.'

Suzanne looked to the sky. It was not yet dusk, but the sun would set soon.

'You do not intend to ask for shelter for the night?'

'They are not our people. So, we should discover what we have come to discover, then continue our journey.' He paused. 'We should have something as a gift for Shansi to show our good will.'

Suzanne thought for a moment, then took out a kerchief from her satchel. White with a *broderie anglaise* trim, a pretty repeated pattern of ovals and lace, her initials were stitched on in green: *SJ*.

'Might this serve?'

Harrie nodded. 'It will do well. And for the clan leader?'

'We might spare a bottle of brandy.'

'Good.'

He led her horse into the copse away from the overhanging rock, then took the musket and hid it in the dead trunk of one of the yellow-wood trees furthest from the encampment.

'Conceal the ammunition, too,' he added.

Suzanne removed the bandolier and wrapped it over, then hesitated before pushing it down into a hole in the ground.

'It will be safer here, less obvious.'

She then placed Louise's diary on top and covered the hiding place with brush and leaves. Of all things, she could not bear the thought of losing that. Like Pierre Jaubert's bible, it had kept her company for too long. She slid her knife round to the back of her skirt, so it was not visible, then stood up and brushed the dirt from her hands.

'Right,' she said. 'I am ready.'

'Follow my lead, miss, if you will,' Harrie said under his breath as they walked into the encampment.

Suzanne nodded. 'I shall.'

The camp was similar to the one they had stayed in the previous evening: a ditch surrounding the *matjieshuis* which had been erected in a circle, facing inwards around a central fire, and a makeshift kraal behind the encampment where the cattle were grazing. As they drew closer, Suzanne noted that the women withdrew into the huts, leaving the men to bid them welcome.

There were three elders, with their distinctive broad and flat faces, and four younger men, one of whom was attempting to stare Harrie down. He had his spear raised rather than holding it to the ground beside him. He looked as if he resented their presence.

Harrie bowed to the clan leader, then gestured to her. Suzanne gave a small bow. A fast conversation followed between the men – the youngest man interrupting several times until the clan chief raised his hand and put it in front of his mouth.

'*Hî-î*, Kmame.' No.

The angry youth stalked away to the edge of the encampment, followed by the three younger men.

Harrie turned to Suzanne. 'They will take you to Shansi now.'

She glanced over her shoulder. 'Who is that disagreeable youth who does not want us here?'

Harrie's expression did not change, though she saw a flicker of warning in his eyes. 'Kmame is the son of the leader of the clan and you are right, he wishes we had not come. But his anger is not directed against you. At least, not only at you. He does not approve of me, either. A *verrader*, as the Dutch would have it.'

'A collaborator?'

'Kmame is one of those who considers any who work for the VOC a traitor to our race.' Harrie shrugged. 'Who's to say? He might be right.'

'You are trying to make things better for your family,' Suzanne said, springing to his defence. 'There is nothing to be ashamed of in that.'

Harrie gave a ghost of a smile. 'Time will tell.'

They followed one of the elders to the hut in the middle of the compound. He called out a greeting. From within, a female voice answered, and they found themselves ushered inside the *matjieshuis*. It was clean and airy, angled so that a gentle breeze slipped through small gaps in the reed walls.

An old woman sat on a mat on the ground, dressed the same as the men outside: a *karros* around her waist, her shoulders and chest bare. Her skin hung in loose folds, like brown velvet, on her arms and belly.

Harrie knelt on the ground in front of the woman, and gestured that Suzanne do the same. At closer quarters, she judged her to be perhaps threescore years, though her lined face might not give a true indication of how many seasons she had lived. Her gaze was direct, inquisitive, and Suzanne felt reassured that she might genuinely have something to impart.

The same conversational dance began again: Suzanne asked a question, Harrie translated, Shansi replied, then her words were spun from Khoi into Dutch. Even though she could understand nothing, Suzanne could tell that Shansi's memory was clear and definite. She barely hesitated in her answers.

Finally, Harrie recounted what Shansi had told him. 'She says that in October in the year of our Lord 1623, her mother Fala was called to assist at the confinement of a white woman, a woman—'

'Forgive me,' Suzanne interrupted, 'but how can she be so precise in the date?'

'It is I who am giving you the date in your calendar from what Shansi has said,' Harrie explained. 'The woman – and another companion – had been granted permission to stay on Goringhaiqua land. Fala arrived when the labour was already far advanced. The birth was straightforward. There was never any fear for the life of the mother or baby. A boy.'

'Shansi is certain her mother said there were two white women, not a man and a woman?' Suzanne asked.

'That is what she says. Two white women, one some years older than the other.'

Suzanne frowned, not knowing what to make of it. 'Can she describe the women?'

Harrie asked the question, listened, then relayed the answer. 'She says they looked the same. One with more lines, taller. A big woman.'

'Anything else to distinguish them?'

Shansi pointed at Suzanne, then laughed.

'She says the tall one had eyes of different colours. Like yours.'

Suzanne caught her breath. There could be no doubt this was Louise. 'And she was the mother?'

Harrie shook her head. 'No, the other woman.'

Suzanne frowned. It made no sense. Louise had never written of another woman. 'And no man?'

'No man,' Shansi repeated in Dutch, then fell back into her own language, talking fast now and with many hand gestures.

Harrie's face grew grave. 'But she remembers there was talk of a man before. There was an argument, somewhere on Goringhaiqua lands.'

Suzanne saw the same realisation in Harrie's eyes that this, at least, tallied with what Tshu had said.

'How does she know this?'

Harrie translated for Shansi, then turned back to Suzanne. 'She says everyone had heard tell of a man with a white stripe in his hair who was looking for the she-captain. She says that the story was passed from clan to clan, that the man found them with the help of someone from the Goringhaiqua. Her mother, Fala, was Goringhaiqua. Shansi says everyone heard that the man found the women and they fought. After that, she does not know.'

Suzanne sat back on her heels. This also chimed with what Tshu had told them about a fight. Did that mean that Phillipe had killed Gilles or vice versa? Or that Phillipe had killed Louise? But who was the second woman who had given birth? Most of all, what had happened to the child?

'When did this happen, the fight, does she know?'

'At the turning of the year,' Harrie replied, 'when it was very hot. Before the child was born.'

'A baby boy,' Suzanne murmured. But not Louise's child, if Shansi's report was to be believed. 'Did she ever hear more of the child?'

Shansi began to talk again, so fast that even Harrie struggled to keep up.

'She says her mother knew nothing of what happened after she left the two women. All she can attest to is that the woman was delivered of a son, healthy and strong.'

'*!Kam*,' Shansi suddenly said.

'What is she saying?'

Harrie listened. 'Shansi is of the opinion that the man came back and killed them all.'

Suzanne's heart skipped a beat. 'Why? Why does she think that?'

Shansi was very animated now, her hands gesturing in the air as she talked.

'Because the women disappeared,' he explained. 'When the clan next travelled back that way, the white people were gone. The buildings, the pen for their animals, had disappeared into the dust.'

'But they could have been hiding?'

Harrie put the point to her. Shansi shook her head. 'She says they would have known. She is certain he murdered them.'

Suzanne fell silent, thoughts spiralling in her head. She didn't want to let Shansi go, but she was unable to think of anything else to ask. She knew these stories were hearsay and grown threadbare down the years. Fragments of information that didn't quite align with what she had been told before.

There had never previously been any mention of another woman close to Louise, not onboard ship nor once the *Old Moon* had arrived in Table Bay. It was, of course, possible that Louise might have picked up another passenger when they over-wintered in Cap Verde. But if that had been the case, surely she would have said so in her diary?

Reluctantly accepting there was nothing more to be gained, Suzanne smiled her thanks to Shansi and held out the kerchief.

'Please could you tell her that I appreciate her kindness and her courtesy. I am in her debt.'

Shansi took the offering with pleasure.

'She wishes you luck in your search,' Harrie said, as they rose reluctantly to their feet.

Suzanne pressed her palms together and repeated what Harrie said, attempting to mimic the clicking sound of their speech.

'*!Gâise hâ re.*' Goodbye.

CHAPTER FORTY-TWO

The moment they stepped back outside into the fading afternoon, Suzanne knew something had changed. The elders had vanished and only the four younger men were now waiting by the cold fire. The air was sharp with menace and threat.

Then she saw Tia, standing with her arms behind her back beside Kmame, and that her mare was now tethered to a post close to the cattle pen. Suzanne stood stock still, her nerves on alert, ready to follow Harrie's lead.

He spoke urgently. Kmame simply laughed and pulled on the rope binding Tia's arms. Harrie stepped forward to remonstrate and was met by three spears pointing directly at his chest. One of the men stepped forward and removed Harrie's weapon from his hand.

'What is happening?'

'Kmame claims we showed ill faith by not bringing Tia to the encampment. He is demanding your horse as recompense for the insult.'

'That's absurd –' Suzanne began, then stayed her tongue. She doubted that could be a genuine cause for offence. It was obviously a ruse. Kmame had been against their being allowed into the camp in the first place. 'Where is the chief?'

Harrie gave a slight shrug, wincing as he did so. 'I can only assume he has been forced to withdraw. Kmame clearly exerts a dishonourable influence over his father for this to be happening.'

Perhaps on hearing his name, Kmame started shouting.

Suzanne tensed. A bully was a bully in any language and, with three young men standing behind him for reinforcements, he was clearly itching for a fight.

'If we allow him the horse, will he let Tia go?'

For the first time since she had known him, Harrie hesitated. 'I do not know.'

Suzanne paused, then stepped forward. 'Translate for me,' she muttered to Harrie, then raised her voice and addressed Kmame.

'Forgive me if I have caused offence. That was not my intention. I wished only to talk to your esteemed elder, Shansi, and I am grateful to your headsman for granting me that honour. Harrie and Tia were acting on my instruction.' She waited for Harrie to finish translating, then continued. 'We journey to the interior and have need of the horse . . .'

Kmame's only response was to click his fingers. One of his men moved to Suzanne and tried to take the satchel from her shoulder.

'*Hî-î*,' she said sharply, remembering the word the clan leader had used earlier. 'No. You shall not have it.'

Taken aback by the force of her refusal, the man faltered. Kmame clicked his fingers again and indicated he should take the bag anyway. Now Suzanne was scared as well as angry: for Tia's safety, for them all. There was nothing to stop Kmame from killing them, leaving their bones to be picked clean by vultures, an inscrutable map of their murders. No one would ever know. She shook her head. She wouldn't inflict that loss upon her grandmother, she could not. And mixed with the fear, was fury.

She watched Kmame rifle through her satchel, whistling when he found her precious eyeglass and another kerchief, then laughing when he found two more bottles of brandy. She was grateful that she had hidden the ammunition in the copse.

'Let Tia go,' she said in a clear and forceful voice, telling herself to exhibit no fear, to treat him as if he was a child to be humoured.

Now Harrie started to speak. Suzanne could not understand what he was saying, but there was a new resolve to his voice. As if he was making some kind of bargain. A negotiation.

Without warning, Kmame suddenly gave Tia a shove in the back that had her sprawling face first into the dust. Harrie leapt to help his sister, but Kmame blocked his way and pointed at Suzanne. She suddenly understood. He would make the white woman do his bidding, as her people forced his to do theirs.

Suzanne helped Tia to her feet. She gestured at the rope binding her hands, mimed untying it, and received a nod in response. With fumbling fingers, she undid the knot and let the rope fall to the ground, then stepped back. Tia rubbed her wrists, shot a furious glare at Kmame, then went to stand beside her brother.

Kmame waved his hand.

'He is permitting us to leave,' Harrie said.

'What of our belongings? My horse?'

'He is keeping those as payment for our trespassing on his lands.'

'His father's lands,' Suzanne muttered under her breath, and saw Kmame move towards her, a look of understanding in his eyes. She turned cold. How stupid to assume he could not speak Dutch. Just because he had chosen not to work for the VOC did not mean he was not proficient in their language.

'Go,' he said, as if reading her thoughts, 'before I change my mind.'

As Suzanne, Harrie and Tia walked away from the encampment, she expected to hear the sound of a spear through the air and the dull thud as the iron tip connected with flesh. Her nerves were taut and each step seemed heavy. But they kept going and made it to the copse of trees. Once they were under cover, Suzanne started to breathe more easily again. Tia burst into tears and threw herself into her brother's arms. Harrie remained impassive.

'What did you say to him to get him to release us?' Suzanne asked.

Finally, Harrie's expression changed. 'That you were a descendant of the woman with Devil eyes and that you would put a curse on him if he did not let us go.'

Suzanne started in astonishment, then laughed. 'And he believed you?'

He raised his hands. 'It appears so.'

The smile faded from her lips. They were safe, but for how much longer?

'How can we know that they won't follow us and attack us on open ground? What are we going to do?'

Harrie's smile faded. 'Nothing. Which is why we will wait until darkness, then we will retrieve what Kmame has stolen.'

Suzanne's eyes widened. 'My belongings don't matter. They are trifles, not worth risking our lives over.'

'He is a thief. And a coward. He will celebrate his triumph over us with brandy. When they are sleeping, I will go back to the camp and take back your horse. If he wakes, I do not think Kmame will argue with the point of a gun.'

She shook her head. 'I cannot allow you to do that, Harrie. I'll go.'

'I cannot permit that, miss. *Mijnheer* Van Dijk would rightly never forgive me.'

'Ah, but Adriaan is not here. Besides, didn't you tell Kmame all manner of falsehoods about me? In his drunken state, if he should wake, he will certainly be more frightened of me than he is of you.'

Dusk fell. Day gave way to night.

Suzanne prepared her musket, in case Kmame's men came for them in the night, then sat down to wait. For some hours, they remained hidden in the copse, listening. The young men were clearly drinking the brandy. The sounds of carousing got louder and louder and Suzanne had to force herself to hold her nerve. She listened as the voices rose and fell. Finally, they stopped altogether.

'How long shall we wait?'

'Until their sleep has deepened,' Harrie replied.

When the last embers of light had faded from the fire in the encampment, Harrie stood up. They had agreed they would all approach the camp together, rather than risk becoming separated in the dark.

On his silent command, they started across the open space between the copse and the encampment, keeping low. This was the first moment of danger. If anyone should still be awake and hear movement in the darkness they would be caught. Suzanne's heart was beating so loudly she thought it would give her away, but she concentrated on each step, and made no noise. The musket was heavy on her back, the bandolier unwieldy, but she managed to find the right equilibrium. Twice, her shirt snagged on a twig and she sent a stone scuffing with her boot, but nothing stirred.

Once they were within striking distance, Harrie indicated that she and Tia should skirt the camp on the right-hand side, and he would go to the left.

Now Suzanne was close enough to see that Kmame and his three companions were lying asleep at the fire. Both her satchel and eyeglass were within striking distance. She tapped Tia on the arm and pointed to the huddle of men. Tia shook her head violently, but Suzanne had already jumped across the ditch and concealed herself between two of the huts.

She crouched on the ground using the shadow of the hut as cover. Carefully, she stretched out her arm. Her fingers found the eyeglass. Slowly, she began to draw it forward, then used it to hook beneath the strap of her satchel.

Kmame suddenly grunted and turned over. Suzanne froze, quickly withdrawing her hand for fear it would be seen. She held her breath as he exhaled and shifted position, before resuming her painstaking recovery of the satchel until, finally, she had it safely in her hands. She leant back against the reed wall of the hut, allowed herself a moment of relief, then carefully slipped back through the shadows and over the ditch.

By the time she came to the top of the encampment, she could see that Harrie had managed to untether her horse and that Tia was carrying her saddle. She waited for them to get further ahead, until she was certain they could no longer be seen from the camp should anyone wake. Then, she made her own move.

Her heart still hammering, she crept soundlessly forward into the darkness, the soft tread of her mare's hooves guiding her way. One step, two steps, she was nearly away.

Then, at the very last minute, there was a movement behind her, and she turned. One of Kmame's men had stepped out of the encampment to relieve himself and stood staring at her. As she saw him open his mouth to shout, Suzanne put her finger to her lips. She could see he didn't have his spear with him and, guessing Kmame would punish his mistake, prayed that his instinct for self-preservation would be greater than his desire for glory. To reinforce her point, she raised the gun and pointed it at his face.

For a moment, everything hung in the balance. Then, with

a nod of his head, the deal was struck. He had not seen anything. She would not kill him. That the gun was primed but not loaded, he did not realise. The man turned and walked back into the camp. Suzanne held her breath, waiting for a shout that revealed he had betrayed her presence.

The night remained silent.

She gave it a moment or two longer, then lowered her weapon and slipped away, convinced that, this night, someone had been watching over her.

CHAPTER FORTY-THREE

GROOT DRAKENSTEIN
Tuesday, 21st December

They rode through the night, Tia sitting with Suzanne on the horse behind the saddle. Harrie walked beside them, though she could see he was weary. But they had to get as far away from the encampment as possible before Kmame and his men woke.

Harrie had told Kmame previously they were headed for Olifantshoek, which was south-east of their encampment. To put them off the trail, they were travelling instead towards Groot Drakenstein, where Pierre Jaubert and three other families had been allocated land. After their experiences at Kmame's encampment, Suzanne wanted to alert her fellow Huguenots in case his men attacked any of the settler farms in retaliation. Such raids had happened before.

From what Shansi had said, she was now certain that Phillipe had found Louise. She had no idea of the identity of the second woman, but Phillipe must have been the father of the baby boy. She also believed that the man from whom Lars Eltorp had acquired his weapon was either Phillipe himself – though his age meant that was unlikely – or that child grown to adulthood.

'Speak to me,' she murmured, but Louise remained silent.

In the star-lit darkness, Suzanne tried to fix her mind on the rumbling of hooves on the dry ground and the hoop of Tia's hands around her waist, Harrie's footsteps as he walked beside them. Each of them was watching for bright eyes in the darkness, a lion or leopard tracking their progress, but nothing impeded their flight.

Her thoughts drifted to her grandmother and their desperate flight across France, the terror of it. At least this time, Florence was safe in their house in the Colony. But Suzanne was increasingly worried for Harrie, though. She had noticed him flinch when Tia hugged him and he was limping on his left-hand side, where Odendaal's stick had done its worst.

At dawn, they stopped to rest the horse and to eat.

'Do you know where your friends are building their farm?' Harrie asked.

'Only that they were one of four families allocated land in the valley close to the Simonsberg mountains.'

He nodded, though his eyes seemed unfocused. 'We will find them.'

It was nigh on eleven o'clock in the morning by the sun, when the footsore and weary party saw a small rectangular hut on the horizon nestled in the fold of two hills. As they drew closer, the outline of the building became clearer. Suzanne thought it looked more like a hide for hunters than a home, but attempts had been made to make it presentable: a flat, matted straw roof; clay walls; a generous window with a wooden shutter and a small bench beneath it. Two earthenware pots stood on either side of the single door.

Suzanne smiled, remembering Pierre Jaubert's protestations at the idea that his wife would have to manage with only half a cooking pot and a third-share in a plough. Now she was out here in this boundless space, it seemed even more absurd that the settlers would have to divide these basic assets between them. How could they share between them when the plots of land were so far apart and the farming seasons the same for each family?

All the same, she had faith that Pierre and Isabeau would make the best of it. And, sure enough, once they were within hailing distance, she saw a makeshift fire with a brace suspending an iron cooking pot. A little further away, a plough with dirt in its teeth suggested Pierre was working hard to till the land. And behind the clay hut, she saw a basic pen with two cattle sheltering from the heat beneath a young karee tree. The thin trunk and sparse leaves provided little shade, but it was better than nothing and Suzanne knew from Tia that these were fast-growing, hardy trees.

Smiling, she dismounted. 'I believe we have found my friends.' She cupped her hands. '*Monsieur Jaubert, Isabeau, c'est moi. C'est Suzanne. Votre voisine du navire.*' Your neighbour from the ship.

For a moment, nothing stirred. At this time of the day, of course, it was more than possible that Pierre himself might be away from the farm. But Isabeau? Surely they would not leave their patch of land unattended.

Suzanne called again. '*Isabeau, tu es là?*'

This time, the door opened. She saw the glint of the muzzle of a musket, and grinned. It seemed that Pierre had managed to take first possession of everything, his third of the musket included.

Isabeau's face peered around the door. She was tanned brown by the sun, but it was the same, no-nonsense stare. The moment she saw who it was, she put down the gun, and rushed towards Suzanne with her arms outstretched.

'I could not believe my ears when I heard your voice,' she cried, enveloping her in a bear hug, 'yet here you are! Why? How?'

Suzanne embraced her. 'All in good time, my friend. Life in the interior clearly suits you, you look well!'

Isabeau laughed. 'I look a sketch, but there is no one here to see it. Give me dry land over the sea any time. And look at you, brown like a peasant. Florence must be in despair.'

Suzanne pulled a face. 'She has not yet seen how the sun has played havoc with my complexion. Let me introduce my travelling companions, Harrie Nemen and his sister, Tia.'

Isabeau peered a little suspiciously. Because the Jauberts had been among the first to leave the Colony, Suzanne suspected they'd had little chance to get to know any of the Khoi women and men who worked with the settlers.

'They are my friends,' Suzanne added.

Still looking nervous, Isabeau nodded. 'How do you communicate with them?'

Now, Suzanne laughed. 'They speak Dutch, Isabeau. Harrie is an interpreter, Tia worked for the *landdrost* in Stellenbosch.'

'Oh. Well, you must come inside. Tell me how you come to be here. I wish Pierre was at home. He has gone to visit Monsieur Grange and Monsieur Malan on the far side of the valley.' She shook her head. 'The soil here is no good. My husband hopes to persuade them to join with him and petition the commander to allocate better more fertile land beside the Berg River.'

'That is where we are headed, to Olifantshoek.'

Isabeau gave a shy smile, then, with a kinder gesture that took them all in, said: 'You must be thirsty and hungry. Sit. I will bring you something. We have little, but what we do have, you can share.'

Suzanne took her hand. '*Mille mercis.* Also, if you have water and cloths, Harrie has wounds that need dressing.'

Isabeau disappeared inside. Once she had gone, Suzanne saw Harrie sway on his feet and nearly fall. She and Tia helped him to sit in the shade of the house and Tia gently removed his shirt. It was an indication of how much pain he was in that he simply shut his eyes and winced.

'Miss . . .' Tia said quietly.

Suzanne glanced at Harrie's back and saw evidence of what she had dreaded. Infection had set in. His skin was swollen and red, yellow pus oozing from his wounds.

'Will he permit you to look after him?'

She waited while Tia spoke to her brother, listening to their whispered conversation. It was a sign of how bad Harrie felt that, although she could tell he was trying to protest, his heart wasn't in it.

But when Isabeau caught sight of Harrie's injuries, she took charge and insisted Tia help Harrie inside the hut. Suzanne heard a murmured conversation but, shortly, Isabeau came back outside. Her expression was grim.

'The man needs to rest and allow the air on his skin. The shirt has been aggravating the wounds. I have a store of herbs that can be made into a poultice to cleanse them. She is his sister, you say?'

'Yes.'

Isabeau nodded. 'I have a little artemisia. Tia is going to make him a poultice. He will rest; the infection is bad.'

'I feared as much.' Suzanne frowned. 'God willing, he will recover. They are good people.'

CHAPTER FORTY-FOUR

Friday, 24th December

For two days, Harrie's fever raged. It was hard to know if Tia's treatment was doing any good – she had made a poultice with buchu leaves and mud from the river to draw out the infection, and changed the dressings every hour. But he could not eat and barely managed sips of water. Suzanne was desperately worried for him – she had seen infected flesh go black and die, and he was afflicted over much of the surface of his back.

Isabeau set up a lean-to shelter for Harrie and Tia at the back of their little hut, so that he could sleep in the open air and let nature heal his skin. Tia never left his side except to fetch water and relieve herself, otherwise she sat beside him on the ground singing haunting songs in their mother tongue. Suzanne had to force her to eat and to drink, too.

Though it was nearly Noel, Pierre Jaubert had not returned. The Provençal Huguenots rejected anything that spoke of papistry, but Isabeau told Suzanne that they intended to gather together in the home of another of the settlers in Drakenstein on the twenty-fifth of December to pray and to thank God for their blessings.

'Though, the Lord forgive me, they are few and meagre,' Isabeau grumbled. Suzanne could see how it was back-breaking work trying to prepare the soil for planting in this arid country-side. Isabeau foraged for edible and medicinal plants – her mother had been a wise-woman – and, each morning, checked their traps for smaller mammals. Suzanne helped her, whilst always keeping an eye for changes to Harrie's condition.

Despite the hardship of her pioneer life, Isabeau was, for the most part, cheerful and happy to share the news that she was expecting a child in the late autumn.

'Who will assist at your confinement?' Suzanne asked.

'Madame Meinard has delivered some ten children in her time, including six of her own. When the time comes, Pierre will fetch her.' She beamed broadly. 'He has managed to acquire a horse, so I need not fear on that account.'

'How so?' Suzanne asked. Horses were rare in the Colony, and expensive.

'In return for services rendered. He hires himself out to help build houses. He persuades the Khoi to trade furs and ivory for timber. In just five months he has made a name for himself. People come to him.'

Suzanne was not surprised. Of all her fellow travellers, she had always believed Pierre Jaubert had the strength of character to make a success of himself.

'And are you happy, Isabeau?'

Her friend met her eye. 'Happy enough. We are safe, the Khoi are mostly willing to trade with us and, otherwise, leave us alone. Some clans are less welcoming of settlers, like the one you encountered.' She pulled a face. 'The stories I have heard, terrible: raids in the night, slaughter . . . And though I would not admit it to any but you, Suzanne, it is a pleasure to live to our own pattern – no pastor telling us what to do or complaining that we have sinned, no endless tolling of bells or old women who scowl at you for even so much as laughing on the Sabbath.'

'Are you not lonely out here, so far from any companionship?'

'A little,' Isabeau admitted, laying her hands across her

stomach. 'But soon my time will not be my own . . . and there are other farms near at hand. Close enough to be there and back within a half-day.'

For a moment, Suzanne contemplated riding back to the Colony to see if she could persuade Jean Prieur du Plessis – the barber-surgeon from the *Oosterland*, whom she had met at the dinner at the Castle in November – to come back with her to Drakenstein. She dismissed the idea as quickly as it had come. Even if du Plessis had been prepared to treat Harrie, she had no doubt he would demand the patient be brought to him.

She suddenly slapped her hands on her knees.

'What?' Isabeau asked.

'There was a name that was familiar, but I couldn't remember why. It has just come to me that I first came across it in the family archive in Amsterdam. Du Plessis was the name of my great-great-grandfather's birth father.'

Isabeau looked at her. 'Does that matter?'

Suzanne looked out over the Drakenstein Valley, remembering too how the man known as Vidal – the first to have the white streak in his hair – had inherited the du Plessis estate as a nephew, robbing her great-great-grandfather Piet Reydon of his inheritance.

She sighed. 'No, not any more. It's so long ago.' She smiled. 'But I am glad to have remembered.'

Saturday, 25th December

The following day was Christmas Day. Pierre had not returned, but Isabeau was confident he would meet them at the farm where the gathering was to be held.

Leaving Harrie in Tia's care, Suzanne and Isabeau left as the sun was rising and walked over the hill to the farm of Jean and Louise Meinard. They had lost two of their sons during the voyage, but their four surviving children were thriving and their daughter, Jeanne, ran to greet Suzanne with flowers in her hands.

Their plot of land looked less welcoming than the Jaubert plot, arid and dry. All the same, Madame Meinard had done her best to mark the day. Small posies of wild flowers and wild herbs were hung from the straw roof and a table had been placed outside on which the visitors were to leave their own contributions: Isabeau put her offering alongside sweetbreads, a bowl of red tortoise berry, roasted fennel, a paste of yellow kei-apple berries. In the shade, a spit had been constructed over a fire and the smell of roasting meat filled the air. It was the largest antelope Suzanne had ever seen.

'It is a kudu,' Isabeau explained. 'Jean and Pierre hunted it together especially for today. It was quite a task to carry it home.'

Suzanne was delighted to see how well Jean Meinard looked. When she had last seen him in the VOC administration block at the waterfront, his hair had hung lank down his face and his bones poked through his pale skin. Now, he was stronger in the shoulders and his skin was brown from the African sun. He looked more like a man in charge of his destiny.

It was wonderful to be reunited with some other of their fellow passengers – the Jourdans and dear Pierre Grange. He, too, had grown in stature and Suzanne passed a pleasant time, answering questions about Florence's health and their lives in the town.

Most of all, it was wonderful to see Pierre Jaubert. It was he who, in the absence of a pastor, led the Noel prayers, his faithful bible in his hands. Suzanne thought how odd it was that the same words kept them company: from La Rochelle to the *China*, from the Colony to Drakenstein, familiar sounds filling the air.

Once the short service was over, the celebrations began. Jean Meinard started to carve the meat and the women corralled the children to stand in a line to fill their platters.

Pierre drew Suzanne aside. They walked a little up the slope and sat on a tumble of rocks looking down over the farm.

'Isabeau tells me you are headed for Olifantshoek.'

'I am. I would have hoped to be there by now, but my guide, Harrie, is not fit enough to travel.'

Pierre shook his head. 'My wife told me what happened, terrible business.'

'Isabeau has been more than kind, letting us stay. We will be gone as soon as we can, though in truth the delay is of concern to me. We are running out of provisions and I fear the longer I leave it, the more I worry that the man I seek will have moved on.'

'That is what I wanted to talk to you about,' Pierre said. 'I have had some dealings with local men – some are prepared to help, others not, as I gather you discovered for yourself. I have heard of the man you encountered, Kmame. He is part of a smaller group that has broken away from the Cochoqua. It is clear he is trying to wrest power away from his father.'

'He has already done so.'

'A bad business. All the same, there are some good men.'

'You mean among Kmame's men?'

'No, elsewhere.'

Suzanne waited, wondering what Pierre was getting at.

'The point is if you need another guide – while your man is recovering – then just say the word. I could arrange it.'

She hesitated, wondering would happen to Tia and Harrie if she left.

'Not to worry,' he said, reading the expression on her face. 'Your people can stay until you return.'

Though Suzanne wasn't sure they would want to stay without her there, what choice did she have? Harrie's wounds were not healing and he was still subject to bouts of fever that came and went. She did not want to rush his recovery, but she was desperate to move on.

'If you're sure?'

'I am.'

'In which case, I will ask them.' She smiled. 'You are a good friend, Pierre.'

'You were kind when my first wife died on board,' he said quietly. 'You accepted my Isabeau and helped us all when we arrived with those Dutch tricksters. That's to say, this is the least I can do.'

'Thank you.' Then, recalling it was Noel, she added: 'And the season's greetings to you, Pierre. May there be better days ahead.'

CHAPTER FORTY-FIVE

It was not until sunset, when the mosquitoes and flies were out in force, that Suzanne, Pierre and Isabeau arrived back at the Jaubert farm. They were footsore and tired from so much talking, but happy.

Tia greeted them with a little hope in her eyes: Harrie was holding steady, and she had managed to persuade him to eat a little bread.

'But he still has a fever, miss. Nothing I do is working.'

'It is working, Tia, otherwise his condition would be worsening,' Suzanne replied, hoping she was right. 'If you are worried, are you sure there is nobody we could fetch? One of your own people?'

'There is no one near.'

Suzanne raised her eyebrows. 'Can that be true?'

'They do not trust us,' Tia admitted.

'Because you work for us?'

She nodded unhappily.

'Well, then we must continue to be patient. Give your herbs time to work. Madame Jaubert will help.'

Tia narrowed her eyes. 'Why do you say that?'

'Because I have to continue to Olifantshoek, Tia, and find the man we're seeking. The longer I wait, the more likely it is that he will have moved on.'

As Suzanne had feared, Tia hated the idea of her going.

'If he lives there, why would he leave?' she cried.

'Well, we don't know if he lives there or if he was just passing through. Can't you see, the longer I delay, the more likely it is that I will miss him. Harrie cannot yet be moved, and he needs you. Madame Jaubert's husband is going to engage another guide for me.'

'What if this person is untrustworthy, what if he is—'

Suzanne put her hand on Tia's arm. 'You can meet him, Harrie can meet him if he is fit enough to do so. But I have to go.'

In the end, Tia conceded her brother was not fit to travel. After further discussion, it was agreed that brother and sister would stay until Harrie improved, then they would follow on to Olifantshoek to meet Suzanne there and escort her back to the Colony.

'And you will come and work for me in our house? Like we said.'

Tia's face lit up. 'You promise?'

'Didn't I give you my word? My grandmother will be delighted to meet you.'

Pierre Jaubert delivered on his promise. Five days later, a Khoi guide arrived at the farm. Tia did not know him, but he was related by blood to their clan, and Harrie was prepared to vouch for him.

Khasso was quietly spoken, his voice a whisper, and he seemed shy even in Tia's company. He was shorter than Harrie, with the same distinctive broad face and a still, unwavering gaze. It was encouraging that he, too, had heard of a white man who lived in the Olifantshoek mountains. This was his territory, and Suzanne took much comfort in that.

Khasso received instructions from Harrie, a price was agreed for him to escort Suzanne to Olifantshoek and to protect her until Harrie and Tia could travel. Later, she explained the plan to Pierre and Isabeau, then retired early to bed leaving her hosts sitting by the fire outside.

As her eyes started to close, she realised she would arrive in Olifantshoek on her birthday – New Year's Day. It would be the first time she had ever spent her feast day apart from Florence. She wondered if her grandmother would light a candle or wait until she returned so that they could mark the day together.

Drifting into sleep, she imagined herself riding into Olifantshoek with the mountains behind her, imagined the farm the Khoi had described. Imagined Louise – or her ghost – waiting for her.

'I'm coming,' she murmured, as she had promised before, 'I'm coming to find you.'

Friday, 31st December

'Come back and see us,' Pierre said with a catch in his voice. 'My wife has enjoyed your company. She will miss you.'

'And I her,' Suzanne replied warmly. 'Again, thank you for your kindness in allowing Harrie and Tia to remain. I warrant it won't be for too much longer. He is strong and determined to heal.'

Pierre held up his hand. 'No hurry, no hurry. *A bientôt.*'

Suzanne hugged Isabeau, took her leave of a weeping Tia and extracted a promise from Harrie that they would not follow after her until he was back to full strength.

At first, they headed due south. Khasso was a silent presence at her side, answering any questions she asked of him, but never volunteering a word otherwise. Suzanne did not mind. She relished the silence.

They travelled all morning until the sun at midday drove them to seek shade. Khasso refused any food and only drank from a stream. Suzanne rested her horse, checked her musket and ammunition, ate a little bread and cured meat, and waited impatiently for the worst of the heat to pass.

They changed their course, now travelling south-east towards the Olifantshoek mountains which loomed grey and green on the horizon. At first, Suzanne noticed nothing different in Khasso's careful and steady gait. But as the ground started to rise, he became jittery, turning his head from side to side as if expecting an ambush.

Suddenly, a blood-curdling scream up ahead stopped them in their tracks. Another scream was followed by a series of grunts, and barks. Suzanne's hand went to her musket slung over her shoulder.

'What is that?' she said quickly, her fingers fumbling with the ammunition in the bandolier.

'Baboons,' he said.

'Are they dangerous?'

'They are thieves. They will try to steal from us.'

'Will they attack us?'

Khasso shrugged. 'You can scare them away.' He pointed to the musket. 'They will not like the noise.'

Suzanne dismounted, then allowed Khasso to lead her horse up the narrow gap between two escarpments until they reached a plateau. Now she could see a troop of baboons, adults and children, settled directly in their path. Their expressions were a mixture of charm and mischief, their faces almost human.

She prepared the black powder and ammunition, blew on the match chord, then pointed the musket into the air and fired. The animals scattered, screeching in all directions, leaping from rock to rock back towards the cover of the trees higher on the ridge. Suzanne thought she could hear the echo of the shot bouncing off the rock, rumbling through the pass like thunder.

Then the smoke cleared and all was still again.

She turned to Khasso smiling, delighted that she had successfully loaded and fired the gun after so long. Adriaan would have been proud of his pupil. To her surprise, Khasso still looked unnerved.

'Is something the matter? Do you think they will come back?'

He shook his head.

'What, then?' she said with a touch of impatience. He seemed rooted to the spot as if unwilling to take another step. 'Khasso?'

Slowly, he pointed to the next range of mountains. 'I cannot go further.'

Suzanne stared at him in disbelief. 'You agreed to take me to Olifantshoek and stay with me until Harrie and Tia arrived. That was our arrangement.'

'Not through this pass.' He gestured to the plains down below. 'We can go another way.'

'But to go round the mountains rather than through them will add days to our journey.'

'Not through the pass,' he repeated.

'But why?' Her voice rose in exasperation.

'It is the wind.'

Suzanne looked up. She realised that, at some point in the past hour, the wind had changed direction. It was now blowing into their faces rather than at their backs.

'When the wind comes from the south-east, the voices of the unquiet dead can be heard whispering through this valley,' he said, so quietly that Suzanne had to strain to hear him at all. 'They are the spirits of those who are destined to roam the earth without rest.' He put his hand to his chest. 'I cannot go further.'

She was dumbfounded. Short of forcing him at the point of the gun to take her further, she did not know what to do to persuade him.

'How long before the wind changes direction again?' she finally asked.

'It could be a day, a week. It could be longer.'

'So, what do you propose?'

Without embarrassment, Khasso met her eye. 'Wait for the wind to change or go around the mountain.' His voice was steady and implacable. He believed what he believed and nothing she could say would make him believe otherwise.

There was, however, a third option. 'How much further is it?'

'Half a day,' he replied. 'You follow this pass. It rises up, then you will be travelling downhill. You will see the farm you seek before sunset.'

Suzanne nodded. 'What are the dangers? Not the spirits you talk about, but predators?'

'Here there are no lions. Leopards, yes, and where there are leopards there will be jackals. Snakes, too, of course.'

She swallowed hard. Was she really going to go on alone for the sake of a few days? She hesitated and she thought of Louise, then decided there was no choice.

'I will continue alone,' she said with more confidence than she felt. 'If you change your mind, come to find me. Otherwise, please wait for Harrie and Tia here and tell them where I am. I will leave some provisions.'

She knew Harrie would have tried to argue with her. He would have worried for her safety and attempted to stop her leaving. But Khasso simply nodded, then sat down to wait.

Suzanne took stock. She could approach under cover of dark, then set up camp within sight of the farm.

And then what? she thought to herself.

With grave misgivings, but also a sense of purpose at her journey's end, on the eve of the new year, Suzanne Joubert rode on alone.

CHAPTER FORTY-SIX

OLIFANTSHOEK
New Year's Day 1689

The sun was going down behind the isolated farmstead between the river and the mountains. After months of searching and hardship, through deep forests and over grasslands, she had found it. Found him.

Suzanne lifted the eyeglass and adjusted the scope. She had been here for much of the day. Watching, waiting. The thatched roof of the farmhouse was cinder black against the blue sky, a wooden palisade for livestock, three straw-thatched huts. It was far grander than the Jaubert farm and looked more established. There was a scattering of bones in what looked like a shallow grave, white markers in the red dust. She almost smiled – blue, white, red, the colours of the VOC flag. She was not superstitious, but surely that meant something?

The gun was heavy in her hands and the leather strap of the bandolier holding the ammunition was cutting into her shoulder. She shifted position. Though she was wearing a man's hat with a broad rim, she could feel the skin on her neck was burning. Her horse was tethered beneath the trees, but she couldn't risk moving into deeper shade. Here she had a good view of the farm.

Kill or be killed.

This was the end to the story that had started several generations ago, more. Ever since that terrible night in La Rochelle, then discovering Louise's diary in the archives in Warmoesstraat, Suzanne's mission had been to do for Louise what she could not do for herself. To right a wrong.

Suzanne felt resolute, determined. Courageous. But it was so silent in the valley and that was beginning to unnerve her. A jackal buzzard spiralled in the hot late afternoon air, the leaves of the silver trees motionless in the punishing heat. How she missed Tia's chattering and Harrie's steady presence.

Then the natural world came to life: the distant trumpeting of the elephants come to calf. Majestic creatures speaking of a time before men walked the earth. The sharp cry of ibis, the shrill call of red-winged starlings, all the colours and songs she had come to know. Vivid and glorious, a beautiful, terrifying world.

As the song of the animals faded, Suzanne allowed herself to wonder how she would feel once she knew the truth. Since setting foot on African soil on that blustery and wet August day five months ago, Louise had never been far from her thoughts. In these past twenty-four hours, she had imagined little else than the pull of her finger on the trigger, the spark of the tip of the match cord as it found the gunpowder, the flight of the ball through the air.

The wind was still blowing from the south-east, carrying the spirits of the undead. Would Khasso still be waiting for her when she returned to the *rendez-vous*? She was not certain. She had paid him well enough, but there was no reason he would be loyal. The Khoi and the San had learnt that the white settlers were perfidious and not to be trusted. Why would she be any different?

Below, there were still no signs of life. Suzanne wondered if the man might have heard whisper of the woman come from across the seas to find him? It was why she had been so determined to keep going, to not allow him to slip through her fingers.

She dismissed the thought. She had mostly kept her own counsel and taken great pains to disguise her purpose. Only Harrie and Tia were aware of her precise progress from west to east – a map of bones, buried in the dust. And though Adriaan, Judith and Florence knew what she intended, she trusted them with her secrets and her life.

Suzanne continued to watch the farmstead shimmering in the heat, allowing the world to shrink to the thudding of her blood, the pump and sigh of her heart, the metallic sweat of the musket in her hands. Though alert to the danger of a boomslang hidden in the scrub, or the hiss of an olive-brown cobra, she was calm and composed. The musket took so long to reload. She would have just one chance, just one shot.

Time passed.

Presently, Suzanne allowed herself to sit. She laid down the eyeglass, sipped a little weak brandy from her water bottle and ate a dry biscuit, the last of her provisions. The sun slipped lower in the west, turning the whitened sky red.

Fire, water, air and earth.

Dusk was falling. The air was soft now, sweet now, on her skin. She listened to the whining of insects, the whistle of a nightjar and the rustling of animals in the fynbos and scrubland. The howl of a black-backed jackal, too far away to be a threat. Leaning against her stone pillow, Suzanne's head began to droop. Her fingers grew loose and she placed the musket beside her, feeling its weight against her thigh. She heard an owl calling to its mate, joyous. Another white owl, perhaps?

Without warning, just as the last vestiges of day slipped from the sky, a sound down below brought her back from her reverie. The door opened. A man was standing in the opening. Suzanne was instantly alert, squinting into the failing light. He was broad-shouldered and tall, a farmer or explorer, wearing breeches and a long leather jerkin, a chemise open at the neck.

Now the moment had come, her resolve faltered. Should she try to speak to him first? Was she allowing her own emotions to cloud her common sense? In the half-light, with the help of the glass, she could see the tell-tale streak of white in his hair.

Suzanne hesitated. Was it a trick of the light, shadows that distorted and concealed in the twilight? She remembered the advice Madame Lombard had given to her when she'd set out on this expedition: 'Man or beast, shoot first, ask questions after.'

All the same . . .

Suzanne intended to shoot to frighten him, not to silence. To warn, not to harm. She needed to persuade him to talk to her.

Quietly, she got to her feet, picked up the gun and slowly crept forward through the grass. She climbed over the dried-out skeleton of a fallen tree, until she was in a perfect position. With steady fingers, she bit the top from the paper cartridge and shook the black powder into the pan, then the remainder into the muzzle. She packed it tight with the scouring stick, making sure the ball was in place, then lifted the weapon to her shoulder. She blew on the match cord, her breath pinking the tip. Moved her finger towards the trigger.

Suzanne leant forward, her eyes fixed on her quarry.

Then, she sensed a movement at her feet and a sound, something like a sigh. She looked down in time to see a flash of speckled brown and white, a thick body, a black-forked tongue. A puff adder, one of the deadliest of all the snakes in the valley. She leapt back, but she was too slow.

Just for a moment, Suzanne thought she glimpsed Louise.

Shining in the shimmering dusk, translucent. And this time, there was a second figure. Indistinct, but beloved. Her grandmother? But before Suzanne had time to wonder what that could mean, the vision faded. She was alone again.

A violent explosion of pain in her leg, two stiletto points piercing the soft leather of her boots. Her finger spasmed on the trigger, the musket fired impotently into the night, Suzanne fell. Then, nothing.

A day to kill or be killed.

CHAPTER FORTY-SEVEN

THE CAPE COLONY
Sunday, 9th January 1689

Marie Lombard rose early on the Sabbath. It was three weeks since Florence had been taken from them and she missed her friend every day.

At this time of year, when the temperature at night was little different from the burning heat of the day, there had been no choice but to bury her quickly. They could not wait for Suzanne to come back – with death came disease – but Marie still felt a lingering guilt she had not been there to see her beloved grandmother laid to rest.

In truth, the matter had been taken out of Marie's hands. Adriaan van Dijk had made the arrangements and chosen a plot in the Christian graveyard where her body could be buried deep enough. At Gallow's Hill, where the slave graveyard was to be found, it was a common sight to see scattered bones torn from the earth by lions and jackals and left to bleach in the hot sun.

Marie dressed slowly, feeling her age in her aching bones. She had no appetite these days, her flesh seemed to hang loose on her once sturdy frame. Grief and the heat had stripped every ounce of energy from her. But she had woken determined that this morning should be different. She would lay flowers on her friend's grave and linger there a while. Perhaps say a few words? Marie was not a woman of faith, but, with Florence gone, she lacked someone with whom to share her otherwise unspoken thoughts.

She walked from her chamber to the living room, realising it was later than she had thought. Only the three youngest orphans were still in her charge, but the house was particularly quiet. Marie realised they must have left her sleeping and gone to chapel without her. Usually, she walked them to the Castle, delivered them into Judith's care for the service, then fetched them home again.

She sat in a chair and poured herself a small cup of watered-down brandy. It was a relief not to have to put on a brave face in front of the girls. Catrina, in particular, was very sensitive to the emotions of others and became easily distressed. Marie did not have the patience for it this morning.

It was not only the heat that made her so fatigued. She knew that the dread of telling Suzanne her grandmother had died lay heavy on her heart. Surely the girl would arrive back in the Colony soon? She had been gone for more than four weeks. In truth, she had expected her before now and sensed the same unease in Judith.

She sipped a little more brandy, letting it calm her nerves, then changed her mind. She would visit Florence's grave later in the afternoon. Better now to go to the Castle, under the guise of meeting the girls after chapel, and try to speak to Adriaan van Dijk. Perhaps he would have heard something?

Marie took her hat, locked the door and set off across the square towards the Castle.

GROOT DRAKENSTEIN

Suzanne's absence was weighing heavily on Isabeau Jaubert, too. Now, a fortnight and more after their arrival, the day had finally come for their visitors to go. Isabeau would miss the steady presence of Harrie and Tia, but she was also relieved. It was not that she doubted the guide her husband had engaged, more that she had come to know and like the brother and sister and trusted them better to look after Suzanne.

Tia had washed their travelling clothes and they were ready to leave. Harrie bowed his head to Pierre Jaubert, before turning to Isabeau with his hands pressed together.

'It is with gratitude that we take our leave,' he said formally. 'Your charity and kindness have been more than I could have expected. I shall make sure all know of it.'

'Maybe not "all",' Pierre laughed with his booming voice. 'We don't want to become a boarding house for everyone who passes through.'

Harrie smiled. 'Maybe not.'

Tia bobbed a shy curtsey, then turned to Isabeau. The Frenchwoman put her hand on the girl's thin shoulder. 'You take good care.'

Tia nodded. 'May God grant you a speedy delivery and a strong child.'

Isabeau smiled. 'May God go also with you.'

Then, turning once to wave over their shoulders, brother and sister began their long walk south.

'I hope all is well,' Isabeau said, the smile fading from her face. 'They have been here longer than I expected.'

'You worry too much,' Pierre said. 'It was sensible for the lad to wait until he was fully recovered. He'd be no use to Suzanne else.'

'Even so.' She took his hand in hers. 'What if the guide turned out to be dishonest? What if he abandoned Suzanne and she has been waiting all this time for Harrie and Tia to arrive? What if—'

'What if you stop worrying about things you cannot change?'

Pierre chided, placing his hand on his wife's swelling belly. 'If there is news, we'll hear it soon enough.'

Planting a kiss on Isabeau's head, he turned and went round to the back of the house to begin dismantling the lean-to shelter his wife had built for Harrie and Tia. He needed the timber for another purpose.

Isabeau stayed where she was, watching the two figures getting smaller and smaller in the distance, until they vanished from sight.

THE CAPE COLONY

'Ah, *mevrouw* Van Dijk,' Madame Lombard said quickly, as the chapel doors opened and the congregation began to walk out into the sun-blanched courtyard. 'Might I have a word?'

'Good morning to you, Madame Lombard, and, please, call me Judith. We can presume on that level of friendship by now, I would hope.' Shielding her eyes against the brightness, she was concerned at how pale the older woman looked, at the dark rings under her eyes. She looked thinner, too. 'Is something wrong?'

'I wondered if there had been any news of Suzanne,' Marie replied, plunging straight in without preamble. 'I had thought she would have returned by now.'

Judith's face grew serious. 'I, too, had expected her presently. Shall we walk?'

They set off across the courtyard towards her chambers.

'Perhaps *mijnheer* Van Dijk has received news from Stellenbosch?'

Judith laced her gloved hands across her growing belly. 'Not unless he has forgotten to inform me of it,' she said. 'He tries to spare me any distress, but he would not keep something like that from me.'

Marie nodded. 'How go the preparations for your confinement?'

Judith's face lit up. 'I think I felt him – or her – move for the first time two nights ago, though it was such a strange sensation. Like a fluttering, so delicate and passing quick. Now the sickness has gone, I am as hungry as a horse and my feet swell to twice their usual size by the end of each day.'

'All very natural,' Marie reassured her. 'And it is good you have an appetite. The more you eat, the better.'

'If it is a boy, we have decided to call him Johannus. After Adriaan's late father.'

'And if it's a girl?'

Judith smiled. 'I feel sure he is a boy. But, if not, we thought to name her Florence. If Suzanne would agree to it.'

To her surprise, Marie felt her eyes prick with tears at the thoughtfulness of the gesture. 'I think she would like that very much.' She gave a long sigh. 'Can we do nothing but continue to wait for news?'

Judith shook her head. 'I will speak to my husband. He is due to ride out to the VOC settlers in Drakenstein – Monsieur Jaubert and others have sent another petition about the poor quality of the soil. Adriaan intends to see for himself if their complaint is justified. Perhaps he might ride via Stellenbosch and speak to *landdrost* Odendaal. He, at least, will know if Suzanne kept to her original plan.'

Marie took her hand. 'See that he does, my dear. I would be reassured to know nothing ill has befallen her.'

CHAPTER FORTY-EIGHT

OLIFANTSHOEK
Wednesday, 12th January

'I think he means me harm . . .'

Suzanne woke with Louise's familiar words going around in her head. She imagined the Justice card pressed between the pages of the diary. The colours were bright at first, then the image started to blur. Red, yellow and blue bleeding into one another until the figure on the card was obscured. For a moment, it was her own face and her own red hair on the card, her silver dagger in her right hand with its garnet in the hilt, the scales of Justice in her left.

She blinked, trying to drag herself up from the heavy sleep that held her. Where was she? Her chamber in La Rochelle? In her semi-conscious state, her head rocked slightly from side to side. Clay walls not white. None of the sounds of the port, no chime from the *grosse horloge* that marked the hours of the day come rain or shine. The rattle of the chain between the two towers that kept the harbour safe.

It had not kept her safe.

Suzanne's thoughts began to race like water over rocks. She was not in Amsterdam, either. There was a smell to that city of adventure, of the sea – and herring when the wind blew in the wrong direction. The Colony, then. Was she in the merchant's house in the square? She reached out for her grandmother sleeping beside her and found only empty space.

She was in some kind of bed, though. She could make out a sloped wooden ceiling with a hole at the top to let in the light.

She blinked again, slowly allowing her eyes to adjust to the semi-gloom. She realised she was lying flat on her back, like an effigy on a tomb. She moved her fingers and felt the rough cotton of a covering pulled up to her chest.

Then, Suzanne tried to move her feet. A lightning bolt of pain shot through the length of her body. Her left leg was on fire, as if her skin was splitting in two like an animal on a spit. A half-memory of being with friends, sharing plates of food, she could almost smell the flames. Sitting on an outcrop of rock talking. But now pain had taken hold. Her whole body seemed to be burning and she cried out with the agony of it.

In the moments before gentle sleep took her again, Suzanne thought she saw a figure standing in the corner of the chamber. A real person, not a figment of her fevered imagination. Then she slipped back beneath the surface, returning to the grey half-light that held her captive.

Groot Drakenstein

Adriaan van Dijk and Pierre Jaubert were sitting on the bench in front of the Jaubert homestead, the official and the farmer. Van Dijk's black clothes were dusty from his two days of riding, from the Colony to Stellenbosch, then north towards the Simonsburg mountains.

Isabeau came out of the house carrying a tray. Two earthenware cups for the wine the VOC man had brought with him and a plate of cold meat from their meagre stores.

'*Mille mercis*, Madame Jaubert,' Van Dijk said, grateful that Suzanne had schooled him in French.

Isabeau nodded and turned to go. Pierre reached out and grabbed his wife's hand.

'Stay,' he said. 'In case there is anything I have forgotten.'

Isabeau upturned a milk pail and sat down.

'*Mijnheer* Van Dijk married Judith Verbeek from the *China*,' Pierre said, smiling. 'They are expecting their first child at about the same time as us, my dear.'

'Congratulations to you both,' Isabeau said warmly.

'God has blessed us,' Adriaan replied, but his mind was clearly elsewhere.

'Tell my wife what you have told me,' Pierre prompted. 'He has ridden from Stellenbosch seeking news of Suzanne.'

'It does not behove me to speak ill of any fellow employees of the VOC,' Adriaan began. 'Having said that, I do not believe the *landdrost* there represents the best of us. He was most obstructive. But in the end, I did discover that Suzanne had left his lodgings with the guide I had secured for her, Harrie Neman. It appears his sister, a young woman called Tia, went with them. Odendaal was enraged by this. He seemed to think that Suzanne owed him compensation for taking the girl away. I sensed there was more to it.'

'That is correct,' Isabeau said. 'On the day they were due to leave, the *landdrost* himself administered so severe a beating to Harrie—'

Adriaan frowned. 'On what grounds?'

Pierre took up the story. 'Two enslaved men had absconded. The *landdrost* believed that Harrie knew something of it. When he denied it, he whipped him in front of the entire household.'

'Suzanne felt Tia's position within the household might

become difficult,' Isabeau continued, 'so she encouraged the girl to leave with them. Harrie's wounds from the beating became infected and, by the time they arrived here, he was very unwell. It is why Suzanne finally set out alone, with a replacement guide. Harrie and Tia stayed here until he was fit enough to travel.'

'Who was the replacement guide?'

'A Khoi man called Khasso, known to me,' Pierre replied. 'Quiet, but a good worker.'

'And when was this?'

'Suzanne left on the thirty-first day of December,' Isabeau said. 'Harrie and Tia only took their leave three days ago, the plan being that they would meet her in Olifantshoek and escort her back to the Colony. They are on foot, so . . .'

Adriaan worked the timings out in his head. 'Which means that Suzanne has been missing for more than ten days.'

'Not necessarily missing,' Pierre protested. 'All being well, she is waiting in Olifantshoek for Harrie and Tia.'

Adriaan could see the logic of this. It was the delay caused by Harrie's injuries that had slowed Suzanne down, and her detour to Drakenstein. It didn't mean necessarily that something was wrong.

'Why did she come here in the first instance? Drakenstein is much out of her way.'

Pierre answered: 'They ran into trouble with another clan, seemingly led by a man called Kmame who has wrested power from his father.'

'It is a splinter group of the Cochoqua, I have heard of him.'

'Suzanne learnt something of her ancestor Louise from one of the female elders of the tribe. The headsman welcomed them, but Kmame overruled his father and confiscated their possessions. They managed to retrieve them, but adjudged it safer to head in the opposite direction from the one Kmame would expect. All this she told us at Noel.'

'She wanted us to be aware,' Isabeau added, 'in case these Cochoqua retaliated by a raid on our farms.'

Adriaan thought for moment. 'Is it possible Kmame might have followed Suzanne to Olifantshoek? If he considered she had humiliated him?'

Pierre now looked worried. 'I suppose so, though would he think it worth the trouble?'

Adriaan could think of several reasons: a young man trying to consolidate his power; a man who hated settlers; a man who had been outwitted by a white woman. Would it be in his interests to let such an insult go?

'Will you go to Oliftanstoek?' Isabeau asked.

'That is my intention.' Adriaan answered. 'My wife will never forgive me if I return without news.'

'Florence must also be out of her mind with worry,' Isabeau said. There was a sudden silence, then she saw the expression on Adriaan's face. 'Oh no.'

'I am afraid Madame Joubert contracted ague. Despite all best efforts, she was taken from us. Madame Lombard was with her until the end.'

Isabeau put her hand to her chest. 'May God have mercy on her soul.'

'Ah, she was a fine woman,' Pierre said. 'Suzanne will feel her loss deeply.' But ever the pragmatist, after an appropriate pause he stood up. 'I will ride with you for a little of the way, *mijnheer*, if I may. We can continue our conversation about why the land we have been allocated here in Drakenstein is not suitable for planting vines.'

OLIFANTSHOEK

When next Suzanne woke, it was dark, though someone had lit a lamp in her room. She was not sure if she was comforted or frightened by the fact. Her eyes fluttered. Perhaps it was a vigil light and she was dead after all? Beneath her sheets, Suzanne shifted position, suddenly terrified at the thought of being buried alive beneath the wet earth with the bones and the worms. Except it wasn't like that here, was it? Here was all sand and red dust and wide horizons.

'Here . . .'

Another glimmering of memory came back to her. She tried to catch the thought, but nothing more came to her to tell her where precisely she was, or how she came to be lying in this chamber.

Her dreams had been filled with memories of happier times: of playing with her great-grandfather, Jean-Jacques, whom she so resembled in colouring and stature. Riding on his back while he pretended to be a lion and, in her clouded mind, another spark of memory formed. She had seen a lion in the flesh, had she not? Magnificent, noble beasts.

Then, in her dreaming, she caught fleeting glimpses of Minou, the great-great-grandmother she had never known. And, standing beside her, Louise, triumphant and fearless. Suzanne smiled. For a moment, in her delirious state, she could all but smell the sea and feel the lilt of the ship, hear the waves crashing against the bow and see the black sky scattered silver with stars. The solitude in the middle of the ocean with no sight of land. Now her beloved grandmother was here, too, holding out her hand and smiling. Calling her home.

When Suzanne put her hand to her cheek, she found it wet with tears.

CHAPTER FORTY-NINE

Olifantshoek Mountains

'There,' Tia whispered. 'Up ahead.'

Tia and Harrie had made good progress in the past three days, trekking south from Drakenstein. The ground was now sloping steeply upwards as they entered the narrow passes that led up and through the mountains. Beyond that, Olifantshoek.

Harrie peered into the dusk, following the line of his sister's finger.

'I see nothing.'

'Look closer,' she insisted. 'By the rock, there is someone waiting.'

He narrowed his eyes and, this time, could just make out a shape leaning against the grey slope. A look-out? If so, there might be others. Harrie shifted his spear in his right hand and nodded at Tia, who drew the knife from her belt.

Careful not to dislodge any loose stones or scree, the siblings moved forward.

'Does he not hear us?' Tia whispered. 'Or sense we are here?'

Harrie shrugged. Certainly, the figure had not moved at all. As they drew nearer, they saw it was a man. He looked as if he had simply sat down, placed his head against the smooth rock and fallen asleep. Harrie could see the *kaross* around the man's waist, though his shoulders were bare and there was no weapon in sight.

He gestured to Tia that she should stay where she was, then continued to creep forward. The man was unnaturally still. Harrie stopped and whispered a greeting. There was no response.

He tried again. '*Halau?*' Hello.

Still nothing. Tentatively, he reached out his hand and touched the man on the shoulder. With a sound almost like a sigh, the man slipped sideways. His chest was completely red as if he had been wrapped in clinging red silk, his neck a gaping wound. Harrie sprang back.

Tia's voice came from behind him. 'Is he dead?'

'Yes,' he said, recognising the guide Pierre Jaubert had engaged to take his place. 'It is Khasso. His throat has been cut.'

Tia looked around as if the assassin might still be somewhere close at hand, watching them.

'He is cold,' he added. 'The stiffness has come and gone.'

'If he had been here long, the animals would have taken him.'

'There are baboons in this valley. They are careful creatures, clever. Perhaps their presence kept other scavengers away.'

Tia drew closer. 'Who killed him?'

'How can I say?' Then he noticed something tucked beneath Khasso's left leg. He reached down and pulled out a kerchief, white with the initials *SJ* embroidered in green.

'This is the one the mistress gave to Shansi in the Cochoqua camp,' Tia said, her voice rising in alarm. 'Is this Kmame's doing? Did he kill Khasso and take her? Is she dead also?'

Harrie put his hand on his sister's shoulder. 'We will keep going to the meeting place,' he said in a level voice, 'and hope she will be waiting for us there.'

OLIFANTSHOEK

The next time Suzanne came to, it was because a noise had disturbed her. Was it the same day, or the next? She didn't know, only that a door was opening. A door connecting this chamber to whatever lay beyond.

Her heart started to race. Footsteps. Now there was someone else in the room with her, not a figure from a dream or a benign ghost. She could hear the rise and fall of their breath. Slowly, she turned her head on the pillow and looked towards the door.

A man of some sixty summers was standing on the threshold, stock still in the flickering light from the candle. He was broad shouldered and tall, a farmer or pioneer, wearing old-fashioned breeches with a chemise open at the neck.

'Who are you?' she asked. At least, she thought she did. She wasn't certain if she had said the words out loud or only in her head. Her voice was cracked and dry through lack of use. Suzanne was about to speak again, when the man stepped further into the light and she saw it: the tell-tale streak of white in his hair. Her breath caught in her throat. 'Are you going to kill me?'

He gave a half-smile. 'If I had been going to kill you, I would have done so eleven days ago.'

It was a soft voice, a gentle voice. And he was speaking in French.

'*Onze jours?*' she said, bewildered.

'You arrived with the New Year. It is now the twelfth day of January.'

Suzanne didn't understand. How could she have been lying in this bed for so long? She struggled to sit up, wanting to be at less of a disadvantage. The man took a step towards her to help, then stopped himself. She was grateful for that, though her arms struggled to take her weight.

'What happened to me?'

'You were bitten by a snake.'

Suzanne blinked, suddenly remembering the flash of speckled brown and white, the thick body, a black-forked tongue. The explosion of pain in her calf.

'A puff adder . . . how am I still alive?'

'It is a miracle that you are,' he replied. 'It was your boots that saved you. The leather prevented the fangs from piercing too deep, so very little poison got into your blood. You were lucky.'

She remembered: the nausea and chills, the dizziness and the sense of floating above her own body. Dreading what she might see, Suzanne lifted the sheet and looked down at her calf. She saw two puncture holes and raised red swelling around them, but her skin was otherwise cool. There was no infection, not like Harrie's wounds.

She smiled. Harrie, she remembered him. And Tia.

'My horse?' she said suddenly.

'Is being looked after.'

On a hook on the back of the door, she saw her riding cloak, her satchel and leather hat. Her other clothes were piled on a second chair beneath a shuttered window, with the boots that had saved her life beside it.

'You have been nursing me?'

The man gave a slight bow.

'Thank you,' she said quickly. He might have saved her, but for what purpose?

Finally, the man moved further into the room and sat down on a chair at some distance from the bed.

'Why are you here?' he asked and Suzanne heard genuine curiosity in his voice. 'In your delirium, you were speaking French, sometimes Dutch. You were talking about justice and women who were lost.'

Suzanne felt uneasy at the thought that she might have betrayed her intentions, but she saw no reason to hide her purpose now.

'I am searching for Louise,' she said simply.

He recoiled as if he had been struck. 'Louise . . .' he repeated the name.

'I thought you were Phillipe Vidal, but you are too young. I think you must be his son?'

'I am Théodore Barenton.' Then he gathered himself. 'More to the point, who are you?'

'Suzanne Joubert. Louise was my cousin. That's to say, my first cousin twice removed.'

For a few moments, he was silent, then he spoke quietly: 'You have the same eyes.'

Suzanne felt a spark of satisfaction. 'So, you did know her.' She paused. 'It is not possible she is still alive, but—'

'You need to rest,' he said abruptly. 'In the morning, we will talk.'

CHAPTER FIFTY

Olifantshoek Valley

The light was fading. It was that time of day when rider or horse might make a misjudgement, stumble or lose the pathway. Nevertheless, Adriaan van Dijk pressed forward, slapping his reins against the stallion's neck to encourage the weary animal to go faster.

Time was snapping at his heels. He tried to balance the common sense of Pierre Jaubert with his own instinct that something was terribly wrong. Though Suzanne's diversion to Drakenstein and Harrie's injuries explained the delay to her journey, Adriaan could still not account for the fact that Suzanne had failed to return to the Colony since then. And the information about the splinter Cochoqua group was disturbing.

During the summer, there had been increasing rumours that Kmame was attempting to oust his father with the intention of causing unrest between the Cochoqua and the settlers. Perhaps even to provoke a third Khoi-Dutch War. Adriaan thought that was a real threat – and had written reports for Commander Van der Stel on the subject. And he knew himself well enough to realise that he felt guilty at having left Suzanne in the care of Odendaal, even though it had been at her request.

Adriaan dug his heels harder into the horse's flank, determined to cover as much ground as possible before night fell. Though

Harrie and Tia had three days' advance on him, they were on foot. If he kept the pace up, he should catch them up by late afternoon tomorrow.

Harrie and Tia had undertaken to convert to Christianity when they started to work for the VOC. It was not mandatory, but those who became co-religionists received better terms of employment than those who did not. It made life easier. It was a matter of pragmatism not faith.

On the barren mountain pass, Harrie had said a Christian prayer over Khasso's body. Then, after a moment's hesitation, he had spoken more ancient words of praise to Tsui-Goab, the supreme creator revered by his Khoi ancestors. He and Tia had covered Khasso's body with rocks to keep predators at bay – a pointless exercise, in truth – and fashioned a wooden cross from two sticks to put at the guide's head.

As darkness had fallen, Harrie and Tia had taken shelter. Leopards mostly hunted at night, particularly in the days of summer heat, and were a danger here. Harrie could just see the imposing blackness of the highest peak they still had to cross. Silently, he prayed that Kmame and his men were not there waiting to ambush any travellers who might come this way. Once through the mountains, they would have a better view over the plain and would be less vulnerable.

Harrie put his arm around his sister's shoulder and felt her grow heavy against him as she fell into sleep. He was resolved to stay awake, keeping watch, his eyes anxiously scanning the dark horizon as he waited for dawn to come.

Adriaan stretched his arms and shoulders, stiff from sleeping on the hard ground. He had never ridden into these mountains before and the vista in this early morning was magnificent.

From his vantage point, he could see all the way down over the Olifantshoek valley.

The beauty of the day lifted his spirits. The grey and red rocks seemed to gleam in the gentle sunlight, as if they had been polished. In the air, the whistles and warbling of red-wing starlings were singing against a sky as blue as the first day on earth.

'God's creation,' he said out loud, wishing Judith were here to share it with him.

Adriaan could see Pierre Jaubert was right. This would be a far better place to settle and to plant vines. Everything was lush and fertile, fed by the tributary from the Berg River. Whoever had allocated the land for the refugees in Drakenstein could not possibly have visited the place in person, or known anything about farming.

Then in the far distance, he saw something moving. Instantly, his senses were on the alert. Animal or human, he could not tell from this far away. Adriaan took out his eyeglass. He could pick out two people in the landscape. On foot, but moving fast. Fearing it might be an advance party sent by Kmame, he adjusted the scope and narrowed his eyes. Now he thought he could discern white shirts and breeches, rather than Khoi capes. He looked again, to be sure, then exhaled with relief.

Harrie and Tia. He had found them.

Then, out of the corner of his eye, he saw something else moving. A knot of men, breaking cover and running from behind towards the brother and sister with spears poised at their shoulders.

Kmame and three of his men?

'*Let op!*' he shouted, trying to attract their attention. Watch out.

But he was too far distant and his warning spiralled unheard up into the air. He shouted again, then pulled his flintlock pistol from his belt, squeezed his finger and thumb, and fired.

For a moment, time seemed to stand still. Adriaan heard the clicking of the wheel, felt the tension of the mainspring, saw the sharp white-hot sparks of the fool's gold as the pyrite hissed and the bullet left the pistol. He had no hope of hitting a target, but surely Harrie and Tia would hear the retort? It might buy them a little time.

Hearing the shot, Tia and Harrie both spun round. Tia screamed and threw herself at her brother just in time as a spear came whistling through the air. It hammered into the ground, sending up a puff of earth. Harrie yanked it free, and started running.

'Head for the trees,' he shouted.

There were four of them. He and Tia had no chance out in the open, but if they could get into the cover of the wood, then perhaps they could evade their attackers.

Tia kept pace with him. At their back, he recognised Kmame's voice shouting an order. Moments later, Harrie felt the same rush of air and the heavy thud of another spear which impaled itself in the trunk of a tree, sending fragments of wood splintering. Tia felt something sharp slice into her arm, and she cried out, but did not falter.

Then, another shot from the gun. Behind them, Harrie heard another of the Cochoqua shout. Still running, he twisted to look over his shoulder and saw one of Kmame's followers was down. Another shot, and a second warrior was hit in the back and fell forward.

'Who is helping us?' Tia shouted.

'Don't look back,' he yelled in reply. 'Run! Keep running.'

*

Adriaan was exhilarated. Two men down, two to go. If Harrie and his sister could stay out of Kmame's reach, then all might yet be well.

He stretched out his arm wide, holding the flintlock pistol well away from his horse's head, and fired again. He could get off three or four rounds before he had to reload.

This time his bullet went wide. His stallion reared. Adriaan dragged the reins savagely to the right, avoiding the spear flying through the air towards the animal's flank by a hair's breadth. He hung on, only just keeping his seat, circling the horse around until he had regained his balance.

'It's all right, it's all right.'

But when he had calmed the horse and looked up, he saw to his horror that Kmame and the remaining warrior were gaining on Harrie and Tia.

'Only a little bit further,' he said in an urgent whisper, as if Harrie and Tia could hear him. He only needed one more clear shot. If he could kill Kmame, the other man would surely surrender.

'Harrie, here!' Tia cried, pointing to the hollowed-out trunk of a tree.

He shook his head. 'No, we need to be higher. Their spears will be less effective if we are above them.'

They kept sprinting over the ground, never losing pace, breath burning in their chests. Tia could no longer feel any pain from her arm, but her shirt sleeve was damp and she could feel the blood trickling down to the inside of her wrist.

She spied a white stinkwood. The branches were low, but it had its summer foliage and there was plenty of cover at the top of the tree. Closing her eyes to the pain, Tia grasped hold of the lowest branch and swung herself up, with Harrie pushing from below. She looked up at the branches towering above her, then started to climb.

'Harrie, come on,' she cried, then suddenly realised what her brother intended to do.

Kmame and his lieutenant had entered the wood. From her vantage point, she could see them scanning left and right, looking for the path they had taken.

'No,' she whispered, now hidden in the leaves, as her brother ran away from the tree, ready to fight.

'Come on, come on,' Adriaan panted, urging his horse forward.

Kmame had entered the wood. Adriaan knew it would be harder to navigate the animal through the thicket and get a clear shot.

He went as far as he could, then dismounted, landing on the ground with both feet. He checked his gunpowder and primed the pistol again, then started to move forward through the trees. His blood was pounding in his ears but, over the sound of it, he could hear the occasional snap of a twig ahead.

Finding a gap between the trees, Adriaan suddenly saw them, like a painted tableau: Kmame standing with his spear raised, Harrie ahead of him with his spear in his hand, the other warrior circling behind. Of Tia, there was no sign.

Adriaan crept forward, knowing he had only a split second.

'*Verrader*,' Kmame spat. Collaborator.

The warrior pulled back his arm ready to throw, as Adriaan pressed his finger and thumb together, and fired. The bullet flew through the air and hit him in the chest. Blood bubbled from the man's mouth, his limbs twitched, then he fell still as Harrie and Kmame both threw their spears. Kmame's glanced Harrie's shoulder, causing Harrie's own shot to go wide. Adriaan took aim again and fired. Kmame threw himself sideways, then scrambled to his feet and ran into the woods. Harrie tried to give chase, but was losing too much blood.

'He's gone,' Harrie panted, then dropped to his knees.

Adriaan lowered his gun, suddenly spent. Never before had he killed a man. Today, he had taken three lives. He closed his eyes and prayed for God's forgiveness.

CHAPTER FIFTY-ONE

OLIFANTSHOEK
Thursday, 13th January

Suzanne realised two things: first, that she was hungry. Second, that a china bowl and jug had appeared on the table. Tentatively, she swung her feet to the ground and tried to stand up. A wave of dizziness sent her falling back to the bed. But she was determined to get dressed.

Like someone finding their sea legs for the first time, Suzanne slowly made her way across the room to the table. She reached out her hand for the back of the chair and sank down onto it to catch her breath. Grateful for Théodore's thoughtfulness, she poured water from the jug into the bowl and, using the hem of her nightshirt as a sponge, began to wash. Only now did she realise she was wearing a man's shirt and blushed: Théodore must have undressed her when she first arrived.

Suzanne washed her face and neck. She had a comb in her satchel, so she could brush out the worst of the knots in her hair. Soon she felt a little more like herself. Still light-headed, she exchanged the man's shirt for her own clothes, fumbling over the hooks and eyes. She examined the puncture marks on her calf, two black spots where the fangs had managed to pierce the skin, but there was little redness or swelling there now.

Suzanne left her boots where they stood. It was already too hot to wear them and she didn't want to aggravate the wound. Then, taking her satchel from the back of the door, she went to find Théodore. She was ready to rejoin the land of the living.

Straight away, she sensed that the house was empty. There was that feeling of stilled air, suspended, as if waiting for people to come to bring it back to life. Suzanne was both disappointed and a little relieved.

She found she was standing in a large single room that served as both kitchen and living space. There were two doors leading to the outside, one at the back and the other at the front, flanked by two large windows. The window shutters were pulled to, but unlatched.

In the middle stood a large wooden table with four chairs set around it, a dresser to the side on which hung several iron pots and cooking utensils. There was a stone fireplace and chimney, with a black pot hanging over the ashes. It was far more comfortable than any of the Huguenot farmsteads she had visited. A larder filled with shelves containing dried herbs, a loaf of bread and a covered plate of dried meat, had a small hatch that gave directly to the air outside for ventilation.

On the far side of the kitchen, opposite her room, was another door. It was ajar, so Suzanne quickly peeked in and saw a second sleeping chamber, the mirror of her own. She wrinkled her nose. Unmistakably it was a man's room, smelling of sweat and leather. It was empty.

Making her way back through the kitchen, she went to the front door, lifted the latch and walked into the world. She had only seen the farmhouse from her vantage point on the hill whilst staking out the farm and blushed to think of how alarming her behaviour now seemed. Without knowing anything about her, Théodore had cared for her – a stranger – and nursed her back to life. How could she admit that she had come prepared to shoot him, perhaps even to kill him? It seemed absurd now.

Suzanne shook her head. She had to trust that she would know what to say when the time came. He knew Louise, his reaction had told her that, and he carried Gilles' family name: Barenton. She had to be bold. She would ask him his story and she would tell him hers.

She stepped out from the shadow of the house and looked around, then murmured in delight when she saw her mare tethered comfortably in an enclosure with another horse.

'*Ma belle!*' she cooed, caressing her neck. She was delighted to see her coat was shining and her eyes bright. She had been well cared for while her own life had hung in the balance.

Suzanne gave the mare a final pat, then she continued exploring the rest of the farmstead. A wooden kraal for livestock stood nearby – sheep by the looks of the droppings on the ground – and three straw-thatched huts. Most impressive was the vegetable garden. Enclosed by thorn trees to protect against scavengers, it was much smaller than the VOC gardens in the Colony, but contained many of the same fruits and vegetables. Not everything was in season, but Suzanne could see cabbage, watermelon, broccoli growing. No doubt, turnips, carrots, beetroot, cauliflower and radish would come. Most surprising of all were the rows of vines stretched on the slope behind the kraal in neat rows.

There were also peach and pear trees growing against the north-facing wall of the house, as well as quince and cherry. As she walked, Suzanne realised that even though Théodore lived here alone, so far from anywhere, he must have traded regularly with VOC and foreign merchants to have created such a garden.

'You are up.'

Suzanne started at the sound of Théodore's voice behind her. He had come from the direction of the woods and was carrying a wicker basket full of branches, and an axe.

'Good morning.' She smiled, feeling strangely shy. 'I am feeling much better.'

He did not return her smile and it seemed to her there was now a wariness in his eyes.

'It is beautiful here,' she said, confused by his change of mood.

'It is,' he said coldly. 'Are you hungry?'

'I find I do have an appetite this morning, yes.'

'In which case, I will prepare some food. And then you will tell me what you are really doing here, Mademoiselle Joubert.'

It was as if the sun had suddenly gone behind the clouds. The brightness of the day faded and Suzanne suddenly felt the precariousness of her situation.

'Of course,' she said, raising her chin. 'I would be glad to, Monsieur Barenton.'

Suddenly, behind them, there was a sound of shouting coming from the woods. She turned to see two San dragging a third man between them.

'We have him!' one of them shouted.

Suzanne looked at Théodore. 'What's happening?'

Théodore fixed her with a stare. 'I was rather expecting you to tell me. My men brought me a report that there was someone on my land. A man known to be a criminal and it seems you brought him here. You came here with a guide, did you not? You talked about it in your fever.'

'But why would—' Then she turned cold as the three men entered the compound. 'Kmame . . .'

'So, you do know him.'

'No, I, at least— It is not what you think.'

He pointed to one of the huts. 'Take him in there and secure him. I will speak to him presently.'

'Théodore, please.'

Now Suzanne felt his hand on her arm and he steered her back towards the house.

'Time to talk,' he said, and now there was no warmth in his voice whatsoever.

CHAPTER FIFTY-TWO

Leading his horse by the reins, Adriaan looked down over the Olifantshoek Valley, shining green in the early morning light.

'Where is he hiding her?' Tia asked again.

After the skirmish with Kmame and his men, Adriaan, Tia and Harrie had spent the hours of darkness recovering in the woods. Adriaan had heard animals feasting on the bodies of the men he had killed and their souls pressed heavily on his conscience. But the night had passed peacefully. The wound on Tia's arm was not deep, and Kmame's spear had only grazed Harrie's shoulder. They had taken it in turns to keep watch until dawn.

Now they were out of the cover of the trees.

'We don't know for sure that he does have her,' Adriaan replied.

Tia gave a scornful laugh. 'He killed her guide and she is missing, what other explanation is there?'

'We will continue to Olifantshoek,' he said steadily. 'See if we can find the man *juffrouw* Joubert was seeking.'

'And what if Kmame is waiting for us with more men, what then?'

'Sister,' Harrie warned.

Adriaan could see he was nervous for Tia. They might have fought side by side the previous day, but Harrie knew better than to assume friendship with a VOC official. He suspected Harrie believed that the Dutch, for all their talk, never let the Khoi forget who was in charge.

'Well, sir?' She spoke with a challenge in her voice.

'Tia!' her brother said sharply. 'Guard your tongue!'

'We will face that challenge if, and when, it happens,' Adriaan replied calmly. Tia had a point. Harrie had told him that Kmame had had three men with him at the Cochoqua encampment, as he had yesterday. But that didn't mean that he didn't have other allies or fighters elsewhere.

Tia's eyes glinted. She said nothing more, but the way in which she stamped out the fire left Adriaan in no doubt that she thought men were fools.

'Do you know where in Olifantshoek this farmstead might be found?' Harrie asked.

Adriaan shook his head. 'No more than when I hired you in Stellenbosch.'

Harrie crouched down, examining the ground. 'It looks as if a person has passed this way. Kmame, perhaps? He was the only one to escape your gun, sir. We should follow, in case my sister is right.'

Adriaan took out his eyeglass and scanned the horizon. There were no signs of human habitation. He looked down at the faint marks in the grass, the blades flattened, imagining Kmame's running feet bruising the ground. He nodded. It was as good a plan as any.

It was downhill all the way and they made good time, Adriaan riding at a steady trot, with Tia and Harrie running beside. Once they reached the river, they stopped to take stock. It was likely any farm buildings would have been built close to the water. The question was should they go upstream, or down?

Harrie pointed to a pile of human excrement, partly covered by leaves. 'Kmame – or someone – was here.'

'What do you advise?' Adriaan asked.

Harrie did not answer, but continued to examine the

surroundings. Shortly, Tia and Adriaan watched him wade knee-deep across the fast-running river and examine the opposite bank. Then he straightened up and beckoned for them to join him. Adriaan mounted his horse to save his boots and Tia tucked up her skirts.

'There are footprints here, do you see?' Harrie said, pointing to where the grass and mud met on the far side of the water. 'More than one pair.'

'You think Kmame found an ally here?' Adriaan asked.

'I cannot say, only that three men were here and they walked in that direction.' He pointed south. 'The prints are not clear once they leave the banks. The ground there is too dry for tracks.'

Adriaan nodded. 'We will go the same way. But we should be on our guard. We might be heading into an ambush.'

Théodore fetched a tray of pears from the sill and put them on the table, together with a loaf and a bowl of dripping. He laid out two cups and two plates, brought a jug of wine, then sat down.

He watched Suzanne eat, then, unexpectedly, he laughed. Did that mean he believed her that Kmame was an enemy not an ally?

'Well,' he said, 'let me hear this story of yours. But tell me the truth, mind. I shall know if you are lying.'

Suzanne looked him the eye. 'I am not accustomed to lying, monsieur, I have no need to do so. As I told you, the man you found trespassing on your land is no friend of mine. His name is Kmame, he is the leader of a splinter group of the Cochoqua.'

Théodore narrowed his eyes. 'I have heard of him. The Khoi say he is attempting to overthrow his father.'

'He has already done so,' Suzanne said, then stopped. 'You speak their language?'

'I do.'

Suzanne put her thoughts in order, then recounted everything that had happened after she and Harrie had talked to Shansi in the Cochoqua encampment. All the time she was talking, she watched Théodore's reactions closely and saw that Shansi's name meant nothing to him.

'So Kmame followed you here?' he said. 'Why?'

'You could ask him.'

Théodore was frowning, still clearly struggling to believe her story. It sounded outlandish that two women and a man would have stood firm against Kmame and three warriors.

'I know it sounds unbelievable,' she said, 'but we had no choice. We could not afford to lose the horse and, well, there were things of great personal importance to me in the satchel.' Suzanne stopped. The moment had perhaps come to begin the conversation that had brought her here in the first place. 'The reason we were there was to speak to Shansi, whose mother, Fala, was a wise woman. She told us that, many years ago, Fala had delivered a baby to a white settler.' She saw him stiffen. 'I think you were that child,' she finished gently, not wanting to provoke him to anger again.

Théodore was silent for so long, that she wondered if he had even heard her.

'I never knew her name,' he began. 'But my mother talked of a Khoi woman who had helped them.'

Suzanne leant forward. 'Louise kept a diary,' she said. 'She started writing it when she was imprisoned, and continued it as a record of her life at sea. I know that all the men of the Vidal family have this white streak in their hair. As you do. Which means, I think, that you are the son of Phillipe Vidal, who sailed to the Cape with my ancestor Louise on the *Old Moon*.'

Suzanne saw a look of revulsion cross his face. 'That is correct.'

She was acutely aware of the silence in the kitchen. She knew she had to tread carefully, and yet she felt she could do nothing more than ask the questions she had carried with her like a burden for so long.

'Monsieur?' she said, when he still did not speak. 'Théodore?'

'Forgive me,' he said, 'I never expected this day to come.'

She nodded, wanting to give him time. 'What I do not understand is this. Shansi said her mother told her there were two women present at the birth, Louise and another. But there was never any mention of another woman in her diary. The only person Louise writes about, save Phillipe, is Gilles Barenton.' She held his gaze. 'You bear his name.'

Théodore's face softened. 'I do.'

'Why?'

He did not answer. Suzanne shook her head.

'I don't understand. You admit Phillipe was your father. Who was your mother, if not Louise?'

Théodore gave a long sigh, as if ridding himself of a lifetime of secrets inside him.

'Gilles Barenton was my mother. And I loved him.'

'There,' Tia shouted, pointing.

Adriaan followed the line of her gaze. In the distance, he could see the outline of a house. A thatched roof, a more permanent structure than the huts built by the Khoi as they made their way across the veldt.

This surely had to be the farmstead Lars Eltorp had talked about? Who else would be living here, so far from civilisation? *Our* civilisation, he corrected himself, imagining how Suzanne would remind him how the Khoi and the San had lived here for millennia. He felt a sudden knot in his chest. What if she was dead? What if Kmame had murdered her, as he had murdered Khasso? How would he ever tell Judith?

'What do you want to do, sir?' Harrie asked. 'Do you think they are there?'

Adriaan shook his head. 'I don't know.' He looked down over the valley. There was no possibility of approaching unseen. The land was too open. If Kmame had other men and had taken the farm, if they were holding Suzanne there, then he, Harrie and Tia needed to wait until cover of darkness to make a move. To do anything else would risk not only their own lives, but also Suzanne's.

'We will wait until nightfall,' he said, 'then attack while they are sleeping.'

Overhead, they heard the first ominous rumbles of thunder.

CHAPTER FIFTY-THREE

Olifantshoek

'Gilles Barenton was your mother? But how is that possible . . .'

Suzanne stopped, words now failing her. Théodore was looking at her with a mixture of sympathy and, she thought, something approaching affection.

'What you are saying makes no sense,' she said, trying again. 'In her diary, Louise wrote of her affection for Gilles, of their . . .' Again, she tailed off.

'All of that was true,' he said. 'Theirs was a love match.'

'So, help me to understand!'

Théodore walked across the kitchen and pushed open the shutter, letting a shaft of subdued light into the grey-shadowed room.

'I grew up hearing stories about Louise,' Suzanne said tentatively, when still he did not speak. 'My grandmother remembers Louise from when she was a child – but it was only when we arrived in Amsterdam last October, and I read her diary for the first time, that she suddenly came to life for me. After that, I read everything else kept in our old family home – my great-great-grandmother Minou's journals . . .'

'Ah, Minou,' Théodore said warmly. 'Louise often talked about her.'

Suzanne smiled, relieved that he was finally engaging in the conversation.

'Also, I read records kept by Minou's sister, Alis, and her

companion, Cornelia van Raay, and pieced together more of Louise's story. It helped me forget . . .' She stopped herself, changed tack. 'It was Cornelia's house in Warmoesstraat where the archives were kept. She and Alis loved Louise, too.'

Outside, she heard a rumble of thunder behind the mountains. Storms clouds were gathering, masking the face of the sun.

'As did I,' Théodore said. 'She and Gilles, they chose to live a wild and different life.'

'From the rumours I have heard since arriving in the Colony, they succeeded.'

'Mostly, yes.'

Suzanne looked at him, trying to understand. 'Have you lived here your whole life?'

'For all of my sixty-five years on this earth. This farm is very close to the original patch of land granted to Louise by an old Goringhaiqua headsman when they first arrived.'

'Which they were forced to abandon after their whereabouts were betrayed, isn't that right?'

Théodore topped up his wine and sighed. 'You have discovered a great deal.'

Suzanne blushed, feeling strangely guilty. 'What I do know – at least, what I *think* I know – is that Louise and Gilles, for whatever reason, were trying to get away from Phillipe. Your father.' She looked him in the eye. 'Is that true, Théodore? Do you know what happened between the three of them?'

He put down his cup. 'You have to understand that much of what took place – I was only told long after the events in question.'

'I understand.'

Théodore took a deep breath. 'Although he lived his life as a man, Gilles was born a woman.'

'What?' the word exploded out of her. 'How can that be?'

'Gilles' mother, who was a vile and debauched creature, forced him to dress as a boy from the age of ten, to gain an inheritance from his uncle. This was in La Rochelle in the summer of 1610.'

Now he had started, the words came easily enough. The story was fantastical, astonishing, devastating in parts, but yet she found she had no trouble believing it. It was as if she had spent days looking at the wrong side of a tapestry, all the colours and threads entangled, obscuring her view, but had now walked round to the other side and seen the image as it was supposed to be seen.

Théodore started to pace around the kitchen. 'Tell me something of your life, Suzanne,' he said, and she realised he was still not quite ready to talk about what had happened on the day Phillipe found Louise and Gilles again. 'Why did you leave La Rochelle?'

She took a breath. 'We lived in Louise's house. She left it to my great-grandfather when she sailed for Gran Canaria.'

Théodore smiled. 'Gilles talked often about the grand house on the rue des Gentilhommes.'

'Things are different now. In their time, La Rochelle was the Huguenot capital of France. Its glory has faded and people of my faith are no longer safe there. Or anywhere. We have all been driven into exile – to Holland or England, Germany or the New World – or made prisoners in our own homes by the *dragonnades*, soldiers who—'

Suzanne broke off.

'Something happened to you,' he probed gently, a statement rather than a question.

'Yes,' she said. It was painful to talk about, but she wanted him to understand how her quest to find Louise was tied up with what had been done to her.

'I am so sorry,' he said, when she had finished.

'It is a common story. Others have suffered just as much, sometimes much more.'

'That doesn't make your experience any the less terrible.'

In the west, the sun was slipping from the sky. Suzanne heard another rumble of thunder, closer now. All the same, she felt calm. Somehow, in these five months, the burden had lifted from her shoulders. What had happened that night – her rape, she could name it now – did not define her. It was one incident, traumatic and violent, but she would refuse to give it more weight than any other experience of her twenty years on the earth.

'What are you thinking?' Théodore asked, noticing the altered expression on her face.

'About being whole again,' she replied, with a catch in her voice. 'About the possibility of beginning anew.'

'Here?'

She shook her head. 'I understand, now, that it lies within me to heal myself. It is not distance that makes the difference, but my own courage.'

Théodore got up, walked to the door and pushed it open to let in a little air. 'You have spoken plainly with me, Suzanne.'

'I have tried to.'

'I owe to you the same honesty. You want to know what happened between Louise, Gilles and Phillipe – how I come to be here?'

'Yes,' she replied simply.

She saw the anguish on his face. 'The fact of the matter is that it is hard for me to speak of it. Indeed, I never have.'

Outside, Suzanne could see how the clouds had turned from grey to black, and were now covering the top of the mountains. There was another cascade of thunder and the first spots of rain started to fall. And Théodore began the hardest part of his story.

'When you were attacked in your home, there was no child?'

Suzanne shook her head. 'That, at least, I was spared.' Then, she turned cold. 'You were conceived – you are the result of . . .' She found she could not say the word out loud.

'A rape, yes.'

'Théodore, I . . . I don't know what to say.'

He sighed. 'I did not learn this until I was an adult, you understand. I knew nothing but love from Louise and from Gilles.'

'Why would Phillipe do something so heinous?'

He held up his hand. 'To make sense of it, we have to go back to the beginning. As you know, Louise and Gilles dropped anchor in Table Bay on the seventh day of May in the year 1622 . . .'

When Théodore had finished talking, Suzanne sat in silence. She hardly knew what to say, how to express what she was feeling. Everything she had imagined was wrong but, at the same time, her instincts had been right.

'I feared that Phillipe had killed Louise, not the other way around,' she said eventually. 'I never imagined . . .'

Théodore's eyes dimmed. 'He was a wicked man, and I regret with every sinew of my body that he was my father.'

She exhaled. 'Thank you for telling me the truth. It cannot have been easy.'

He gave an exhausted smile. 'It was easier than I thought it might be. Given what you have suffered, I thought you would understand.'

Suzanne took Louise's prison diary from her satchel and pushed it across the table to him. 'When I found this in the archive in Warmoesstraat, it became the focus of my determination to find Louise.'

Théodore stared at the leather cover as if he was scared to touch it.

'There is also this,' she added, taking out the Justice card. 'I don't know why it was so important to Louise, nor why she kept it. She never struck me as a superstitious woman, but it must have meant something for her to have gone to such lengths to preserve it.'

Théodore's weather-worn face lit up. 'It did mean something, but not to Louise. It belonged to Gilles. It was the only thing he possessed from his younger life in La Rochelle.'

Suzanne passed it across the table. 'You should have it. It rightly belongs to you.'

He smiled. 'The card meant a lot to him. To them both, the ideal of justice. It is what they fought for all of their lives.'

Suzanne watched as Théodore went into his bedchamber, then returned moments later with a book with plain brown boards, like a child's school jotter.

'Louise continued to keep a diary of our lives here,' he said. 'It was the reason I accompanied Gilles to Table Bay from time to time, to trade furs and timber for the paper and ink the ships brought back from China.'

He put it into her hands, then went to the door.

'Where are you going?'

'To give you time to read this. While you do so, I will check on the animals and pay a visit to our house guest. The storm is nearly upon us.'

'There he is,' Harrie said, pointing as a white man came out of the farmhouse.

Adriaan, Tia and Harrie watched him head first to the animal pen to check on the sheep, then to lead the horses from the kraal to a shelter behind the house. This had to be the man Eltorp had met near Stellenbosch several weeks before.

'He knows the storm is coming,' Tia said, as a roll of thunder echoed overhead.

The man then headed to the nearest hut. Adriaan watched the two San get to their feet, then all three went inside. Moments later, they came out with another man between them.

'Is that Kmame?' Adriaan asked.

'That is him,' Tia hissed behind him.

Adriaan was failing to understand the relationship between the four men. They had been working on the assumption that Kmame had more warriors at his command and that he had kidnapped Suzanne. Tia was certain that was what had happened. Now Adriaan wasn't so sure. Kmame was holding his hands behind his back. He couldn't tell if they were bound there or if it was simply how he was standing. Might he be a prisoner rather than captor? And what of the white man? Adriaan knew Suzanne had been convinced that he was someone connected to Louise, but had not made it clear if she thought he was someone she could trust. Perhaps it was he, rather than Kmame, who had kidnapped Suzanne to ransom for a reward?

If she was there at all.

Suddenly, a huge fork of lightning split the grey sky and thunder erupted almost directly over their heads. Rain started to fall: furious, torrential, blinding.

Kmame took advantage of the diversion and started to shout. There was an altercation between him and the white man, who turned his back and started to walk towards the house. He had nearly reached the door, when there was another clap of thunder.

Then chaos broke loose.

Kmame screamed at the top of his voice, a battle cry to chill the blood, then swung round with what looked like a rock in his hand. He smashed it once, then again, into the face of the San warrior closest to him, who fell to the ground without a sound. The other guard readied his spear, but he was too slow. Kmame delivered a ferocious blow to the side of his head. He bought the rock down on the back of his neck until the second San also lay motionless in the dirt.

All this had taken no more than seconds.

The white man was running back to confront him, but Kmame grabbed the spear of one of the fallen San.

'Stop him!' Adriaan shouted at the top of his voice.

Harrie instantly broke cover, racing down towards the farm, slipping and sliding in the mud. Adriaan followed, his pistol in hand but, in the driving rain, he couldn't get a clear shot.

Then, to his amazement, he saw Suzanne standing in the doorway of the farmhouse with her musket in her hand. Adriaan saw Kmame pull back his arm and aim the spear directly towards the white man, who threw himself to the ground as the iron point whistled past his ear. Harrie burst into the compound and tried to reach Kmame, who now had the second spear in his hand.

Then, he saw white smoke and the explosion as the ball left the muzzle of the gun. Suzanne's aim was true. Kmame's body was thrown back by the impact and fell, bleeding red into the dirt. His legs twitched, his feet tracing patterns on the drowning land, then nothing.

Adriaan watched Suzanne slowly lower her arm. Then, as carefully as if she was releasing a child, she put the musket down on the ground. The white man pulled himself to his feet, then he opened his arms as Suzanne ran to embrace him. They stood there for a moment, drenched by the driving rain, then stepped apart.

'Miss!' screamed Tia, hurtling past her brother and throwing herself at Suzanne. 'You're alive!'

Suzanne was in shock. She seemed barely to notice the rain pelting down upon their heads.

'Adriaan, may I present Théodore Barenton to you,' she said, as if they were at a reception at the Commander's residence. 'He is a distant cousin of sorts. His father was Louise's half-brother, though what relation that makes us to one another, I cannot say.'

'Suzanne, are you . . .?' he began.

'Théodore,' she continued in a daze, 'this is Adriaan van Dijk, the husband of my dearest friend in the Colony. It is he who taught me how to shoot on the sand dunes at Gallow's Hill.'

The two men looked at one another, then Théodore put out his hand. 'In which case, *mijnheer* Van Dijk, I am very much in your debt.'

Finally, Suzanne's composure cracked. She began to laugh until the tears mixed with the rain on her cheeks.

CHAPTER FIFTY-FOUR

Friday, 14th January

In accordance with tradition, Tia and Harrie cleaned the bodies of the two fallen San and buried them that same evening. Suzanne, worn out by everything that had happened, sat silently with Adriaan, while Théodore prepared a meal for them all.

'Théodore's mother—' she started to explain, then stopped. It was all too complicated and too shocking. She realised she wanted to keep all that she had learnt close to her heart until she had absorbed it properly herself. She found a safer topic of conversation. 'Gilles Barenton was brought up by his uncle, who was a vintner in La Rochelle, and he passed on that skill to Théodore. Given the interest Commander Van der Stel has in cultivating vines, Adriaan, you will find his success interesting. Théodore's vineyard rivals what the Company has achieved in the Colony. Would you like to see it?'

Adriaan nodded. 'If Monsieur Barenton would be kind enough to show me, I would.'

Théodore lit a lantern and they walked out into the soft night. Everywhere smelt fresh and clean. Suzanne said little, but listened as the two men fell into an easy discussion about irrigation and crop yield. The details did not interest her, and both her mind and her body were exhausted. But she thought the wine Théodore was producing was as good as anything that might grace a table in La Rochelle and hoped that, by piquing Adriaan's interest, she might help Pierre and Isabeau Jaubert and their fellow refugees.

'What do you call your farm?' Adriaan asked as they returned to the main house.

Théodore hesitated. 'It has never needed a name. We made wine for our own table, nothing more. But perhaps it should.' He looked at Suzanne. 'What about La Justice. Do you approve?'

She smiled. 'I cannot think of a more fitting name.'

'Very well.' Théodore nodded. 'Are you coming in?'

'If you might give me a moment with Suzanne,' Adriaan said.

Suzanne looked at him. All evening, she had felt him darting anxious looks at her. And his relief at finding her alive and unharmed was clearly tempered by some other consideration. Then, suddenly, she knew what he was going to say.

'Sister, I do not know how to tell you this, when you have been through so much,' he began, 'but Florence—'

Suzanne put her hand on his arm. 'It is all right. I saw her in my dreams, standing side by side with Louise and Minou. She is at peace now.'

They remained with Théodore for a few days. Suzanne was still not back to full strength and Tia's arm needed time to heal.

Suzanne and Théodore talked most of the time, as he went about the chores on the farm. She read Louise's Olifantshoek diary detailing their arrival in the Cape and their lives on the farm. For his part, Théodore asked many questions about La Rochelle and Amsterdam, about her experiences in the Colony.

By and by, Suzanne felt strong enough to leave. Early one morning, holding a bouquet of wild flowers, she walked to the small planted copse of oak saplings behind the farmhouse. Théodore had offered to accompany her, but she wanted to make this last pilgrimage alone. It would be her final act of remembrance for Louise, and for Gilles, on African soil.

With the peaks of the Olifantshoek mountains behind it, Suzanne found the glade easily enough. In the centre was a small sign made out of yellow-wood beneath a spreading aloe tree. The inscription on the board was plain: carved, she knew, by Gilles, showing simply the dates of Louise's birth and death. Beneath that, three words in block capitals:

CAPTAIN AND COMMANDER

Lower still, inscribed by a different hand, Gilles' name and dates had been added a decade later: Just one word underneath in the same block capitals: BELOVED.

Suzanne lingered a while, thinking of the love Louise and Gilles had found and fought for, the love that had held them fast for all of their lives. And she thought of their son living his solitary life in the valley where they had made their home. All in all, despite the hardships and the tragedies, it was a good life.

She bent down and laid her flowers on the grave. She would never again stand here, but that didn't mean her quest had failed. Far from it. She was ready to let Louise go. She had discovered what she needed to know and had laid her ghost to rest. Her own demons, too. Now, after all the words that had been written and spoken and imagined, there was only one word left to say.

'Goodbye,' she whispered.

Wednesday, 19th January

On Wednesday, the nineteenth of January, Suzanne, Adriaan, Harrie and Tia took their leave of Olifantshoek. Théodore had provided a horse for Harrie and Tia to ride as far as Stellenbosch, saying that he would collect the animal from there when next he ventured west. The travellers should be back in the Colony before the Sabbath.

'Are you certain you will not come with us?' Suzanne asked.

Théodore shook his head. 'I am content here. I am not made for the city.' He turned to Adriaan. 'But you will always be a welcome visitor, *mijnheer*.' He nodded to Tia and Harrie. 'As will you.'

'And you in the Colony, Monsieur Barenton, should we ever persuade you to venture so far,' Adriaan replied. 'My wife would be pleased to make your acquaintance. Perhaps I might seek your further advice on the land here for the refugees to farm?'

Suzanne rested her hand on Théodore's arm. 'And you are quite sure that you do not want me to leave this with you?' She had spent the past days copying out Louise's Olifantshoek writings, and had offered to leave Louise's diary from the *Old Moon* with him. It seemed to her that they all belonged together.

'You are kind, but no. Louise did not intend for it to remain here, given she sent it back to Amsterdam with her ship.' Théodore held up the Tarot card between his thumb and forefinger. 'This is enough for me.'

'La Justice,' Suzanne said and smiled, taking in the surroundings with a final look. 'The first wine farm in Olifantshoek.'

CHAPTER FIFTY-FIVE

THE CAPE COLONY
Sunday, 20th March 1689

Eight weeks after returning to the Colony – and precisely one year to the day that the *China* had left Rotterdam bound for the Cape of Good Hope – Suzanne Joubert was ready to depart. Her friends were waiting to see her off. She was sad to be leaving those she had come to love, but she would carry them with her in her heart. Both the living and the dead.

It was not the end of the story but a beginning.

It was a beautiful autumn day, warm and tempered with a light breeze, so unlike the day of their arrival in the Colony. Out in the bay a *spiegelretourschip*, the *Gouw*, under the command of captain Joost Barend, was preparing to return to Amsterdam. The *Gouw* had come from the East Indies via Batavia, loaded with cloves, nutmeg, anise and cinnamon to be auctioned in Dutch markets. Once her last passengers had embarked, she would sail.

'Do you have everything?' Judith asked for the hundredth time.

Suzanne laughed and took her hands, taking delight in the full swell of her friend's belly.

'You promise me that you will write and let me know when you are safely delivered? Send letters via the next ship. Girl or boy, one thing is for certain, he will have his father's wonderful blue eyes.' She turned to Madame Lombard. 'I am relying on you to take good care of them. And Isabeau Jaubert, if you could ever be persuaded to travel outside the Colony to see her. She is due at much the same time as Judith.'

Madame Lombard grunted, her sharp eyes glistening. 'You can trust me, child. And to tend your grandmother's grave.'

Suzanne bowed her head. 'I am grateful to know she will not lie forgotten in the ground.'

Finally, she turned to Adriaan. In many ways, he was the person she would miss the most. 'You have been like the brother I never had,' she said, emotion catching in her throat. 'I can never thank you enough for all that you have done for me. And remember, Théodore Barenton is a good man. He can help you.'

'We will miss you,' Adriaan said, then turned away, so she should not see the dew in his eyes. She heard him clear his throat, then he slapped Harrie on the shoulder. 'Harrie has agreed to come to work for me, did you know? And Tia will be a companion to Judith.'

'I think it a marvellous idea. When I am lonely, I will think of you all together and that will give me comfort.' She held out her hand. 'Thank you, Harrie, for everything.'

'The honour has been mine.'

Tia stepped forward, then her composure broke and she threw her arms around Suzanne's waist.

'Come, come, this will not do,' Suzanne said softly. 'You need to care for *mevrouw* Van Dijk now. She needs you more than I.'

Tia wiped her eyes. 'I know, miss, but—'

'You will be always in my heart.'

Slowly, Suzanne turned to face the vista that had first welcomed her, seeing it now through altered eyes. Today, no cloth of cloud covered Table Mountain. Now, she had been beyond the mountains and had seen the red earth and the veld for herself, seen the fynbos and animals which came from the beginning of time.

Her satchel was slung over her shoulder, Safe inside were Louise's prison diary and her own silver dagger. She would give it into the care of the captain once she was on board. Her portmanteau with her other possessions, and the written notes she had made during her time in the Cape, had already been loaded into the rowing boat.

Suzanne took a deep breath as she allowed the sailor to help her down and looked up to the little group standing on the jetty.

'Farewell,' she called up to them. 'I will never forget you, my friends. Never.'

PART TWO

One month later

THE HIGH SEAS & CORNWALL

April–July 1689

CHAPTER FIFTY-SIX

THE ATLANTIC OCEAN
Wednesday, 20th April

They had been a month at sea.

Suzanne had settled easily into life on board the *Gouw*. The ringing of the ship's bell, the changing of the watch, the sound of the sailors' bare feet as they ran up and down the deck, the crack of the sails and the whistling of the wind through the rigging. The captain was firm, but fair, and his men respected him. He raised his voice when it was necessary, administered punishment for serious infractions, but otherwise let his mariners work the ship.

They took advantage of the trade winds, changing direction to avoid storms and ride the ocean currents, and the weather was mostly kind. It was a very different experience from Suzanne's voyage one year ago. Then, the fear and destitution of the Huguenot refugees – the women and men who had become her friends – had hovered over the *China* like a black mist. This time, there were no more than a handful of passengers, all of them, like Suzanne, paying their own passage: VOC officials returning home; sons sent from the Colony to be educated in the Fatherland; daughters to be married to Amsterdamers. It made for a calm ship, a working ship.

Suzanne found herself enjoying the journey. On the *China*, there had always been some human tragedy being played out below deck. And she'd had Florence to talk to, to take her mind off the rolling and listing of the ship. On the *Gouw*, she was alone with her thoughts and memories. But she was not lonely, because Louise and Gilles were her constant companions now, Tia and Judith, Adriaan and Harrie. It was only when she thought of her grandmother that she felt her heart contract.

When the weather was good, Suzanne sat on the starboard side, knowing that the Portuguese gold coast was far off to the east, out of sight. Further north, lay Dakar in its sea of sands. She imagined the maps in her mind and traced their journey in her imagination. No one paid her much attention, no one bothered her and she wrote down everything she had seen, everything she had been told, everything she felt.

They made it through the doldrums, where the south-easterly trade winds met the north-easterly trade winds of the northern hemisphere, finding themselves becalmed for no more than a couple of days. Then on to the Las Palmas de Gran Canaria, where Louise had been put on trial for having forced slaver ships to abandon their vile trade in those waters.

April into May, May into June. Day after day, the sun rose in a milky sky and set over the endless horizon. Suzanne relished the glorious isolation, surrounded on all sides by the dark, shifting ocean. Some days, the sea was a deep green, purple in places, crested by white waves. At other times, when the black clouds gathered, it was a turbulent and broiling black, as if monsters from the deep were whipping the waves into a frenzy. She remembered paintings in Amsterdam, portraits of the sea, and knew that there was nothing that an artist could create that would capture the ocean's majesty and awful power.

June eased into July, sailing from autumn in the south to summer in the north. Dusk to dawn, Suzanne watched the sky turn from royal blue to misted grey. Spirits were high as they sailed close to the coast of Portugal. The *Gouw* was a lucky ship, the sailors told her, hadn't their progress so far proved it? She knew storms could whip up out of nowhere in the Bay of Biscay and even seasoned sailors would cross themselves when they saw the clouds chasing in from the Atlantic. But, she was not concerned. The sky remained clear and the seas remained calm.

The days passed in endless motion. Every part of the vessel seemed to sing – creaking, lilting, moving, moaning – the rise and fall in the waves, bouncing and crashing against the swell.

Their luck changed as they sailed north from the Bay of Biscay. It began to rain. Huge waves rolled in from the Atlantic. Steep and unforgiving, they set the *Gouw* bobbing like a cork. Waves broke across the waist of the main deck, making all movement perilous. Then the wind veered round so they were battling into a north-easterly, threatening to blow them back into the open ocean.

'Welcome home,' somebody said, and everyone laughed.

Somewhere out of sight, they passed the rocky coast of Brittany and, for a day or two, they were blessed with a westerly wind. Relations between France and England were difficult, meaning the Channel was often a watery battleground.

'Will we sail directly to Amsterdam?' Suzanne asked the captain, knowing that ships were sometimes forced to detour up the coast of Ireland, around Scotland and through the North Sea to avoid possible conflict.

'From what we were told in the Colony, there have been no reports of foreign vessels in the Channel so far this year,' he replied. 'Or pirate ships. All being well, we will dock in Amsterdam by the beginning of next month as scheduled.'

CHAPTER FIFTY-SEVEN

THE LIZARD PENINSULA, CORNWALL
Thursday, 7th July 1689

The storm hit at three o'clock in the morning. A single gust of wind, a warning shot across the bow, then the *Gouw* started to dip and plunge, then rear up. Suzanne found herself smashed leeward, then thrown in the opposite direction as the tempest started to build.

She rushed up on deck. 'What is happening?'

'Stay down below!' the captain shouted. 'Stay out of the way!'

Within moments, the ship was flanked by water, rolling black walls of green and purple as high as the mast. Caught in the maelstrom, the *Gouw* began to fight for her life. She was twisting, sliding, crashing into the waves that threatened to sink her.

Suzanne disobeyed the captain's orders, feeling safer on deck than below. She clung to the taffrail, watching as the crew struck the sails and battened the hatches. Every rope was tied, every lantern secured, starboard and portside. She saw the lights guttering in their wooden cages before being extinguished by the sea. Monstrous waves, crested with white, hovered and loomed over them, before thundering down again and again onto the deck.

She had never heard such a roaring, the hammering of rigging and rope. With every crack of thunder, every fork of lightning, every vertiginous plunge that sent the *Gouw* down into the depths, it seemed impossible the ship would not crack in two.

The captain was at the helm, with his first lieutenant beside him. Men were scooping up water with wooden pails, trying to clear the deck.

'Do what you can!' a sailor shouted, pushing a bucket into Suzanne's hands. 'Stay away from the side and be careful not to slip.'

Down below, she could hear men working the bilge pump, driving the metal lever up and down to rid the lower deck of seawater. It made little difference. Water was sheeting down from the quarterdeck and back under the door of the captain's cabin, the sandbags offering little protection.

For hour after hour, the wind was relentless. Vicious, unpredictable, unyielding. Even below deck, water foamed as high as a man's knee, finding every crack or chink in the wood. Suzanne felt as if the ship herself was drowning. She saw the cabin boy thrown against the mizzen mast, cracking his head. She rushed to help him, dragging him along the deck to relative shelter below the bridge.

Lurching like a drunken man, Suzanne made her way back to the bow, which was now part underwater. Then, above the sound of the storm, a cry went up.

'Land ahoy! Land ahoy!'

Her initial relief turned to terror when she realised that they were going to be blown onto the rocks. The westerly wind was now their enemy, driving them relentlessly forward towards the jagged coast of Cornwall. All around her, Suzanne could hear panic in the crew's voices, their desperate shouts, as they vainly tried to keep control of the ship. But the wind was too strong, the tide was too fierce. There was a deafening crack and the *Gouw* listed dangerously to starboard. Everyone was tipped down onto the deck, sent slamming against the taffrail. Others were thrown into the sea.

'Man overboard! Men overboard!'

Suzanne grabbed a rope that had come loose. The cord tore at her skin, burning her palms, but she did not let go. For a moment, she seemed to be flying free in the air with every roll of the ship. Then, another twist in the swirling current, and she fell heavily. She felt her head strike the deck. She felt pain reverberate through her bones as the ship tilted to one side. They were sinking. As she started to lose consciousness, her only thought was that she should not let go of the rope.

Then, she was in the water. Everything changed. The tempest, the wind, the desperate cries of the sailors, the death throes of the ship, all of it was happening somewhere else. The shock of the cold on her face did not matter, the seawater replacing the air in her lungs.

Images tumbled through her mind: the green forests of the Cape and the white houses of the Colony, the grey stone façade of their old house in the rue des Gentilshommes and the candlelit library in Warmoesstraat.

Now, all was silence. Down into the darkness of the sea, to the underground caverns where the fish and ancient sea-monsters dwell, Suzanne had never known such quiet, such peace. Voices, now, whispering in her head. The sounds of all those who had taken this path before her, the glorious dead coming to make her one of their own. Citizens of the sea, honoured guests in the watery halls that stretched further than any man had ever imagined. You are safe, now. You are home, now.

'Do not fear death,' the voices seemed to whisper. 'Do not fear death by drowning.'

Then, her instinct for self-preservation kicked in. Suzanne had gone to the Cape to find Louise, a woman who had loved the sea and lived her life by its rules. If she drowned here, then Louise's story would be lost, too. It would all have been for nothing. Suzanne's hand instinctively clutched at the leather strap of her satchel, before remembering she had given it into the captain's safe-keeping. What hope that Louise's diary and her own silver dagger might be saved even if she was not?

But Suzanne wanted to live. Her limbs were cold and heavy. She struggled with the buckle on her cloak until she managed to release the clasp. She kicked off the boots that previously had saved her life, then looked up towards the hull of the ship and the water's surface.

'*Post tenebras lux.*' After the dark, the light.

She had not defeated her demons, had not survived what she had survived, to die now. Suzanne clawed at the ties on her skirt until she could wriggle free of the heavy fabric that was pulling her down. Then she started to swim. Her arms and her legs thrashing, strong after her months in the Colony, her lungs screaming, she battled her way back up to the surface.

Then, she was gulping at air. All around her, she saw the wreck of the *Gouw*. Splintered planks, the cracked hull, the magnificent vessel was lying on its side in the raging sea. Lamps, boxes, provisions were bobbing in the tempestuous current.

Suzanne had very little strength left now. She would not survive for much longer unless she could reach land. Then, in the darkness and the driving rain, she saw the pennant of the main mast, red, blue and white in the water. With her last scrap of energy, she kicked her feet and stretched out her hands. But in the roll of the waves, her fingers could not get purchase.

She tried again, reaching out until she felt something solid beneath her hands. Hauling herself forward, she managed to throw her arms around the broken mast and raise her chin above the water. Then she closed her eyes, and laced her hands together, and prayed that the storm would pass.

'Do not let go,' she muttered over and again, like a prayer. 'Don't let go.'

Suzanne had no idea how long she clung to the wreckage. Only that, as the first hint of morning broke over the rocky coastline, suddenly there was calm. With the light, the wind died down and the swell began to subside. She raised her head and found that she had drifted close to the shore. She could see rocks, sand, the wreckage from the *Gouw* washing up onto the beach. The captain's chest, too?

She could hear men's voices now, shouting to one another. Speaking in English. Could that be right? Weren't they supposed to be in Amsterdam? Suzanne wanted to call out, but she found she had no voice. Then, she felt strong hands beneath her shoulders, pulling her to shore.

'This one's alive,' she heard someone shout.

It was the last thing she remembered.

PART THREE

One hundred and seventy-three years later

CAPE TOWN,
STELLENBOSCH
& FRANSCHHOEK

January–March 1862

CHAPTER FIFTY-EIGHT

CAPE TOWN
Saturday, 18th January 1862

Isabelle Joubert Lepard stood with her hands on the taffrail looking across the still water of Table Bay to Cape Town. Wearing a wide-brimmed hat, a brown high-necked dress with a lace collar and buttons to a narrow waist, wide pagoda sleeves and a full skirt too heavy for the African summer, she was a woman of angles and bones in a Victorian world that appreciated delicate features and plump femininity.

Forceful and determined, Isabelle had spent her childhood demanding equal treatment with her older brothers, a request her forward-thinking clergyman father had acceded to. With no mother to provide a civilising touch in the nursery, and a well-meaning but ineffectual nanny, Isabelle had been allowed into the schoolroom to learn beside them, and studied botany and natural sciences as well as languages and the classics.

When the boys had been sent to boarding school, she had pestered her father to have her enrolled in a girls' day school in Fleet Street, within walking distance of their house. An avid reader, Isabelle devoured anything and everything, from adventure stories to articles in science magazines. In her studies, she particularly sought out women who had refused to live a sheltered life bound by drawing rooms and church: Grace O'Malley, ruling the seas off the west coast of Ireland in the days of Queen Elizabeth; or pirates Anne Bonny and

Mary Read who had terrorised the Caribbean Seas a century later.

Most of all, she was fascinated with the warrior women in her own family: her distant ancestor Minou Joubert, who had lived through the violent and turbulent years of the wars of religion in France; Minou's granddaughter Louise Reydon-Joubert, a she-captain herself; and Louise's first cousin twice removed, Suzanne Joubert, who had gone to the Cape Colony in search of her elusive cousin.

Isabelle had grown up in the sooty streets of London, in a comfortable Georgian house in Bouverie Street where the Lepard family had settled as Huguenot refugees a century before. Originally paper makers and book binders, they had become printers and pamphleteers. It was there that she had learnt her love of words, growing up among the heat and the hiss of the printing presses and with the conviction that words mattered. By the time she was twenty, Isabelle had travelled the world in her imagination without ever setting foot outside England. And she had developed a passion for recording her thoughts and impressions on the page. Was she not descended from a family of women writers?

The turning point in her transition from reader to writer had come five years before. In 1857, a four-day gala had been held on the banks of the Thames to celebrate Mrs Seacole's contribution to the war effort. A British nurse from Jamaica, Mary Seacole had set up her own field hospital in the Crimea, known as the British Hotel. Since both of Isabelle's brothers had died in the Crimean War within a few weeks of one another – one on the Black Sea of injuries sustained in battle and the other from disease – Isabelle had wanted to pay her respects to the brave woman who had done her best to nurse British soldiers back to health.

On the first day of the gala, she had sneaked out of the house unchaperoned, returning at ten o'clock that night full of everything she had seen. It was the one and only time she had ever seen her gentle-mannered father lose his temper. He had been beside himself, imagining all the things that might have happened to a young lady alone in the city, and had confined her to the house for a week.

Though she hated having caused him distress, Isabelle smiled at the memory. It had been worth it. Like all of London, she had devoured Mrs Seacole's life-story, *Wonderful Adventures of Mrs Seacole in Many Lands*, and determined to become a writer herself.

A few months after attending the gala, Isabelle had published her first pamphlet, a record of the day. Several pen portraits of women she admired had followed: the abolitionist and fellow Huguenot Harriet Martineau; Mary Wollstonecraft; and blue-stocking Hannah More. Finally, she had persuaded the Editor of *The Leisure Hour* to publish her own stories. Anonymously, at first, next with her initials appended alongside – IJL – then with her name: Miss Isabelle Lepard. She was now thirty years of age and was still thrilled by seeing her name in print.

But, even when her father was alive, she'd had bigger ambitions. Isabelle was descended from one of the great, lost, Huguenot families of France and was in sole possession of the substantial archive passed down through the family by Suzanne Joubert and her Lepard descendants. The collection – which contained all of Minou's journals, Louise's prison diary and Suzanne's notebooks, written over many years in England – told of the Joubert family's flight from Carcassonne to Puivert, Puivert to Paris, Paris to Amsterdam, Amsterdam to the Cape and back again. But the key piece of the story, what had happened when Louise and Gilles first set foot in the Cape, was still missing. Isabelle intended to solve that mystery and then endow her own Family Archive and Reading Room. A space open to all, dedicated to the history of the women of her family.

Standing on deck beneath the fierce African sun, Isabelle grew sombre. Her dear father's death, and the legacy that had come to her, were the only reasons she could afford to travel. She wished it might have been possible to have the one without the other.

After her father's funeral, Isabelle had wasted no time. She had no other close family and a significant inheritance. She had never travelled beyond the British Isles before – family holidays to the Lake District and Cornwall, weekend trips to Sussex to visit a cousin who was a canon at Chichester Cathedral, philanthropic visits to Rochester in Kent where many Huguenot refugees of earlier centuries had first found sanctuary remained the extent of her travel. But she considered herself brave, an excellent horsewoman and believed she would be able to tolerate discomfort and hardship well enough.

Last July, Isabelle had travelled to La Rochelle by rail, then on to Toulouse and Carcassonne, where the Joubert family originated. She had visited Minou's grave in Puivert, in the shadow of the Pyrenees, and seen the magnificence of its now ruined castle. In August, she had returned home via Amsterdam, visiting the house on Warmoesstraat where the family archive had begun, retrieving the documents from storage. In her spare time, she walked the streets that Minou had described in her journal and visited the dock from where Louise had sailed on her own ship, the *Old Moon*.

Returning to London in September, Isabelle reread Minou's journals and Louise's prison diary, which had survived the shipwreck and been washed up on the shores of Cornwall in a metal-lined chest after the ship bringing Suzanne back to Europe had foundered. She spent hours with Suzanne's notebooks describing her time in southern Africa and, later, her dramatic rescue from the sea, telling of how she had married an English Huguenot refugee and settled in London. Isabelle became obsessed by the rise and fall of their family's fortunes, with the feud between her own Protestant family and a Catholic family that had lasted generations and cost the Jouberts so much.

More than three hundred years of history until, finally, she was ready.

Two months later, at the tail end of November 1861, Isabelle had bought herself a first-class ticket and boarded the ship *Recorder* in Portsmouth bound for the Cape of Good Hope. The only document she had brought with her was Minou's original journal. It had a soft tan leather cover, held shut by a strap wrapped twice around, and some of the pages were loose, their corners spiking out like the yellow points of a diamond. It detailed the beginning of the centuries-old feud between two families, the Joubert family and the Vidal family. And sewn inside the covers was the last Will and Testament of Marguerite de Puivert, Minou's birth mother, written on the thirty-first day of October in the year 1542. The day Minou had been born.

Isabelle watched as a small boat came out to greet them.

'The harbour master,' one of the sailors explained as he ran past her to secure the mooring ropes. 'He is here to ascertain that we have no infectious diseases on board.'

Isabelle knew that a ship from India had docked in Cape Town in 1713 bringing smallpox to the Cape. It had been the first of three epidemics, killing half of the settler population and wiping out whole clans of Khoi and San people.

Reluctantly, Isabelle stepped away from the taffrail and took her place in the queue of passengers waiting to disembark, hoping that her luggage would find her. Her leather satchel – a modern version of the one her ancestor Suzanne Joubert had taken with her to the Cape – was slung across her shoulders. As well as Minou's journal, it contained her papers and everything she would need for the journey to the interior. Her travelling clothes and other essentials were stowed in her chest that would be taken directly to her lodgings in Adderley Street.

The order was given to prepare for disembarkation. From the Castle of Good Hope, the Noon Gun was fired, overwhelming the ringing of the ship's bell. Isabelle joined the first-class passengers, walking carefully down the gang plank into the melee and organised chaos of the African waterside.

Half an hour later, standing surrounded by luggage and porters, by the stink of the harbour and the horses and carriages lined up to take disembarking passengers to their lodgings, she was smiling. Isabelle remembered Suzanne's account of her own arrival into Table Bay on the fourth day of August 1688.

Finally, she was here too, on African soil at last. She was following in the footsteps of her pioneering female ancestors. Already, in her mind, she was writing the scene in her head, intertwining it with the stories of Louise and Suzanne who had come before her. Their extraordinary lives deserved to be known, deserved to be celebrated on the pages of a book just like Mrs Seacole's best-selling memoir.

Isabelle was the person to do it.

CHAPTER FIFTY-NINE

Cape Town
Sunday, 26th January

Isabelle spent a week in Cape Town, now a sprawling city beneath the mountains, with impressive buildings and a bustling community. In the mornings she visited all the landmarks Suzanne had written about, from the Castle of Good Hope to Gallow's Hill where her friend Adriaan van Dijk had taught her to shoot. The afternoons she spent making plans for her journey to Stellenbosch and Franschhoek, where Louise, Gilles and their son Théodore had lived two centuries before.

But there was a restlessness in Cape Town, a sense of things being unsettled. Two weeks previously, Sir Philip Wodehouse had taken over as the new Governor of the Cape Colony. His appointment was unpopular, relations between the Boers – the descendants of the original Dutch settlers – and the British were poor, there had been a series of skirmishes between the displaced Khoi population, and the new immigrants from India sailing into Natal were not being welcomed. The atmosphere was charged, as if even the slightest spark might make the whole city explode.

There were two incidents that added to Isabelle's general sense of disquiet. First, she was sure that, several times, she had seen the same man looking up at her hotel window: loitering in the shadows, a broad-brimmed hat obscuring his face, watching. He always wore a battered jacket and long leather waistcoat, knee-length black boots. After the third time, she went down to the lobby to report her concerns to the manager. A weasel-faced man, with suspicious eyes and brusque manner, he dismissed her concerns.

'There are any number of drosters hanging about the town, scoundrels with no appetite for work,' he said, his breath stinking of yesterday's brandy.

'Droster?'

'It's the old name for outlaws who used to live in the hills. Villains, Black and coloured, runaway slaves, cattle thieves. These days they hang about the town menacing decent folk.'

'But this man appears to be watching my window.'

The manager snorted. 'I'm sure he is not, why would he? He'll be on the look-out for any foreigner stupid enough to carry their valuables in plain sight.'

Isabelle tried to forget about it and dismissed the ineffectual manager from her mind. But two days later, when she returned after a tiresome morning trying to deposit funds at the Cape of Good Hope Bank, a private institution recommended by her London solicitors, she found her door standing open. The maid had serviced her room earlier and Isabelle knew she had not left the door unlatched.

'*Hallo?*' she said in Afrikaans. Tentatively, she stepped inside. 'Is anyone here?'

The room was empty. Isabelle exhaled with relief, hung her bag over the arm of the chair, removed her hat and her gloves, then looked around. At first glance, everything looked in order. But then she noticed that the papers on her desk were not quite where they should be. The first draft of a letter was no longer on the top and the top drawer of the bureau was not quite shut. Her father's bible was still on her bedside table, but it was now facing the wrong way. Her notebook was still where she had left it, but she could see her handkerchiefs and stockings had been disturbed. She was relieved that she always took Minou's journal with her, but the thought of some unknown person handling her personal possessions turned her stomach.

Furious, she stormed down to the lobby and once more demanded to see the manager.

'I am telling you that someone has been in my room,' she insisted, refusing to allow him to dismiss her complaint this time. 'Items have been moved.'

Chewing a match in the corner of his mouth, he narrowed his eyes.

'Has anything been taken, Miss Lepard?' he said slyly, stressing the word 'miss'.

'Well, no. But that is not the point.'

'To be clear, you are not accusing members of my staff of acting improperly?'

'I have already said not. All the same, someone has been in my room, searching through my belongings.'

The manager held her gaze. Isabelle refused to look away. Finally, he turned and pulled a piece of paper across the counter.

'I will make a note of your complaint,' he said, making it clear that he considered her protestations a waste of his time.

'Mind that you do!'

Frustrated, Isabelle turned on her heel and returned to her room.

That night, her last in Cape Town, she pushed a chair against the door and wedged it beneath the handle. She had Suzanne's dagger in her possession which she hid under her pillow, but she still slept badly. Every noise made her jump, every creak of the landing floorboard had her senses on high alert. She tried to tell herself she was imagining things, but she was glad when the morning came.

CHAPTER SIXTY

STELLENBOSCH
Friday, 31st January

To Isabelle's delight, there was a daily omnibus service to Stellenbosch, made possible by the new road over the Cape Flats.

She arrived in Stellenbosch mid-afternoon on the last day of the month, the route taking them through a sea of vines stretching in all directions beneath the Simonsberg mountains. Instantly, Isabelle fell in love with the town: its lime-washed gables, the curves and lines of the white Cape-Dutch houses with pediments and drip mouldings, the glorious cast-iron lacework decorating shady verandas and stoeps. She found it hard to picture the single wagon trail and the *drostdij* built on Simon van der Stel's orders a matter of years before Suzanne wrote about her time spent in the original settlement on the banks of the Eerste River.

Isabelle took lodgings on Dorp Street. Her boarding house, which advertised itself as a home-from-home for British travellers, was a two-storeyed building with a white gable and an arched doorway with two long-paned windows either side. Her room on the first floor looked out over a line of green oak trees and little rills of water running alongside. Isabelle adored the room on sight: a ceiling of yellow-wood, a dressing table and wardrobe fashioned from the same; wooden shutters and a small but comfortable four-poster bed. She secured it for two weeks, intending to make it her base from which to travel to Franschhoek and back.

'Might I have a table brought up?' she asked the landlady, a red-faced English woman who had emigrated to the Colony as a child from Portsmouth and married a German settler. 'I am a writer, but I would not wish to monopolise the desk in the parlour.'

'A writer, who'd have thought that.'

Isabelle smiled sweetly. 'Might that be possible?'

'Of course, of course.' The landlady wiped her hands on her apron then rang a bell. A young Black man, dressed in a white shirt and white culottes, instantly appeared. 'Jacob, fetch a table for Miss Lepard's room. The round one from the back parlour will do.'

Deciding it would be sensible to wait out of the way in the hall while the furniture exchange was taking place, Isabelle continued the conversation with her landlady.

'Where do you come from, Mrs Müller?'

'Chichester, Miss Lepard,' she replied. 'I don't suppose you know it.'

Isabelle grinned. 'In point of fact, I do. It is a delightful city.'

'Oh, it is, it is,' Mrs Müller sighed. 'There is a great deal of opportunity here, of course, but I miss Sussex. The Downs and the Marshes. Old Stellenbosch was destroyed by fire in 1710, then the great flood of 1768 swept away the bridge, and on top of that, the hurricane forty years ago flattened nearly a hundred buildings. Everything here is so new in comparison to Chichester.' She shook her head. 'Do you come from Sussex, Miss Lepard?'

'No, I live in London. But I visited often with my father. My cousin is a canon at the cathedral.'

The landlady looked up the stairs as Jacob arrived with the

table. 'Take Miss Lepard the embroidered chair, too,' she said, before turning back to Isabelle. 'It will be more comfortable for your working.'

As Jacob trudged away, Mrs Müller sighed again. 'My folk come from Fishbourne. Christie was my maiden name, one of the oldest families in the village we were. Very well thought of. But my father believed he would have a better chance here, so here we came.'

'It is very beautiful.'

'I suppose it is.' She straightened her apron. 'Well, I mustn't keep you, Miss Lepard. Let me know if you need anything, anything at all. We serve a cold supper at six o'clock every day and the front door is locked at eight. After that, you will have to ring the bell.'

'Thank you. Might it also be possible to have a glass of wine?'

Mrs Müller looked surprised that a young lady might be drinking alone in the middle of the day, but she made no comment.

After a late luncheon of bread and cheese, Isabelle went out to explore her surroundings. Dorp Street was the original wagon trail leading from Cape Town to Stellenbosch. The oak trees were in full leaf, shading the buildings and walkways, and the husks of last year's acorns crunched underfoot. Isabelle was sure that this was the road along which Suzanne had walked with her friend Adriaan van Dijk as she planned her journey to Olifantshoek, a place now known as Franschhoek in acknowledgement of the Huguenot refugees who had settled there.

Stellenbosch felt cultured, welcoming and it was bigger than she had expected, boasting a hotel, several inns and boarding houses. There were two distilleries, a butcher's shop and a post office, pharmacies and two physicians. Isabelle counted four bakeries and as many blacksmiths. Residents would have little need to ever leave the town.

Here, perhaps even more than in Cape Town, Isabelle could see the influence of generations of Dutch and German immigrants. In between the colony houses that spoke more of Amsterdam than Africa, were many private residences in the Cape style. The most magnificent building was the Oude Leeskamer, the Old Reading Room, on the corner of Dorp Street and Drostdij Street, with its latticed balconies and long sash windows. She also passed the Stellenbosch gaol though, from Suzanne's descriptions of the fledgling town in 1688, Isabelle doubted it could be the place where Lars Eltorp had met his end. A little further and she came to the Old Police Station, which had housed a school for the children of enslaved people – testament to the vigour of German missionaries who believed that education was the path to godliness.

Hidden behind walls in the residential quarters, Isabelle could see evidence of kitchen gardens: the green and silver tips of orchards, medlars and red wemmershoek apples, saffron pears. Exuberant oleanders and japonicas, and butterflies half the size of her hand provided beautiful bursts of colour. Layered beneath the sounds of servants gossiping on the street and ladies walking to and fro in the shade, was the squawking of hens and geese and a raucous shrieking from the long-beaked birds they called ibis.

As the shadows lengthened, and the mission bell rang the labourers home from the fields, Isabelle returned tired, but content, to her lodgings and slept the clock round.

CHAPTER SIXTY-ONE

Sunday, 2nd February

After luncheon two days later, Isabelle went to church. She put on her Sunday best and finest blue lace gloves and, holding her father's bible before her like a shield, made her way to the afternoon service. Building work was about to begin on the new Dutch Reformed Church on Kerk Street, which meant that all services were being relocated to other venues in the town for the duration.

The afternoon services were held in the Lutheran Church in Dorp Street, not far from her lodgings. As Isabelle took a seat in an empty pew, she looked around her. The pews at the front were filled by British, Boer and German families, their Black servants sitting at the back of the church. From Suzanne's notebooks, she knew about the early history of the Colony, and from the newspapers, she was aware there was currently great opposition to British rule, particularly from the Boers in Natal, and that those disagreements over land and sovereignty were widespread. Here in Stellenbosch, though, the atmosphere seemed less bellicose.

Nevertheless, Isabelle was aware that her presence was attracting notice. She supposed it was natural enough in a small town. One man in particular seemed to be staring intently. Isabelle looked away, then back again to find his eyes still fixed upon her. She tried to tell herself she was mistaken, but he looked very similar to the man who had stood beneath her hotel window in Cape Town. Unlike every other man in the congregation, he had not removed his hat.

For the entire service, Isabelle felt his eyes drilling into her back. She tried to ignore him, focusing instead on the white walls and the way that the wood seemed to shine in the afternoon sunlight. The service was in Dutch, so Isabelle understood little of it, but she recognised the psalms and bowed her head at appropriate moments.

Isabelle allowed her mind to wander. She had come to church for reasons of tradition and propriety, but also to enquire about someone who might help with arrangements for her journey to Franschhoek. She wanted to keep her true business to herself so far as possible. Although she was open about the fact that she was here as a travel correspondent, she did not want anyone in Franschhoek to know she was coming. Isabelle had discovered there were still Barentons living in the valley on the site of Théodore's original wine farm, La Justice, and realised there might conceivably be a concern that she was here to stake a claim to the land. She had been told that there was a deal of sensitivity about French descendants of those original Huguenot families, believing ownership belonged with them and not the Boers who had owned the land since.

At the end of the service, Isabelle spoke to the pastor at the door. He had good, but strongly accented, English.

'I wonder if I might ask your advice?' she asked. 'I am a visitor from England, hoping to travel to Franschhoek. I need a reliable guide to take me there.'

Johannes Neethling looked down his red, bulbous nose. 'Indeed.'

She smiled. 'I am writing a travel article for a London periodical, so I would do the country and its people justice. I regret my knowledge of Afrikaans is meagre, so if there was someone who spoke passable English?'

Neethling looked at her for a moment longer. 'Leave it with me, Miss . . .?' He left the question hanging.

She bowed her head. 'Forgive me. Isabelle Lepard. From London.'

'Very well. If you would come to the Parsonage at ten o'clock tomorrow morning, Miss Lepard, I will see what I can do.'

CHAPTER SIXTY-TWO

Monday, 3rd February

Isabelle slept well again and was ready in good time for her appointment.

A Black maid showed her into a gloomy parlour with heavy curtains. A beautiful longcase clock at least six feet tall dominated the room. Fashioned, she thought, from oak, Isabelle could hear the pendulum swinging ponderously in the tower. The dial was highly ornamental: roman numerals to mark the time and, inset into the face, paintings of two figures – a man holding a panel with tiny numbers showing the month, a woman opposite showing the day and date. But what made it exceptional was the tableau of delicate wooden ships, like children's toys, set above the clock face against the backdrop of a painting of the harbour at Amsterdam seen from the water.

Entranced, Isabelle stepped closer. She did not know Amsterdam well, having been there only once last year, but she could identify several landmarks, including the spire of the church of Sant Nicolas and that of the Oude Kerk just a little way behind. The purpose of her trip had been to retrieve the precious Joubert family journals and writings, not to mention Louise's prison diary, and arrange for the complete archive to be shipped back to England. The documents had been languishing in storage for many years, having been removed from the house in Warmoesstraat when the property was sold in the early 1800s.

'Miss Lepard, I am sorry to keep you waiting.'

'Pastor Neethling, not at all. I was just admiring your magnificent clock.'

'Ah, not mine, I regret. I inherited it from a predecessor, who had it brought here at great expense. Perhaps he was missing his homeland? It is a beautiful piece of work, all the same, and it keeps excellent time.' He gestured she should sit. 'Do you know Amsterdam?'

'I have made one visit,' Isabelle replied. 'I was particularly enchanted by the religious community, Begijnhof.'

Neethling nodded. 'Such an interesting history. After the Alteration of 1578, when the city transferred from Catholic to Calvinist rule in the space of an afternoon, it was the only papist institution allowed to remain for the sisters to continue to live there. Subsequently, the chapel was ceded to the English, I regret to say, rather than the Dutch Reformed Church. There are, I understand, very few beguines left in the community now.'

'Your knowledge far exceeds mine. My Huguenot ancestors were given sanctuary in Amsterdam during the sixteenth century, so the city holds a place in my heart.'

'Quite so.' Neethling rang the bell. 'Might I offer you a little brandy?'

Although Isabelle felt it was rather early in the day, she accepted.

'Thank you. If it is not forward of me to say so, your English is very good.'

He smiled. 'I shared rooms with an English missionary when I was studying in Utrecht. And these days, of course, it is useful to be able to speak the language of the administration.'

The speed with which the maid arrived suggested that Neethling perhaps often had a restorative at this time of day.

Isabelle removed her gloves and hat, and accepted the glass of brandy.

'Why did your ancestors go to England rather than remain in Amsterdam?' Neethling asked, once he had taken a sip.

'It was not by design. My family is part Dutch, by blood as well as adoption. Two of my ancestors came to the Cape after the Revocation of the Edict of Nantes. One died here, the other was shipwrecked returning to the Netherlands and found sanctuary in England.'

'On which ship?'

'The *China*, which sailed from the Rotterdam Chamber in March 1688 and arrived in Table Bay in August of that same year.'

Neethling frowned. 'But I do not believe I have encountered the name "Lepard" before . . .'

'My family name was Joubert.'

Neethling put down his glass. 'Joubert?' he asked, with a new interest. Isabelle knew that the Joubert family – descendants of Pierre Jaubert, who had also sailed on the *China* – was now one of the most well-known and powerful families in the Cape.

She laughed. 'I regret I am not related to *that* Joubert family. My antecedents come from Languedoc, Carcassonne and Puivert. It is a coincidence of name, nothing more.'

'Yet you are English?'

'As I mentioned, the ship on which my relative, Suzanne Joubert, was returning to Amsterdam was blown off course in 1689. The *Gouw* was wrecked off the coast of the Cornwall with the loss of almost everybody on board. Only my ancestor and three or four sailors were saved.'

'In which case, if you do not think it impertinent, might I ask why you have come, given you have no family in our country now?'

Isabelle gave her most engaging smile, the one that had first persuaded the Editor of *The Leisure Hour* to publish her journalism.

'As I mentioned yesterday, I am a writer. I have a commission to produce a travel piece for a London periodical.'

'I have heard travel writing is quite the rage in England,' Neethling said as if it was beyond his comprehension as to why anyone would want to read about foreign places. 'In Germany, I believe they have even begun to produce travel guides.'

'My articles are published by a periodical that has links with the Religious Tract Society. My father was a clergyman and much engaged with missionary work. Much travel writing these days is in that vein.'

'Your father has not accompanied you on this voyage?'

'He went to the Lord last year,' Isabelle replied, using a form of words she thought Neethling would appreciate.

'Oh. May he rest in peace.'

She nodded her thanks. 'I am a stranger in this country, pastor Neethling, so I need a guide to take me over the mountains to Franschhoek. I do not believe there is a hotel there, so I would be grateful for the recommendation of a Christian family who might give me lodgings. I have funds enough to pay. I cannot imagine I will be there for more than three or four days.'

Neethling pressed the tips of his fingers together in thought. 'Franschhoek is a newer town than Stellenbosch, you understand. First, it was simply land given to Huguenot refugees and German immigrants to cultivate wine and fruit. The community has grown, however, and now there is a church and a chapel, even a school. There are several respectable boarding houses, so accommodation should not be a problem.'

'That is good to hear.' Isabelle took a tiny sip of her brandy. 'Can you help with securing me a guide?'

Neethling nodded. 'There is a man I think would be suitable for what you have in mind. He is one of your compatriots, who married a local girl of Dutch origin. Leave it with me. You are boarding with *mevrouw* Müller I believe?'

'I am.'

'She is a good woman.' He drained his glass and stood up. 'I will send word to you there. Good morning, Miss Lepard. It has been a pleasure to meet you.'

Isabelle also stood, leaving her brandy almost untouched. The next part of her adventure was about to begin.

Isabelle considered herself patient – though she could imagine her beloved father raising his eyebrows at such an assertion – but the thought of sitting in the parlour or her bedroom at the boarding house until there was news did not appeal. She knew from Suzanne's notebooks that she had felt the same. Besides, she needed to absorb as much local colour as she could for her travel article for *The Leisure Hour*.

Isabelle resolved to do another circuit of the town. It was hardly likely pastor Neethling would be able to organise what she needed immediately. Even if he did, she had no doubt Mrs Müller would be happy enough to take a message.

Monday was clearly a busy day in Stellenbosch and there was a certain amount of traffic on Dorp Street – carriages, carts, a cooper rolling barrels, a gaggle of geese hissing and spitting. Clusters of bare-footed Black children were playing in the rills and flustered clerks, with starched white collars and sunburnt foreheads, were delivering messages to the professional offices. Outside the bakeries and the butchers' shops, there were lines of women, mostly Black. Servants, she assumed, from the bigger houses.

As she walked, Isabelle noticed details she had missed on her first perambulation of the town: the elegant gable on *La Gratitude* and the *Schreuderhuis* on Van Rynveld Street, with its charming thatched roof and white walls. On Die Braak, Isabelle strolled to the gates of the VOC arsenal, the *Kruithuis*, with its white domed vault used to house ammunition.

The Braak was the largest remaining open green space within the town. Lined with the ubiquitous oak trees, it was used as a military parade ground and for any large municipal celebrations. Dodging carts and carriages with their hoods raised against the fierce sun, Isabelle walked across to admire the Rhenish Mission Church. An imposing white building with a thatched roof, neo-classical gables and a double campanile, it was some sixty years old and dominated the square. Its Anglican neighbour, St Mary's, was smaller and more modest, built ten years previously with donations from England and English-speaking local residents, Mrs Müller included. Isabelle knew how important subscriptions to a cause could be. Without them, her own plan to create a Joubert Family Archive and Reading Room would come to nothing.

Knowing her father would wish her to pay her respects, Isabelle doubled back across the square towards the church. Suddenly, she had that same sensation that she was being watched. The short hairs on the back of her neck stood on end. Pretending to consult the list of sights Mrs Müller had provided, Isabelle slowly stepped into the shade beneath a towering oak, and feigned interest in the paper in her hand whilst gazing surreptitiously around the square.

At first she saw nothing to disturb her, just the people of Stellenbosch going about their ordinary everyday business. But then, standing slightly apart from a group of men close to the stream and the water mill, she saw him. Her heart contracted. She would not swear that it was the man she had noticed in

Cape Town, but it was certainly the same man who had been staring at her in the Lutheran church yesterday.

Her initial alarm gave way to fury. She would not be intimidated. Striding out of the shadows, she started to walk towards the stream. The man at first pretended not to see her then, when it became clear that she intended to confront him, he slipped away.

Isabelle picked up her pace, determined to catch him, but he was faster and clearly knew the town well. By the time she got to the corner, he had vanished.

Later, in her room, she tried to rationalise what she had seen. What she *thought* she had seen. Why would anyone be following her? She was one of increasing numbers of English visitors to the Cape, nothing marked her out. She had told no one but pastor Neethling of her Huguenot antecedents and, even if he had been loose-lipped, the man had already been on her tail in Cape Town.

Isabelle sat up late in her room that evening, drinking a rather blowsy red wine and writing her notes by the light of a candle. Only when fingers of light started to slip through the shutters did she extinguish the flame and creep into bed. Her dreams were full of images of pursuit and chase. Running through the fynbos and rows of vines, unable to see where she was going. Images of lions and hyenas and jackals, a leopard with red-tipped claws and sharp teeth, with the face of a man.

CHAPTER SIXTY-THREE

Monday, 17th February 1862

'It is a day's ride, no more,' said John Turner. True to his word, pastor Neethling had secured the services of an Englishman, who was married to the youngest daughter of a manager on the Spier wine farm, one of the oldest in Stellenbosch.

The interview was taking place in the stuffy parlour of Mrs Müller's boarding house. Turner was a presentable man in his mid-twenties, with a mop of blond hair and an appealing, boyish face. Isabelle had taken to him straight away.

'And will we break the journey?' she asked. Though Isabelle was a competent horsewoman, she had grown up in London and most of her riding had been in Hyde Park or on the Sussex Downs between one country house and the next. She had never before trekked through mountain passes nor over such wild terrain. She was not anxious as such – it would all be good copy – but she did want to be clear as to what she was letting herself in for.

'There is a farm halfway between Stellenbosch and Franschhoek,' Turner replied. 'My wife's family lives there, and will be happy to provide us with a bed for the night. It's a pretty place, though rather isolated. Nothing fancy, mind, but it will be clean and comfortable enough. My proposal is that we should leave here at midday on Wednesday, stay one night at Klein Bethlehem, then ride on to Franschhoek, arriving at the end of that same day.'

Recalling Suzanne's account of her own arrangements to travel from Stellenbosch to Franschhoek, Isabelle smiled.

'That sounds just the ticket, John, thank you. Please confirm the arrangements. And we must agree an advance payment for your services, too. You must let me know how much you need.'

The young man blushed. 'Thank you, miss. Glad to be of service.'

Tuesday, 18th February

In the next two days, Isabelle was very busy. She was in good spirits, heartened by the fact that there had been no further sightings of the man who been following her. She came to an arrangement with Mrs Müller to store her excess luggage and keep her room for another few days during the first week in March on her return from Franschhoek. She acquired a printed map of the region, clearly showing the terrain between the two towns and the mountain passes. On the Tuesday afternoon, she paid a visit to pastor Neethling to thank him for his assistance.

From him, she learnt that the wine farm at Bethlehem – where she and John Turner were to lodge for the first night – had first been granted to Pierre Simond, the French Huguenot pastor who had sailed to the Cape on a ship docking two weeks after Suzanne's ship, the *China*. Isabelle had tried to converse in French with a few of the French-named shopkeepers in Stellenbosch and discovered that the language simply was not spoken any more. In a matter of a few generations, it had died out almost completely.

'How did that happen? I would have thought they would have fought tooth and nail to preserve their heritage.'

'It is an irony,' Neethling agreed. 'Your ancestors fled here to be allowed to worship in their own language, yet the VOC was determined that they should fully integrate. Within a hundred years, all teaching in schools and seminaries was in Dutch. Only the French names remain.'

'That seems a dreadful pity.'

Neethling nodded. 'Though bear in mind that many of your forebears did not really speak French at all. Pierre Jaubert, from whom you are *not* descended –' he paused to allow Isabelle to smile at his joke – 'Jaubert and his co-religionists spoke Provençal. Others Flemish or Occitan.'

'Will this be the case in Franschhoek, too?' The town's name – meaning 'the French corner' – had given Isabelle to hope that she might be able to communicate more directly with its inhabitants. She had discovered there was resistance to speaking English and she had no more than a few words of Afrikaans, certainly not enough to ask the questions she needed to.

'There are perhaps more French speakers there than in Stellenbosch, to be sure,' he replied. 'But it is rare. Now, may I offer you a little something?'

Wednesday, 19th February

As the mission bell rang for eleven o'clock, Isabelle set out from Stellenbosch in the company of John Turner. She was riding a pretty piebald mare, Ana; Turner, a bay called Minx.

She took little with her, only what she could not have borne to lose – her father's bible, Minou's journal and Suzanne's dagger with the red garnet in its hilt. The blade was blunt, and its use more decorative than protective, but Isabelle liked to have it with her.

John Turner was, as she had hoped, pleasant company, neither too talkative nor overly taciturn. The sun was not too fierce and their ride from Stellenbosch towards Klein Bethlehem was enjoyable. The open terrain between the towns was, she realised, relatively unchanged since Suzanne had made the same journey. The significant difference was the lack of Khoi clans or San, who had been driven north by the colonisers, their communities decimated by smallpox, and conscripted as foot soldiers in the wars between the Boers and the British.

They rode on, mile after empty green mile. Isabelle had glimpsed a distant lion on the Cape Flats when leaving Cape Town a couple of weeks before. Now, while they had seen various species of antelope, she had yet to see either a leopard or an elephant. Since the Huguenot settlers started to farm the land along the Berg River in Olifantshoek, the big game had moved to a safer place to avoid the hunters and their guns.

'It is baboons that cause the most mischief,' Turner said, 'and snakes that are the most dangerous. Cobra, puff adder, boomslang, black mamba, they all can be found hereabouts.'

'What should I do?'

'Watch where you put your feet,' he replied with a grin.

Remembering Suzanne's near fatal accident, Isabelle whistled. This was one way in which she did not want to mirror her ancestor's experience.

KLEIN BETHLEHEM

They arrived at Klein Bethlehem at dusk, when the mosquitoes were out in force. Isabelle was glad of the protection of her gloves and the netting around her hat.

John dismounted, then held her piebald so she could jump down from her saddle. An enormous red wheaten ridgeback dog came bounding towards them. John caught the dog's muzzle in his hands to stop him jumping up at Isabelle.

'He is friendly,' he said, 'just rather boisterous.'

A small, plump woman in a pale blue-and-white-striped dress, and a hard-working apron that told the story of many meals cooked, came bustling out to greet them.

'*Hallo, hallo!*'

'Miss Lepard, may I introduce you to my aunt? Griet van Aarnhem.'

'Please to meet you, Miss Lepard,' Griet said in hesitant English.

Isabelle smiled. 'The pleasure is mine, *mevrouw* Van Aarnhem. It is kind of you to let me stay.'

'She is my wife's aunt rather than my own.' Turner put his arm around Griet's shoulders. 'They can trace their ancestors right back to the days of Simon van der Stel.'

Isabelle smiled, then gestured at the land lying around them. 'Is this Pierre Simond's original wine farm?'

She had thought that it would be far grander and more substantial. Simond had not only become a successful wine maker, but also a significant slave owner. How this squared with his Christian beliefs, Isabelle could not imagine.

Turner translated for his aunt, who laughed and rattled a reply in Afrikaans.

'*Geen, geen.*' No.

'This is Klein Bethlehem, little Bethlehem,' he replied. 'The actual farm is further up the valley. This patch of land was granted to a relative of my aunt some fifty years ago, an overseer who had served a previous owner faithfully. They grow only what they need for themselves. My cousins and uncle work in the vineyards belonging to the main farm.'

Griet gestured for Isabelle to follow. 'You come. Come.'

She was shown to a very basic, but clean, little cottage with a single pallet bed, a net over the window, a chair on which to put her things, a washing bowl and jug, and a beef tallow candle, set on a spindly legged table.

'If you come back to the house when you are ready, miss,' Turner said, 'my aunt has prepared us some supper. You can meet the rest of the family.'

When they had gone, Isabelle's spirits dipped a little. It was more of an outhouse than a cottage, though she supposed this was what she had determined upon. This was her first true experience of the real adventurer's life. She pressed her hand to the mattress. It was hard, but would be comfortable enough. The pillowcase smelt of fresh air and soap, and the embroidered covering looked as if it had been put on that day.

Isabelle washed her face and hands, tidied her blonde hair into a bun at the nape of her neck, then took her satchel and went to join the others. Suzanne's notebooks had prepared her for the fact that a day in the saddle was hungry work.

CHAPTER SIXTY-FOUR

Isabelle passed a pleasant evening in the company of the Van Aarnhem family. Griet's husband Hans was a big, comfortable man with skin the texture of cracked leather from working in the fields. He had risen to a senior position in the Bethlehem wine farm and was highly valued. His English was good, thanks to his having to negotiate with the British, and he explained that this was the busiest time of the year, bringing the grape harvest in. The two sons – Piet and Jan – smiled shyly when she caught their eye. They were as broad and sandy-haired as their father, and Isabelle found it hard to tell them apart.

The kitchen was plain but welcoming. Dried herbs hung from the rafters, both medicinal and for cooking: buchu, wild wormwood, blue sage, wild sorrel and bunches of *bokkom*, strips of dried and salted mullet. Beside the hearth stood a large *vetpot*, used for storing rendered animal fat. On a sideboard, Isabelle saw metal moulds filled with beef tallow, much like the candle in her cottage.

Waving away Isabelle's offer to help, Griet served a platter of poached red prickly pears and blackberries from wild brambles. Rather than wine, they drank Arak, a strongly flavoured rice spirit of brandy and anise that made Isabelle's head spin. There was also *tameletjie*, a kind of sweet toffee confection, which Griet explained was made with pine nuts, dried ginger, butter and water.

'You should not have gone to so much trouble,' Isabelle protested.

Griet smiled, then spoke to her husband.

'She says she likes to cook,' John translated, 'and you have a good appetite for an Englishwoman!'

As soon as the meal was over, and Van Aarnhem had finished his pipe, he got to his feet.

'We must be back at the farm before first light. At this time of the year, there can be sudden rainstorms, so we have to bring in the grapes as quickly as possible. This is a good farm. The owner allows us to have regular breaks. So, if you will excuse us?'

'Of course. Good night, *mijnheer* Van Aarnhem. Gentlemen.'

When father and sons had retired, Isabelle offered to help Griet wash the dishes. Her offer was again declined.

Thinking it would all make good copy for her article, she asked Griet questions about her life and John translated easily. Little by little, she built up a picture of an uncomplaining, hard-working woman, much on her own, but fiercely proud of her home and her family. It was clearly a tough life, not much easier than that of those first pioneers trying to eke out a living in a new and inhospitable land. Suzanne had written of Isabeau Jaubert, the Meinards and the Malans, foraging for food to eat, trying to protect their farms against raids and wild animals, always reliant on the harvest not failing. In nearly two hundred years on the veldt, not much had changed.

'Do they have trouble with drosters?' Isabelle asked when Griet had retired to bed. Then, seeing the look of surprise on John's face, added: 'It was a word the manager in my hotel in Cape Town used.'

He pushed some tobacco leaves into his pipe, lit it with a faggot from the fire, then sat back in his chair opposite her.

'This region was a hotbed for the drosters many years ago, but not so much now. There was one nest, as the communities were called, in the Simonsberg Mountains, in the lost world of deep *kloofs* – gorges – and unscaled precipices.'

'Who were they?'

'Men who'd deserted from the army, Dutch and French, German labourers who refused to pay taxes, runaway slaves. Many San and Khoi formed nests too, but it was mostly white settlers. They would descend from their hideaway, steal livestock, burn farms and terrorise families living on the veldt.'

'What happened to them?'

'The authorities organised units to hunt them down. The last stronghold I heard survived was between Waaihoek and Wagenmakersvallei, some way north of here. But that was thirty years ago or so.'

'So, there are no drosters any more?'

Turner shook his head. 'There will always bands of renegades, those who want to live outside of society. But at this time of year, when workers are in the fields day and night, it is harder for thieves to pass undetected. You are safe enough here, and I will be sleeping outside to keep guard.'

'I'm sure there is no need.'

'There is no room in the house and I'm happy to sleep under the stars. Pastor Neethling would never forgive me if I didn't deliver you safely back in one piece.'

He walked her to her cottage, a lamp lighting the way.

'Goodnight, miss,' he said, pushing open the door for her to step inside. 'Should a snake find its way in, try not to panic. They react to movement. If you stay still, more likely than not it will simply move on. Oh, and shake your boots out in the morning before you put them on.' He touched his forehead. 'If there is anything, just shout. I'll be here.'

Isabelle left the candle burning, wedged the chair against the door and put her satchel below to block up the gap through which a snake might get in. John had closed the shutter, although there wasn't a latch, and she pushed the net into the corners to fill the holes. Then she climbed into bed, fully clothed, with Suzanne's dagger under her pillow. With the distant sound of a jackal howling and the sweeter song of nightbirds, she drifted into a fitful sleep.

It was still dark when Isabelle woke with a jolt. Some new sound, or different sound, piercing her subconscious had disturbed her. The candle had almost burnt down, casting no more than a pool of light on the table, so the room was mostly in shadow.

Mindful of John's advice, she lay very still, listening for the tell-tale slither of a snake on the beaten earth floor, but heard nothing.

Her pulse racing, she lay in bed with the covering pulled up to her chin. A shiny black-backed beetle skittered up the wall beside her. She hated it, the rustling and scuttling in the darkness, then despised herself for being so easily unnerved. She thought of Louise and Gilles, of Suzanne, and compared her relatively comfortable situation with theirs. They had been true pioneers. How could she claim to be following in their footsteps if her nerves were put on edge by the most harmless of insects?

Isabelle made herself think of pleasant things – her own bed in Bouverie Street, the building on the corner with Temple Lane where she hoped to establish the Joubert Family Archive and Reading Room. She would need subscribers, of course, to underwrite the cost of the refurbishment, but with her inheritance and her journalism for *The Leisure Hour*, she thought she would be able to raise the extra funds she needed easily enough.

She started to picture all the wooden shelving they would

need to house Minou's journals, Louise's two diaries, as well as Suzanne's notebooks written over her long life in England.

Isabelle smiled, now imagining a published book with her name on the front cover. It would be a history, a memoir, about the women of the Joubert family, putting their stories back centre stage. She would give a lecture series and offer to speak at her old school in Fleet Street to inspire girls to be ambitious. What would the book be called? Perhaps *Miss Lepard's Amazing Adventures in the Cape*? Or maybe *The Joubert Family Chronicles* would be better?

The candle guttered and died, but she no longer minded. Perhaps she would call her memoir *The Map of Bones*, as she followed her ancestors from resting place to resting place? For wasn't that what she had come to the Cape to find? The grave that Suzanne had looked for, the honouring of a woman long dead?

She was just drifting back into sleep when she heard a creak. This time, she knew it was not an insect. Someone was pulling open the shutter from the outside. Moments later, she saw the netting move and a hand reaching down into the room.

Isabelle screamed.

Pulling the knife from beneath her pillow, she acted on pure instinct and struck out, but found only air. The intruder was gone.

CHAPTER SIXTY-FIVE

Straight away, there was a knocking at the door.

'Miss Lepard?' John was calling. 'Are you all right?'

Her heart hammering, Isabelle leapt from her bed. 'I'm coming.'

Feeling the rough dust beneath her feet, she pulled the chair and satchel away and John burst into the room.

'What is it? Are you hurt?'

'Around the back! Someone was trying to get in. I saw his hand reaching down inside the window.'

John turned on his heel and rushed round the cottage. Isabelle shook her boots, then put them on and followed him outside.

'Did you see anyone?'

John came back round the corner of the building. 'No, but there is a box upended beneath the window.'

Isabelle wrapped her arms around herself, relieved that she hadn't been imagining the intrusion and frightened by what it might mean.

John looked mortified. 'I cannot believe any of the servants would do such a thing.'

'I am sure they would not.'

The door to the main house opened. Hans stood there with Griet, holding a lamp.

'What is it? Are there intruders?'

'A peeping Tom, Uncle,' John said, running towards him. 'Someone opened Miss Lepard's shutter.'

Griet bustled towards them. 'Why didn't the dog bark?'

John shook his head. 'I don't know.'

Van Aarnhem called inside to one of his sons. 'Piet, go and see.' He turned back to Isabelle. 'We'll rouse the servants and search the farm, he can't have got far.'

'I want to help,' Isabelle said.

He shook his head. 'I don't want to be worrying for your safety. John, you stay here too, in case the intruder comes back.'

Moments later, they heard a cry from behind the house. Piet came stumbling round the side of the building holding the body of the ridgeback in his arms, the dog's head lolling over his strong arms.

'He's been poisoned!'

Jan ran to his brother and pressed his hand against the animal's chest. 'He's still breathing.'

'We need to make him sick. Quick,' Griet said, taking charge. 'Leave the dog with me. You boys go with your father.'

As Jan rushed to fetch lamps, Van Aarnhem turned to Isabelle. 'Was he alone, Miss Lepard?'

'All I saw was a man's hand, his right hand, reaching down through the window. It was white-skinned and –' she frowned as the memory became clearer – 'I think the lower half of his little finger was missing.'

Van Aarnhem fetched his rifle from inside the house then, with Piet and Jan holding the lamps, he summoned three Black servants who were carrying sticks, and the party headed up into the scrubland behind the cottage.

Isabelle saw the lamps jerking in the darkness, two spots of light receding against the dark beyond. The men were shouting, a kind of hunting cry, as they thrashed through the scrub.

'John, will you help?' Griet said.

Isabelle watched as Turner carried the dog to the side of the house, while Griet went to fetch a pot from the kitchen. 'A paste from the cork-bark bird-berry tree,' he explained. 'It's a good purgative.'

With her nephew holding his head, Griet spooned the mixture into the dog's mouth, then massaged his throat to help it go down. She kneaded his pale stomach until he started to retch, then John hauled the animal upright. They both stepped back as the dog suddenly vomited.

'There,' Griet said, standing up and wiping her hands on her apron.

The dog shook its head, then circled around.

'No, you don't,' John said quickly. Griet reached for a pail of water and sluiced the mess away. He pointed. 'That's what did it.' Isabelle peered at some remaining chunks of undigested meat, barely chewed. 'Your intruder fed him something to put him to sleep.'

'But why?'

John shrugged. 'So he would not alert us, I suppose.'

'Come inside, Miss Lepard,' said Griet. 'I make tea.'

Isabelle took a last look into the darkness. In the heat of the moment, she hadn't thought of anything more than to protect herself. Even though drosters no longer existed in their hundreds, any farm might fall victim to a night-time raid. Now, a cold trickle went down her spine. What if it was nothing to do with Klein Bethlehem? What if it was the same man who had been following her since Cape Town, somehow knowing she was here?

Galloping bare-backed on the bay horse, leading the piebald by its halter, the man cleared the boundary of Klein Drakenstein. He found the wagon trail, and kept moving. He was not worried about anyone seeing him. Farmers went to bed early and rose with the light.

He did not regret trying to steal the Will. His informant in

Cape Town had told him it was tucked inside an old leather journal. But he had not expected the woman to be awake, nor to have a knife so easily to hand.

The theft of the horses would at least slow them down. And that would give him time enough to position himself in a spot on the outskirts of Franschhoek. He would ambush them there.

While they waited for the search party to come back, Isabelle drank some sage tea sweetened with honey, and listened while John and Griet talked. She could only make out one or two words, but got the impression that Griet's main concern was that they had failed as her hosts.

Finally, they heard the tramp of boots outside. Isabelle sprang up as the men came into the house.

'*Hoe is . . .?*' Piet asked immediately.

'The dog seems fine,' John replied in Afrikaans. 'Poisoned meat, but only to make him sleep. There should be no lasting damage.'

'Did you find anyone?' Isabelle asked, seeing the grim look on van Arnhem's face.

'There was a trail of broken twigs and a path down through the scrub. I regret to say the horses are gone.'

'No!' Isabelle cried out. Without them, they would not be able to continue on to Franschhoek.

'But if he was merely a horse thief,' John observed, 'why was he trying to break into Miss Lepard's cottage? Why draw attention to himself?'

Isabelle was certain it was her fault that trouble had come to the farm.

'I might know who the man is,' she began, and felt five pairs of eyes fix upon her like a searchlight. 'I don't know his name, but I noticed him first in Cape Town.'

CHAPTER SIXTY-SIX

Tuesday, 25th February

Over the next six days, there were no further sightings of a stranger at Klein Bethlehem, though they all remained watchful.

While John and his uncle tried to secure fresh horses, Isabelle determined to make herself useful. Because John had taken the bridles and saddles into the barn on the night they arrived, the thief hadn't taken Isabelle's side-saddle. It was a significant stroke of luck. It would have been a near impossible task to find another so far from the town. Griet had moved her sons into one bedroom and insisted Isabelle take Jan's bed, rather than have her sleeping away from the main house in the cottage. Though she had protested, Isabelle felt relieved.

She persuaded Griet to let her help with some of the chores around the farm. She learnt how to milk a goat, fetched eggs from the hens in the morning, mended the kitchen reed broom handle with a strip of rawhide. The enforced delay was frustrating, but working helped keep her spiralling thoughts under control. She was certain it was the same man who had been following her, though what he wanted was still unclear. If it was he who had searched her room in Cape Town, and had attempted to get into the cottage on the evening they had arrived, it suggested he was looking for something particular he believed she had in her possession. Stealing the horses might have been for gain but Isabelle thought it more likely to be an attempt to stop her travelling to Franschhoek. Why that should be, again she could not say.

Each night, after the evening meal, Isabelle recorded her impressions. Her admiration for Suzanne's fortitude, in coming to the Cape to find Louise and bring her story back into the light, grew stronger with every passing day: the hardships she had faced, her courage and refusal to give in until she had found her ancestor. It made Isabelle even more determined than ever to do both women justice – Louise and Suzanne, and all the women of the Joubert family in whose image she was made.

Thursday, 27th February

A week and a day after they had arrived at the farm, Isabelle and John Turner left Klein Bethlehem and rode east towards the rising sun.

Isabelle was sorry to leave, having become fond of Griet, and her husband, and their sweet, silent sons. She had felt herself at the heart of a family again, something she had not known since she was a little girl before her beloved older brothers had been sent to boarding school.

After they had died, her loneliness had deepened. She and her father had been left alone in Bouverie Street with their ghosts. Isabelle knew that this was, in part, why Minou, Louise and Suzanne meant so much to her. She had never known her grandmothers, or her mother. These distant relatives were the female family she had never had. But, in this out-of-the-way farm, part way between Stellenbosch and Franschhoek, for a few special days she had felt part of something larger than herself again.

DRAKENSTEIN MOUNTAINS

As they rode away from the Drakenstein mountains, Turner told Isabelle that they were nearing Pierre Jaubert's original plot of land.

Away from Klein Bethlehem, her nerves were on edge. She thought John felt the same. He carried a rifle across the front of his saddle and was always alert, flicking his gaze this way and that as they rode over the veldt towards the rockier passes that led towards the Berg River, and then to the smaller tributary that ran down through the town of Franschhoek.

Her thoughts were much occupied. Partly she was thinking about her destination and what she hoped to find. Once she had located Louise's grave, if she *could* locate it, that would be the moment to try to make contact with the Barenton family and explain who she was. She was also constantly worried about the possibility of the stalker making another assault on them. In a way, she would almost welcome it. It was the not knowing where he was, or what he wanted, that was so unnerving. At least if she could come face to face with him, she would feel less powerless. As it was, she felt like an antelope being stalked by a leopard, a constant prickling at the back of her neck and the sensation that somewhere, hidden in the hills, was a person who meant her harm.

Isabelle knew that, during Suzanne's nine months at the Cape from the winter of 1688 to the following April, she had succeeded in learning what had happened to Louise. Later, having survived the shipwreck of the *Gouw*, having married and then lived in London, with children of her own, Suzanne had written an account of Louise's life.

But she had left gaps, not least of all a record of the final confrontation between Louise and Gilles and Phillipe. That diary, written in Louise's own hand, had remained in Olifantshoek in the possession of Théodore Barenton and it was this that Isabelle hoped to find. In it, she believed the final chapter of the story of the feud between the Joubert and Vidal families going back generations would be explained.

Isabelle pressed her satchel into her side, feeling the comforting bulk of Minou's journal. This told the story of a Catholic priest, Vidal, and the feud that had begun in Carcassonne when a Catholic girl, Minou Joubert, had fallen in love with a Huguenot boy, Piet Reydon. From that one chance moment of instant connection, on a misty February evening before France descended into religious turmoil, everything had followed.

Though both the Vidal and the Joubert families had been wealthy and influential in their time, there was nothing left now, no inheritance, no land: the Joubert estate in Puivert had been seized during the first religious war in 1562; and the Vidal estates outside Chartres had been lost during the Revolution two centuries later. Isabelle didn't care about any of that. What she cared about was the truth.

Isabelle brought herself back to the present. She looked at the fynbos, the green foliage punctuated by pink sugarbush and laurel-leaf protea and *kloof* pincushion blooms. She saw *waboom*, wagon trees – so-called because its wood was used for wheel rims and brake blocks – and reddish-brown assegai, wild olive and magnificent yellow-wood trees. It was a vista that could not be more different from the cobbled streets of the medieval citadel of Carcassonne where Minou had grown up, or La Rochelle, where Suzanne had been born, or her own home in London. Those worlds seemed so far away now.

'How much longer until we arrive?' she asked.

John looked up at the sky. 'There is a storm coming from the south-east. Rainstorms are pretty common at the tail-end of summer, and it will make the passes dangerous. When it comes, we will have to take shelter and, depending on how long the storm lasts, either ride hard to escape it or, more likely, wait until morning.'

'If at all possible, I would keep going.'

To be so close, and yet so far, was unbearable to her. And she did not like the idea of spending a night out in the open.

'There are shepherds' huts where we might wait out the storm,' John said, as if reading her mind. 'But it would be unwise to travel at night. There are too many wild animals. Hunters, too.' He pointed ahead. 'That is the Berg River. Can you see?'

'I think so.'

'If we can reach it before the rain starts, there is grassy pasture down there. That will be the safest place to spend the night.'

Isabelle dug her heel into her horse's flank and set off across the veldt, John following in her wake.

CHAPTER SIXTY-SEVEN

Andries Barenton watched them from behind the cover of the river reeds, swaying in the gathering wind. A storm was coming. He waited a moment more, then stepped out of the cover of the ironwood tree and knelt down.

They were still too far away.

He was a skilled hunter and an excellent shot. His military rifle, taken from the dead hands of a British soldier in an ambush, had an impressive range, but it was not accurate at much over nine hundred yards.

He needed to be patient. He got back to his feet and laid the gun across his arms. He was still weighing up whether to kill the woman first, or the man? He flushed in anger when he remembered how she had taken him by surprise on die Braak in Stellenbosch. She had a knife, he knew that now, and was prepared to use it. But the man would be stronger and, no doubt, carry a firearm. It might be better to eliminate him first.

'*Kom op*,' he urged as they came closer into view. Come on.

He was still smarting from his failure to steal the Will at Klein Bethlehem and, before that, in Cape Town. The vein in his forehead started pumping and his face reddened. La Justice had been in his family for nearly two hundred years, on the site of an even earlier farm. Yet this English *hoer* thought she could arrive with a piece of paper – a French document at that – and take away all that his family had built.

He would not stand for it.

Andries had heard how several decent Boer families had had their livelihoods taken from them by claimants come from Europe. Whispers carried on the wind from settlement to settlement. One German farmer, faced with the loss of his farm, had taken his shotgun and killed his wife and three daughters, before turning the gun on himself. From then on, Andries had vowed he would not be cheated in the same way. He would do anything necessary to protect what was his. Though he was no thinker, he was cunning. Some years ago, Andries had put in place an arrangement with several hotels to be notified about new arrivals from France or England. It had cost him, but it was worth it. So, as soon as the message arrived that there was an English woman with a French name asking questions about Franschhoek, he had ridden to Cape Town. The maid at the hotel in Greenmarket Square, who was walking out with one of his informants, reported that there was a Will among the woman's papers in her room. Andries didn't know anything more than that, but he was not prepared to take the slightest chance. Her name meant nothing – Lepard was not a name he had ever come across – but the maid said her middle name was Joubert, and that name carried great weight.

Andries steadied his breathing and fixed his gaze on his quarry as they came closer, closer. His grip tightened upon the trigger. He set his eye along the muzzle, kept his arm steady and prepared to fire.

A sudden rumble of thunder in the mountains broke his concentration. Andries took aim once more as the first spots of rain began to fall. Slowly at first, then faster and harder, hammering down onto the dry land and obscuring his sight.

Reluctantly, he let his arm drop as the storm took hold. He stepped back under cover, slung the rifle over his shoulder and took shelter beneath the branches of the ironwood tree. He rubbed the raw stump of his little finger.

He would have to wait.

Isabelle heard another rumble of thunder, an ominous growling in the mountains, like a giant waking from sleep. Above the wild torment in the skies, she thought she could hear the sound of elephants calling to one another across the valley.

'There,' John shouted, pointing at a clump of wild olive trees. 'We'll shelter there until the storm passes.'

The storm was intensifying. Isabelle could not believe that the sky could contain so much water. The rain was coming down in sheets, as if they were standing beneath a waterfall.

At last, she huddled with John under the olive trees, each soothing their horses as the thunder cracked overhead, shivering in the chilled air.

'How long do such storms usually last?'

'Impossible to say,' he replied. 'It could last until morning, or else the wind could blow the clouds through in the next few hours.'

Isabelle looked around the little grove. 'So, will we set up camp here?'

'I think we had better. It is not ideal, but the weather should keep the worst of the predators at bay.'

Isabelle nodded. 'The fallen twigs closer to the trunk should still be dry enough for a fire.' She stared up at the tiny black olives. 'And at least the rain has driven the mosquitoes away.'

In his hideaway beside the river, Andries Barenton kept watch.

He'd seen them change course and head for the clump of wild olive trees. As the light faded, he had seen the first sparks of a fire, bright in the darkness of the storm-drenched veldt at night. He had seriously considered sneaking up on them. They had no dog, just two horses, and the fire betrayed their position. But caution had prevailed. Though the storm would most likely keep the larger predators at bay, he could hear a pack of jackals, not too distant.

He sat back with his rifle across his knees. He was not worried his quarry would escape him. They would not risk leaving in darkness and he would wake with the first rays of the sun.

CHAPTER SIXTY-EIGHT

FRANSCHHOEK VALLEY
Friday, 28th February

Isabelle awoke to the sound of birdsong.

She looked out on a world painted new and clean. Everywhere was evidence of the storm – branches down, silver pools of rainwater on the veldt – but it was glorious. Isabelle did not think that she had ever visited so startlingly beautiful a country as southern Africa: the sheer scale of it, the glory of it, the strangeness of it, quite took her breath away. She inhaled, filling her lungs with fresh air, and raised her face to the rising sun.

John had already saddled the horses and was waiting.

Isabelle lifted the edge of her damp skirts and laughed. 'Although the sun is often too strong for me, I could do with a little this morning to dry myself out.'

'It will be hot later. It usually is after a storm clears the air.'

'How far is Franschhoek from here?'

'No more than an hour or so, all being well.'

As she stamped out the embers of the fire, Isabelle realised she was smiling. She was almost there, the place where Louise had lived and died, the place to which Suzanne had found her way. Soon, she would be there, too, and would lay flowers on the grave.

Both the end of her quest, and its beginning.

*

The wind had changed direction, so Andries could just make out their voices. Indistinct words carried across the rain-washed valley and down to the river where he was camped. Then, the woman laughed.

The sound enraged him.

He emerged from the reeds and resumed the position he had taken last evening, down on one knee with his finger on the trigger. It was a clear day, he ought to be able to get a clean shot.

Suddenly, Andries knew that he was being stalked. He had been so focused on his own prey, that he had failed to pay attention to his surroundings.

Slowly, with no abrupt movements, he turned. There was a leopard only some thirty paces away, moving sinuously along the bank of the river. Their eyes locked for an instant. Then everything seemed to happen at once. Sensing his prey, the leopard sprang, accelerating along the path in a blur of gold and brown. Andries raised his gun and fired.

Blood exploded from the creature's chest, red against the tawny pelt. For a moment, he seemed to hold the animal's gaze, eyes wide and white as its body hung in the air, like a marionette. Then, the leopard fell heavily to the path in front of Andries.

Shaken, he lowered his gun. He, who was an expert tracker and hunter, had let his guard down like a novice. That lapse in concentration had nearly killed him.

He looked down to check the leopard was dead. In normal circumstances, he would find a way of transporting the carcass back to town. Or else, skin it here for the pelt. But these were not normal circumstances. He dragged the animal into the reeds. If other predators did not find it first, he would return and skin it later.

For now, it was more important to get to Franschhoek before his prey and be ready for them.

Isabelle jerked round in the saddle. 'What was that? It sounded like a shot.'

John did not look concerned. 'Hunters, probably. They mostly go out early in the day. Or a farmer scaring jackals away from his livestock.'

'It was very close.'

'Sound travels differently here.'

Isabelle peered across the veldt. 'I can't see anyone.'

'They are more likely higher up in the Franschhoek pass. It's nothing to worry about.'

She nodded. 'Nearly there,' she muttered under her breath. 'Nearly there.'

FRANSCHHOEK

An hour later, as the mission bell was ringing for eleven o'clock, Isabelle and John rode into the small frontier town.

Her first impression was that Franschhoek was a place of white and blue. Cape Dutch architecture, of the kind she had seen in Stellenbosch and Cape Town, buildings with gables and peak-arched windows. Everything seemed so new. The church less than fifteen years old – the date of its construction painted black on the white pediment – stood startling bright on Victoria Street, proud against the cloudless blue sky. The houses were mostly single-storeyed and also painted white, simple and comfortable dwellings for the growing population of the town. They were more modest than in Stellenbosch, some with wrought-iron trellises and stoeps at the front. Beyond the houses, stretching right up to the foothills of the mountains, were fields of vines and farms.

There were little children and their nurses, servants in white bonnets and aprons, ladies out taking the air. Yet it was very quiet. The cypress trees in the graveyard were almost black in the strengthening sun. And all around, the magnificent mountains bounded the settlement, their limestone slopes painted copper by the morning sun.

Isabelle exhaled, finding herself moved by this visible evidence of her own history. For these farms surrounding the town were the original plots of land granted to the Huguenot refugees – La Dauphiné, Bourgogne, La Bri, Champagne, La Motte, Cabrière and La Provence, where Pierre Jaubert had subsequently lived. Their lost villages remembered in the names they gave to their new homes. And, if Suzanne's description was accurate, La Justice would be found at the end of the old wagon trail.

'There is a boarding house on Dirkie Uys Street,' John said, breaking into her thoughts. 'Uys was a Voortrekker, a hero of the Great Trek. They should have rooms and stabling for the horses.' He dismounted. 'Will you come with me now or shall I fetch you once I have made arrangements?'

Isabelle swung her leg over the pommel and jumped down to the ground. She sorely needed a wash and a change of clothes, but she wanted to visit the graveyard first. Everything about her journey had led to this point. She didn't want to wait another moment.

'I will go to the cemetery,' she said. 'Come and find me there once our rooms are ready.'

'Very good, miss.'

While John led the horses away, Isabelle made her way along Victoria Street towards the graveyard at the edge of the town, where she believed Théodore Barenton once had lived.

CHAPTER SIXTY-NINE

Isabelle stood alone beneath the endless blue sky. Evergreen cypress and rough grasses bounded the graveyard. The few grey headstones had been bleached the colour of bone by the fierce Cape sun.

Hier Rust. Here lies.

She bent forward to read the names and dates on the tombstone, obscured by lichen or moss. Between her high white collar and the dust-caked brim of her leather hat, her skin on the back of her neck was burning. The African sun was too strong for her English complexion and she had been riding across the veldt for days.

Isabelle removed her riding gloves, folding one inside the other. She had mislaid too many in her travels to be careless. She dropped them to the ground at her feet. A powder of copper-red Cape dust puffed into a cloud, then settled. A black beetle, hard-backed and resolute, scuttled for cover.

Isabelle drew breath, allowing everything to still for a moment.

She had followed this trail from the banks of the Thames to the Aude, to the Garonne and the Amstel, across the English Channel and over the wildest seas to where the Atlantic Sea meets the Indian Ocean. Sometimes the trail had blazed bright. The story of two families and a secret passed down from generation to generation. More than three hundred years of women's lives, lost and now found. Some of their names had been obscured by time, taken up in those of their husbands and brothers and lovers, but their spirit lived in her.

Finally, her quest had come to an end here. In Franschhoek.

Ci gît. Here lies.

Isabelle removed her leather riding hat and fanned herself. The wide brim shifted the blistering air, but there was little respite. She wiped her forehead with a stained handkerchief and her blonde hair was damp with sweat. She cared little for her appearance. She had survived this journey, survived the assaults on her person and the attempted theft of her possessions. All to bring her here.

To this unkempt cemetery in this frontier town.

Still, Isabelle could not bring herself to look at the name on the gravestone. Wishing to savour this last moment a little longer, she undid the buckle on her satchel and reached inside. Her fingers skimmed the small antique bible that had once belonged to her father, but it was Minou's journal that she took out. The words were etched on her heart, the spidery browned ink, the antique language reaching forward to her across hundreds of years. She knew every syllable like a catechism learnt in Sunday School from the last entry to the first.

This is the day of my death.

She heard the whistling of a red-wing starling in flight at the boundary of the cemetery. Her knuckles were white, clasped tight. What if, after all this, there was nothing left to find?

As the Lord God is my witness, here, by my own hand, do I set this down. My last will and testament.

Isabelle did not pray. Though she was the daughter of a clergyman, the history of the injustices done in the name of religion to her Huguenot ancestors surely proved that there was no such thing as God. For what God would allow so many to die in agony and terror in His name? Besides, she was a blue-stocking, a scholar educated in natural sciences and philosophy. Superstitions – old mythologies to keep women in their place – were not for her.

All the same, Isabelle glanced heavenwards. The sky here in Franschhoek in February was the same vivid blue as it was in Carcassonne. The same kind of fierce winds caught the dust in the hinterlands of the Cape of Good Hope as they did in the garrigue du Midi. She belonged in neither place – she was English to her bones – yet she could see that the two landscapes were mirror images of one another, Languedoc and southern Africa. This was her heritage.

The air was still. Little was stirring in the graveyard in the heat of the day. Almost all living creatures had taken shelter in the shade. Iron railings marked out each plot – the de Villiers family, the le Roux family, the Malan family, the Jourdans, the Hugos and the du Toits, the Retiefs and the de Villiers – all those of the Reformed Religion who had fled France in search of sanctuary in the year of Grace of the Lord 1688.

Her ancestors, too.

Finally, having prepared herself, Isabelle crouched down and traced the letters carved on the headstone. And saw the names she had hoped to see. She gave a long sigh of relief. It was all true, then. The two names she had hoped to find inscribed in stone. This had been the very first grave in the cemetery, built on the land of the first wine farm in Olifantshoek.

'La Justice,' she said, remembering what Suzanne had written in her notebooks.

Isabelle was so absorbed, so held by the moment, that she did not hear the footsteps behind her in the dirt. She did not register the sudden shadow blocking the sun, nor the smell of sweat, of clinker and leather, of a long journey across the veldt. She noticed nothing until the push of the muzzle of a gun was at her neck.

'*Staan op.*' A man's voice speaking in Afrikaans, then in English. 'Get up.'

Isabelle tried to turn, to see him, but the cold metal jabbed against her skin and, momentarily, she glimpsed the deformed little finger on his right hand.

Slowly, she did what she was told.

'Give me the Will,' he said. 'If you do, I will not harm you.'

She knew he was lying, for there was too much at stake now. He had been following her for several weeks.

'Give it to me. Slowly, now.'

Instinctively, her grasp tightened on Minou's journal and the precious papers contained inside. After all that she had endured, Isabelle refused to surrender it. But now his fingers were pinching at her shoulder, driving into the muscle hard and fierce, through the cotton of her shirt. Her grip could not hold. The journal fell down onto the dirt and burst open, scattering the Will and other papers into the dust of the graveyard.

'Did you follow me from Cape Town?' she asked, in hesitant Afrikaans – 'kitchen Dutch', as the English called it.

He did not answer.

Isabelle had Suzanne's knife concealed in her boot. When he leant down to pick up the papers, she whipped out the dagger. If she could disable him, if only for a moment, she might steal the journal back and run.

But he had anticipated such an attack and shifted his weight sideways. She was aware, just before it connected with the side of her head, of the downward strike of his arm, and a glimpse of his black hair, divided by a seam of white. Then an explosion of pain as the pistol made contact. She felt the seep of blood on her temple, the heat of it, then nothing.

In her last seconds of consciousness, Isabelle grieved to think this was how the story would end. In a forgotten corner of a graveyard on the other side of the world.

This is the day of my death.

CHAPTER SEVENTY

When she came to, Isabelle found she was lying on a bed, beneath a white sheet in a white room, dreaming of colour. Caught between sleeping and waking.

She lifted a cautious hand to her head. Though she could feel the split skin on her temple, and the ridge of the blow, there was no fresh blood. In a swoop of despair, she remembered how Minou's journal had fallen down onto the red soil. That was the last thing she remembered.

She opened her eyes, surfacing from a place of shadows to a world of harsh light. The space was unremarkable and unfamiliar, but it was a typical room in a Cape Dutch homestead. White walls, plain but for a piece of embroidery with verses from the Bible on the wall. Bare-board floors, a chest of drawers and a nightstand made of stinkwood.

Isabelle sat up, sending her head spinning. She took stock. She was robust and strong, not a feeble creature addicted to *sal volatile*. She swung her legs off the bed, wiggled her toes, then felt the wooden floor through her stockinged feet, relieved that everything seemed to be in working order. Her white shirt and her riding skirt were stained with dust, but someone had removed her boots and placed them at the foot of the bed. She saw her leather hat was hanging from a hook on the back of the wooden door.

Slowly, she took stock of the room, taking in every tiny detail. There was a brass tray with an earthenware jug on the chest of drawers. She went to investigate and found, beneath the cloth, local wine the colour of cherries, a piece of white bread and strips of dried beef.

Isabelle did not understand. Was she prisoner or guest?

Still a little unsteady on her feet, she moved to the door and found it locked. Then she heard a chattering of starlings outside. She put on her boots, then walked to the window. A small square frame with thin metal bars on the inside.

To keep her in or to keep others out?

She reached through the bars and pushed open the rough glass. The sky at dusk in the Cape was the same as it was in Languedoc. White, with a wash of pink as the sun set behind the mountains. She could just make out the chapel, with its thatched roof and peak-arched windows either side of the arched wooden door. The sight of it gave her hope, for at least she was still within the boundaries of the town. If the man meant to kill her, surely he would have taken her up into the mountains? Away from prying eyes.

Isabelle could make out the fruit orchards, too, Cape damsel and damask plums, sweet saffron pears and apples hanging from the trees. The rise and fall of girls' voices playing a skipping game, communicating in a mixture of Afrikaans and English, no French, the legacy of years of struggle for control of this stolen land. Further away, she could make out the plangent singing of the men coming home from the fields.

She decided she must have been unconscious for six or seven hours at least. Her feeling of relief was fleeting. Quickly, it gave way to anger at what she had lost: Minou's journal, and the precious Will and Testament, which had been in her family for hundreds of years. Isabelle could almost hear the voices of her ancestors calling to her across the centuries.

Then, her despair at the loss of the documents turned to fear.

If he had not killed her yet, it could only be because there was something more he wanted from her. She wished she had been quicker in the graveyard, more alert. She remembered reaching to scrape the lichen from the stone, then the feel of the cold muzzle of the gun and the sound of his pitiless voice. She'd managed to draw her knife, but only grazed his hand. It was not enough. She wondered if John was looking for her? When he went to the graveyard and found her missing, surely he would have tried to find her?

The light was fading from the sky. The still air was filled with the whining and the buzzing of insects. Through the bars, Isabelle watched the children being taken inside and pinpricks of light appearing in every house as candles and lamps were lit. Though she was tired, she kept vigil at the window, drinking only a little of the smooth Cape wine. She could not afford to dull her senses.

The bell in its solitary white tower marked the passing hours. Nine o'clock, then ten. Outside, darkness fell and the mountains faded into shadow. On Victoria Street and the criss-cross of smaller roads and alleyways, the flames in the houses were being extinguished one by one. Franschhoek was evidently a town that went to bed at dusk and rose with the sun.

It was not until past two o'clock, when Isabelle was battling sleep and the throbbing in her head had started again, that she heard a sound from inside the house. The creak of the floorboards on the other side of the door, someone walking carefully, as if trying not to be heard.

Although she'd had hours to decide what to do, it was instinct that took over now. Isabelle grabbed the wine jug and slipped behind the door. She listened to the rattle of a key being pushed into the lock, then the clunk of the catch as it gave. The door slowly opened inwards.

She could not see clearly, but she glimpsed the streak of white hair in the dark and smelt the leather of the man's jacket. This time she would not be bested. The instant he was within reach, she launched the earthenware jug at the height of his head. In the poor light, she misjudged, striking only a glancing blow. Though the man staggered, he did not fall.

Isabelle launched herself towards the open door, intending to try to get past, but he was faster. He grabbed her wrist and pushed her backwards into the room, clamping a hand over her mouth.

'Be quiet, you little fool! You'll get us both killed.'

Immediately, she was still. It was a different voice. Speaking English, not Afrikaans. And in the moonlight filtering through the window, she could see his right hand. No half-missing finger.

Seeming to trust her not to run, the man released her and took a step away.

'Forgive me,' she said in English. 'I thought you were him.'

Now, in the silver shadows, Isabelle could see his face. He was shorter than her attacker in the graveyard and his black hair was longer, though split through by the same twist of white.

'You do look like him, though.'

'Yes.'

She waited for him to say more, but he didn't speak.

'Why am I here?'

He held up his hand. 'We have to go.'

Isabelle shook her head. 'Not until you tell me who you are.'

'We—' He hesitated. 'I saw what happened in the graveyard. I've had to wait until now. He is my brother.'

Isabelle froze, not knowing whether she should trust this man or not.

'We do not see eye to eye. He has firm opinions and, well, once he has made his mind up, he cannot be swayed . . .' His words tailed off. He glanced to the door and seemed restless to be gone.

'Whose house is this?' she asked.

'It belongs to our mother. She is all but bedridden. None of this is her fault.' He briefly touched her arm. 'Please, come with me. I will answer all your questions once we are safely away from Franschhoek.'

'Where is your brother now?'

'Drinking, as is his custom. Once he starts, he cannot stop. But he will be back at any moment. It is late. We must leave.'

Isabelle hesitated. 'And if I don't come with you?'

The man looked directly at her and she saw the determination – concern, too – in his eyes. 'Then I fear he will kill you.'

The calm statement convinced her more than any entreaty or fierce persuasion could have done. She had no idea what was happening, but better surely to take her chance with this stranger than to remain here, waiting for what the dawn might bring?

Isabelle took her hat from the back of the door. 'Will you tell me your name?' she whispered, as she followed him along the dark corridor and towards a door at the rear of the house.

He put his finger to his lips.

'Will you at least tell me where we are going?'

He hesitated, then answered. 'To the old stone bridge across the ford. The others are waiting there.'

'What others? What bridge? I don't understand.'

'Jan Joubertsgat,' he replied, as if surprised she didn't know. 'It is where Jan Joubert died.' He turned. 'Isn't that why you are here?'

Isabelle stopped dead. 'You know who I am?'

Unexpectedly, the man smiled. 'Of course,' he said, unhooking the latch and pushing open the front door. 'Everyone knows who you are.'

CHAPTER SEVENTY-ONE

JAN JOUBERTSGAT
Saturday, 1st March

Isabelle followed her rescuer silently out onto the road.

'Is this Dirkie Uys Street?'

'It is.'

It crossed her mind that she should try to leave a message for John, telling him she was all right. Hadn't he said he was going to secure them rooms here? She was sure he would be out of his mind with worry. But, just as quickly as the thought had come, she dismissed the idea. She had no idea where, precisely, John had intended them to stay.

Perhaps she should make a run for it? How could she be sure this man and his brother were not in league together? She only had his word that he meant her no harm. But instinct told her that he was to be trusted. And despite all that had happened to her, Isabelle felt alert and alive, curious to know what was going to happen. Wasn't this what she had been looking for? The truth of her family history? She would learn nothing by being timid.

'How far is it?' she asked.

'It will take us two hours on foot.'

Isabelle looked down at her boots, at the uncompromising back of the man striding in front of her, then stopped. 'I am not going a step further until you tell me your name. And why we are going to Joubertsgat.'

In the delicate light from the new moon, she thought she saw the amusement in his eyes.

'You are very forthright.'

'A woman has to be.'

He gave a short laugh and slowed his pace, though he did not stop.

Isabelle hesitated, then ran to catch him up. 'Well?'

'Joubertsgat – or Joubert's Bridge – is a stone bridge over a *kloof* in the Franschhoek pass, built nearly forty years ago. It was so called because a frontiersman by the name of Jan Joubert died there when the shaft of his wagon broke.'

'What does that have to do with me?'

'You are a Joubert, are you not?'

Isabelle sighed. 'I am not part of that family—'

He held up his hand. 'Yes, I know. You are not descended from *our* Joubert family in the Cape, but you are a Joubert all the same.'

In a rush, everything made sense. Of course, Isabelle had known from the moment she had seen her assailant's hair in the graveyard. And this man had the same white streak, too. It was just that, in her concussed state, her thoughts had been dulled.

'As are you,' she said.

He nodded. 'Xavier Joubert Barenton. My brother, whose acquaintance I regret you have already made, is Andries.'

'Barenton.' Isabelle caught her breath. 'It is you I have come to find.'

'I know.'

'You do?' She frowned. 'Why did your brother attack me? I have given him no cause.'

'He believes you have come to make a claim on his land.'

'*His* land?'

'He is my elder by five years, so Andries inherited the farm when our father died.'

'I have said or done nothing to give him that impression,' Isabelle protested. 'I have never written to him, nor had a conversation with him. He has been following me,' she said, suddenly angry. 'I saw him outside my hotel in Cape Town, then again in Stellenbosch. He stole our horses in Klein Bethlehem.'

'I can only apologise.'

'Could I not talk to him? Persuade him of my good intentions?'

'Once an idea is fixed in my brother's mind, it is impossible to shift. He had an accident some years ago, fell into a ravine and hurt his head. He was not expected to live. He did survive, but was never the same. He became obsessed with the farm and believed everyone was plotting to take it away from him. Even our mother is afraid of him.'

'And you?'

'I keep out of his way,' Xavier replied in a level voice. 'Unless I am given no alternative.'

'Like rescuing me.'

'Quite.'

'How did you know what had happened?'

'Word reached me.'

Isabelle saw they had now come to the outskirts of the town. Ahead, a path wound silver up into the mountains, a ghostly white beneath the thin moon.

'You should save your breath,' he said. 'We have a hard climb ahead of us.'

'But where are we going?'

'To find what you seek, I think. Louise's account of her time in the Cape. I hid it so my brother would not find it.'

Isabelle felt a shiver go down her spine. 'Louise's diary,' she whispered, and focused with renewed energy on the climb ahead.

*

Andries Barenton hurled the jug at the wall. He had been away longer than he had intended, then come back to find the woman gone.

'Where is she?' he shouted at his mother, a shrivelled woman cowering in a wheeled chair.

'I don't know! I heard nothing,' she whimpered.

Andries grabbed her arm. 'Who unlocked the door, then, you tell me that?'

The old woman shrank back even further into her chair. 'Who is she?' she whispered.

'It doesn't matter. What matters is that I asked you to watch over her and you have failed.'

'I fell asleep,' she protested, but her excuses only enraged him further. She felt silent. She had been on the receiving end of his fury too many times not to read the signs. 'I do not know how she got the key. Did you leave it in the lock?'

'Of course I did not,' he shouted, though in his inebriated state he realised he wasn't sure. Perhaps he had left the key in the lock and she had worked it loose? 'Go back to bed,' he spat, striding towards the door. 'You're no use to me.'

'Where are you going?' she cried. 'Don't do anything you'll regret, son.' She held up her worn hands, as if to protect herself. 'I don't want you to get into any trouble.'

Andries gave a bitter laugh. 'It is a bit late for that, Mother dearest.' Then, with a lightning change of mood, he suddenly leant down and patted her on the cheek. She flinched, fearing a blow.

'Go to bed,' he said, almost tender now. 'There is nothing for you to worry about.'

*

His dark mood returned the instant he was back in the street. He knew his anger at his mother was mostly anger at himself.

Andries blamed himself for his indecision. He should have killed the woman when he'd had the chance. It was only because it had been broad daylight when he found her in the graveyard that he had decided to take her instead to his mother's house in the centre of the town. His intention had been to wait until night and deal with her then. But one thing had led to another, and he stayed drinking with his friends for longer than he had intended, secure in the knowledge that the Will was now in his possession. Andries had considered burning it – if it didn't exist, then how could it be used against him – but something had held him back.

But now the woman had escaped. She could testify against him, speak of his attack on her person and the theft of her possessions. She was English and the administration would therefore take her word over his.

He had to find her and silence her.

Standing beneath the thinnest of new moons, a little unsteady on his feet, Andries tried to decide what to do. The wine had dulled his senses. He put his fingers to his temples and pressed, as if he could force his thoughts into order.

'The man who was with her,' he muttered, as a plan started to form. Perhaps her guide had somehow found her and set her free? Perhaps he had seen them in the graveyard and followed them to his mother's house?

Andries began to feel more hopeful. It would be a simple matter to investigate the few boarding houses with stables in the town. He was a hunter. If he could find the horses, then he could find the man.

*

'Is it much further?' Isabelle asked. Her head was pounding and her legs felt like water.

'They will be waiting for us with food and drink. You can rest then.'

All these things sounded good to Isabelle – rest, drink and food – though she was still none the wiser as to why they were climbing to Joubertsgat at all.

'Who are we going to meet? I am trusting you, should you not return the compliment?'

He hesitated, then answered: 'My wife.'

'You have a wife?'

'I do.' She heard the amusement in his voice. 'And a daughter, too.'

'Where do they live?'

Now he laughed. 'With me.'

'Where is that?' she asked impatiently. She was becoming tired of his elliptical answers and how he seemed always to be mocking her.

'We have a farm higher in the valley, but I cannot take you there. It is one of the first places my brother might think to look.' Xavier turned on the steep incline. 'As I told you, what you want is hidden at the bridge. It seemed safest for us to meet there.'

Isabelle looked up at the rock face looming above her head and hoped she could find the strength to make it to wherever they were going.

'For Suzanne,' she muttered. 'For Louise.'

CHAPTER SEVENTY-TWO

It was still pitch-black as they turned a corner at the top of the path and Isabelle finally found herself on level ground. She was exhausted, but determined not to show it.

'Here we are,' Xavier said at last.

Isabelle sat on a rock to catch her breath. Below her, she saw nothing but darkness with only one or two lamps burning in the houses in Franschhoek below.

Xavier cupped his hands together and made a sound, mimicking the call of an owl. Isabelle was pierced by a sudden memory as she remembered how Suzanne had seen a white owl so many, many years before. Some said it was a good portent, others claimed it was an omen of death.

For a moment, nothing stirred on the rocky mountain.

Xavier repeated the call. This time, from beneath the underhang of a rock, came an answering sound. Isabelle watched as a dark-skinned woman came out of the darkness. A little behind her, a child of some ten or eleven years old followed, paler than her mother and with her father's eyes. She was carrying a lamp.

Xavier turned to Isabelle, his face softened with affection. 'This is my wife, Maya, and my daughter Magdalena.'

The little girl bobbed a curtsey and Maya inclined her head.

'It is a pleasure to meet you, Miss Lepard,' she said, in faultless English.

'The pleasure is mine,' Isabelle replied formally, feeling oddly at a disadvantage. Though mixed marriages were not forbidden by the British administration, Isabelle had learnt enough in her short time in the country to know that they were certainly frowned upon. From her colouring, Isabelle imagined that Maya was descended from some of the earliest slaves who had been brought from Madagascar, but she did not feel it would be appropriate to ask. In any case, how did it matter?

'Was there any trouble?' Maya asked her husband *sotto voce*.

'I did not see him,' Xavier replied, 'though he will have discovered Miss Lepard is gone by now.'

Maya nodded. 'I left instructions with the servants to inform him, should he come to our farm, that we were in Wagenmakersvallei.'

He leant forward and kissed his wife. Feeling as if she was intruding, Isabelle turned away.

'You must be tired after the climb, Miss Lepard,' Maya said. 'Will you rest a while or take a little sustenance? We have bread and cheese, some pears and a little of our own wine?'

Isabelle smiled. 'That would be most welcome.'

Maya led her to a small clearing by the rock face, where a cloth and a picnic had been laid out. Isabelle, imagining Xavier's wife and daughter making the preparations for their arrival, was touched by the trouble they had taken.

Maya took the lamp from her daughter's hand and put it on the ground. 'Please, do sit. My husband told me what happened in the graveyard.'

'I am tired,' Isabelle admitted. 'My experiences in Franschhoek so far have been challenging, to say the least.'

Isabelle and Xavier ate in silence, watched over by Maya and Magdalena. The girl was clearly shy of their English visitor, but was also full of curiosity and spirit. She kept darting inquisitive glances at Isabelle, then looking away when she caught her eye. She did not seem to be frightened to be in the mountains at night, even when a jackal started to howl.

'It's a long way distant,' Xavier said, as if reading Isabelle's mind.

Now they were safely away from the town, and from his brother, she observed that Xavier was a different man. Sitting with his eyes half closed, the flames from the lamp lighting his face, he was calm, exhibiting none of the tension he had shown during their flight from his mother's house to this hidden eyrie.

Isabelle, on the other hand, felt her nerves were stretched tighter than ever. She had imagined this moment for so long – holding in her hands the record of what had happened to Louise and Gilles. But she also feared to read it. Having seen their names on the gravestone, everything felt so final. For a moment, she was happy to sit quietly, putting off the moment, regaining her strength, while Xavier and his wife talked.

Finally, the first rays of the sun began to climb above the highest tips of the mountains. She supposed it must be six o'clock in the morning, or thereabouts. Brushing the crumbs from her skirt, she put down her cup.

'You said you had hidden Louise's Olifantshoek diary here?'

Xavier got to his feet and walked towards the Joubertsgat. Isabelle followed, watching as he stepped down from the road and swung himself under the bridge. In the gathering light, Isabelle could see the flat stones on the river bed and the white water rushing over the stones, the green trees and bushes on either side of the narrow stream. Xavier's boots echoed beneath the underside of the bridge as he waded into the shallow water and disappeared from sight.

'There is a gap in the wall,' Maya explained, as she came to stand beside her. 'Xavier found it some time ago. He has used the hiding space from time to time to keep things safe.'

'From his brother?'

'Andries is a difficult man. It is sometimes easier to avoid confrontation than to be ensnared in his machinations.'

Wanting a better view, Isabelle threaded her way down the steep bank, holding onto the shrubs and small trees growing in the poor soil of the gorge to keep her balance. Now she could see Xavier working loose a stone in the underside of the bridge. He placed it carefully to one side, before reaching in and pulling out a small metal box.

He waded back through the water, passed the box up to Isabelle, then, using the roots of the same shrubs as handholds, hauled himself back up the bank until he was standing beside her on the ground above the bridge.

'Allow me.'

Xavier took the box from her hands, then they walked back to where Magdalena was clearing away the remnants of their breakfast meal. He took a small key from a chain around his neck, unlocked the padlock, reached inside and lifted out a brown diary. Isabelle saw that it was covered in plain board, much like a child's schoolbook.

'So far as I can tell,' Xavier said, 'this diary was kept by Louise and the last entries finished by her companion.' He stopped, perhaps unsure as to whether or not Isabelle knew the nature of the relationship between them. 'Finished by Gilles.'

'I know their story,' Isabelle said gently. 'Who they were to one another. It is what happened to them when first they arrived in the Cape that I have come to discover.'

'I am sure the answers you seek will be here,' Xavier said.

'Haven't you read it?' she said, surprised.

He shook his head. 'I do not understand French.'

Realising this made the stakes even higher and Isabelle took a deep breath.

'Then I shall translate it for you.'

She opened the diary, looked down at the familiar handwriting – picturing Louise's prison diary in her mind's eye and seeing the echo and shape and substance of those words on the page before her.

Isabelle began to read. And, suddenly, like a miracle, Louise was there, her voice filling the air as if she was sitting between them.

'It is the seventh day of May in the year of our Lord sixteen-hundred-and-twenty-two. Our voyage is at an end but our troubles, as I feared, are far from over. For it is clear, now, that he will never let me go.'

CHAPTER SEVENTY-THREE

THE CAPE COLONY
7th May 1622

Dressed in her captain's breeches with her red scarf tied around her head, Louise Reydon-Joubert stood on the sand and looked out over the sea of pavilions and huts. Gilles Barenton, in his customary black doublet and breeches, a white stock at his neck, was at her side.

It was a bright autumn morning and the mountains were painted gold by the sun. The limitless blue sky was broken only by thin threads of white cloud like a veil of gauze.

'It is beautiful,' she said to Gilles, for a moment forgetting the cares on her shoulders.

To Louise's eye, the scene looked as much like a muster for an army as anything else: people and animals everywhere, flags and pennants cracking in the wind, hawkers and traders laying out their wares, the smell of roasting meat. It might have been the Fleet Fair on the waterfront in Amsterdam were it not for the fact that there were no buildings and every face she saw was Black or brown.

Louise smiled. She was here. This was the Africa she had read about in books. Members of her crew, who had sailed around the Cape of Good Hope before, had told her the local people were called the Khoi, an ancient race who had lived on this continent for thousands of years. They waited on the shore for any passing ship – Portuguese, Spanish, English, Dutch – ready to trade: spices for iron, china and precious silks in exchange for fruit and vegetables and fresh water. Louise feared they were doomed to be disappointed when they discovered the *Old Moon* had nothing to trade, even more so when they learnt that the ship was going to set sail on the first tide to return to Europe.

Her spirits started to sink. She and Gilles had talked and talked, whenever they could find a private corner of the ship to do so. Though it would break her heart, they had agreed this was the only way they could ever be rid of her half-brother, Phillipe Vidal. It would mean Louise forfeiting everything she had worked for, but it was the only way they would ever be free. As important, was for her loved ones in Amsterdam to know what had happened. Her plan would ensure that Alis and Cornelia did not go to their graves in ignorance of what had befallen her. She wanted them to know how she thought of them often, and loved them always.

'Here he comes,' Gilles murmured in her ear. 'As I knew he would.'

Louise turned to see her half-brother disembarking from the rowing boat onto the sand, attended by his odious servant, and her heart sank further. She had prayed that Phillipe would stay on board. He had been afflicted with some kind of ague which she hoped would have kept him confined to his cabin. It was an unwritten rule that anyone suffering from sickness remained with the ship.

'I suppose it was too much to think that he would put the well-being of others before his own desires,' she replied.

'He would never do that,' Gilles said bitterly.

Louise's lieutenant, Tom Smith, was at the oars. He was the only member of the crew they had taken into their confidence. She knew Tom did not understand her intentions, but he would follow her orders to the letter. He had suggested an alternative way to solve the problem, but Louise could not allow him to damn his soul for her. It was one thing to kill in battle, another to take a life in cold blood.

Tom caught her eye and mouthed an apology for bringing Phillipe to shore. She gave a slight shrug, acknowledging that it was not his fault.

'Ah, sister,' Phillipe called out, walking towards her. 'You should have waited for me.'

Despite having been seven months at sea, Phillipe still managed to look as if he was walking along the boulevard St-Germain in Paris: his servant kept his clothes pressed, and his cuffs and ruff were somehow passingly white. The silver cross he wore around his neck glinted in the soft sunshine. He looked every bit the Catholic nobleman and Louise hated him for it. All the same, she forced a smile in greeting.

'Forgive me, brother, I thought you were resting.' Over their time at sea, she had learnt to hide her true emotions from her half-brother. He, somehow, had a gift for weaselling out secrets and she did not want him on his guard. 'I had not thought you intended to come ashore since we are here for so short a time. And since you are unwell . . .'

'I find I am much improved,' Phillipe replied with a thin smile that did not reach his eyes. 'Though I am surprised that you did not think to change your attire. What will these people think?'

Gilles gave a hollow laugh. 'I cannot imagine that the Khoi care a jot for fashion!'

Phillipe glared at him. 'When I wish for your opinion, Monsieur Barenton, I will ask for it.'

Louise touched Gilles' hand, warning him not to be drawn into yet another battle of wills that left him exhausted, and Phillipe exhilarated. It had been some weeks into their voyage from Gran Canaria to Cap Verde before she had accepted that her half-brother actually enjoyed sowing discord and setting everyone at one another's throats. She had done her best to neutralise his malign presence on board, but it was like fighting air. He was manipulative and sly, and left people doubting themselves as well as their previously firm friendships. It had led to an unhappy ship.

'Since you are here, shall we venture out?' Louise said, hoping Gilles would take the chance to speak with Tom without being overheard. Though she had hoped their original plan would succeed, she and Gilles had discussed other eventualities should Phillipe not remain on board. Louise slipped her arm through his. 'I would see the beads and ivory, and learn a little more of the people who live here.'

'I do not understand, sir,' said the lieutenant. Tom Smith was an honest fellow, and loyal, but could be dogged. 'Can you tell me again?'

Gilles bit his tongue, then repeated Louise's instructions as to how they intended to dupe Phillipe back on board the *Old Moon* without them.

'Young Pieter will have to take on the disguise,' he repeated patiently. 'He is the only crew member with the colouring and stature to match.'

'You want the boy to pretend to be the captain?'

Gilles held his gaze. 'I know we are grasping at straws, Tom, but there is no better option. From a distance, if Vidal sees someone of similar stature standing on the deck wearing one of the captain's red scarves, he will assume it is her. Surely you can see that?'

'But as soon as the rowing boat gets close, Monsieur Vidal will see that it is not.'

'Before they come alongside, Pieter will go to the captain's cabin. He must lock the door from the inside. You must explain that Louise has been taken suddenly unwell and has given you orders to pilot the *Old Moon* out of the bay. Put it out that it was something that she ate on shore.'

Smith was shaking his head. 'But everyone on board will know.'

'The only people who matter are Vidal and his servant,' Gilles said firmly, hoping he was right. 'And they will be on the second of the rowing boats coming back to the ship. If we can trick them back on board, and you can weigh anchor, then the captain will be safe.'

Tom mimed slitting his throat. 'I offered to—'

'I know,' Gilles interrupted. He sighed. 'And I am grateful to you for it. But she – we – cannot allow you to take such a risk.'

'The crew would be glad to see the back of him.'

'Even so, it is better that you sail the *Old Moon* back to Amsterdam as we agreed. The captain has given her diary into your safe keeping, has she not?'

'Yes, sir. I am to deliver it to an address on Warmoesstraat.'

For a moment, the two men stood in silence. Then Smith asked: 'I know it's not my place, but what are you going to do here?' He gestured around them. 'How will you survive?'

Gilles gave a sad smile. 'It will not be easy, I know that. But the Khoi have lived in these lands for thousands of years, Tom. We will find our way. The captain cannot go back to Europe, you know that. The terms of her release from the court in Gran Canaria prohibit it.'

'But you could sail on to the East,' the lieutenant protested. 'Find some vestiges of civilisation there.'

'Perhaps we will.'

'Or come back with us and settle elsewhere,' Tom persisted. 'Not one of us would betray her, you know that.'

'I do.' Gilles put his hand on Smith's arm. 'You are a good man, Tom, and a loyal friend. But her mind is made up to stay here. Please, help.'

The Englishman hesitated, then he nodded. 'Of course. Whatever the captain wants, sir.'

CHAPTER SEVENTY-FOUR

JAN JOUBERTSGAT
Saturday, 1st March 1862

Isabelle paused to catch her breath, leaving Louise's words hanging in the air. Maya offered her cup and Isabelle took a sip of wine. She felt light-headed, giddy from the experience of being taken into the heart of Louise's world over two centuries before. When she looked at Xavier's face, she could see he felt the same.

'I'm not sure how much you know of your – our – ancestors' first years here . . .'

She left the question unfinished. It was possible that Xavier knew nothing of the feud between the Joubert and the Vidal families.

'I know that Théodore Barenton, from whom I am directly descended, was the first owner of the wine farm La Justice. Théodore spoke of Louise Joubert and Gilles Barenton as his parents, though his blood father was in fact Phillipe Vidal. I also know that Vidal, from whom I inherited the streak of white in my hair, was not a good man.'

Isabelle nodded, relieved that she was not about to shatter any illusions or destroy the reputation of someone Xavier had long revered.

'The feud between the two families began during the Wars of Religion which tore France apart in the sixteenth century. Suzanne Joubert, Louise's first cousin twice removed, came to the Cape in the winter of 1688 in search of Louise and Gilles.'

Xavier nodded.

'Suzanne found Théodore, as you know. She gave him Louise's prison diary to read and he showed her this in return.' Isabelle patted the diary retrieved from beneath the bridge. 'Later, once she had found asylum in England, she wrote down what she remembered. I have those notebooks in London. But there were gaps, times when she skates over what had happened – the circumstances of Théodore's birth, Phillipe's death. I'm not altogether sure why.'

'Maybe it was too private?' suggested Xavier.

'Or Théodore asked her to keep his confidence,' Isabelle said. 'That Gilles gave birth, we know. That Phillipe was the father, we know. But how that came about . . .'

For a moment, they were silent.

'What happened to Suzanne?' asked Maya.

'The ship on which she was sailing back to Amsterdam, the *Gouw*, was wrecked off the Lizard Peninsula in Cornwall in 1629. She was one of few to survive. Fortunately, she had given Louise's prison diary – and, indeed, her own precious dagger – into the safekeeping of the captain and his chest was washed up on the beach. But all her writings from the Cape were lost, however, hence her having to write her reflections from memory. Suzanne found her way to London. In time, she fell in love and married another Huguenot refugee, William Lepard.'

'And so here you are,' Xavier said.

Isabelle smiled. 'All the oldest sons in our family have the Christian name William. They were men of faith, but most joined the Anglican Church rather than worship within Huguenot communities. My own dear father was a parish priest.'

'He did not wish to come with you?' Maya asked.

'I regret to say he passed away last year. Both of my brothers were lost in the Crimean War. It broke his heart.'

Maya instinctively drew her daughter to her. 'I am sorry.'

Isabelle smiled wistfully. 'I still find myself saving snippets of information to tell him, forgetting he is gone. He would be so proud of me having come this far.'

She gathered her thoughts and returned to the diary on her lap. 'The next entry is written two days later, the ninth of May 1622, when it seems that Louise's and Gilles' plan is to be put into effect.'

Isabelle began to read again, translating the text as she went:

'These have been the longest hours of my life. Phillipe never leaves my side, and will not allow me alone with Gilles. It is not that he forbids it, but rather that he is always there: talking, asking questions, insinuating and casting a shadow over everything that is said and done. Reminding me constantly, without ever saying as much, that I owe my life to him.

'Today, of all things, he presented me with my dagger with the emerald at its hilt. It was confiscated by the court in Gran Canaria and I thought it lost for ever. Now, it seems Phillipe had it all along. Of course, I had no choice but to thank him – and, in truth, I was delighted to have it in my possession again – but it is typical that he would have held back returning it to increase my sense of gratitude and of debt. It is a power play.

'Well, I have his measure and know that everything he does, he does only for himself. At first I gave him the benefit of the doubt, now I check every action for an ulterior motive. So, I thanked him courteously enough, but coolly. I refused to give him the pleasure of showing my genuine delight. That, needless to say, put him in an ill humour.

'I am watching the sky, praying that the wind will turn and that the Old Moon *can sail on the next tide. Only when Phillipe is gone, will I be able to breathe easily again.'*

CHAPTER SEVENTY-FIVE

THE CAPE COLONY
9th May 1622

The last of the afternoon was slipping from the sky as the rowing boat forged its way through the choppy waters of Table Bay towards the *Old Moon*. Louise could see it in miniature through the slit in the pavilion where she and Gilles were hiding.

Though the Dutch flag still snapped atop the main mast, the flag at the stern was unique. Designed by Gilles, and stitched by one of the crew members who had once been a tailor, it displayed a three-masted sailing ship with a woman in a red headscarf standing on the deck. She wished she could have taken it as a memento of those glorious months in the waters surrounding the Islas Afortunadas last year, when she had been a pirate queen, commander of her own ship, running the slaver corsairs to ground.

In the grey light of the tent, Louise took Gilles' hand. She had no doubt they were doing the right thing. How else could they be together, how else could they be free? But the prospect of watching her beloved ship sail away was even harder than she had imagined it would be.

'We will be all right,' he said. 'We will build a good life here.'

'I wish you had not relinquished your talisman, your card,' Louise replied. 'It means so much to you.'

'We agreed that if Phillipe saw both your diary and the Tarot card, he would have no reason to suspect we are not on board.'

Louise turned to Gilles and cupped his face in her hands. 'It is going to be very hard, one of the hardest things we have ever done. You do understand that? Even if I do manage to negotiate a parcel of land from the Khoi, and ask to be under their protection, our lives will be like nothing we have known.'

'But we will be together,' Gilles said simply.

Louise smiled with gratitude, then turned back to look out into the bay. The rowing boat now seemed no larger than a bird caught in the furrows between the waves.

'They are almost there,' she said.

Louise remained at her post, unwilling to take her eyes off the ship. She knew it would be the last time she set eyes on the *Old Moon*, her companion for so much of her adult life. She had to take comfort in the fact that the vessel was returning home to Cornelia and Alis in Amsterdam, and that they would cherish her.

Finally, as the last rays of the autumn sun vanished behind the mountains, Louise heard the cannon fire. The shot echoed across the bay and set a flock of seabirds on the shore to flight.

'They are about to weigh anchor,' she whispered, feeling relief but also an immense sense of sadness pressing down upon her chest as she bid her old life farewell.

As the smoke from the cannon dissipated, Vidal came striding across the deck of the *Old Moon*.

'What is this? I demand to see my sister.'

'I am sorry, sir, I am just following orders,' Tom Smith replied. 'The captain is indisposed. She would not risk your health by coming into contact with you. Some sickness from contaminated food, or foul air encountered on shore. It is why she came back early to the ship.'

Tom was aware that the crew were listening as they awaited

their orders. He also knew that he was talking too much, making too many excuses, but he was not skilled in subterfuge. And Phillipe Vidal made him nervous. The Frenchman always seemed to know a man's weakness and then pricked at it until it bled. On many occasions on their voyage south, Smith had been called upon to calm tensions between members of the crew who had previously been boon companions. All because of Vidal's serpent tongue.

'I do not believe my sister would keep me from her chamber,' Vidal said coldly.

'In ordinary circumstances, no. Indeed, the captain asked me particularly to pass on her apologies to you, monsieur, but she would hate for you to see her in so parlous a condition.' Smith swallowed hard. 'She knows it would cause you distress and would spare you.'

As Vidal glared at him, Smith forced himself not to look away.

'How long is this indisposition expected to last?'

'She very much hopes it is a passing affliction and to be quite restored to her usual self by the morning.'

'Is Barenton with her?'

'No, sir. The captain wanted to be left quite alone.'

Phillipe Vidal tapped his fingers on the taffrail, considering the situation. Perhaps looking for his advantage, Tom thought.

Then Vidal nodded. 'And you are to pilot us out of the bay?'

'Yes, sir.'

'These are her orders?'

'They are,' Tom replied.

A moment passed, then another.

'Tell me the instant she is improved, do you hear?' Vidal snapped. 'If I find she has been asking for me, and you have neglected to inform me, it will go the worse for you.'

'Very good, sir.'

The question of what would happen once the Frenchman discovered he had been duped, Tom had yet to confront. Despite his commander's objections, he would willingly kill Vidal with his own bare hands. Originally from Cornwall, Smith had lost his entire family and been taken captive by Barbary corsairs and survived the galleys. By rescuing him, and others of the crew, Louise had given him a new purpose and a new family. He would do anything for the captain, not least rid her of her villainous brother.

'One step at a time, Tom,' he muttered to himself, then raised his voice. 'Weigh anchor! We sail with the tide.'

CHAPTER SEVENTY-SIX

JAN JOUBERTSGAT
Saturday, 1st March 1862

In the summer's morning on the mountain, Isabelle looked at Xavier. They were both wondering the same thing.

'So, what went wrong?' he said.

'That is precisely the point at issue. We know Phillipe was not on board when the ship docked in Amsterdam,' Isabelle replied. 'And Tom Smith did deliver Louise's prison diary and Gilles' Tarot card to her great-aunt Alis and her friend Cornelia in Amsterdam after they arrived, but does not mention Vidal. So, either Vidal died *en route*, or he did not sail on the *Old Moon*.'

'Or he boarded, but disembarked and returned to the mainland,' Xavier added. 'Though is it possible that . . .'

Isabelle completed the thought for him.

'That Gilles was already in the family way before the *Old Moon* sailed? Yes, I considered that, too. That it happened on board, not once they were in the Cape.' She shook her head. 'But everything Louise writes makes it clear how much Phillipe and Gilles hated one another, and how both Louise and Gilles distrusted him. And at no point does she say that her half-brother realised that Gilles was biologically a woman.'

'No, but would Louise dare write such a potentially explosive truth in her diary?' Xavier countered. 'There would be no privacy on the ship and the fear of Vidal reading it must have always been on her mind.'

'I agree. It's why I rejected that idea. Besides, if we assume that any relations between Gilles and Phillipe were not consensual – and I think we can – then surely Smith, or another, would have dispatched Vidal there and then?'

Xavier nodded.

'But the main reason against the child having been conceived on board,' Isabelle continued, 'is that Suzanne relates the story of how a Khoi woman delivered a baby to a white woman in October 1623, which means Gilles could not have been with child in early May 1622. The dates do not fit.'

'Which means . . .?'

Isabelle frowned. 'I think Vidal somehow came back to the Cape, either immediately after the *Old Moon* had sailed or a little while later, determined to find them and make them pay for duping him. It is clear that he was obsessed with Louise, that he thought in some way that he owned her because he had saved her from the gallows.'

'And Gilles?' Xavier asked.

Isabelle looked up at the mountains, taking comfort in the beauty of the day while her head was filled with such troubling thoughts. 'If Phillipe wanted to punish Louise, what better way than to hurt Gilles,' she said, aware that her thoughts were turning back to Suzanne's story many years later. Suzanne, who had been raped in her own home, and found a way to survive. Isabelle ran her fingers across the page of the book. 'If I read on, I think we will find the answer. But do you want to continue, Xavier? We can stop.'

He shook his head. 'I would rather know.'

Isabelle nodded. 'Very well. The next entry is not until three months later. The seventeenth day of August. Mid-winter.'

CHAPTER SEVENTY-SEVEN

OLIFANTSHOEK
August 1622

'It is bitterly cold, but we have much to be thankful for.'

Louise laid down her quill. It was hard to write when her fingers were like ice.

The flames of the fire outside were flickering wildly, sending shadows up and along the walls of their reed hut. She rubbed her hands together and pulled her shawl over her shoulders, wishing Gilles would return.

Even though the wind was whistling through the gaps, she looked around their little home with pleasure. They were together, with no prying eyes watching them. They foraged and hunted and trapped for what they needed, answered to no man, lived a life in tune with the patterns of day and night. All the same, Louise would be glad when summer returned. She had not thought the valley would be so chill in winter. And the ever-present fear of hungry animals was worse in the cold weather.

They kept the fire burning day and night, and Louise had bartered the last of her gold coins for a musket. They had dug a pit around their tiny encampment and covered it with reeds from the river. So far they had been lucky. The Khoi had told them that elephants should be feared the most, their sheer size making them unstoppable should they decide to attack.

Louise pushed the fear from her mind. She had survived the ocean, the storms and the pirates, she had survived the noose, they would survive this. Soon spring would come again, bringing a carpet of flowers to the slopes of the mountains. The sun would return.

Although the pain of the loss of the *Old Moon* three months past still lay heavy on her heart, there had been little time to grieve. The relief at seeing the ship quit Table Bay, taking Phillipe Vidal with it, had quickly given way to the need to find a place to settle, safety.

Louise and Gilles had been presented to a leader of the Goringhaiqua, one of the most populous of the Khoi clans in the region. A few days of negotiations and a bargain had been struck. For *reales* and the jewels that Louise and Gilles had concealed in their clothes when disembarking the *Old Moon*, the clan leader had allowed them a dwelling on the lands over which his people travelled. He ruled that they should be left in peace and that no one would reveal their presence on pain of banishment. The oath was to be passed down to his sons, and to their sons, too.

Louise judged the Goringhaiqua to be people of honour and the headsman had been as good as his word. His men had brought them here two months ago and they had rarely been disturbed. She had a stick on which she counted the days, scoring the bark, so that they kept some connection with the world they had left behind. And their bodies helped them keep the measure of the months.

Louise did miss the company of other people and had wondered if they might occasionally venture back to the waterfront and the traders' pavilions. Gilles had cautioned against it. Even though they had seen the *Old Moon* sail away, he still could not let down his guard. But when they lay in one another's arms at night, with no pretence and no fear of being caught, they were happy.

'We could go when the weather is more clement,' Louise had suggested the previous night.

'Perhaps.'

'But there is no danger now.'

Gilles had stroked her cheek. 'Let us stay hidden a while longer.'

Louise got up and added another log to the fire outside. Soon, they would have exhausted their supplies of paper and ink. The only way to acquire more would be to go to Table Bay when one of the ships coming from the East was due to dock and barter. She would raise the subject with Gilles again in a month or so.

Sitting back at her table, she imagined how proud her grandmother, Minou, would have been. All those years spent trying to cajole her into doing her lessons in the old house in Amsterdam, and now keeping a diary was something that gave her much pleasure.

She heard footsteps outside, then Gilles appeared in the doorway of the hut.

'It is wild out there,' he said, pulling a hare from his bag. 'But I have something special for the pot.'

'That is marvellous, my love,' she said. It had been some days since they had last tasted meat. 'Do you need any help?'

Gilles shook his head. 'You continue with what you are doing.'

Louise picked up her quill, rolling it between her fingers to warm the shaft, then began to write again.

'It seems impossible that this will be our life for ever. We will manage, we will. But how I miss the sea, how I miss our friends on the Old Moon.'

CHAPTER SEVENTY-EIGHT

JAN JOUBERTSGAT
Saturday, 1st March 1862

Isabelle stood up. With the after effects of the attack and her sleepless night, she felt suddenly nauseous.

'You must be worn out,' said Maya.

Isabelle gave a wan smile. 'I am a little.'

'Would you like something more to eat, to drink?' Xavier asked, getting to his feet.

'Actually, I would like to wash my face and stretch my legs. Is there anywhere I might walk for a moment or two?'

Maya looked concerned. 'There are many baboons here. Though they are not dangerous, they can be spiteful to humans who venture into their territory.'

'You could go down to the riverbed beneath the bridge,' Xavier suggested. 'The water there is fresh and cool.'

Isabelle smiled. 'I will not be long. I just need to be alone with my thoughts for a while, you understand?'

'I do.'

And, of course, he did. Xavier, even more than Isabelle, had reason to fear what they might find out. It was the story of his family line. He was a direct blood descendent of Phillipe Vidal.

Xavier accompanied her to the bridge, pointing out the safest way down to the riverbed. For a while, she simply stood on the dry stones in the stream, letting the sound of the water soothe her. She breathed in deeply, then out again, then crouched to hold her hands in the current to wash the remnants of the midnight feast from her fingers. She knew she was simply delaying the moment where she would finally read, in Louise's own words, what had happened. Filling in the silences that Suzanne had left.

'This is what you came here for,' she said to herself. Louise, Gilles, Théodore, Suzanne, they were all long in the ground. The truth could not hurt them now.

Isabelle clambered back up the bank and along the track to where the Barenton family sat waiting.

She reopened the diary and skimmed the text. She could not translate it all, not here under these circumstances. There would be time enough to dwell on Louise's words at a later date. It was information they needed now, not reflection.

'Louise did not make an entry every day,' she said, turning the pages quickly until she reached the date she was looking for, 'but she writes clearly. She describes their day-to-day lives, how the leader of the Goringhaiqua clan sent men to teach them how to hunt more efficiently, to track animals through the scrub, and wise women to show them which herbs were good and which berries were poisonous. And although Louise often says they lived hand-to-mouth, it is clear that she also got great pleasure from learning to adapt. But then . . .'

Xavier leant forward. 'Go on.'

'But then Phillipe found them.' She took a deep breath and squared her shoulders. 'This entry comes in January, after Louise and Gilles had been in Olifantshoek for six months:

'I no longer know exactly what day it is. I abandoned my makeshift calendar during the winter, there seemed little point. But it is somewhere towards the end of January in the year 1623. I can be no more precise than that.

'I am writing this several days after the most terrible hours of our lives, and the worst may not yet be over. I do not say this lightly, for Gilles and I first met on the night that his uncle was murdered in front of his eyes in La Rochelle. I hold the memory of the trauma I witnessed as a child and suppressed for many years, as well as the death of Gilles' mother at my hands. An accident, but the body bleeds just the same.

'The words I spoke at my trial before the court in Gran Canaria were true. On that day in October, I testified that I had killed, but only in self-defence or to protect those whom I love. They did not believe me and found me guilty for a murder I did not commit.

'But now? Now, I have so much blood on my hands that I do not think even Cornelia's intercessions and her contributions to the offertory plate in the Oude Kerk could possibly buy my place in heaven.

'I do not care. I would do the same again.'

CHAPTER SEVENTY-NINE

OLIFANTSHOEK
January 1623

'Gilles?' Louise called out as she approached their little compound.

The homestead had grown. Alongside their original reed hut, some of the Goringhaiqua had helped them build a larger dwelling in which to live. They now used the original hut as a larder, storing preserved meats and herbs, piles of precious wood for the winter. There was also a small kraal for their goat and for two sheep the chief of the clan had promised.

Little remained from their life on board ship, only one of Louise's red scarves and the dagger that Phillipe had returned to her. Everything else – maps, instruments, jewels – they had bartered. But Louise was deeply grateful to the Goringhaiqua clan leader. Without his patronage, they would not have survived out here in the veldt.

Louise had gone out at first light and been away for much of the day, taking advantage of the relatively cool weather after days of fierce summer heat. She had returned, the hunter from the plains, bowed down with her day's bounty: wild pears, apples, pointed buchu leaves for their medicine chest, and sour figs; and a young antelope, which she was dragging in a blanket behind her.

'Gilles?' she called again, surprised that he had not come out to greet her. Usually he was at the door of the hut waiting before she even appeared at the top of the hill. 'I'm back.'

Louise left the antelope carcass outside the larder, then stepped inside to begin unpacking. She placed the produce on wooden slatted shelves that Gilles had constructed from olive branches, allowing the fruit to air so they did not rot, and reached up to tie the sorrel and the buchu from the reed struts of the hut.

Six months living off the land had made Louise even stronger. Her forearms and face were as sun-tanned as they had been when she had stood on the bridge of the *Old Moon* with her face raised to the east, her calves and bare feet, too. Even Gilles had forsaken his black secretarial clothing and taken to wearing an open shirt and breeches, though he continued to wear his black-buckled shoes despite the heat. Louise teased him for it.

Her tasks accomplished, she stepped back outside and looked around their tiny patch of land with pleasure.

'Where is he?' she murmured, patting the goat over the low palisade of the kraal. 'Still abed, I don't think so . . .'

Above her head, an ibis screeched, so close that it made her jump. As the sound echoed away into silence, Louise felt an unaccustomed shiver of alarm go down her spine. Why had Gilles not come to meet her?

'Gilles,' she said, this time his name catching in her throat.

Louise ran into the big hut and almost laughed out loud at how she had frightened herself for no reason. There he was, lying on their bed. Where else would he have been?

'I thought you had vanished,' she said lightly, walking towards the bed. 'Come on, wake up, *marmotte*.' Sleepy head.

But Gilles did not stir. A knot twisted in Louise's stomach. 'Wake up, my love,' she said, putting her hand out and touching his shoulder.

'She can't hear you.' The voice came from behind her.

Louise's breath froze in her chest. She started to shake Gilles, roughly now, until his head fell back. There was a gash on his temple and clotted blood around his hairline. Now, Louise could see that his shirt was open and he was naked from the waist down. Blood on his thighs. But from the rise and fall of his chest, Louise could see he was still breathing.

She steeled herself, then turned around to face the intruder.

'Phillipe.'

Louise gasped at the sight of him. The elegant, urbane Frenchman had gone, replaced by a man who would not have been out of place with the prisoners in the *oubliettes* of Paris. His eyes were burning mad, his hair matted and wild. His clothes were filthy and his left hand was clutching the silver cross around his neck, so she could see his fingernails were black with dirt. In his right hand, he held a pistol.

'What have you done?'

He gave a hollow laugh. 'Did you really think you would deceive me with so juvenile a trick? Forcing the cabin boy to dress up in your clothes. Pathetic.' He glanced with distaste at the bed. 'But then it appears that you quite revel in deception.'

'But I saw you sail away,' she said, struggling to keep her voice steady. She could show no fear, knowing that might only spur him on to further acts of cruelty. 'You were on the *Old Moon*.'

Phillipe rubbed his thumb and forefinger together. 'I was. But it always comes down to money in the end,' he said, his eyes glinting. 'It was easy enough to add a little something to your devoted lieutenant's bumboo once we were out of Table Bay. Out like a light. Such a loyal man, Tom Smith. But such a stupid one.'

'If you have harmed him I'll—'

'You will do what?' Vidal sneered. 'You, sister dearest, are not in a position to do anything.' He waved his hand dismissively. 'To answer your question, it was simple enough to find two members of the crew who, for a consideration, were happy to take me in the rowing boat to the Portuguese island. Few of your faithful mariners were prepared to argue with the point of a gun.' He sighed. 'Sadly, I was not able to let them return to the ship.'

'You killed them?' Louise said, conscious all the time of Gilles' ragged breathing behind her. But she had to keep Phillipe talking until she could work out how to disable him.

'Not immediately. Not until we reached the mainland.'

'Does your Catholic faith not tell you the price you will pay in the afterlife?'

'Do not be so naive.'

Louise bit her tongue. 'How did you find us?'

'Same answer, sister mine. Lucre. You have a terrible tendency to think the best of people. It is a weakness. The youngest son of the chief who has so graciously bestowed his patronage on you has an eye to the future. He is not content to live in the manner of his forebears, but is looking for more. He was very happy to trade information about the two white people who had travelled into the interior. Though he was under the impression that it was a woman and a *man*.' He stopped and Louise saw the rage in his eyes. 'As were we all.'

'Is that what this is about?' Louise said in disbelief.

Phillipe lunged towards her, jabbing a finger in her face. 'I will not be made a fool of!' he screamed. 'That you had immoral relations with a man far inferior to our family's worth was bad enough. But to learn you were dabbling with an invert – or whatever you call a whore like that.' He pointed his gun towards the bed. 'To learn that you had disgraced me by such behaviour, that I could not allow to pass.'

Louise stared in horror. He had not killed Gilles yet but, in such a mood, he still might.

'Brother—' she began.

He lurched backwards. 'Keep away from me! You have shamed me, shamed our father's name.'

Louise held his gaze, trying to work out how best to disarm him. 'That was never my intention. For any offence I have caused, forgive me. I did not stop to think of how it would reflect on you. And we are so far away from home, you and I.'

Louise could not tell if he was being soothed by her words or not. She took another step closer, careful not to startle him.

'Everyone laughing at me, jeering.' He was muttering, his voice losing some of its heat. 'All I wanted was to look after you, but that, that . . . that creature came between us.'

'I would like you to look after me,' Louise said. 'We can live here together. Would you like that, Phillipe? Would you like to stay here with me?'

He nodded and, for a moment, she saw the boy inside the man. Then his face hardened again. 'But just us.'

He raised the gun just as Louise leapt forward, pulling her knife from her waistband. Phillipe was so focused on taking aim at Gilles, that he didn't move to defend himself. She thrust the blade up through his open doublet into his heart. He gasped. She withdrew the knife and struck again, this time at his side.

He staggered back, his eyes wide in surprise. 'I thought you loved me,' he cried as he fell to his knees.

'I love Gilles,' Louise said, and drew the dagger for a final time across his throat.

Louise's first priority was to tend to Gilles.

Averting her eyes from Phillipe's corpse, she used an ancient Khoi remedy made from buchu leaves steeped in honey to clean the wound on his temple, where Phillipe had struck him with the pistol. His hands were scratched and bleeding, where he had tried to fend off the attack, and his little finger was broken. There was also terrible damage where Phillipe had violated Gilles, a man taking revenge on a woman in the only way he knew how. Caught between grief and rage, Louise was gentle and made a pad of cotton to soak up the blood, and found herself praying.

All the time Gilles hovered between sleep and unconsciousness, and Louise was glad of it. So long as no infection took hold, his body would mend. The damage to his spirit would be harder to heal and Louise did not know how he could recover from that.

A wave of horror at what had happened suddenly overwhelmed her, and she stumbled. But her relief that Gilles had not died was stronger and gave her the courage to apply herself to the grisly task that lay ahead: disposing of Vidal's body. The smell of blood and rot would attract predators. She had to get the corpse as far away as possible and he was heavy, almost too much for her to move on her own. But she had no choice.

Louise went outside to fetch the blanket in which she had dragged the antelope and rolled the body onto it. She tied the corners around her wrists, then began the back-breaking task of hauling the body out of the hut into the open air. Through the compound, over the narrow piece of earth between the ditch surrounding their camp, then up towards the mouth of a gorge higher in the mountains.

'A little further,' she said, with every step, reminding herself that the further from the camp she went, the better. She remembered hauling wet ropes across the deck of the *Old Moon*, recalling how she and Gilles, and her faithful crew, had worked together to hold the mainsail steady in the teeth of a hurricane. She could do it. 'Just a little further . . .'

Her hands rubbed raw by the knot in the blanket, Louise

finally reached the top of the hill. She paused next to a precipitous drop to catch her breath then, holding tight to the blanket, rolled Vidal's body over the edge. She stood and watched as it ricocheted off the rocks, down through the scrub and pink and white flowers, until it landed at the bottom of the gully. Then, she turned away and walked back down to the compound, secure in the knowledge that the remains of Phillipe Vidal would not be there in the morning.

CHAPTER EIGHTY

JAN JOUBERTSGAT
Saturday, 1st March 1862

Isabelle felt hollow. Though she had guessed what must have happened, seeing the truth set down in black and white, Louise's account of the attack and its aftermath, made the terrible events real in a way that they had not been before. Vivid, vile, true. And, as she was reading, she had held Suzanne's ordeal in her mind, too. No wonder she had found it too hard to write of Gilles' experience. A binding history endured by women through the generations. Would nothing ever change?

Isabelle sat up, enraged. She would be like Louise and face her enemies head on, like Suzanne. Whatever happened, they both had kept fighting.

'We will have to confront your brother at some stage, Xavier,' she said quietly.

'I know.'

'I refuse to be intimidated,' she said, with more confidence than she felt. 'When we are finished here, I will seek him out. Between us, we might be able to persuade him that he has nothing to fear from me. I will make him listen.'

She saw Xavier and Maya exchange a look, but they said nothing. Still fired up by her anger, Isabelle held out her cup. Maya refilled it without a word, then Isabelle continued reading.

Olifantshoek
Spring 1623

'It was, of course, far from over. Although Gilles' physical injuries healed quickly, and well, his spirit was broken. Phillipe's attack had forced him to confront his physical nature in a way he had not since he was ten years old. He was born a woman, but had lived his life as a man. Phillipe had taken away his identity from him. Nothing I said, or did, seemed to make any difference. I could not bring him back from the place he had gone to.

'He was not angry. That, I could have understood. Rather, he was silent. He was like a ghost in his own life. He moved about the farmstead, he did the same chores, but it was as if he was not there. Nothing moved him, nothing stirred him, and it broke my heart to see Phillipe's malign presence still dominating our lives thus.

'As I write this, you will think me foolish. Think us foolish. But, understand this. We had both lived our lives differently from most women. We did not recognise the signs. So, although Gilles' courses had hitherto come from month to month, he said nothing to me when they stopped. And I did not think to ask.

'As the first winds of autumn were beginning to blow through the valley, I returned from hunting one day and looked at Gilles as if for the first time. Standing like a student before a painting, seeing the lines and shadows of his face, the shapes and the contours of his body. Then I knew.

'Gilles would not accept it. When I ventured to suggest there might be a child, he turned away and would not

speak of it. But his belly continued to grow, his face grew round, and I knew I was right.

'Though it rained and rained, it was a mild winter. September was warm and October came in with a blaze of summer colours. When the time came, I told him I would go and fetch help. He said nothing, but I thought I saw the gratitude in his eyes.

'I had no idea where the Goringhaiqua were camped – they moved across the land according to the seasons and the movement of the animals – but I was lucky. Some two days' walk from our encampment, I found the clan who had, with the one exception, watched over us, and explained what I needed. A young woman, Fala, strong and with a gentle expression, agreed to come with me. Leaving her baby daughter, Shansi, with the other women of the clan, we trekked back over the mountains.

'As we approached our encampment, I felt a stab of fear. Except to fetch us the food and water we needed, I had barely left Gilles' side for nigh on nine months. I suddenly remembered coming back into the camp that day in January and calling his name. How he had not answered. What if he had gone? What if his life was such a burden to him that he had taken advantage of my absence and . . .?

'"Gilles?" I cried out, my voice shrill with alarm, and ran into the bedchamber.

'"I am here, Louise," he said quietly. "Though I would be rid of this world, I would never leave you. You should know that."

'We were only just in time, for his pains had already begun.'

*

For hours, Louise went to and fro fetching water in the heavy-bellied tin pail, replacing the stained cloths with fresh strips of cotton bleached white by the sun. Fala was measured and steady, every action quiet. Louise loved her for it. 'Is this normal?' she wanted to ask. 'Does it always take so long for a child to come?' But they had no language in common, just a few words, hand gestures and smiles.

Louise had no idea how old Fala might be, but she believed she had helped bring many daughters and sons of the Goringhaiqua clan into the world, and she told herself this birth would be no different. Gilles was strong, despite the attack in January. The only question was whether or not the child would be born healthy. Despite everything, Louise was astonished that she so strongly wanted the baby to live.

She stroked Gilles' head and whispered encouragement. 'You are so brave,' she whispered. 'You are nearly there.'

Gilles roared again as another contraction took hold, and squeezed Louise's hand. She flinched, unable to believe that this was all natural and that all was well. Fala, seeing her worried expression, nodded.

'*!Gâi.*' Good.

The sweat-soaked blankets were changed, the reeds were cleared from the floor and fresh matting laid down. Louise wiped Gilles' forehead with a damp cloth.

Suddenly, Gilles opened his eyes.

'*Î*,' said Fala. Yes. Signing to Louise that she should climb onto the pallet and sit behind Gilles, Fala knelt on the ground and put her hands on Gilles' hips. The baby was coming.

'This time, try to push,' Louise said, when another contraction came.

She could see Gilles was now lost in the moment, allowing each contraction to come and go, pushing, getting closer each time. She had no idea how much time was passing, only that the world had shrunk to the three of them. Nothing else mattered. The past was erased, the future was yet to come. There was nothing but now.

As the last of the light slipped from the sky, plunging the bedchamber into shadow, and the cicadas began their night-time song, Gilles cried out again, not in pain this time, but release.

'It's a boy,' Louise cried.

Fala swept the child up, quickly tied the birth cord, cut it, then placed the baby tenderly on Gilles' breast.

'He seems to have a good colour.' Louise put out her little finger against the tiny hand, and he grabbed it. She laughed. 'And has a strong grip.'

Emotion caught in her throat. Her fear had been that Gilles would reject the child, but one look at her lover's face told her that there was no question of that. She felt as if her heart would burst with love and with pride.

'Your son is beautiful,' she said in wonder, looking at them both.

Gilles smiled up at her. '*Our* son. Théodore, a gift from God. Théodore Joubert Barenton.'

CHAPTER EIGHTY-ONE

JAN JOUBERTSGAT
Saturday, 1st March 1862

Isabelle closed the diary. When she looked up, she saw Maya had tears in her eyes and that Xavier was looking into the middle distance, clearly trying to control his emotions. While she had been talking, Magdalena had slipped away.

'From what Suzanne wrote,' she said, 'it's evident that the Goringhaiqua continued to protect them. Fala told everyone that the women had gone, or had possibly been killed by a white man who had been told of their whereabouts by the chief's younger son. Whether she did this to protect Gilles and Louise, or whether she simply confused the sequence of events and thought Phillipe had come for them after Théodore had been born, I do not know.'

'But it left them free to live,' Xavier said.

'It did,' she agreed. 'By all accounts, a long and happy life. Later, they built a new house on the site of the original hut, which is where Suzanne found Théodore all those years later. Your family farm.'

'And they are buried in the graveyard below,' Maya said.

Isabelle nodded. 'It wasn't a graveyard then, just a single plot. Théodore planted saplings to provide shade and replaced the wooden cross with a carved headstone.'

Xavier exhaled. 'How old was Louise when she died?'

'She died when she was seventy years old.' Isabelle looked

down at the book on her lap. 'After Louise had gone, Gilles wrote the end of the story. He survived her by ten years.'

Her ears were ringing with the voices from the past, from the weight of history. The thought, too, that while Théodore had been the first of his family, she was the last of her own.

Then her reflections were shattered by a scream, close at hand. Instantly, Maya was on her feet.

'Magdalena!' she cried, running towards the sound. Xavier followed.

Isabelle stood up, not sure what to do, then she froze. Coming around the curve on the track was Andries Barenton, dragging little Magdalena by the arm. At her neck, the point of his knife.

'Andries, no,' Maya was pleading. 'She is your niece. Your family.'

'Where is she?' Andries demanded in his clumsy English.

Isabelle stepped into the middle of the path.

'Let her go. It's me that you want.' Her heart was thundering with fury – with herself for having brought danger to Xavier and his family, but most of all for the man standing in front of her. 'Let her go and we will talk. I am not your enemy. I want nothing from you.'

She bent down to retrieve the diary. Thinking she was reaching for a weapon, Andries jabbed the point of the blade at his niece's neck. Magdalena whimpered. Isabelle heard Maya gasp.

Isabelle was frightened for the girl, but was determined not to let it show. Holding her hands up, so that he could see she was no threat, she kept her eyes fixed on his face.

'I understand that you wish to protect your farm, your birthright. I know that there have been others – from England, from France – who have come here and attempted to take what was not rightfully theirs. I am not like them. The Will that you sought, that you took from me, is a very old document pertaining to land in Puivert in the mountains of the Pyrenees that was lost a long time ago. It is nothing to do with your farm, La Justice. I give you my word that you have nothing to fear from me.'

She took a step closer, hoping to forge a connection with the wild-eyed man standing in front of her. It did not work. He shook Magdalena's arm roughly, making the girl cry out again.

'Please, Andries,' Maya begged. 'Let her go.'

Isabelle looked down at Louise's plain brown diary. 'This is what I came for,' she said, careful not to make any sudden movements. 'Not for your land, not vines. Now I have read it, I will be returning to Cape Town. I came in search of the story of my family and I found it. That is all.'

Finally, Andries spoke. 'You are lying,' he spat, shaking his head. 'If I let you go, you will inform the authorities. They will come for me and I will lose my farm all the same.' He spun round and shouted at his brother. 'And you, you would work against me with this foreigner. You have always resented me, always wanted to take the farm for yourself. For her.' He glared at his hostage. 'I have no children. You are just waiting for me to die.'

'Andries, put down the knife,' Xavier said. 'Let Magdalena go. No one wants to deprive you of what is rightfully yours, not me, not Miss Lepard.'

'I don't believe you!' he shrieked. 'I don't believe—'

His words were cut off in mid-air. Isabelle didn't understand what was happening. One moment Andries had been there, shouting. Now there seemed to be nothing but empty space.

Then the world came rushing back. Magdalena was running into her mother's arms, weeping; Xavier was wiping his face;

Andries was lying on the ground, blood seeping into the dirt. And behind it all, Isabelle saw John Turner, with Andries' rifle in his hand, his face as white as milk with shock.

'I didn't mean to kill him,' he said in a daze, 'but I didn't know how else to stop him.'

Isabelle gently took the weapon from his hands. 'You saved Magdalena's life, John,' she said. 'We are all in your debt.'

Franschhoek

Xavier and John made a litter from their jackets and two sturdy branches to carry the body down from the pass to Franschhoek.

'We will take him to my mother's house and lay him out there,' Xavier said in a flat voice. Though he and his brother had been estranged, Isabelle could see how much Andries' death, and the manner of it, had distressed him. 'He was not a bad man,' he said suddenly, 'not at the heart of it. It was just that the accident damaged his wits. His life had become a burden to him and it made him mad.'

'I understand,' she said, though she wasn't so sure.

In town, though the solemn procession attracted the curious looks of women and men going about their daily business, no one stopped them. They parted at the door to the house where, only the previous day, Isabelle had been kept prisoner. Seeing it in the light, it looked ordinary.

'Did you find rooms in Dirkie Uys Street?' she said, looking to John.

He nodded. 'It's the one with a blue door and a *stoep* at the front and side.'

'I will wait for you there.' She turned to Xavier. 'We should tell someone what happened. Report the accident.'

'Yes. I will fetch the pastor, once I have told our mother. Despite everything he had become, she will feel the loss of her son keenly.'

Xavier went inside and, moments later, Isabelle heard a heart-breaking wail. With a heavy heart, she turned away as the bell began to toll for midday as if for a funeral cortège.

Some two hours later, and after several cups of hot, China tea, Isabelle took herself to the swinging chair on the veranda of the guest house.

She was glad to be on her own. For she felt she owed it to Louise, and to Gilles, to read to the very end of the story, and Isabelle wanted no witnesses to that.

She turned to the end and saw the different handwriting. Not Louise's open, sometimes chaotic, hand, but rather a clear and elegant manuscript, precise words set down in the closing pages. Isabelle smiled. This was the handwriting of someone who once had worked as a secretary for his living. Before love took him away to sea, and he turned pirate.

CHAPTER EIGHTY-TWO

OLIFANTSHOEK
December 1655

'Is there anything I can do?' Gilles asked. He knew it would not be long. 'Anything that you need, my love?'

Gilles thought it strange how his thoughts kept returning to when he and Louise had first met. They had lived in Africa for more than thirty years, but it was the cathedrals and churches of La Rochelle and Amsterdam that filled his mind now. Perhaps it was natural, he thought, that at the end our hearts went back to our beginning?

He rubbed his face, then got up from the chair and pushed open the shutter to let in a little air. He was exhausted. He had barely slept for days, wanting to be available at any moment Louise might stir. Since dusk on the previous evening, though, she had not moved. She was no longer drinking, no longer speaking. He rearranged the blanket, pulling it up to her chin and laying her hands on the top. It was a hot day, but Louise was never warm any more. Her skin hung loose over her bones; her flesh had wasted away. Her extraordinary eyes, one brown and one blue, were dulled now.

He did not know how he could bear to live without her.

Louise knew her time was coming and had tried to prepare them. Gilles had taken longer to accept it, trying every remedy the Khoi had to offer, even travelling with Théodore to the new

Colony being built by the Dutch in Table Bay in search of modern medicines that might help. Nothing had made any difference.

'I am old,' Louise had said, placing her hand against his cheek. 'I have had my time. I am ready to go.'

'But I am not ready to lose you,' he'd cried. He was ashamed of that now, putting his own feelings before hers. 'And what of Théodore?'

Louise had smiled that slow, wise smile of hers. 'Our son is a grown man, Gilles, a fine man. You will comfort one another, and walk forward into the future together. Find him a wife. He deserves to have a companion.'

When Gilles had relayed the conversation later, Théodore had laughed and said he had everything he needed. But the idea had lodged in Gilles' mind.

Now Théodore came quietly into the chamber. 'Is there any change?' he asked quietly.

'No change,' Gilles replied.

Half sleeping, half dreaming, Louise was running through the cobbled streets of Carcassonne where, in the summer of 1610, she had stayed with her beloved grandmother, Minou, and her grandfather, Piet, after the assassination of the old king. Louise had been twenty-five and Minou had been dying.

Then, she had not understood Minou's determination to prepare her family for her passing. Now she did. She knew how hard it was to watch someone you loved suffer, she could see the pain of it in Gilles' drawn face and Théodore's over-bright eyes.

Louise was comforted by the thought that Minou was waiting for her on the other side. Her grandfather, too, and her mother,

Marta. And Alis and Cornelia, whom she had not seen since she had sailed from Amsterdam in the spring of 1622.

Remembering the conversations she and Minou had had in the tiny house in Carcassonne with wild roses around the door, Louise had tried to do the same for Gilles and for Théodore. But she did not think it had made any difference. Their hearts were breaking, as hers had done so many years before.

Louise was proud of the life she had lived, a wild and exceptional life. She had refused to be bound by the limits the world put on a woman's existence. She had loved and she had fought and she had survived, she had lived a good life. There could be no better epitaph than that. If it had been possible, she would have wanted her body committed to the sea. For she still missed the roll of the waves beneath her feet, the buck and the tilt of the ship, the solitude of the night watch and the black sky painted silver with stars. The endless, treacherous, beautiful shifting water.

But she would be content to be laid to rest in African soil, here where she and Gilles and their son had made their home. No monument for her, no effigies of weeping angels. Just a simple wooden marker set in the land she had come to love.

Gilles put his hand on Louise's cheek, as he had done so many times before, and instantly knew something had changed.

'Louise?' he said, his voice rising like the wind in autumn, calling her name louder and louder. 'Louise, Louise . . .'

The sound brought Théodore running to the bedside. He put his hand on his mother's shoulder, then dropped his head and started to weep.

'Go in peace, my love,' Gilles managed to say. 'Go in peace.'

Outside, the December sun sank behind the hills on the longest day of the year.

They buried Louise the following morning, as she had wished, on the small patch of land above the farmstead in the shadow of the Olifantshoek mountains. They lowered her down into the grave, her red scarf around her head, and placed her silver dagger in her hands. Neither spoke, they just stood with their heads bowed in front of a wooden cross:

LOUISE REYDON-JOUBERT
14TH MAY 1585–21ST DECEMBER 1655

Beneath that were three simple words that said everything:

CAPTAIN AND COMMANDER

They weighted down the grave with stones to keep predators away and, in the spring, a carpet of pink and yellow flowers sprang up in the cracks between the slabs. Théodore planted saplings around the grave and it became a place of comfort, where he would go to talk to Louise when he was lonely or worried.

When Gilles' time came, a decade later, Théodore laid him to rest beside the woman he had loved: Louise and Gilles, reunited in death as they had wanted. As the Colony grew, Théodore ventured out from the farm, making occasional visits to the new town of Stellenbosch. On one such visit, he acquired a piece of granite. By the light of a candle at night, and the warmth of the sun in the daytime, he made a new headstone for them both. Beneath Gilles' name and his dates, just a single word was carved in the same block capitals:

BELOVED

Franschhoek
Saturday, 1st March 1862

'Are you all right, Miss Lepard?'

In her mind's eye, Isabelle had been back in the cemetery, where she had stood twenty-four hours previously. It was a surprise to find herself on the pretty veranda of the boarding house with John Turner's worried face looking down at her. A climbing fig wrapped its tendrils around the wrought-iron lattice work and a row of wild olive trees separated the house from the street. She was aware of the humming of the bees and the gentle chirruping of songbirds in the trees.

'Miss?'

She smiled, breaking the spell. 'I am fine, John. Thank you.'

'You have everything you need?'

'It has been quite a day,' she replied, unable to think of anything better to say. Then she added: 'You mustn't worry. We will see you right. No blame will be laid at your door.'

'Thank you, miss,' he said, clearly relieved. 'These small towns, they protect their own.'

'Andries Barenton's character was well known. Xavier and his wife will speak in your defence. You have nothing to fear.' The young man was still holding his cap and looking at his feet. 'Is there something else?'

'I wondered how long we might be here? The landlady was asking and I said I would find out.'

Isabelle nodded. 'Please tell her that I would be grateful for rooms for two nights, tonight and tomorrow. There are still some matters outstanding. After that, we will return to Stellenbosch, where I will take my leave of you.'

'Are you going back to Cape Town?'

'I'm going home to England, John.' She patted the diary on her lap, her eyes shining. 'I have a book to write.'

CHAPTER EIGHTY-THREE

FRANSCHHOEK
Monday, 3rd March 1862

Isabelle waited until after the funeral before leaving Franschhoek. Andries had been buried privately and without ceremony in the same graveyard where Louise, Gilles and Théodore lay, the first inhabitants of that city of the dead.

It was emotional taking her leave of Xavier, Maya and Magdalena. They all knew it was unlikely that they would meet again, but Isabelle promised to talk of La Justice in Cape Town. Now the farm had passed to him, Xavier had ambitious plans of how the farm could expand and bring prosperity to Franschhoek. He had retrieved Minou's journal, with the Will and Testament, from where Andries had hidden it in their mother's house. On their last night together, he had also given her Louise's Olifantshoek diary to take back to England after learning about Isabelle's intentions to write the history of their family, and endow an archive and reading room in the Joubert family name.

'I would rather the diary be there, where everyone can see it,' Xavier had said. 'And how proud we will be to see it there in pride of place if we ever visit London.'

STELLENBOSCH
Wednesday, 5th March

Isabelle parted company with John Turner in Stellenbosch. Of all of the people she had met on her journey, Isabelle realised she would miss him the most. He had been a steady, loyal presence and his quick thinking – both in Klein Bethlehem and at Joubertsgat – had saved her life, as well as that of Xavier's and Maya's daughter.

'I wish you the very best, John,' she said, as he helped carry her luggage from Mrs Müller's boarding house.

'It has been an honour, miss,' he said, blushing.

He waited with her for the service to Cape Town, then stood watching as she waved goodbye to the beautiful white town set in the sea of vines.

CAPE TOWN
Monday, 10th March

Back in Cape Town, Isabelle found political tensions were still running high. There were rumours of unrest in the Transvaal and daily complaints about the Governor, Sir Philip Wodehouse. There were a great many soldiers on the streets and the Parade Ground was busy with drills and military manoeuvres. Isabelle shut her eyes to it all. She booked herself into a different hotel in Buitengracht Street, refusing to give her custom to the odious manager who had betrayed her to Andries Barenton.

As Suzanne before her, Isabelle started to write her story, meticulously recording everything that had happened since her arrival in southern Africa. She retrieved her bonds and possessions from the Cape of Good Hope Bank, booked herself a first-class ticket on the next steamship sailing from Port Natal in Durban via Cape Town to Portsmouth at the end of the month, and settled her accounts. In the early evenings, she ate in the hotel dining room, then retired to the lounge to write letters to her solicitor and her editor in London – just in case anything should happen to her on the voyage home. She compiled a list of possible benefactors and started to sketch out the design for her Archive and Reading Room.

Finally, there was just one last task remaining.

In the years after the collapse of the VOC and the arrival of the British in the Colony, many records and archives had been lost. The Castle of Good Hope had fallen into disrepair. But, with a great deal of persistence and the help of a secretary at the British Consulate, Isabelle had discovered that some VOC archives from the Castle had been rescued and were stored in an administration building on Adderley Street.

On the morning of Monday the tenth of March, Isabelle presented herself at the featureless building at the commercial heart of the city. She rang the bell and was admitted into a long dark corridor. Her heels echoed loudly as she followed the servant to a desk at the rear of the empty building.

'A visitor,' he said, then turned on his heel.

A pale, snub-nosed clerk in a uniform too big for him looked over his pince-nez. 'May I help you?'

'I very much hope so,' Isabelle replied brightly.

With her blonde hair drawn into a coil at the nape of her neck, she was wearing a pale blue hat, blue buttoned jacket and full skirt and black patent buttoned boots. She looked every bit the Victorian lady, nothing resembling the woman who had ridden across the veldt with the wind in her hair and a knife at her side. 'I am a travel correspondent from England. I write for a periodical, *The Leisure Hour*. Perhaps you have heard of it?'

'I have not,' he said, barely troubling to hide his lack of interest.

'I wish I had thought to bring a copy,' Isabelle said, refusing to be discouraged. 'I am here to visit the VOC archives. I have a letter of authorisation from the British Consulate.' She paused a moment. 'Please do forgive me for the imposition. I appreciate the pressure this puts upon your valuable time. I assure you I will be as quiet as a mouse and will take up as little of your time as possible.'

'We are more than usually busy,' the clerk said, though she and he appeared to be the only two people in the building.

'It must be so difficult,' she said disingenuously. 'And too often the powers-that-be fail to understand the hard work and the effort that goes in to making such a facility as this run smoothly.' She leant forward, as if afraid they would be overheard. 'It is much the same in London, I regret.'

The clerk's eyes brightened. 'Is it, is it indeed? Well, in point of fact, I would say that our systems are far superior to anything one might find in England. Was there anything in particular you were looking for?'

Ten minutes later, Isabelle was seated at a large table in an otherwise empty room with four dusty ledgers in front of her. Many of the Huguenot refugee families had grown prosperous and become families of distinction in the Colony, their deeds recorded. But others who had touched the lives of Louise and Suzanne had disappeared from sight.

Isabelle opened the first ledger and began her search, patiently tracing her finger down the columns of names and dates until she found one of the things she was looking for. She smiled: to Adriaan and Judith van Dijk, on the fourteenth day of June in the year 1689, a daughter: Florence Suzanne van Dijk.

Isabelle felt tears well in her eyes. Adriaan and Judith had not forgotten their friend and she thought Suzanne would have been delighted. Had she ever known? She had found no mention of the baby girl in Suzanne's notebooks, but she couldn't help but hope they had managed to exchange letters despite the thousands of miles between them. Isabelle ran her eye down the rest of the column and found that little Florence was the first of four daughters and five sons born to Judith and her husband.

'Rather her than me,' she murmured into the cavernous room, then put that ledger aside.

The second task, she knew, would be harder. Maybe impossible. Away from the main Colony in the countryside, births and deaths often went unrecorded. Life was hard, many children failed to survive in the harsh conditions, their names were never written down. And when women married, if the union was recorded at all, they were subsumed into their husband's families. But, ever since Isabelle had stood in the graveyard in Franschhoek thinking about the Barenton family line, she had pondered the identity of Théodore's wife or lover. That there had been someone was not in doubt: Xavier and Andries, with the white strip in their dark hair, were evidence of that.

She doubted if she would find Théodore in the records – he had lived for most of his life outside of VOC jurisdiction. But he had known Adriaan van Dijk and he had, from time to time, come to Cape Town. People must have seen him. It was how Suzanne had tracked him down.

Isabelle had no luck with the second ledger. Among marriages between VOC employees, she saw no names she recognised. The third was the same. Tired now, with her fingers stained black from the ink and dusty pages, she pulled the final ledger towards her and started to run down the names . . . 'Yes,' she whispered with triumph. It was as she had suspected, as she had hoped. The record of a marriage on the third day of August 1690, a Khoi servant in the employ of the Van Dijk family of Cape Town had married a bachelor residing in the municipality of Stellenbosch.

Tia Nemen and Théodore Barenton, the founders of a new dynasty.

EPILOGUE

Ten years later
London
September 1872

Bouverie Street, London
Thursday, 19th September 1872

It was a quarter to four in the afternoon and Isabelle was relishing the last moments of quiet before her guests arrived. She was on pins, but excited too. This was the day she had been dreaming of for more than a decade: the official opening of the Joubert Family Archive and Reading Room, and the launch of her memoir.

Usually, when travelling or lecturing, Isabelle dressed for comfort rather than style. Today, she wanted to make her father proud. Though he was not alive to see what she had achieved, she felt his gentle presence in the room. She looked elegant and appropriate, a respectable Victorian lady. She was wearing a green silk day dress with a fitted bodice and square neck, sleeves that flared at the wrist and two embroidered buttons at the top of her bustle. A supporter of women's dress reform, advocating for clothes that allowed freedom of movement, Isabelle drew the line at the tassels, bobs and bows that were currently in fashion. Her thick blonde hair was gathered into a chignon at the nape of her neck. Isabelle grinned. It had taken her maid many hours and countless spoiled pins to fix it into place.

The high windows in the main room of the archive faced west, so the late afternoon sun was shining down in broad slants, making the motes of dust dance in the air. The room itself seemed to gleam. Polished wooden shelving rose floor to ceiling on three sides. In the past ten years, Isabelle had built up a significant collection of books in several languages about southern Africa, memoirs and works of natural history, as well as travelogues about Amsterdam and La Rochelle, Languedoc and the Pyrenees. She also had a good selection of contemporary titles by women on history, suffrage and education. Books about her own Huguenot ancestry, too.

Mahogany display cases filled the centre of the room, the glass cleaned this morning with lemon juice – or so her archivist, Anna Peake, had told her – so that the exhibits could be clearly seen. Originally from Manchester, Anna had come to London as one of the first women to be accepted at the University of London. The daughter of a botanist, she had approached Isabelle after a lecture they had both attended at the Royal Geographical Society. She was brilliant and efficient and Isabelle felt lucky to have her.

Slowly, Isabelle walked around the room taking pleasure in the empty space for one last time. She paused before the cases holding the most precious items: Minou's sixteenth-century journal lay on white satin, opened at the first page. In the case beside it was displayed the Will and Testament that had nearly caused Isabelle's death in Franschhoek ten years ago. In another case, below the tallest stacks at the rear of the room, Suzanne's silver dagger with the red garnet was on show and a note explaining how it had been miraculously rescued from the sea during the shipwreck of the *Gouw*.

A third case was dedicated to Louise, the pirate queen of the seventeenth century. There were nautical maps of the routes the *Old Moon* had sailed and a replica of the ship itself, created by a toy maker in Holland from the descriptions in Louise's prison diary. That was here, together with the diary from Olifantshoek that Gilles had finished. Isabelle had also commissioned a watercolour portrait of the court house in Las Palmas de Gran Canaria where Louise had been put on trial.

Most of all, Isabelle loved the long, narrow display case that greeted visitors on their first arrival: a woven tapestry showing Minou and Piet and their two oldest children, rescued by Alis from the castle in Puivert; and a family tree of the Joubert family going back to the early years of the sixteenth century. All the names were here – Joubert and Reydon, du Plessis and Barenton.

For a moment, Isabelle allowed herself a moment of regret. She was forty years old and had no intention of marrying. Her name would die with her. Then she thought of Xavier's and Maya's daughter, Magdalena, and smiled. Different branches of their family would rise, and would fall, but the spirit that linked them all together would never be lost.

Anna came striding into the room.

'Mr Macmillan is here.'

Isabelle felt a flutter of unaccustomed nerves. 'Is everything ready?'

The archivist nodded. 'The wine is poured and there are soft drinks for those who are teetotal.' Anna sniffed with disapproval. 'Temperance types and the like.'

Some two weeks previously, a consignment had arrived from La Justice, a gift from Xavier Barenton to bring the family's best wishes for the opening of the Archive. Isabelle had been touched by the gesture, though tasted the wine with trepidation, aware that its long journey from Franschhoek to Cape Town, Cape Town to London, might well have spoilt it. In fact, it was delicious, brimming with African sun, so she had decided to serve it at the opening.

'Another gentleman from the publishers has set up a desk in the hall for those who want to purchase copies of your book,' the archivist added. 'I have put the pamphlet about the Archive there too and suggested he might consider slipping endowment forms inside, in case there are any new potential subscribers.'

Isabelle took a final look around. 'Then we are set.'

'We are. It's going to be wonderful,' Anna replied. 'Shall I show Mr Macmillan in?'

'If you would.'

Moments later, Alexander Macmillan, white-whiskered and with sparkling eyes, came bustling into the room. Still nominally in charge of the publishing company he and his brother had founded nearly thirty years ago, he was gradually passing on control of the thriving business to his sons and nephews. But as an old friend of Isabelle's late father, he had taken a keen interest in her writing career and offered to publish her family memoir without hesitation. Isabelle was very fond of him.

'Isabelle, my dear,' he said, his Scottish accent little dimmed by his years in London. 'What a day, what a day. You look absolutely charming, if I might say. Your father would be proud.'

She put up her cheek to be kissed. 'Thank you for coming, Alexander.'

'I would not have missed it for the world. Have you got a good crowd in?'

'I think so, if everyone who has accepted makes an appearance.'

'They will, my dear. We have invited some of our bigwigs, Lewis Carroll and Christina Rossetti included, although of course *she* won't be able to come. Her health is not what it was. But the Reverend Kingsley is in town, so hopefully he will find time to grace us with his presence. We've issued invitations to one or two select gentlemen of the press. And all your subscribers will be here, will they not?'

'Most of them, yes. People have been very generous.'

'Well then,' he beamed, 'it is all going to be tremendous.' He looked towards the hall. 'Now, what about a glass of that family wine you have been telling me about?'

An hour later and the room was filled to the gunwales. Isabelle was delighted to see that most guests were clutching a copy of the museum pamphlet and a fair few had a copy of her book under their arms, too. She didn't expect her family history to be a bestseller like Mrs Seacole's memoir, but she hoped it might find a modest audience.

Anna was conducting a tour of the section devoted to Suzanne's notebooks. A knot of male students, possibly her friends from the university, were peering into the display case containing Suzanne's dagger.

'Of course, Miss Lepard herself has visited all of these places,' Isabelle heard Anna say. 'Her recollections are from first-hand experience.'

Isabelle glanced at the clock on the wall above the door, watching the hands move inexorably towards five o'clock. It was then that the speeches were due to start. She had a list in her pocket of all the people she had to thank, all those who had invested in the Archive or donated money. Only when that was over would she be able to enjoy herself.

Too nervous to stay still, Isabelle continued her circuit of the room. She was pleased to see the Director of the French Hospital, La Providence, was among the guests. A Huguenot almshouse for poor French refugees, it had recently taken possession of new purpose-built premises in Hackney, in East London. Isabelle had not yet found the time to visit, but she had continued her father's commitment of making a donation to the almshouses every year in remembrance of their Huguenot antecedents.

She noticed her former editor at *The Leisure Hour* talking to one of her fellow contributors and was pleased to see that Charles Kingsley, author of *The Water Babies*, had indeed come and was deep in conversation with her solicitor, Samuel Watson. The firm Watson & Sons was resident in Bouverie Street and old Mr Watson had been a friend of her father's, even though the family was non-conformist. Isabelle smiled at Sam and nodded to his wife, Lily. A self-possessed, thoughtful young woman some ten year's Samuel's junior, she had given birth to their first child, a daughter, last year. Since they lived out in the country in Brixton, Isabelle was surprised – and pleased – that Lily had accompanied him today. She was someone Isabelle would like to know better. Perhaps she would invite her to tea when all this was over.

Isabelle felt a touch on her elbow.

'Mr Macmillan would like to know if you are ready?' Anna asked.

'As I'll ever be.'

She took a deep breath, then walked to the back of the room where a small platform had been set up. Alexander smiled encouragingly, then stepped up to the podium brandishing a copy of her book in his hand.

'Ladies and gentlemen, esteemed guests,' he boomed. 'On behalf of Macmillan and Company, it is my very great pleasure to be welcoming you here today. We are honoured to be publishing the travel memoir of Miss Isabelle Lepard, *The Joubert Family Chronicles*, and to be playing a small role today as we gather to celebrate the opening of this magnificent Archive and Reading Room.'

While he talked, Isabelle watched the expressions on the faces of the guests in the room: curiosity, pride, interest. These were the women and men who had believed in her and she was grateful to every one of them.

'Ladies and gentlemen,' Macmillan concluded, 'I give you Miss Isabelle Lepard.'

She felt a hush fall over the room: the slightest chink of a glass being put down; the ruffle of a brochure being used as a fan; somebody cleared his throat, another sneezed.

'Ladies and gentlemen . . .'

Isabelle looked down at the list in her hands. She knew the speech she was supposed to make, but it didn't feel right. There would be time enough to thank everyone and say all the official things that needed to be said. Now, though, what she wanted to do – what she *had* to do – was to explain why she had dedicated ten years of her life to this project. She had to explain why it mattered. She put her list away.

'Friends, you are most welcome. Today is an important day in my life. For I come from a line of extraordinary women. Loyal, courageous, brilliant women who refused to allow their lives to be circumscribed or limited by the societies in which they lived. My ancestor Louise Reydon-Joubert, in the early years of the seventeenth century, captained her own ship, the *Old Moon*. We might say she was an early abolitionist, hunting down slaver ships in the Atlantic Ocean.'

Several of the audience clapped, Lily Watson among them.

'Looking back through my family history,' Isabelle continued, 'I began to ask myself why the names of the women in my family – Florence Joubert, Minou Joubert, Louise Reydon-Joubert, Alis Joubert, Cornelia van Raay, Suzanne Joubert to mention but a few – were forgotten. Why were their names missing from the history books? Why were their extraordinary achievements not lauded and praised?

'You may say that it is impossible to honour everyone. You may say that, if a person's contribution is great enough then it will be remembered. But there are many, and various reasons, why this is not always the case. For too much of human history, women have not had access to paper and pen, to archives and libraries. It was Minou Joubert who, some three hundred years ago wrote about the importance of women telling their own stories, of not allowing the words of others to stand for us. She understood that without education, without the means to record our experiences, then much of her daughters' lives, her granddaughters' lives – so many women's stories – would be lost. For history to mean anything it needs to include us all, women as well as men.'

Anna cupped her hand round her mouth. 'Hear, hear!'

Isabelle smiled and held up a copy of her book. 'This is a record of how our stories are passed down the generations, beginning in the earliest years of the religious wars that tore France in two during the sixteenth century. Carcassonne, Puivert, Toulouse, the Islas Afortunadas, the Cape of Good Hope – these might be places known to you only by name. But I have stood before the graves of my ancestors and pieced their stories together, a map of bones, if you will. It is my hope that, by the time you have read my book, their stories will be as familiar to you as your own. It is also, of course, the story of persecution, of how my Huguenot forebears were forced to leave the land that they loved, and the countries such as Britain and Holland who gave my ancestors sanctuary.'

Isabelle paused to allow her words to hit their mark.

'Many of you have known me since I was a child. You have supported me. You know I was fortunate enough to be brought up by a father who believed that I should have the same opportunities as my brothers. Many girls do not. And even now, in 1872, most libraries are closed to us. Institutions of learning are only just starting to accept female students, though not on equal terms. This is why I founded the Joubert Family Archive and Reading Room, to honour the women of my family, those past as well as those still to come. It is my great hope that it will become a meeting space where the female scholars of the present, and the authors of the future, can come to learn, to exchange ideas, to write.' She looked across to the crowd of young male students standing by the stacks and smiled. 'Though you are also most welcome, gentlemen, if you will walk beside us.'

Isabelle stopped, overwhelmed by the significance of the moment. 'That is all I want to say. I am grateful to Macmillan and Company for their support of my work, and to all of you for putting your faith in me.'

As the room erupted into enthusiastic applause, with whoops and cheers led by the young men and Anna, Alexander Macmillan hurried back onto the podium and raised his glass.

'A toast, ladies and gentlemen,' he said, shouting to make his voice heard. 'To the Joubert Family Archive and Reading Room and to our own dear Miss Lepard.'

Someone thrust a wine glass into Isabelle's hand.

For a moment, the noise was too much, the sea of faces, the lack of air. But then, just for a moment, she imagined she saw the outline of three other guests standing in the open doorway. They were smiling at her, shimmering white in the September afternoon: Minou and Louise and Suzanne, the mighty women in whose footsteps she walked.

Isabelle lifted her glass. 'To you all,' she whispered, 'from us all. Thank you.'

ACKNOWLEDGEMENTS

The inspiration for *The Joubert Family Chronicles* came from a visit to the Franschhoek Book Festival in 2012, when I first fell in love with the history of the handful of Huguenot refugees who had sailed to the Cape after the Revocation of the Edict of Nantes. It is with both satisfaction and sadness that I'm bringing to an end a series whose characters have kept me company for twelve years from the initial glimmerings of an idea to typing the last full stop. Many people have supported me on the way, so my thanks to:

My agent and friend Mark Lucas, and all at The Soho Agency and ILA including Nicki Kennedy, Jenny Robson, Benedict Clark, Alice Saunders, Niamh O'Grady, Sophie Laurimore and Helen Mumby; the amazing team at Mantle, not least my brilliant editor Maria Rejt, and the Pan Macmillan team including Lara Borlenghi, Joanna Prior, Christine Jones, Stuart Dwyer, James Annal for the wonderful jacket, the amazing sales reps, Sara Lloyd, Claire Evans, Lucy Hale, Jamie Forrest, Michael Davies, Jonathan Atkins, Cormac Kinsella, Poppy North, Becky Lloyd, Leanne Williams, Lucy Grainer, Christian Lewis, Nick Lee and copy-editor extraordinaire, Marian Reid.

I am lucky to have so many exceptional foreign publishers.

For this book, a special shout-out to Terry Morris and her team at Pan Macmillan South Africa – and to Veronica Napier, who took me to Jan Joubertsgat. Also, to my friends and long-term supporters at Meulenhoff-Boekerij, especially Maaike le Noble and Frederika van Traa, and everyone at Sonatine, Newton Compton and Planeta. Also in South Africa, a huge thank you to Mark and Deirdre Simpson, who showed me around Stellenbosch and introduced me to so many brilliant people, most especially Gawie Groenwald, who gave brilliant advice on history, language, landscape and Huguenot history, and Pietman Retief, for his fabulous tour and historical knowledge – our Monday trip was one of the most enjoyable research days I have ever spent. Thanks, too, to Anna Rita van Der Westhuizen for showing me her glorious farm in Wellington and advising on flora and fauna; to Duncan Brown, of the University of the Western Cape, for his helpful editing; to Daniel Malan Jacobs, Archivist at Babylonstoren for a wonderful morning in the archives; to Elsa Vogts, Museologist at Babylonstoren, for a superb tour of Soetmelksvlei; to everyone at the Huguenot Memorial Museum in Franschhoek; and, in the UK, Professor Murdoch, Chair of the Huguenot Museum in Rochester. Any mistakes are mine and mine alone.

In Carcassonne, *mille mercis* to our old friends Pierre Sanchez and Chantal Bilautou, and to Alain Pignon.

To my friends and neighbours, thank you: first amongst equals are Jon Evans, Clare Parsons, Tony Langham, Anthony Horowitz, Jill Green, Saira Keevil, Lucinda Montefiore, Robert Dye, Syl Saller, Sylvia Horton, Sally Clay and Linda and Roger Heald. Love to the legendary Granny Rosie, to my wonderful cousin Dr Philippa Towlson-Mulbregt (for revolting descriptions of malaria!), my fabulous sisters Beth Huxley and Caroline Matthews, my brothers-in-law Mark Huxley and Benjamin Graham (who helps keep the home fires burning), and my nieces and nephews including Thea Huxley and Ellen Huxley (for the Scrabble!), Rick Matthews, Lottie Ockleton and Bryony Dunk.

Finally, as always, there would be no point to any of this without my beloved Greg Mosse – my first love and first reader – magnificent Martha Mosse and brilliant Felix Mosse, as well as wonderful Ollie Halladay and the joyous Finn. Thank you all for your love, support and care. I am more proud of you than I can say.

ABOUT THE AUTHOR

Kate Mosse CBE FRSL is an award-winning novelist, playwright, essayist and non-fiction writer. The author of eleven novels and short-story collections, her books have been translated into thirty-eight languages and published in more than forty countries. Fiction includes the multimillion-selling Languedoc Trilogy (*Labyrinth*, *Sepulchre* and *Citadel*), The Joubert Family Chronicles (*The Burning Chambers*, *The City of Tears* and *The Ghost Ship*), and number one bestselling Gothic fiction. Her highly acclaimed non-fiction includes *An Extra Pair of Hands* and *Warrior Queens & Quiet Revolutionaries: How Women (Also) Built the World.* The Founder Director of the Women's Prize for Fiction and the Women's Prize for Non-Fiction, she is also the founder of the global #WomanInHistory campaign. A Fellow of the Royal Society of Literature, Kate is a Visiting Professor of Contemporary Fiction and Creative Writing at the University of Chichester, President of the Festival of Chichester, an Honorary Fellow of the Society of Authors and a Trustee of the British Library. She was awarded a CBE in the New Year Honours List 2024.